Siren in Waiting

Other Books By Lexi Blake

ROMANTIC SUSPENSE

Masters And Mercenaries
The Dom Who Loved Me
The Men With The Golden Cuffs
A Dom is Forever
On Her Master's Secret Service
Sanctum: A Masters and Mercenaries Novella
Love and Let Die
Unconditional: A Masters and Mercenaries Novella
Dungeon Royale
Dungeon Games: A Masters and Mercenaries Novella
A View to a Thrill
Cherished: A Masters and Mercenaries Novella
You Only Love Twice
Luscious: Masters and Mercenaries~Topped
Adored: A Masters and Mercenaries Novella
Master No
Just One Taste: Masters and Mercenaries~Topped 2
From Sanctum with Love
Devoted: A Masters and Mercenaries Novella
Dominance Never Dies
Submission is Not Enough
Master Bits and Mercenary Bites~The Secret Recipes of Topped
Perfectly Paired: Masters and Mercenaries~Topped 3
For His Eyes Only
Arranged: A Masters and Mercenaries Novella
Love Another Day
At Your Service: Masters and Mercenaries~Topped 4
Master Bits and Mercenary Bites~Girls Night
Nobody Does It Better
Close Cover
Protected

Masters and Mercenaries: The Forgotten
Memento Mori, Coming August 28, 2018

Lawless
Ruthless
Satisfaction
Revenge

Courting Justice
Order of Protection
Evidence of Desire, Coming January 8, 2019

Masters Of Ménage (by Shayla Black and Lexi Blake)
Their Virgin Captive
Their Virgin's Secret
Their Virgin Concubine
Their Virgin Princess
Their Virgin Hostage
Their Virgin Secretary
Their Virgin Mistress

The Perfect Gentlemen (by Shayla Black and Lexi Blake)
Scandal Never Sleeps
Seduction in Session
Big Easy Temptation
Smoke and Sin
At the Pleasure of the President, Coming Fall 2018

URBAN FANTASY

Thieves
Steal the Light
Steal the Day
Steal the Moon
Steal the Sun
Steal the Night
Ripper
Addict
Sleeper
Outcast, Coming 2018

LEXI BLAKE WRITING AS SOPHIE OAK

Small Town Siren
Siren in the City
Away From Me
Three to Ride
Siren Enslaved
Two to Love
Siren Beloved
One to Keep, Coming August 7, 2018
Siren in Waiting, Coming September 4, 2018
Lost in Bliss, Coming September 25, 2018
Found in Bliss, Coming October 9, 2018
Siren in Bloom, November 6, 2018
Pure Bliss, Coming December 4, 2018

Siren in Waiting

Texas Sirens, Book 5
Lexi Blake
writing as
Sophie Oak

Siren Enslaved
Texas Sirens Book 3

Published by DLZ Entertainment LLC

Copyright 2018 DLZ Entertainment LLC
Edited by Chloe Vale
ISBN: 978-1-937608-91-0

This is a work of fiction. Names, places, characters and incidents are the product of the author's imagination and are fictitious. Any resemblance to actual persons, living or dead, events or establishments is solely coincidental.

Sign up for Lexi Blake's newsletter
and be entered to win a $25 gift certificate
to the bookseller of your choice.

Join us for news, fun, and exclusive content
including free short stories.

There's a new contest every month!

Go to www.LexiBlake.net to subscribe.

Dedication

For my husband – who understands a little about the addictive personality since he has to live with me. As always, thanks to everyone who makes my life work – Chloe Vale, Shayla Black, Kris Cook, my mom and kids.

Dedication 2018

As I went through this book again, I realized Trev is the first time I had the courage to write an addict as a hero. Since then I've done it several times, but Trev still holds a place in my heart. Over the course of my life, I've been lucky enough to have had relationships with a couple of remarkable men. One was my college boyfriend. He formed the core of Trev, the idea of a golden boy who fell and had the heart and soul to pick himself back up, to find a way to be kind, to have seen the dark core of himself and still have faith.

This book is for everyone who lives one day at a time, for everyone who stumbles and falls and picks themselves back up.

This one is for Kevin.

Prologue

San Antonio, Texas

Trevor McNamara looked around the office he found himself in. Found was the right word since he definitely hadn't meant to be here. It was a pristinely kept workspace, neat and pin perfect, much like the man who sat behind the opulent desk—a man Trev was sure had to be joking. "I'm sorry. What did you say?"

The general manager of the San Antonio Bandits leaned forward. There was a slightly sympathetic look on Curt Goff's face as he steepled his hands together. "You're fired, Trevor."

"You can't fire me." His brain was still trying to process those two words that threatened to end his football career.

The words didn't end your career, idiot. You did that when you started in on the coke. The booze wasn't enough, was it? You just had to go for more.

"I think you'll find I can," Curt said, his voice sure. "In your contract, there's a clause that states plainly if you flunk three drug tests in a row, I can fire you."

Trev's head pounded. How had he flunked the last drug test? He'd paid the tech off to switch the results. Or he'd had his assistant pay the fucker off. Had he forgotten? Panic threatened to swamp

13

him. He couldn't get fired. He had bills to pay. Lots of fucking bills. "I'll call my union rep."

Curt nodded as though this move had been anticipated and potentially blocked. Once upon a time, Goff had been the San Antonio Bandits' quarterback, but he'd retired a few years back and now ran the front office. Everyone in the business considered the man a shark. "I assumed as much. I think you'll find the contract is ironclad. It's possible the union will sue for you, but I intend to go to court and I'll make that plain. I won't settle. I've talked to Frank, and we've decided that we'll spend what it takes in order to enforce your contract."

His stomach turned over a couple of times, and he wondered if the contents of his last meal weren't about to come back up. Frank Boyle was the owner of the team. He owed Trev ten million dollars on the last year of his contract. A protracted legal fight could cost Frank much more. Why would he do that? How could this be happening?

"It's happening because you can't control yourself, Trevor." Curt's eyes pinned him.

Damn, he was far gone. He hadn't even realized he'd said the words out loud.

"I'm going to call my agent." He pulled out his phone and glanced down at the screen. Fifteen messages. "You're going to have to deal with my agent. He won't put up with this shit. You can't treat me this way."

Curt's face hardened. Trev had heard rumors about the man. He was into some strange shit. Supposedly he tied up his wife and spanked her on a regular basis. Of course, there were other rumors about his perpetual houseguests. Two of the veterans on the team lived at Curt and Tess Goff's multimillion dollar compound and had for years. *Pervert.*

"I think you're going to find out that your agent quit after this morning's headlines." Curt's words fell in the silence with all the subtlety of a buzzsaw.

Bile crept into his throat. Headlines? He didn't remember much about the night before. He'd gone out with some friends. Friends. He didn't have friends. He had people who hung around because he paid for shit. He'd woken up in bed next to some bleach blonde with fake tits this morning. He didn't remember her name. She could definitely be a stripper. Shit. What had he done?

He hadn't gotten arrested. He would remember that. Fuck, when had he started to think a night when he didn't get caught was a win? "Bullshit. Marty wouldn't dump me."

"No. Not bullshit. Marty has moved on to greener pastures. I informed him this morning that we would be using the clause in your contract to release you. The Internet is already full of stories about what you did last night at a strip club. It wasn't a particularly upscale one, hence the fact that they have photos. There's a good one of you doing lines of cocaine off a stripper's body. It's not the image this club wants or needs. You tested positive for cocaine and marijuana. We didn't run a test for alcohol, or you might have broken the equipment. Can you honestly tell me you're not drunk right now?"

He'd only had a couple. Or three. It was the only way to deal with the hangover. It didn't matter. He hadn't driven himself anyway. He had a driver. Yeah, he wasn't going to be able to pay the driver anymore. "I'll go to rehab. I can be out in three weeks and ready for the season."

He hated the whine in his voice. He hated rehab. It didn't work. He'd be fine for a week or two, and then the need for a drink would call to him again. The pressure would build, and he would have to have that first drink. It never ended with one. It ended in bottles, and when the alcohol stopped working, he moved on to the harder stuff. Just last night, he'd thought about sticking a needle in his arm to see how high he could get.

God, he was going to kill himself.

"You've been three times, and it hasn't worked. I don't think conventional rehab works on someone like you." Curt's voice had softened slightly.

He didn't have any money. He'd spent it all on the house, the cars, and the parties. The drugs. He'd spent so much on drugs. He owed more than he had. How had it all gone to shit?

"Trev, I have an offer to make you. You know my wife is a therapist, right?"

Curt's wife was a pretty blonde named Tess. She'd run a few team-building exercises in the three years Trev had played for the Bandits. She was some sort of best-selling author. He remembered how Curt's eyes had lit up when she walked in and started talking. Of course, Mike Cabrerra's and Kevin Best's eyes had lit up, too. How did that work?

Trev had never looked at a woman the way those three men looked at Tess. What would it feel like to love a woman so much he was willing to share her?

"Yeah. You think she can fix me?" He laughed as he asked the question.

Trev doubted it. A strange sense of fatalism fell over him. It was done. His career was over, and now he could find a bottle and never stop. It was where he'd been headed since that first beer. He'd been on a path, and now he could follow it without the pesky frustrations of having a career. He could focus on what was important. Liquor had always been more important than football or family or any girl. When he'd been in high school, his so-called friends would put beer after beer in his hands. In college he'd discovered whiskey. When he'd gotten to the pros, he'd found even harder stuff.

For some strange reason, he remembered an old friend from high school named Bo O'Malley. Bo had been a freshman when Trev was a senior. Bo had been a scrawny kid at the time. He'd tried so hard to make the football team that Trev had taken the kid under his wing. For a brief period of time, he'd felt like someone needed him for something other than his throwing arm. Trev remembered Bo was funny, and when he'd hung out with Bo, he hadn't felt the need to drink.

He'd dumped Bo when he went off to college. He hadn't needed a puppy-like high school kid hanging around no matter how much he behaved like a brother.

He sincerely hoped Bo was doing better than he was.

Curt's voice drew Trev back to reality. "She doesn't do this type of work, but she's come up with a plan. You might think it's a bit radical. Here's the deal. I hired a psychologist. He's worked with men with impulse-control issues. He works in an odd place, though.

16

It's a BDSM club."

Trev threw back his head and laughed. "That is a brilliant plan. Put the addict in a club."

Curt's expression could have been cut from granite. "I assure you, you won't be allowed to drink in this club. The owner has agreed to take you under his wing and teach you a thing or two about control. His methods are far from standard, but I believe they will work for you."

"I'm not going to go to some club and let some asshole I don't know talk me to death." There was no way. He was going to fight this. Marty hadn't really dropped him. There was still time. His QB rating had tanked toward the end of last year, but he was young. Everyone needed a quarterback.

"If you go through the treatment and remain sober for three years, you will receive the rest of your contract."

Trev felt his eyes widen. Ten million dollars. For staying sober. Hell, he probably couldn't do it for all the money in the world.

Something inside him was broken. He was deeply flawed. He wasn't sure how or why it had happened. His father had loved him. He'd died far too young, but Paul McNamara had loved his family. His mother and sister had loved him.

He was the problem and he always had been.

"Why the hell would you do that for me?" The words felt heavy in his mouth. A weariness had invaded his bones, making him feel so much older than his twenty-six years. He was twenty-six, and his career was over.

He was over.

"I believe in second chances." Curt leaned forward, his hands on his desk. "Or, in your case, third or fourth chances. You had enormous talent. You couldn't handle all the crap that went with it. It doesn't have to mean your life is over. It simply means this isn't the life for you."

He was an idiot. That was what Curt was saying. And Trev knew it. He was a dumbass. The only things he'd ever been good at were football and working a herd. His father's herd was gone now because he'd gone off to play football and left his mom and sister with no one to work the ranch. It had been sold off to some organic co-op. There was nothing to go back to. He wanted to call his sister, but he couldn't tell her how badly he'd fucked up.

The papers would do that job for him. There would be no way Shelley didn't find out, and she would be ashamed. She still lived in the tiny town they'd grown up in. They would give his sister hell, making her pay for his sins. He let his head fall to his hand.

"If you say yes, you can be in Dallas tonight, beginning your treatment. You would have to stay for at least a year."

He looked up. "A year?"

"I believe I mentioned this isn't standard treatment." Curt pressed a button on his desk. "You need to make a decision. This offer is only available for the next five minutes. If you don't accept it, you're on your own."

Anger threatened to shove aside the panic. The cage door was closing, and he wasn't sure he could get out. "You have no right to do this to me."

"If I give you time to think about it, you'll come up with a million ways out. I'm closing off all the exits. You can fix yourself, or you'll have nothing. You'll walk out of here and lose your house, your cars, all those fancy clothes. You'll find solace in a bottle. You'll drink all you can, and when that stops working, you'll do whatever it takes to find that oblivion you seek. You'll sell whatever you have left, including yourself. You'll drink it, snort it, and when that doesn't work, you'll inject it. You'll do it until one day you don't wake up."

Trev could see it, the rest of his life laid out in a neat pattern. He would do everything Curt said. He would use until he died. He would try to find that place where nothing mattered and no one cared.

He was going to kill himself. He was going to waste everything he'd been given, and he would never even know what it meant to really give a damn.

What the hell did he want?

"I'll do it." The words came out of his mouth, but they felt foreign.

"See, that's what I wanted to hear." A new voice spoke from the corner of the room. Trev turned and saw what he hadn't before. A man stood in the corner. He was roughly six foot four with dark hair that hit his shoulders. Despite his long, slightly curly hair, the man had a military bent that couldn't be denied.

"Who the fuck is that?"

Curt smiled and held out his hand. "Meet Leo Meyer. He's the man who's going to fix you."

Leo Meyer nodded toward the door. "So, you ready to go? It's a long way to Dallas."

What did he really have to pack? Some clothes? He would have to sell the house and everything in it. None of it mattered.

"I can go now."

Trev stood and walked toward a man he didn't know but hoped would show him the way home.

He didn't have anywhere else to go.

* * * *

Eighteen Months Later
Deer Run, TX

Bo O'Malley felt the smile come over his face as Mouse walked into the tiny church. She wore a gray skirt and white blouse. Both were too big for her. Her brown hair was pulled back in an old-lady bun, but she was still the sweetest sight he'd seen all day. It meant he wasn't alone.

No one else from town had shown up. Bastards.

"Mouse." He felt himself relax for the first time all morning. He never had to pretend with her. Of all the people he'd known in his life, Mouse Hobbes was the only one who had accepted him with a whole heart. Her father stood beside her, leaning heavily on his cane.

She smiled shyly, but then everything she did had a shy quality to it. "Hi. We're not late, are we?"

Only Mouse would ask that question when it was blatantly obvious that one side of the church was empty. The groom's side. Well, one of the grooms. Lucas had several coworkers and apparently he knew a whole security team. They were a fun, sarcastic group who'd take up most of the only motel in town. Lexi's family and a few friends—including a scary, dark-haired dude in a suit who reminded Bo of a mobster—had come. But Aidan had almost no one. Certainly no one from here in Deer Run. Even the pastor had been imported from Dallas. Bo had heard the only way they had gotten the church was Jack Barnes's generous contribution.

He reached out and took her hand. Mouse's hand wasn't as soft as the hands of some of the women he'd dated. She worked hard. Strange then that he'd always liked holding hers. She was the sister he'd never had.

Except that sometimes he thought about doing things to Mouse that he wouldn't do to a sister.

"No. You're right on time. Lexi is almost ready." Bo turned and greeted George Hobbes. He looked frail but dapper in his suit. The suit had probably been in his closet since the seventies. George Hobbes was what people in Deer Run called an "individual." It was not necessarily a compliment. "Thanks so much for coming, George."

George held out his slender hand and shook Bo's. "Anything for you, son. You always watch out for my girl."

Bo lightly gripped the hand in his. George was under a few mistaken impressions. He believed that Bo was dating Mouse. He wasn't going to correct the man. Bo and Mouse had been friends since their junior year of high school when she had gotten him through chemistry. And algebra. And English. He had a high school diploma because Mouse hadn't let him fail. He'd had a deep affection for her ever since.

And besides, George Hobbes was dying. The cancer was slowly eating away at his health, and it was only a matter of time. If believing Bo would take care of his daughter made that easier on him, then he wasn't about to take that away.

"Did you manage to get your father here on your handlebars?" He grinned as he asked the question. Mouse wasn't big on driving. She had a license, but she greatly preferred her bicycle.

Her face scrunched up sweetly at his teasing. "I can drive. I just do it slowly."

"Hello, Bethany, Mr. Hobbes." Aidan walked up looking tidy in his monkey suit. Bo hated his, but Aidan seemed to like wearing a suit all right. He and Lucas were dressed almost identically. "It's nice of you to come."

"We wouldn't miss it. I've come to really like your Lexi," Mouse replied.

In the months since Lexi and Lucas had come to live at the O'Malley Ranch, Mouse had gotten close to Lexi. He was grateful for their budding friendship. Mouse had offered to help Lexi by reading some of the stories she wrote. The two had bonded over their love of romance novels. Without Mouse, Lexi would probably feel alone.

Deer Run was a small town, and they didn't take well to outsiders—especially outsiders who lived openly in a polyamorous relationship.

"She likes you, too." Aidan smiled warmly at her. "We were going to do this in Vegas, but my mother-in-law wouldn't hear of it. And don't try telling Abigail Barnes what she can't do. I tried to explain that it would be difficult to get married in Deer Run. Abby sicced Jack on everyone, and presto, here we are getting married."

"And how does this work, Aidan?" George asked. "Marrying two people?"

Coming from anyone else, the question might have sounded judgmental. From Professor Hobbes's mouth, it was a mere curiosity. Aidan didn't even blink.

"Lexi is going to be formally married to my partner, Lucas. Lucas has already changed his name legally to O'Malley. Lexi won't be married to me in the eyes of the law, but our hearts are a different matter."

George smiled warmly. "That sounds very nice. I'm happy for all three of you. Beth, dear, I believe I should find a seat."

Mouse took her father's hand and led him down the aisle to find a place to sit.

Aidan frowned at Bo. "When are you going to let that girl go?"

"Mouse?" Bo asked. "She's my friend. Why should I let her go?"

He actually couldn't imagine his life without Mouse. Mouse

21

was always there. Mouse was the one person he could count on.

"Because that woman is in love with you. And her name is Bethany. Why you insist on calling her by that ridiculous, demeaning nickname, I have no idea. She's a nice lady. She's smart and kind. She deserves some respect."

"Hell, Aidan. I like the hell out of Mouse. I don't mean any disrespect. It's what everyone in our class has called her since first grade."

She'd been as quiet as a mouse. Their teacher had called her a little mouse and the name had stuck. He didn't mean it as an insult. It was simply who she was. He'd known her most of his life, couldn't remember a time when he didn't. She'd always been there, in the back of the room, a quiet presence he could count on.

"Do you understand what she is?" Aidan asked, his face taking on that serious look he got when he was about to launch into a fatherly lecture.

Bo sighed. They'd been over this before. "She's not a submissive. I don't believe in that bullshit. I'm fine with whatever you, Lucas, and Lexi want to do in the bedroom, but don't treat it like it's a religion or something. Mouse doesn't want a man who chains her up and spanks her ass."

"Have you asked her?" Lucas asked, walking up. Lucas was a mystery. He liked the man, but Lucas had a perpetual amusement with the world that he simply didn't understand.

"Hell, no, I haven't asked her," he shot back at his almost brother-in-law, partner-in-law. Hell, he still didn't know what to call Lucas. It was all a mess, but it seemed to work for them. Not for him though. He wasn't getting involved in any of that kinky stuff. "And I'm not going to. As far as I can tell Mouse isn't into anything physical, and I'm fine with it staying that way."

Lucas wouldn't be swayed. "I wasn't merely talking about her sexuality, though I bet it's in there. She would likely be as submissive in bed as she is in her life."

They'd been over this argument numerous times, and he was starting to get annoyed. "I told you, Mouse isn't submissive. She's just real nice."

"I disagree, but you're taking advantage of her niceness, as you call it," Aidan insisted. "If her father weren't sick, I would seriously consider sending her back to Dallas with Julian. She needs a Dom. I've heard Taggart has a couple of friends looking for a permanent sub. You can't help her the way she needs to be helped or give her what she truly needs. You should encourage her to go to Dallas when she can."

Bo felt the sudden need to punch his brother in the face. "I will not allow her to go."

Lucas stepped between them. Despite the fact that Bo had healed the breach with his brother months before, they were still brothers. They still fought on a regular basis.

"How about we shelve this fight until after we get married?" Lucas straightened Aidan's tie. "I believe our bride is ready."

A smile crossed Aidan's face as his hand found the back of Lucas's neck. Bo had never seen anyone smile the way Aidan did when Lucas and Lexi entered a room. He might not understand what those three had found, but damn, he envied it. Bo didn't even look away when his brother leaned in and kissed Lucas.

He was getting used to his brother's peculiar life. The town of Deer Run, however, was not. A wedding was a big event in a small town, but everyone was ignoring this one. It had to hurt Aidan. It hurt him.

"Let's go get our girl," Aidan said to his partner. He turned to Bo, placing a hand on his shoulder. "I'm glad you're here. I know this makes it hard for you in town."

It did. His buddies gave him shit about it all the time. When Bo settled down, he was going to find a woman who truly fit into this town. He loved his brother, but he didn't want to be an outcast. "I wouldn't be anywhere else. Now you go and get married."

Bo was supposed to sit up front with the family, but the truth was Lexi's family scared him. He felt way more comfortable with Mouse and her dad. He slid in beside her.

When her hand found his, he let his fingers curl around hers. His whole body relaxed, and he could breathe again. That was what Mouse always offered him.

And she wasn't going anywhere. She was going to stay right here in Deer Run. And maybe, when he was ready to settle down, if he hadn't found anyone else, maybe he would talk to Mouse about getting married. That thought brought a little smile to his lips.

"What's so funny?" Mouse asked.

"Nothing," he replied, taking her hand more firmly in his own. "I had a silly thought."

Except when Lexi walked down the aisle, he couldn't help but wonder how Mouse would look in a white dress.

Nope. She wasn't going anywhere.

There wasn't anywhere else to go.

Chapter One

Deer Run, TX
Six Months Later

Mouse Hobbes stared at the house in front of her, excitement growing. The key in her hands felt a bit unreal, but this was happening. She was doing this. Her house. The old Bellows place was hers as of noon today. Every board, every piece of furniture, everything in the house was hers. All of the land along with a detached garage and a barn that looked like it might house a serial killer was hers.

It seemed like a mighty big adventure.

"Are you sure about this?" Bo stood at her side, his handsome face staring at the house like it might jump out and bite him.

It wouldn't bite him. But pieces of it might fall on him. Even now, one of the shutters banged against the side of the house in rhythmic time to the wind. She was definitely going to have to fix that.

She'd bought all the house's problems at auction, too.

"Totally sure." She'd been dreaming about buying a place and fixing it up for years.

She didn't buy the rumors that the place was haunted. It was simply a little run-down. Like all things in this old world, it needed a bit of love and attention. She had both of those, and no one left to spend them on. She relished the idea of taking the big farmhouse and turning it into a place for a family to live in.

And the money she would make by fixing it up and reselling it wouldn't hurt, either.

"It looks like it might fall down around you." Bo kicked at the porch step. She was happy when it held up. His eyes glanced over the yard. Along with the house had come two acres of property. "I wouldn't be shocked if old lady Bellows didn't leave you a couple of surprises, if you know what I mean."

"Those are rumors." Surely Maudine Bellows hadn't really laid bear traps around the grounds of her house in order to keep children from coming onto her lawn. "You don't happen to have a metal detector, do you?"

That smile of his lit up her world. "You want me to do a perimeter sweep? I bet you can find about a hundred baseballs and footballs. Kids in this county have been terrified of Maudine for years. I know she scared the hell out of me the one time I was brave enough to try to sell her popcorn when my Boy Scout troop was raising money. She opened the door with a shotgun in her hand and told me popcorn killed her last cat."

She walked up the steps. Despite the decrepit look of the stairs, they were solid under her feet, like the house itself. The huge wraparound porch likely needed nothing more than a coat of weatherproof paint. The cornices were in superb shape. She was going to have to work to save the stained glass, but it was worth it.

The porch overlooked the huge yard. In her mind's eye she could see a couple of rockers sitting on the porch. They would be there when she watched the sunset with her husband. Who always looked like Bo.

Stop. You are not keeping this house. This house is your key to the future. You sank everything you had into this house.

And Bo won't ever be more than a friend.

She often thought her inner voice was far too practical. Her inner voice was always angelic. She wondered if she'd been born without the devil others seemed to have. A little devilish voice might be fun from time to time.

"What the hell are you planning on doing with all these rooms?" Bo stood, scratching his head and looking up at the second story. "I heard there are five bedrooms in this place. You planning on getting a couple of cats or something?"

She wrinkled her nose at him. She wasn't ready to become an old woman with too many cats. She was only twenty-five. And she had a million ideas on what to do with the rooms. "I'm going to fix them up."

Bo tried to open the screen door. The handle came off in his hands. "I don't know about this. I think an apartment might have been a better idea. I heard the complex on Oak Street has a vacancy. I don't know if I like the thought of you living here all by yourself."

The building was called the Oak Street Manors. There was nothing manorial about the place. It was gray and boring. Every unit was exactly like the next. She wanted something beautiful in her life. After two years of hospitals and sick rooms, she needed to build something lovely and amazing. She'd watched her father die. It was time to bring something to life.

"Forget I said that." He set the screen door handle aside. Bo stood, looking at her with his hands on his hips. "I can't imagine you in one of those tiny things. You wouldn't have any place to put your books. When am I supposed to move all those boxes, by the way? Please say Saturday. I played poker with Lucas last night, and he lost. I made him promise to help me move you."

She smiled at the thought. She liked the idea of Lucas O'Malley helping her move. Oh sure, he was her part-time boss's husband, but he looked awfully nice without his shirt on. Maybe there was a little devil in her, after all. "Saturday it is, then. I don't have to be out of Dad's place until next week."

Her father's place. She had lived there for almost twenty-six years. She had never known another home. All of her memories were wrapped up in that little two-bedroom house. She'd shared a room with her sister for years. She'd grown up in that house.

She'd watched both of her parents die in that house.

The small, ranch-style house on Pine Street held her whole childhood, but it was past time for Mouse Hobbes to become a woman.

"Did I ever thank you for helping me with the funeral?" It had only been a month since she'd buried her father. Tears pricked at her eyes. Her dad. She missed him with every fiber of her being. Her sister, Bonnie, had stood beside her, but Bonnie had a husband and a strong circle of friends. Bonnie was the golden girl. She'd left home as soon as she was able to. Mouse had stayed behind. Mouse had nursed her mother and then her father as cancer ravaged them both.

It hadn't been Bonnie who sat beside her in the funeral home making arrangements. It had been Bo O'Malley.

"You know I'd do anything to help you, girl."

Anything but sleep with her. Oh, she had to put that out of her head. "I know. I wanted to say thanks though."

"Well, you're welcome. It's the least I can do." His cell phone rang. He looked down at the number, and a little smirk took over his face. She knew what that smile meant. She felt her whole soul sag as he answered the call. "Hey. I wasn't sure you were going to call me, pretty thing."

Bo winked at her and held out a hand that let her know he'd be back. He walked off, talking to some girl. He would have met her at a bar or a party. Places where Mouse never went.

He was never serious about those women, but one day Bo O'Malley was going to fall in love, and it wouldn't be with her. He considered her a friend, a sister. They had an odd relationship, and there was no way it would last. When he found a serious girlfriend, she would be out.

She looked up at the house she'd bought. This house was her future. When she had enough money, maybe she would leave and find some new place.

Or maybe she would stay because she could change locations, but things would always be the same if she herself never changed.

"Hey, I gotta go, Mouse. Clarissa is waiting for me," Bo said, walking out to his truck. "You want me to take you back home?"

Clarissa Gates. Perfect hair, perfect nails. Daddy's little princess. At twenty-seven, she had never had to leave her prom queen crown in the closet. Since Karen Wilcox had imploded a couple of years back, Clarissa had taken over as the town's queen bee. And now she was after Bo, and Bo seemed perfectly happy to get caught.

She shook her head. She had some work to do. The boxes held the contents to make the master bedroom livable. She could spend the night here if she wanted. The bedroom and the master bath were the only parts of the house that weren't falling apart. "No. I think I want to stay here for a while."

Bo frowned. "Come on. Let me take you home."

When he pushed her, she always caved. The impulse was right there. She wanted to get in the truck and let him take her home because he would worry. He would worry about her, but that wouldn't stop him from chasing after Clarissa. She was damn tired of being everyone's friend. She thought about the plan she'd come up with the night before. Bo wouldn't like it, but she wasn't Bo's responsibility.

It was time to stand on her own. "No. This is home."

"Fine. But I'll pick you up for dinner. I'll be back here at seven o'clock." Bo shook his head as he walked away.

Mouse fit that key into the lock, turning it and opening the door with pure satisfaction. It might fall down around her, but this was home for now.

* * * *

Trev stopped the truck in front of the big, rambling ranch house. It was no longer attached to a ranch. The land had been sold long ago, but the house still stood. There was still a tire swing hanging from the branches of the giant oak tree. How many times had he pushed his sister in that swing? Looking at it now, he could still see her pigtails hanging down as she threw her body back. She had been the worst giggle bunny. She would laugh and laugh as he got that old tire to go higher. They would run and play until Momma finally called them in for dinner, her head shaking at how dirty they were.

How had he gotten so lost?

His hands trembled slightly around the steering wheel. Too much caffeine. He always had too damn much of something. He put the truck in park and slid out.

29

Who lived here now? Shelley had put the house up for sale after Momma had passed. His mother had died while he was in the hospital detoxing. He'd had to come to her funeral with a "handler" and a bunch of security guards to keep the press out. That had been his contribution to the passing of his beloved mother. Leo Meyer had been quiet, helpful, and unobtrusive, but the fact that Trev hadn't been able to help his sister out had just about killed him.

What was he doing here? He'd been offered a job in Dallas, but the call of home had been too much. When his mentor had mentioned he could get Trev work on a ranch, he'd jumped at the chance. He'd only ever been good at two things in his life—football and handling cattle. He could never walk on the football field again. He knew that now. The pressure was too much. Fame had proven to be far too much for him to handle.

When he'd left this place, he'd been a hero. He'd been the first boy from Deer Run to get a full-ride scholarship to the University of Texas. After leading the Longhorns to a conference championship, they'd given him a parade.

No one had even talked to him at his mother's funeral. After ten years away, he was back, and he was utterly unsure of his welcome.

The door to the house opened, and two women walked out. He thought about jumping back into his truck and riding away, but before he could manage to move, he recognized one of them. Straight, dark hair and a wide smile. She didn't wear pigtails anymore, but damn, he loved his sister.

"I thought you might stop here." His sister waved to her friend and started walking down the path toward him.

She'd lost weight. Mourning seemed to have aged her a bit, but he could see the girl in her face when she smiled at him. She was a year younger and worlds smarter than he was. She had looked up to him once.

"Did you? I wanted to see the old place." He glanced up, but the woman who owned the house had gone back inside. "I needed to stand here for a minute. Please tell your friend I won't ask to come inside or anything."

She frowned. "She's the head of the church social league. I'm afraid she considers you a bit of a sinner."

A bit? Hell, he'd been the chief number one sinner for so long it was probably tattooed on his backside. It would take a while to convince these people he wasn't still going straight to hell in a designer handbasket. "Is she going to give you trouble?"

"No. This town knows sin and gossip, but they also know about family. It's going to be all right, Trev. Give it time."

He had plenty of time. Days, hours, weeks, years. They stretched in front of him. A lifetime of penance for the man he was trying to become. "How did you know I was coming in early?"

"I called your friend, Leo. He's very polite, that one." Shelley held her arms out for a hug.

He pulled his kid sister into his arms. It felt good to hold her. Tears misted his eyes.

He didn't mention that Leo was intensely attracted to her. There was no way he could miss the way Leo's eyes lit up any time he mentioned Shelley. He'd seen it even at his mother's funeral. Leo would never admit it, but even in Trev's shaken, detoxifying state, he'd seen the effect his sister had on his mentor. Leo had watched her the whole time. Now Trev understood why. He'd never considered it before, but his sister, for all her fire, was probably submissive. And he wasn't going to think about that.

His sister was also married. Sure, Bryce Hughes was the biggest asshole in the county, but she'd married him and showed no signs of divorcing. Leo was shit out of luck.

"Leo prides himself on his manners." He moved his hat back. The early fall heat was making a sweaty mess of his hair. The air conditioner was out on the old Ford. He would need a shower before he met with Bryce. "So, he told you I left early?"

"Yep. He gave you up fast, big brother. Now, can you explain why you're not staying with me?" She pulled back and put her hands on her hips.

Leo hadn't been happy about his living arrangements, either. But there was no way Trev was going to upset his sister's marriage. Bryce had been his biggest fan at one point in time, but he'd fled along with all the rest. Shelley would fight for him, but in this case, he didn't want her to.

"I have to be on my own at some point." It scared the hell out of him. He'd spent the last two years of his life under careful scrutiny. He'd stayed on at The Club for a whole year after the initial period because he liked the routine. He hadn't had a chance to fuck up. Now he was out on his own. The only thing that kept him from a bottle was his willpower.

He wasn't sure that was enough.

"I know that and I think you're going to be fine," she said. "But I thought it would be nice to have you around for a couple of days until you find your footing."

Yeah. Bryce had made it plain at the funeral that Trev wasn't welcome. His brother-in-law had called him a loser and an addict who'd failed everyone.

All of that might be true, but he knew his limits. He didn't need to be around Bryce.

"So you're going to live out on the O'Malley Ranch? I've heard some crazy stuff goes on there."

Trev stared at his sister. He sincerely hoped she hadn't given in to small-town small-mindedness. "Lexi O'Malley is a nice lady."

He'd met her a couple of times along with her husbands. He'd spent a bit of time with Lucas O'Malley. He knew Aidan in passing. He knew Aidan's brother, Bo, better, but Aidan seemed all right. He was a good Dom. That meant something to Trev.

Sometimes being a good Dom was all he had.

Shelley shook her head. "I know she is. I like that girl. She's the funniest thing to hit this town in forever, but you should know that not everyone accepts what goes on at that ranch. They tolerate her because everyone knows her stepdad can be one mean son of a bitch when he thinks his family is being mistreated. I don't know if they're going to be any nicer to you, brother."

They wouldn't. It would be worse for him. He didn't have a mean son-of-a-bitch stepdad with more money than god backing him up. He could handle it. He'd earned their disdain in a way Lexi hadn't.

He was used to people turning up their noses at him. He'd found out the only thing people hated more than a fuckup was a fuckup who had it all at one point in time. People gloried in the fact that he had fallen from grace. His screwups had been played out in all the tabloids until Julian Lodge had taken over his life. There hadn't been a single newspaper story about him since the day he'd walked into The Club. Trev was very aware that he owed his life and his sobriety to two men. Julian Lodge and Leo Meyer had taught him how to control himself. He would never forget that. His sobriety was a gift he worked to earn every damn day of his life.

"Well, I don't care what everyone else thinks. I'm going to be the foreman of that ranch. They can like it or leave it. It doesn't much matter. The cattle don't care what goes on in the ranch house." And they wouldn't give a damn that he'd had it all and thrown it away for a momentary high.

Shelley grinned. "You have to get me invited to dinner. I'm so curious I could scream. I hear they spend a lot of time at that club where you worked. I would give a lot to find out what goes on there. Does Leo work there, too?"

He felt his brows draw together. "It's a BDSM club, Shell. I hardly think your husband is going to show his face there."

Her whole body seemed to deflate. He wished he hadn't said it. It was a harmless fantasy for her. Wasn't she entitled to that? "I guess so. I'm a small-town girl. That's a bit out of my league."

"Hey, if you want to go, I'll get you in. Hell, I'll have Leo give you a tour." If his sister wanted to leave the rat bastard she married for Leo Meyer, Trev would facilitate her adultery. It wouldn't be like she was cheating on a faithful man, from what he'd heard. It was another reason he didn't want to stay with his sister. He was worried the temptation to kill his brother-in-law might prove too much for him to resist. He wasn't good at resisting temptation.

She patted his chest. "No. I don't think Bryce would much like that. I'll have to live vicariously. Now, do you want to tell me why you came home early but didn't bother to mention it to your only sibling?"

"I didn't want you to make a big deal out of it." If he knew his sister, she would have met him on the outskirts of town with balloons and a cake. "It's best if I come in quietly, like I intend to live."

"You can't let them intimidate you." Shelley had always been a bit of a rebel. Her good looks and sweet nature had ensured her place in the pecking order, but she tended to push the boundaries.

He intended to make sure she didn't get in trouble because of him. He'd already caused his family enough heartache. "Don't worry about me. I don't intend to leave the ranch much. I'll have a lot of work to do. From what I hear, O'Malley's been without a foreman for a year. I'll have my work cut out for me."

It was exactly what he needed. A lot of ridiculously physical work. Ranch work would take up all of his time and leave him without the strength to even think about drinking at night. Or during the day. It was always there at the edge of his consciousness, teasing him, taunting him. He longed for the day where he didn't think about a bottle.

The mischievous imp was back. Shelley's eyes lit up. "I still wouldn't mind coming out to that ranch sometime. They say it's a den of inequity. Did you know that Lexi calls both those men her husbands?"

Oh, it was worse than that. Trev had watched Aidan top his subs at The Club. Aidan and Lucas were lovers, too. A true threesome.

Trev had zero interest in sleeping with another man, but he envied Lucas and Aidan's camaraderie. He'd liked the way they both worked to love and care for their wife. Maybe if he had someone like Lucas, he wouldn't be so afraid he would fail a woman. He'd played with subs once he'd been given the go-ahead to work in The Club, but he hadn't formed any kind of relationship. He wasn't cut out for that.

Yeah, his BDSM past really would help his standing in the community. Hell, as far as he could tell, no one was going to talk to him, much less be friends with him. And he deserved it. He'd said some hateful things about his hometown when he was less than in control. He imagined he wouldn't be forgiven for that either.

"I'll see if I can get you invited out to dinner sometime." Trev was looking forward to getting to know Aidan O'Malley. At least he had one person in this town he had a lot in common with. They had never said more than a passing hello while at The Club. Though they were from the same town, he'd been a couple of years behind Aidan in school.

He'd been surprised Aidan wanted him to be his foreman. He'd always assumed Aidan didn't like him. It was nice to be proven wrong for once.

"Stay the night with us tonight." Shelley practically pleaded with him.

It was a righteously bad idea, but she was his sister, and he'd been planning on spending the evening at a cut-rate motel since his meeting with Aidan wasn't until tomorrow. "All right."

Maybe it would be fine. Maybe he and Bryce would get along and he wouldn't have to worry about causing his sister more trouble.

She hugged him. "I'm glad you're home."

He hoped she wasn't the only one.

Chapter Two

Mouse put the finishing touches on the master bedroom. She'd cleaned the whole thing from top to bottom, and with a brand-new pillow-top mattress and satiny soft sheets on the big bed, it looked comfy and homey. She'd gotten rid of the heavy drapes and the dark quilts. Now the room looked light and airy, despite the ornate nature of the furnishings. Once she'd stripped and refinished the antique bedroom set, it would be perfect. For now, she was satisfied with her afternoon's work. The bedroom was fresh and feminine, and the bathroom fixtures all worked. She'd scrubbed the bathroom until she was sure her arms would fall off, but it sparkled now. The antique claw-footed tub was a beautiful monstrosity. She couldn't wait to soak in it, but she'd been practical. She'd used the shower.

She moved in front of the window unit, allowing the cold air to caress her skin. She felt different somehow.

Stronger.

She had a home, and it was all hers. Despite the fact that the majority of her belongings were back at her parents' house, she intended to spend the night here. She had an overnight bag with some clothes and her personal items.

Of course, she could always try on the clothes she'd found. Her eyes strayed to the trunk she'd discovered in the back of the master closet. She'd felt odd opening it, like she was spying on someone, but according to the contract she'd signed, the trunk and all its contents now belonged to her. Maudine Bellows only had one relative, and he'd died six months before she had. Even if Barry Bellows hadn't been killed in a car accident, she seriously doubted he would have wanted his elderly aunt's clothes. The property was another matter. He would have been interested in that. Barry Bellows had run a real estate agency along with his partner, Bryce Hughes. Bryce had already offered to take the place off her hands.

She wasn't interested in making a quick buck. If Bryce Hughes got his hands on the place, he would probably tear it down and put in a convenience store or a fast-food restaurant. The last thing Deer Run needed was another place to get a ninety-nine-cent burger.

She let the thought go. It was nicer to think about the trunk. It had been like finding a treasure trove. Gorgeous, classic clothes. Vintage designers. She knew a couple of the names. Chanel. Givenchy. Everything looked like it had come straight out of a Doris Day film. Or Audrey Hepburn.

Old lady Bellows had secrets she'd hidden.

And the pictures. She'd found wooden boxes with stacks of pictures. She'd stared at them in shocked disbelief. Apparently during Hollywood's heyday, Maudine Bellows had worked in Dallas for Republic Pictures. The old black-and-white photos told the tale. Maudine was smiling as she stood next to John Wayne and Clark Gable.

Maudine had lived a life.

She couldn't help but wonder why Maudine's final years had been lonely and bitter. The woman smiling in the pictures alongside Claudette Colbert bore little resemblance to the Maudine Mouse had known.

Along with the clothes and photos, she'd found a thick book. A diary. Maybe the truth of Maudine's life was in there. She'd only glanced at the first page, the lines written in a flowy, feminine hand. The first words of the diary had been written on July 5, 1956.

This is my diary. I will kill anyone who reads it. Yes. That means you.

Yep, there was a reason Maudine Bellows had never been

married. Mouse touched the book and slid it into the dresser drawer she'd cleaned out earlier. It was now free of old antacids, a mildewed V.C. Andrews paperback, and a hideous set of what Mouse was pretty sure were bottom-teeth dentures. She'd handled those with care. There was a rumor that Maudine had eaten several local children with those false teeth.

She sighed and decided to get dressed. Bo should be here any minute. She picked out a skirt and a T-shirt. It was boring, but that was who she was.

Was that who she had to be?

She stared down at the vintage clothes. They looked like they might fit. Many of them were far too formal for dinner at Patty Cake's, but there was a pretty yellow-and-white sundress. The skirt was gathered, and the neckline was far lower than anything she'd worn before. Surely it wouldn't fit, but did it hurt to try?

Twenty minutes later, Bo knocked on her door. She let him in, grateful that a couple of lamps in the parlor worked. The hall light didn't, but she had enough illumination from the parlor and the living room. She strode toward the back of the house to the living area and shut off the lamp, leaving only the soft light from the parlor on.

"Damn, girl, where did you get that dress? Why are you wearing a dress at all? You do know we're going to Patty's, right? Was I supposed to take you somewhere else?" Bo stood in her dilapidated hallway with a quizzical look on the face she loved.

Bo O'Malley was proof positive that the universe loved some people. He was six foot three, with a crop of perfect gold hair and a drool-worthy body. No one would ever think to compare him to a rodent. He looked down at her, his blue eyes wide.

"No. I just thought it would look nice." She felt self-conscious all of a sudden. She was well aware that her breasts were far more exposed than she was used to. The bodice of the sundress formed a deep *V*, and the dress clung where her usual clothes hung down. She normally wore shapeless clothes that gave the illusion that she weighed more than she did. Her breasts seemed curvy and round now. A moment ago, she thought they looked a little sexy. She'd stood in front of the mirror and vamped, giggling at the thought that

Bo might take one look at her and fall at her feet.

Bo didn't look like he was interested in her new look. All she could read on his face was disapproval. Maybe she didn't look as pretty as she thought.

His face was set in deep lines. He finally waved his hand as if dismissing the whole thing entirely. "It does look nice. I'm surprised is all. Um. I didn't think you cared about looking nice."

That was typical. Bo didn't even see her as female. "Well, maybe I'm changing. I'm almost twenty-six. Maybe it's about time I started dating."

It was time. She had several plans in place.

Bo actually laughed.

"I'll put something else on." She started to turn and realized the choice she was facing. She could change back into her old clothes, but her mind would be working all night. At this point, all she would think about would be the fact that Bo didn't find her attractive. He couldn't help that. Maybe she needed a bit of distance. "You know what, I think I'll eat here. You go on. I'm sure Clarissa needs a dinner date."

His hand came out and caught her elbow. "Don't be like that, Mouse. I was surprised. You never seemed interested in dating before. I'm sorry. Come on. I don't want to eat dinner with Clarissa. I want to spend some time with my best friend."

Her heart softened. It was a strange friendship that she and Bo had formed, but she depended on it. "All right."

And she didn't want to be alone tonight. She'd been alone far too often since her father passed. The quiet had begun to eat away at her. It was all right when she had something to do, but at night when she was all alone, she felt the heavy weight of her loss.

"Besides, I'm meeting Clarissa at the honky-tonk after I drop you back off. I might not want to spend a lot of time talking to the girl, but she can sure dance." Bo gave her a wink and opened the door.

Mouse sighed. It looked like she was in for a long night.

* * * *

39

Trev kept his eyes on the menu, though he didn't really need to. The menu at Patty Cake's hadn't changed in thirty years. He had it memorized, but looking at the menu meant he didn't have to deal with his brother-in-law. Or the fifteen other people staring a hole through him. It was way too much to think that the good people of Deer Run were above reading tabloids.

"And now you're going to run someone else's ranch?" Bryce's voice sounded nasal to Trev's ears.

He glanced over the menu at his brother-in-law. Bryce Hughes was handsome in an antiseptic fashion. He was always fastidiously clean. Bryce had come up from Houston and started a real estate company. He'd done well for himself. Even when the market had fallen out, Bryce seemed to make money.

He had no idea what his sister saw in the man.

"It's called being a foreman. I know ranching." At least he used to. He'd spent a couple of weeks at a ranch in Willow Fork recently. He'd been happy that it had all seemed to come back to him. He'd even enjoyed the easy camaraderie he'd had with the other hands. He was genuinely looking forward to getting started at O'Malley's ranch.

"Yeah, well, I would have said you knew football, too," Bryce grumbled.

"Stop," Shelley said under her breath. "You promised."

It had been like this ever since he'd walked in the door of his sister's house. Bryce had tried to cut him down in a million different ways. Bryce had come home and immediately asked if Shelley had hired a new lawn-care man because the truck in the driveway obviously belonged to the help and should be parked in the back of the house where it wouldn't offend anyone.

Yeah, he loved hanging out with his brother-in-law.

"Football and I didn't get along." He looked back at the menu. There was no point in going deeper than that. Bryce wouldn't understand the myriad of reasons he'd left behind a profitable career. He had the talent for the game, but he couldn't handle the pressure. Leo had tried to get him to understand that didn't mean he was a failure. The words still rung hollow.

"Trev always was a cowboy." Shelley seemed determined to put

40

a positive light on everything. "He used to ride the fences with Daddy every morning. He wasn't even eight years old, but he would get up before dawn and help out."

He'd liked that time with his dad. Everything was peaceful and quiet. Later on in the day, his father had a million responsibilities, but in the pale light right after dawn, it had been just Trev and his father.

Maybe if he hadn't discovered he could throw a damn football, he would have been riding the fences that morning his father had a heart attack. Maybe his father wouldn't have died and Momma wouldn't have had to find him out in the south field, his old horse nudging him like the damn thing was trying to wake the man up. Trev had started junior year two-a-days earlier that week. He'd rarely talked to his dad after he'd started football, but the old man had come to every game.

"Trev was always a natural with horses, too. He always did ride better than me. I miss riding." Shelley took a sip of her tea. "Maybe Lexi wouldn't mind if I came out and used her stables. I know they've got some well-trained horses out there."

"I don't think that's a good idea," Bryce said, frowning. "We talked about this, babe."

A bit of Shelley's light faded, but she smiled anyway. "Of course. I have things I need to concentrate on, anyway. I got a new client. The mayor asked me to redesign his office."

Bryce nodded. "Yes, that's right. You need to concentrate on your business. Hey, did you hear the Hobbes girl bought old lady Bellows's place? I had hoped we could snap that sucker up. I assumed the auction would be months out, but they got that will through probate damn fast. Who would have guessed the old lady would leave everything she had to a damn animal shelter?"

"I thought it was smart of them to auction it all off. They made a bundle," Shelley said.

Bryce's eyes narrowed, his irritation plain. "I would have paid them more. It's the perfect place to put a strip mall."

Shelley rolled her deep-brown eyes. "Yes, tear down the gorgeous house to put in a strip mall. We need another dollar store."

The bell rang as the door to the diner swung open.

"Speak of the devil." Bryce turned to greet the newcomers.

Oh, but what walked in that door didn't even vaguely resemble a devil. He felt every nerve in his body go on high alert as a brunette breezed through the doorway. She wore an old-fashioned yellow sundress that showed off an hourglass figure and complemented her complexion. The sweet-looking dress nipped in her middle and plunged exactly where it should, emphasizing her waist and her luscious breasts. Most women in his life didn't have curves like that. Even at The Club in Dallas, he'd been surrounded by wealthy, fashionable women. They tended to be slender and well made-up. Most had had a nip and tuck by the time they hit twenty-five.

Not this woman. She was natural. As far as he could tell, she wasn't wearing any makeup past a touch of mascara. Her skin was fair, with an almost translucent quality. No spray tan for that lovely lady. He let his eyes roam as she glanced around, obviously looking for a table. A waitress approached, and the woman got the sweetest smile on her face. Her eyes glanced down before she forced them back up. Even then she spoke quietly.

He'd been trained to look for signs, and every bit of that training told him he'd just hit the jackpot. There was a sure intelligence in her brown eyes that coupled with her obvious submissive nature made her exactly his type. If the universe had reached into his libido and pulled out his perfect lover, the woman would be damn close to the woman in the yellow dress.

Her hair was pulled back in a bun. If she was his, he would walk straight up to her and tangle his hands in it. He would force her hair to spill over her shoulders, drowning her in brown and gold silk. From the massive size of that knot at the back of her head, he would bet that hair reached almost to her waist. And it would be soft, like the woman herself. She would be silky and sweet. She would kneel at his feet, and when she looked up at him, he would feel ten feet tall. He wouldn't feel like a failure. He would feel like her Master.

This woman was soft, so soft it practically poured off her. When her lips turned up in a shy smile, he wondered what they would feel like on his cock.

Fuck. It had been too damn long since he'd had sex. He thought about the small bag he'd brought with him. Julian Lodge had given it to him the day he'd finished his training and was allowed to work with subs in The Club. Leo had laughed and told him never to be caught without his kit. At one point in time, Trev had always carried around an athletic bag. Now he carried a small leather one with lube and ropes and a whip.

You never know when a little sub is going to need some discipline, Leo always said.

He imagined her tied up and spread on his bed, awaiting his pleasure.

And then he noticed the man beside her. A tall, strong cowboy in Levi's, a western shirt, and well-worn boots. Blond hair curled out from under his Stetson.

Bo O'Malley.

The exact person he didn't want to see. He owed Bo O'Malley one of those long, rambling apologies he never seemed to get good at. It was something every addict got used to, but he wasn't looking forward to it. He'd forced himself to apologize to many people, but he was pretty sure Bo O'Malley wasn't going to listen.

Bo put a hand to the pretty woman's waist and started to lead her to an empty booth on the opposite side of the diner. The woman's head turned. Her eyes trailed back and locked on to him. They widened in recognition.

He felt his stomach knot. He couldn't change his face or his past. He hated the way people looked at him now.

Except she smiled shyly, as though she was looking at a stranger and trying to be polite.

Damn, but he wanted to eat her up.

"Do you know Mouse?" Shelley asked, an expectant look on her face.

"Mouse?" He had to force his eyes away. The woman with the brown hair scooted into her booth. She faced his way but looked at Bo. Was she his wife? Shelly hadn't mentioned Bo had married.

Bryce snorted. "Mouse Hobbes."

He searched his brain, trying to connect that face to a name. "Bethany Hobbes?"

A vision of a ridiculously shy girl from his high school whispered across his mind. She'd been younger than him. She'd been smart, but quiet. Utterly ignored. He couldn't ignore her now. He hadn't reacted this way to a woman in years. His hands tightened around his coffee mug. Despite the ache in his groin, it felt damn good to want something, anything besides a drink.

Bryce continued. "Poor girl's been chasing after that cowboy since they were kids from what I hear. I have no idea why he lets her hang around. She's been his shadow for years."

"She's not his girlfriend?" His cock had been at half-staff, but the idea that she was unattached had an effect on him. His cock hardened to the point that he could probably pound nails with the damn thing.

Submissive. The word floated in his brain like a butterfly. That woman right there was submissive, and she probably had no idea what the word meant. He could show her. He could train her.

Now Bryce outright laughed. "Mouse? Mouse doesn't have a boyfriend. I don't think the girl has ever even been kissed. Who the hell in this town would kiss old Mouse?"

Trev could think of a couple of places he'd like to kiss her. Those full lips. Her round breasts. She probably had a plump pussy. He could put his mouth on all of those places. Never been kissed. Never been fucked. Never knelt at her Master's feet. That fact should have sent him running. It didn't. It merely made him think about the fact that she knew absolutely nothing about a lifestyle she might enjoy. And he could teach her.

But apparently she was in love with Bo. Hadn't he taken enough from Bo?

"Her name is Bethany." He didn't like the nickname. It smacked of a put-down. He might not get to know the woman, but he wasn't about to allow anyone to put her down around him. He knew the way things worked. If she was submissive and no one watched out for her, she could get ground beneath everyone's feet.

Bryce snorted. "Good luck with getting that to change. She even calls herself Mouse."

If she was his, everyone would change or they would have to deal with him. And that included her sweet ass.

"So, do you really want to order from a Podunk, piece-of-shit, hole-in-the-wall?" The waitress stared down at him. He hadn't seen her walk up. He'd been far too taken by this sweet little Mouse. Bethany. Her name was Bethany. He was going to give her the respect she deserved.

Damn. The waitress's words reached his brain. He'd called this place a shithole in fucking *People* magazine. He'd said a lot of things in the tabloids he shouldn't have said. The reporter had practically cackled as she wrote the story. And he'd fucked her. And gotten high with her.

He turned his face up to meet the waitress's glare. Patty's hair had more gray in it, but she still looked like she could kill a man with nothing more than her glare. "I am sorry, ma'am. I've always loved this place, ever since I was a kid. I didn't right know what I was saying at the time. I pretty much hated myself, so I said awful things about everyone."

She simply stared. "Well, I could certainly see why you would hate yourself. Do you want to order something, or do we small-town idiots not even know how to make a burger?"

He wasn't going to win with her. "I would love a burger."

Hopefully she didn't spit in it.

Shelley ordered, her mouth tight and tense. Bryce simply sighed and chose not to eat.

Patty walked away, her feet beating against the linoleum.

Bryce scooted out of the bench. "I should go back to the office. You two enjoy your time together. I hope once Trevor gets to work, he won't have much time for us."

"You hope?" Shelley asked.

"I meant suspect. I suspect." Bryce shrugged as though it didn't bother him. "He's going to be living at the ranch. I doubt he'll get out much. I mean, ranching is such hard work. That's what everyone tells me."

Bryce pivoted on his expensive loafers and walked away.

Shelley turned sad eyes his way. "Don't mind him. He hasn't been the same since his best friend died. He's been a bit lost. Barry was his business partner. He died a few months back. Bad accident. He's had a lot to deal with."

And Bryce had obviously dealt with it by being the biggest asshole known to man. He leaned forward and took his sister's hand in his. "Are you happy with him?"

She suddenly seemed to find the tabletop endlessly interesting. "He's my husband."

He tightened his fingers around hers. "That doesn't answer my question."

She pulled away. "You weren't around when Mom got sick. You don't know what it was like. I needed someone, and Bryce was there. He isn't the best husband in the world, but damn it, he was there when I needed him."

He sat back, his stomach in knots. Of course. Shelley had married right around the time their mother had been diagnosed with stage three esophageal cancer. Trev had been drunk off his ass the night his mother had called to tell him. He was pretty sure he'd hung up on her and went right back to his party.

When the bills from her treatment had kicked in, he had been almost tapped out. He'd sold his house and only managed to give his sister a measly ten grand after he'd paid off all his bills. Bryce had probably had to pay the balance. No wonder the man hated him.

"Sorry. I won't mention it again." Small talk. He needed small talk. His eyes strayed to Bethany. He wanted to ask about her. She'd been so smart in high school. Why hadn't she gone off to college? Why was she still hanging out in Deer Run? He didn't ask, though. She wasn't his, and he fucked up everything he touched. He would leave her be. "So, I heard the rodeo was great this year."

Shelley reached out. "I didn't mean to make you feel bad."

He ached inside. "Not at all. It's all right. Now tell me about the rodeo."

* * * *

Bo managed to not roll his eyes as Bryce Hughes approached. He was a pretentious son of a bitch who always overdressed for the occasion. The man wore slacks and a blazer to the annual county fair. And he always looked down on cowboys.

"Mr. O'Malley." Bryce greeted him with an unctuous smile on his face. Unctuous. Bo grinned. He only knew what that meant because Mouse used it an awful lot. She was fond of big words.

He'd learned a lot from her.

Now he was learning about jealousy because that unctuous asshole was looking at her breasts. He might have learned what "unctuous" meant from Mouse, but the word "asshole" had come with the territory. Bryce Hughes was a married asshole looking at a younger woman's tits.

"Mr. O'Malley's my brother," Bo said between clenched teeth. "You can call me Bo."

Bryce seemed unconcerned with his show of defiance. "Well, I wasn't sure what your brother had done about his name given his marital status. He might have taken on his wife's name. Or the other fellow's."

And that was the crux of Bo's whole world. His brother wasn't normal. His brother lived an alternative lifestyle. His brother was always a badass who didn't mind throwing his power around, so Bo took the brunt of the nastiness. They were afraid of Aidan, but they let Bo know exactly what they thought.

"His name is still O'Malley." Bo felt his eyes narrow. He'd seen Bryce as he'd walked in. He knew exactly who Bryce had been sitting with. He hadn't missed a damn thing. "And I would watch where you decide to throw stones. Your brother-in-law is the most hated man in the county."

"Bo." Mouse gasped. The prim set of her mouth let him know he'd done something she considered impolite.

Well, he didn't care. Trev McNamara was an asshole addict who should never have shown his face in this county again. Didn't he have strippers to screw? It seemed the man even neglected his strippers. What was the world coming to?

"It wasn't my idea to have him come back here," Bryce said, adjusting his tie. "Trust me, when I married his sister, I thought I was gaining an asset. He was the hero of Deer Run when he signed that contract with the San Antonio Bandits. I imagined his face on my billboards telling everyone to come to Hughes-Bellows for all their real estate needs. Life doesn't always turn out the way you think it will. How is that new house treating you, Mouse?"

He had the insane urge to get Mouse a sweater despite the hundred plus degree heat. The neckline plunged down, showing off

47

a crazy amount of creamy, smooth skin and the rounded tops of breasts he hadn't imagined were really there. She always wore loose clothes. He'd thought she was on the chubby side. This dress dispelled those mistaken impressions. She was curvy and female and Bryce noticed.

What had she been thinking putting on that dress?

"I love it." Pure pleasure could be heard in her voice. Her lips curled up in a strangely attractive smile, like she had a secret. He'd never seen Mouse smile like that. "It's the most beautiful house ever."

"I'm surprised it wasn't condemned. Well, when you figure out it's more trouble than it's worth, you go on and give me a call." Bryce held out his card. Mouse's hand came out obediently and took it.

Bryce walked away without saying good-bye.

"Why didn't you tell that fucker to shove his card up his ass?" Something nasty was brewing in his gut. He almost never cursed around Mouse. He tended to like the person he became when she was around, but tonight he felt like fighting.

He didn't fool himself. He felt like fighting because he was in the same room with Trev McNamara.

They'd been friends once. After Aidan had left for college, Trev had practically become his big brother. Trev had been the quarterback. Bo had been a freshman in need of a mentor. They had bonded because unlike a lot of senior players, Trev hadn't ignored the underclassmen. He'd taught Bo a lot about football. After a while it had been easy to hang out with the older student. There was a picture somewhere of himself and Trev smiling on the day Trev graduated from high school. He'd told Bo that his door was always open in Austin. That had been a bold-faced lie. He could still remember Trev telling him to go away that night when Bo had needed a friend. When he'd needed someone to save him.

"I won't call Bryce. He would try to talk me into a bad deal." Mouse still tucked the card into her purse. "But I certainly don't see any reason to be impolite."

"He's a dickhead. Everyone knows it." He couldn't help but notice the fact that Mouse's eyes kept straying away from him.

48

"What's got you so distracted?"

"Is that who I think it is?"

She was looking at him. The fucker. "Yeah. That's Trevor McNamara. Haven't you seen an addict before?"

Her mouth turned down. "I've seen him before. We did all go to the same school. I wasn't close to him or anything. It's been years since I saw him on anything but a magazine cover or the television. I never thought he would come back. He looks good. He looks healthy."

"He shouldn't have come back. After what he said about this town in *People* magazine, I'm surprised he would show his face."

She shrugged. "He was a different person. And he didn't say anything so awful."

"He called us all small-minded rubes."

Mouse stared.

He hated it when she made him feel like a dumbass. "I know what a rube is."

He sure did now. He'd looked it up after reading that article.

She picked up the menu. "Well, if you know what it means, then you know he was mostly right. And he was definitely right about the small-minded part. Hasn't the way this town treats your brother taught you anything? They haven't exactly been tolerant. If you don't fit a very narrow criteria, you don't get to belong here. I should know."

Mouse did know. She never had fit in, but that wasn't her fault. She was too quiet, too odd to find a place here. Trev was a different story. He'd been the damn king of Deer Run in his day. Trev had it good and he'd thrown it all away.

He didn't like the way she was looking at Trev.

"He's an addict, you know. He got kicked out of the pros. Do you know how bad you have to get to be kicked out of football when you have an arm like his?"

"He went to rehab," she argued.

"Three times. It never took. He's an addict. It's all he'll ever be." Trev was an asshole, too. But he hadn't always been. Bo remembered a time when Trev had been a goddamn lifeline. Trev had reached out and pulled him out of the abyss.

And then tossed his ass right back in. Trev was like everyone else. Everyone left. Everyone but Mouse. Even though his brother was back in his life, Aidan had Lucas and Lexi. He didn't have time for Bo.

"He's obviously trying to get better. Why else would he be here?" she asked.

Sweet, naïve Mouse. "He hasn't got anywhere else to go. No one will have him. He got dropped by everyone. He got fired from his job, and his agent quit on him. All of his sponsorship deals dried up. He's got nothing."

A gentle smile crossed her lips. "And now he's come home. This is where he should be. This is where he can find himself again. Everyone deserves a second chance."

But Trev had had more than his share of chances.

"You used to be friends with him, right?" Mouse asked the question as Darlene, the waitress, put a Coke in front of her.

Darlene, Patty's daughter, was the biggest gossip in town. She smiled conspiratorially as she pulled out her notepad. "Are y'all talking about Trevor McNamara?"

"No," Bo said immediately. The last thing he needed was to get caught talking about that idiot.

"Yes." Mouse leaned in close to Darlene.

Darlene chose to ignore Bo. "My momma says he's not welcome in this town anymore after all the bad things he said, but damn, that man is hot. And he has a reputation, if you know what I mean."

"Yeah, he has a reputation. As a cokehead and an asshole," he complained.

Mouse ignored him, too. "I don't know what you mean."

Darlene's blonde ponytail bobbed as she got to one knee. "I'm talking about sex, Mouse. He's got a real bad reputation when it comes to sex. And by bad, I mean good."

He thought seriously about poking out his own eyeballs with the knife on the table. Then he wouldn't have to see his best friend glancing that jerk's way and blushing. Blushing.

"He's good at sex?" Mouse asked, her breath hitching.

Darlene nodded. "The way I hear it, he can go all night. Some of the women who went to high school with him talked about the fact that he liked a lot of foreplay, but once he got in there, he didn't leave for a long time. I know that everyone in this town hates him, but I think that won't keep some of the women from crawling into his bed, real quiet like."

Women. They were so much worse than men. "Darlene, I'd like to order now."

She popped back to her feet. "Of course."

He gave her his order, and she took Mouse's, too. The minute she bounced off, Bo turned to his best friend. He gave off what he sincerely hoped was an air of paternal authority.

"Darlene is talking crap, you know."

Mouse's eyes trailed off. He knew who she was looking at. "I don't know about that. Why would she lie?"

"Because that girl likes to gossip more than she likes to breathe. All right, let me let you in on a little secret. A man like Trev McNamara is never going to be good in bed."

Now he had her attention. Her face caught his. "Why?"

So naïve. She really did need him. "Because he doesn't have to be. That man sitting over there was born with everything he needed to attract a hundred women at a time to his bed. He has looks and athletic ability. He can be a charming bastard when he wants to be. From what I've heard, the asshole's even got a monster cock. No man who has all those things is going to give a damn about foreplay. He doesn't need to. All he has to do to get a woman to open her legs is to smile at her. That's going to be his version of foreplay."

"How do you feel about foreplay?"

A sudden vision of stripping Mouse down and finding out if she tasted as innocent as she looked assaulted him. He loved to eat pussy. He could spend hours with his tongue on a woman. Would Mouse taste sweet and delicate? Or would she get wet and creamy and tangy? How long would he have to lick her before her juices flowed over his tongue?

Fuck. He was thinking about Mouse and getting a goddamn hard-on in the middle of the diner.

"Sorry," she said, looking down at her hands. "I didn't mean to embarrass you."

She'd utterly misread him, but then he knew she probably did that a lot. She had next to no experience. He wanted to let the whole conversation drop, but his hand came out and slid over hers.

"I like foreplay. When you decide to make love for the first time, you need to tell that man that you want a lot of foreplay. Don't let him cheat you out of that."

What was happening between him and Mouse? God. He wasn't sure if he was ready for this. He wasn't sure of anything at all. He loved Mouse. He knew that deep down. He loved her probably more than he'd loved anyone in his life.

But he wasn't ready to commit to anyone. Hell, if he did commit to her, it didn't mean everything would work out. He could ruin the only good relationship in his life by letting his dick lead him on.

Besides, if he slept with Mouse, it would mean something. She wasn't a good-time girl. She wasn't someone he could fuck and laugh when the next night she fucked one of his buddies. If he spent the night inside Mouse, it would mean she belonged to him. It would mean everyone would know about them. Right now, they were a weird pair. His friends and the rest of the town thought Bo was nice taking care of the odd girl. It would be different if they knew he loved her. He would be lumped in with her—an odd, misfit outcast.

Damn, he hated himself sometimes.

"I want to go to the honky-tonk tonight."

Bo let go of her hand. "What? Why?"

She didn't belong at The Rusty Spur. It was a dive bar located right outside the county line. It was one of his favorite places in the world. It was also the part of his life he kept hidden from Mouse.

She leaned back in the booth. "I've never been. I'm almost twenty-six years old. I haven't lived at all. I've spent every ounce of my energy taking care of my parents. I didn't do a lot of the things other women my age have done. I want to see what it's like."

It was smoky and nasty. It was filled with energy and life and beer and a whole bunch of men who would be all over her in a heartbeat. No way. No how. No go.

"You've never been to a crack house, either. That doesn't mean you should go. You can cross that right off your bucket list. I'm not taking you." He was supposed to meet Clarissa. He was going to drink for a while and then head on back to her place for a nice long screw. He wasn't sure how that would work when he explained he needed to drop off Mouse before they got to the fun bit.

Her chin came up. "Fine. I can go by myself."

Had something happened to her in that house? Where was this coming from? He stared at her like he'd never seen her before. "How are you going to get there? You don't even like to drive."

Those smooth, white shoulders shrugged. "I can drive when I want to. Or I can ride my bike."

He slapped his hand on the table. This was getting ridiculous. "You will do neither one. That road is dark and dangerous. You could get killed."

She bit her bottom lip, and a frustrated huff left her mouth. "I could get killed walking down the street. I want to go, Bo. I'm tired of being alone. I want to meet someone. I joined this online dating service, but they haven't sent me a good match yet. It seems like we're a little isolated. I've exchanged a couple of e-mails, but no one lives close enough for me to date."

He felt like his head was about to explode. "You did what?"

He'd practically screeched. He toned it down. Everyone in the restaurant was looking at them now. Mouse had turned a spectacular shade of red.

She kept her voice low, but he couldn't miss the irritation as she explained herself. "I joined this nice dating site. I got a check from Lexi and I bought a new computer. She showed me how to set everything up. She said the site I picked was reputable, but I'm not supposed to meet anyone without Lucas running a background check. Lucas says his law firm works with a security company and they'll vet anyone I date."

He was going to kill his brother. Aidan was behind this. He just knew it. Master Aidan had to stick his nose into everything when it came to a submissive woman. And Lexi. Bo should never have allowed Mouse to work for Lexi. Lexi wrote BDSM romance novels. He loved his sister-in-law, but she was proving to be a bad influence on Mouse.

"Yeah, I bet Ted Bundy could have passed a background check.

Serial killers who haven't gotten caught don't show up in the system. That's a real nice plan there, Mouse. Real smart. Let me get this straight. You've decided you want to get laid and the best way to do it is to meet some man on the Internet you don't know from Adam. Since that hasn't worked out for you, you're going to pick a guy up in a skank-ass bar. That's real classy."

Tears pooled in her eyes. "You go to that bar all the time. You sound very hypocritical right now."

He knew he did. He sounded like an asshole. But he couldn't stand the thought of some jerk who'd had one too many using his girl. His girl. It was happening too soon. They had been building to this for years, but now Bo knew he wasn't ready. He wasn't ready to give up the life he had for the one he would have with Mouse. Why couldn't things stay the same? Why had she put on that dress? Why did she have to look so fucking pretty? Why did he have to be such a goddamn coward?

"Hey, if you want to get a reputation, you feel free to go to that bar. Those men will screw almost anything that walks in the door. You won't have to look long before one shoves you up against the wall and fucks you right there. Is that what you want? You want to lose your virginity in a honky-tonk? Hell, if all that matters to you is the sex, I can call up five of my friends and set it up for you."

"Is there a problem here?"

Bo hadn't realized he'd had an audience. Trev McNamara and his sister stood at their table. Trev's jaw was clenched, and there was a dangerous glint in his eyes as he looked down at Bo.

Mouse gamely attempted a smile that didn't reach her eyes. Her nose had turned red. She wasn't the type of girl who cried pretty. When Mouse cried, she really cried. "No. We're fine, but thank you so much for asking."

Trev's whole face softened when he looked down at Mouse. "Are you sure, ma'am?"

She nodded, but the tears were streaking down her face.

"This is none of your business." Bo practically growled at the man, but it was Trev's sister who replied in a low tone.

"You've made it everyone's business by yelling. You've humiliated her. I don't know what this is about, but no one misunderstood the fact that you called her a whore in front of the whole diner. Patty's already on the phone." Shelley pinned him with her dark eyes. She put her hand out and took Mouse's. "Hey, let's go fix your mascara, Mouse."

Trev cleared his throat.

"Bethany," Shelley corrected. "Sorry. My brother doesn't like the fact that people call you Mouse. He doesn't understand, but he can be immovable about some things. Come on."

Mouse and Shelley disappeared into the ladies' room.

"You stay out of this, Trev. And you stay away from her. She isn't one of your strippers."

Trev frowned down at him. Bo wished he was standing. He knew even standing, Trev's six foot five topped him by an inch or two, but now the former quarterback loomed over him. "I realize that. Don't throw this on me, O'Malley. I'm not the one calling her a whore in public."

"I didn't do that." He certainly hadn't meant to. "I was trying to talk her out of making a terrible mistake. You know all about mistakes, don't you?"

"I do, indeed, and you're making a huge one. This scene is going to haunt her. No one will think less of you, but they'll talk about her. She's going to feel this scene for a long time. Now, we can go a couple of ways. You can shake my hand, and we can pretend this was all a misunderstanding and then people will start talking about us. Or you can prove yourself to be less of a man than I thought you were and you can keep spitting bile."

Trev was right. If he held out his hand, people would talk about how Bo O'Malley was the dumbass who welcomed the bad boy of Deer Run back to town. Or he could leave Mouse high and dry to take the brunt of his temper.

Bo cleared his face and put a friendly smile there. He held out his hand. Mouse had been through enough without having to listen to gossip about herself. His buddies would give him hell, but he could survive it.

"You always were a good man, Bo," Trev said solemnly as he shook his hand. "Even when you were a boy. Scoot over and Shelley and I will eat with you two, and the scene will be utterly forgotten."

Bo wasn't sure why, but he did it. He let the bastard sit beside him. He tried not to think about the fact that Trev McNamara calling him a good man had nearly brought a tear to his damn eye. He'd looked up to this man at one point. And he'd been brutally let down.

When Mouse returned, she sat across from Bo, quieter than she'd been before.

"Mouse, I'm sorry," he said, his voice barely above a whisper.

She shook her head. "It's okay. I won't mention it again. You're right, that kind of stuff isn't for someone like me."

His heart ached. That kind of stuff. Sex and affection and love.

She turned to Shelley and politely asked about her job. Shelley started talking about her redecorating efforts, and the two were off. He and Trev sat there not talking. But he couldn't miss the way Trev's eyes nearly ate up Mouse.

When his burger came, Bo found he wasn't hungry anymore.

Chapter Three

Mouse eased up the road. The pavement had ended about a mile back, and she was struggling to pedal on the gravel. There was a reason most people didn't ride bikes out this far. Several cars had already passed her by. Bo had been right about this. She could get run down on the road, but now she could hear the music. It seemed foolish to have come all this way only to turn back.

After Bo had dropped her off, she hadn't been able to sit still. She'd tried to read, but the words had swum before her. She was reading Lexi's new manuscript, highlighting the phrases that didn't work and making notes on what she liked. It was part of her job, being Lexi's assistant. It was only part-time for now, but she hoped one day she could quit all the contract accounting work she did and concentrate on helping Lexi. She usually enjoyed beta reading, but not tonight. Tonight she couldn't get the fight with Bo out of her head.

The idea of going to The Rusty Spur had tickled her consciousness.

He'd told her not to come. Bo didn't have any right to tell her what to do. He was only her friend. She'd read enough of Lexi's books to know a bit about Lexi's lifestyle. Aidan called the shots when it came to Lexi. But Aidan loved her. According to Lexi, he loved her often and with many toys. Bo didn't want her like that, so it didn't seem to her like he had any right to tell her what not to do.

She wasn't going to go in. Well, maybe for a moment. After all, she had ridden her bike over three miles to get here.

Surely it couldn't hurt too much to walk inside and see what was going on. She walked the bike up the gravel road. The honky-tonk was nothing more than a prefab building. It wasn't big. No bigger than a house really. The neon red sign illuminated the parking lot. It proudly claimed that this establishment was The Rusty Spur. The walls fairly vibrated with twangy, bouncy country music.

She'd already spied Bo's truck in the parking lot. He was here. He was probably drinking with his buddies. He had muttered an apology as he'd dropped her off, but he'd still held to his plans for the evening. Bo's plans included Clarissa Gates.

The door opened and music seemed to spill out. Two women dressed in tight jeans stumbled into the parking lot.

"Are you sure you want to share him?" the girl in the white jeans asked.

There was a loud laugh as the second woman lit a cigarette. "Trust me, Melody, Bo O'Malley can keep up with two women. Did you see the look on his face when I suggested it? I think he died and went to heaven."

She tried to shrink into the background. Clarissa and her friend Melody stood outside the doorway. Clarissa looked ready for action. Her blonde hair was teased sky-high, and her jeans looked painted on. She was the picture of a small-town princess walking on the wild side. She took a long drag on her cigarette.

"I think after I get through with old Bo, I might have to give Trev a whirl. My big sister said he was a stud back in high school."

Trev McNamara. She'd sat across from him all through dinner. He was so beautiful it almost hurt to look at him. Of course, she had a streak of masochism. She'd stolen glances all night. Trev was a huge man. He'd looked almost too big for the booth, but he hadn't complained or seemed uncomfortable. His shoulders were broad. His face looked like it should be on a movie screen. He had dark hair that was a tad long. It curled over his ears. His deep-blue eyes had seemed on the weary side, as though he'd had as much of the world as he could take, yet he kept on. But when he'd smiled at her, those eyes had lit up, and she hadn't thought about Bo for a while.

Idiot. If she couldn't handle Bo, she definitely couldn't handle a former star quarterback.

And it looked like it took two women to handle Bo.

"Well, don't let anyone know if you screw Trev. You don't want to get a reputation," Melody complained.

Clarissa's laugh split the air. "I already got a reputation, hon. I'm making damn sure I live up to it. Now, how about we get Bo and show him a real nice time."

The women tossed their cigarettes to the ground and turned to go inside. Mouse breathed a sigh of relief.

"Is that Mouse Hobbes?"

Oh, she wished she'd stayed at home.

Clarissa cocked her head. "Mouse, what the hell are you doing here?"

There was nothing to do but brazen her way through. "I thought I would get a beer."

Clarissa's eyes rolled. "No, I think you thought you would pull your crying act and get Bo to come home with you. Do you have any idea how pathetic you are? Everyone in the county laughs about it. You follow that man around like a sad puppy. He's never going to fuck you, hon. He likes real women, not pathetic losers."

Melody shook her head. "It's so sad how you use that man. He can't have a real life because he feels sorry for you."

Clarissa stepped forward, her eyes narrowed. "You aren't talking to him tonight, Mouse. In fact, as long as he's with me, I don't think I want you around him at all."

"Bethany?"

Tears blurring her eyes, she turned at the deep voice calling her name. Trev stepped out of the shadows looking long and lean and slightly dangerous.

"I thought we were going to meet out back. I was worried you stood me up. Now, come on. Let's get out of here. You know I can't hang out in a bar." He held out his big, callused hand.

It was the second time in one day that he'd saved her.

Clarissa took a step back. Her mouth firmed as she looked him over. "Damn, Trev. You look fine. How are you doing? And what are you doing here? I should have known all that sobriety shit was for show. Nothing ever stopped Trev McNamara from having a good time. Hey, dump the mouse and come inside with us."

Mouse waited for him to do exactly that, but his hand pulled her close. His arm went around her waist. She felt tiny and petite next to him. Her head barely came to his shoulders.

"I think we'll pass. I want to spend time with Beth. I don't think this establishment is good enough for her. After all, I've seen the clientele."

Clarissa's mouth dropped open. "You're a bastard."

"Everyone knows that," he replied with a shrug.

Mouse didn't. She was pretty sure he was her guardian angel. Clarissa turned on her heels and flounced back into the bar, Melody right behind her.

Trev immediately stepped back, and she missed the heat of his body.

"I'm sorry, Beth. I didn't think about how this was going to look. She's probably going to march in there and start telling the tale about how she saw you with me. I wasn't thinking. I heard what she said and I couldn't let her get away with it." His deep voice had a gravely quality to it that she found oddly soothing even when he was stumbling over words to apologize.

She stared down at his boots because she worried she might drool if she kept looking at his face. "It's okay. The worst that might happen is they think old Mouse Hobbes finally found someone who can stand to sleep with her."

His hand came out, and he lifted her chin. She was shocked at the dark look on his face. His hands came down and curled around her shoulders, his grip the slightest bit harsh. It got her attention.

"Don't you dare say such things about yourself. Not around me. And your name is Bethany."

Her heart did an odd pitter-pat, like it couldn't quite find a rhythm. "I like Beth better."

His mouth curved up, and the hands on her shoulders relaxed. "All right then, Beth. No more Mouse. And no more calling yourself old. God, girl, you're practically a baby compared to me. Spare an old man, please."

"Yes, Trevor. You look like an old man."

"I feel it. Never doubt that I feel it." His face closed off, and she wished he was smiling again. "Did you drive here? I'll follow you home. This isn't a good place for a woman on her own, and I really can't go in that bar."

She reached around and pulled out her bike. It had been her mother's at one point in time. It was a feminine bike with a comfy seat and a basket on the front. It was painted a muted green and white.

A single eyebrow arched as he looked over her favorite mode of transportation. "Are you serious?"

She shrugged. "I don't like to drive much. It scares me."

"And being on the highway on a bicycle in the middle of the night doesn't?"

Now he sounded like Bo. "I can handle it. I'm responsible for myself, sir."

"Fuck." He said it under his breath, but she caught it. He shifted as though he was in a little pain. "Give the bike to me. We can put it in the back of my truck. I'll take you home. Unless you really were planning on walking in and hauling Bo out of there."

She couldn't stand the thought that Trev believed that. "I didn't come here for Bo."

"You seem pretty close to him." His eyes became hooded.

"He's my friend. I will admit that I care about him. But he doesn't want me like a man wants a woman. He sees me as his sister. I didn't come here for him."

"Why did you come here, Beth?" The question rolled out of his mouth like a silky temptation, as if he knew what she was looking for, but he was going to make her say it.

"I didn't want to be alone tonight." She forced the admission out. Maybe Clarissa was right. Maybe she was pathetic, but by god, she was honest about it.

He took her bike, easily picking it up with one hand. He didn't roll it along. He simply lifted it as though it had no real weight. "Come on then, darlin'. I don't want to be alone, either. You're sure you don't belong to Bo?"

"I don't belong to anyone." She didn't anymore. Her family was all gone. Bonnie loved her, but it was in a distant way. And Bo was too busy having crazy ménage sex. She was never going to be enough for him. She belonged to herself. She was responsible for her own happiness.

Trev stopped in front of a battered old Ford pickup. It was green and white. It was lovely. Trev hefted the bike up and gently put it in the back of the truck.

"This is yours?"

He smiled, one eyebrow cocking up. "I hope so, darlin'. Otherwise I just gave away your preferred mode of transportation."

She let her hands find the truck's body, remembering everything she loved about this model. 1970. Green body. White trim. Bench seats. "My granddaddy had a truck like this. I remember how it felt to sit beside him as he drove through town. I felt like I was bigger than everyone else. He always played Loretta Lynn."

Trev grimaced. "I don't have that, darlin'. The only thing I've spent money on in this car is a CD player. I'm afraid the best I can do is Miranda Lambert. My sister gave me her CD for my birthday."

"Same difference. The point is, I love your truck. It's been a long time since I saw one like this."

"It's a mess. It needs to be fixed up."

"I like to fix things up. It's so much better than buying something new."

Trev stopped and stared. "You know, you're just about perfect for me. Where did you come from?"

"Deer Run. I was born here." It wasn't surprising he didn't know much about her. They had lived in the same town their whole lives, but she had never really spoken to him. He might have occupied the same space, but his world had been completely different.

He laughed, throwing that gorgeous head back. "I'll buy that, darlin'. I will. Now take a seat and I'll get you home. Buckle up."

Trev jogged around the truck and managed to get to the passenger door before she could. He opened the door and held out his hand to help her up.

"Thank you, sir."

He sighed again. "Beth, you're killing me."

She wasn't sure why, but it felt nice when he handed her up. He pulled the seat belt out and buckled her in. His hand sliding across her waist sparked something odd and primal in Mouse. Her skin sizzled everywhere he touched.

She tried to turn her attention away. "What were you doing here?"

Was he already slipping? She found that unaccountably sad. He didn't seem drunk. The cab of his truck smelled like coffee, rich and warm. She didn't see any evidence of a drinking binge.

"I was sitting out here staring at the bar."

It was a stark admission. His eyes trailed back toward the honky-tonk.

Without really thinking about it beyond the fact he seemed to need it, she brought her hands up to his cheeks and gently forced his head to turn to face her. "Why?"

"I was trying to decide whether or not I would go in and have a drink. I sat here and sipped my coffee and made a deal with myself. I would wait five minutes and then I would go in and have a drink. And then I would decide to wait another five minutes."

He was on the edge of something bad, yet he'd managed to treat her with genuine kindness. "Are you all right?"

He hadn't tried to move out of her hold. He simply stared at her, the moonlight illuminating his gorgeous face. "No, Beth, but that's not your problem."

But Clarissa hadn't been his problem. "I want to help you if I can."

Now he did take a step back and ran a hand through his hair. He wasn't wearing a hat. His hair tumbled over his forehead. "I don't think that's such a good idea. I think I should drive you home, and then I should probably stay away from you."

He closed the door to the truck and walked around to the driver's side. He hopped in, but he didn't say anything, merely turned the engine over and started out of the lot, gravel crunching beneath the tires.

He asked for directions to her house in a controlled, quiet voice, but she knew that easy intimacy they had found in the parking lot was gone. He was doing her a favor. He was cleaning up the small mess she'd made by trying to go somewhere she shouldn't.

She stared out of the window. The moon was huge and full, hanging low in the sky. She was right back where she had started. She would spend the night alone, like she spent all her nights.

But at least now she knew once and forever that Bo wasn't going to be hers. It was long past time to let that dream go. He was a nice man who had been a good friend to her, but she couldn't compete with the Clarissas of this world. She didn't have a lick of experience with anything but taking care of sick people, running her boss's errands, and accounting. She had a wonderful, sexy degree in accounting from an online college. Yep, she was going to attract a man like Bo with her innate ability to add.

The drive was over all too soon, though she knew it was for the best. Trev McNamara wasn't for her, either.

He pulled the truck to a stop.

"Isn't this the old Bellows's place?" He put the truck in park and killed the engine. "I heard my sister's husband say something about you buying it."

She undid the seat belt. Now that she was home, she wanted to get inside quickly and put the idiocy of the night behind her. Trev had already said he didn't intend to see her again. She would go back to her life, a little wiser than before. She would concentrate on her new house.

"I bought it in an auction." She'd used all of the insurance money she'd inherited. She would be forever grateful to Bonnie, who hadn't taken her half of the money their parents had left them. If she had, Mouse wouldn't have been able to afford the house. Her sister had hugged her and told her she deserved the money. Even as it was, she needed another loan to make the improvements. "It was a last-minute kind of thing. I was lucky. Not a whole bunch of people showed up to the auction. I think most folks around here think this house is haunted. If Bryce had shown up, I doubt I could have afforded the place."

She opened the passenger side door, but Trev put a hand on her arm.

"Did you leave the front door open?"

She looked out the window. He was right. Sure enough, the front door was wide open. She scrambled to get out. Her sandals hit the ground, and she started to sprint toward the house. Was someone in there? Was someone stealing the antiques? She didn't have much in the house of her own, but she'd bought the place and it was all she had.

A big arm clotheslined her midsection. Trev caught her and tightened his hold.

"Let me go. I need to get in there," she pleaded.

"Not happening." Trev set her on her feet but kept his hands on her. "I'm not about to let you go into that house. You stay here. If you hear anything funny, call 9-1-1. Do you understand me?"

She nodded as he shoved his phone in her hand. He was right. If there was someone inside, exactly how did she intend to deal with them? A politely worded request for them to leave probably wouldn't do it.

She opened her mouth to call him back, but he was already on the steps by the time she thought of it. He turned, his big body shadowed.

"And, Beth, if you come in here after me, you will not like what I do to your backside. Is that understood?"

She nodded, not trusting her voice. He turned and disappeared inside.

Had he threatened to spank her?

The phone in her hand trilled. She looked down at it. Someone named Marty was calling. She slid her finger across the phone to answer. "Hello?"

"Thank god. I've been trying all week. Who is this? I need to talk to Trevor." The man had a slick-sounding accent, like he was from back East. He spoke in the quick cadence of a man used to having his needs met.

Trevor might be fighting for his life. Her stomach turned. "He's unavailable right now."

There was a humorless huff on the other end of the line. "That's not surprising. Tell me something, is it booze, or is he back on the coke?"

"No, I think he's drinking coffee. And at dinner he had a Dr Pepper."

There was a long pause. She gave serious thought to disobeying Trev. He wouldn't really spank her. That was an empty threat. What if he needed her help?

She started to walk toward the house as the voice on the other end of the phone kept talking.

"Are you serious? Listen, when he comes to, tell him to call me. I have a team in LA desperate for a veteran QB. I'm hopping a flight from JFK to DFW in the morning. He needs to be ready to head out to LAX by afternoon. Got that, doll? And I'll bring him a little pick-me-up. He needs to look good for these guys."

The connection was cut without a good-bye, and Mouse grasped the phone. She might need it. She was on the first step, trying to move quietly, when she heard a voice.

"You are not where I left you, Beth."

She shrieked. He'd caught her unawares. Her heart felt like it would pound out of her chest. Trev stood in the doorway glaring at her.

"It's my house. You can't expect me to stand in the yard while someone murders you," she said, breathless.

"I expect my direct orders to be obeyed." His sculpted arms crossed over his chest.

"Should I call the cops?" She tried to avoid the whole discussion about direct orders. Something about the way he was looking at her made her a little breathless.

His head shook. "No one's in there. Are you sure you locked it?"

She bit her bottom lip and tried to remember. "I think so. But maybe not."

His face hardened. "You live alone in this big house and you didn't bother to lock up?"

"Well, nothing much works in this place. And the door isn't very sturdy. Even if I did lock it, it wouldn't take much to get in. It's on my list of things to replace. I don't think the back door even has a lock." She laughed a little. Now that the threat had passed, it seemed silly to have panicked. She'd watched too many movies. "Well, I thank you for the ride."

She started to move past him, but he stood there in the doorway, an immovable hunk of granite.

"We're not done here, darlin'. You can't expect me to walk away. Anyone could come in here while you're sleeping. You could be raped."

She laughed outright at that. "Didn't you hear what Clarissa said? I think I'm safe. No one is going to touch old Mouse Hobbes."

"I warned you."

She gasped as Trev pulled her wrist into his hand and started to haul her into the house.

* * * *

Trev felt his blood pressure threaten to hit the roof. It was all too fucking much. First, the altercation with Bo O'Malley, then after they'd gotten back from the diner, he'd had to listen to his poor sister fight her husband over having Trev in the house. Then there were the calls from Marty. That had really threatened to send him over the edge. Marty had left about thirty messages promising him money, women, and all the coke he could snort if he would meet with the general manager of the LA team about taking over their QB position.

Too much.

He'd found himself sitting outside The Rusty Spur before he really knew what was happening. He'd sat there for at least an hour, staring at the building. It had been a goddamn relief when he'd realized Beth was standing at the door. He hadn't seen her approach, but he'd heard that bitch Clarissa try to drag her down. He hadn't thought twice. He'd inserted himself into the situation.

"Trev, what are you doing?"

Beth's voice came out as a squeak. He could feel the trepidation coming off her in waves. He knew he should slow down, but they needed to make a few things clear.

"I'm giving you the lay of the land, darlin'." He found the old sofa in the living room. He'd nearly tripped on it earlier because apparently the overhead lights didn't work in here. He pulled her over his lap. Bethany Hobbes's round ass was right over his knee.

Yes. This was exactly what he needed to get his mind off everything. When he was balls deep in Beth's ass, he wouldn't be thinking about a drink. He would only be thinking about how long he could last and how many times he could take her.

"I think the land is laid out enough. Now let me up, please." Even across a man's knee, she was polite.

Damn, but she needed a keeper.

"Call me Sir." He wanted to hear it again. She said it to be polite. She couldn't possibly know what it did to his dick.

"If you're trying to show me all the bad things that could happen to me, then I get your point. You're bigger and stronger than I am. You don't have to make a fool out of me."

He heard the slight hitch in her voice. He had been trained to read women. Beth wasn't even close to being aroused. She was sad. Her body was slumped over as though she was merely waiting for whatever happened to her.

The discipline would have to wait.

He helped her to her feet.

"Thank you. I think you should go now. I promise I won't get into trouble again." She smoothed down the skirt of that fluffy, yellow sundress.

There were a few problems with that scenario. "I told you I can't go. I can't leave you alone here."

"This is my home."

His dick didn't like the idea of leaving her, but if he had to, he couldn't simply walk out. "What's your dad's number?"

"My father passed away."

His heart clenched. She was truly alone. She didn't have anyone to watch out for her. What the hell was he thinking going after a woman like Beth? She was soft and sweet and deserved way more than he would be able to give her.

And yet, it was so obvious there wasn't a decent prospect for her on the horizon.

He liked her. He should treat her the way she should expect to be treated, and that meant getting her out of a house that was obviously dangerous. His only other option was to stay here and watch over her. But if he stayed with her, he wasn't sure he would be able to control his baser instinct. His cock was already aching.

"I'm sorry to hear about your father." He forced the Neanderthal inside him to take a break. He reached over and flicked on the lamp, praying it worked. It didn't offer much by the way of illumination, but it was better than nothing. And then he caught sight of the monstrosity over his head. "What the hell is that?"

She looked up and a smile curled her lips. He was happy to see it since her face had paled when she'd mentioned her father. "It's Maudine Bellows's version of high art, I'm afraid."

It was a chandelier of sorts, only where there should be crystal dripping down, someone had made the whole damn thing out of deer antlers. They pointed up, down, and every which way, as though the "artist" hadn't been able to decide on a direction and simply shoved a mass of sharp antlers into a bundle, parked some lights here and there, and hung it from the ceiling.

It sort of creeped him out. "I think that's a whole herd."

Beth simply shrugged. "She didn't have the best taste, I'm afraid. And the actual lights don't work. I'm going to replace it with something more modern and less dead."

That seemed like a good idea. Now that he had a real look around, it was obvious the house needed a lot of work. It looked like the set of *The Addams Family*. Beth was a ray of sunshine in amongst the gloom. And he couldn't leave her. "Why don't you get some things and I'll take you back to Shelley's with me?"

He hadn't intended to go back, but he would for Beth. Tomorrow, after he'd met with Aidan and set everything up, he would install a new door and bright, shiny locks.

And maybe he could take her to dinner if she honestly didn't care what people thought.

She shook her head. "I'm staying here."

"That's a bad idea. Anyone could walk in."

"I'll be fine. Nothing happened. It was probably the wind. I'll move one of the bookshelves in front of the door, and it will be safe."

"I can't leave you here alone." He took a deep breath. Honesty was always best. "And I can't stay with you, either. If I stay in this house, I'm going to end up in bed with you."

Her eyes flashed to him and then back down, but not before he'd seen the interest there.

Damn. He needed to walk away. She was so naïve. So fucking innocent, but she wasn't a girl. She was a woman. She was a woman on her own.

He should walk the fuck away.

His hand came out and lifted her chin up. "I would love to spend the night with you, but you have to understand what that means to someone like me."

"I suspect it would mean sex." She said it quietly, but there was a sparkle in her eye.

He loved the way her eyes lit up. She wasn't thinking about everything she'd lost now.

"I need to be in control. I wanted you the minute I saw you, but you should know that going to bed with me tonight would be about more than simply wanting you."

"You want the distraction." And she wasn't a fool. His Beth was smart.

His. Sometimes he was sure he was two utterly different people. There was the dumbass addict who didn't care about anything beyond his next high, and the caveman who thought everything belonged to him. Those two sides of him fought constantly for control. He needed to make her understand.

"Every second of the day is a fight. It's my first night on my own and I ended up sitting in front of a bar. If you hadn't come along, I don't know what would have happened."

"I do," she replied with surety. "You would have kept pushing the decision out until it was too late. You would have sat there until the bar closed."

She had more faith in him than he did. "Why on earth would you say that?"

"Because you're here. Because you did it. You went to rehab, and you're sober. You fought it."

"I fight it every day, baby. You have to understand that. This isn't something that goes away. I'm an alcoholic and an addict, and I will be until the day I die."

70

She seemed to think about that for a moment. "I think we all have our flaws. I'm way too shy."

"It's not the same thing. Your shyness never caused you trouble."

"My shyness never did a thing at all. And I'm addicted to it. I can't quite give it up. I don't even try. So don't say it hasn't caused me trouble. It means I'm a twenty-five-year-old virgin who can't stand up for herself. You had to change or you would die. If I don't find a way to change, I'm never going to *live*."

She stood there, the moonlight from the window making her skin seem translucent, and Trev knew there was no way he was going to walk away from her. He wanted her. He needed her.

And it appeared she might need him, too.

"If I scare you, you have to tell me. No safe words tonight. A simple 'no' will stop me."

Her eyes went wide. "Safe word? Like in Lexi's books?"

He felt himself smile. Lexi's BDSM romances had become quite popular in the erotic community. He could see Beth reading one. If she was curious, that was all the better for him. "Yes."

"You really were going to spank me, weren't you? That wasn't about trying to teach me a lesson. You wanted to spank me."

His cock pulsed at the thought. "Yes, darlin'. I wanted to flip that skirt up and push your panties down. I would have tangled them at your ankles so you couldn't fight me. Your ass would have been in the air. I would have touched you, and then, oh then I would spank you. Over and over, you would have felt the slap of my hand against your flesh. Yes, Beth, I wanted it. And I was absolutely trying to teach you a lesson, just not the one you think."

"I think you would spank me to teach me that you're the Dom."

Such a smart girl. "I am. Make your decision. If you want to think about this for a while, I'll understand. You can go and pack a bag and sleep out at Shelley's. Tomorrow, I'll make arrangements for some sturdier doors and better locks. And we can have dinner. Like a normal couple."

He could do normal. He could treat her like the sweet virgin she was. He didn't have to spank her and tie her up and teach her what it meant to take her Dom's cock up her ass.

71

No. He didn't need that at all.

"And if you stay?"

He swallowed. If he stayed, it would get serious. "I want you kneeling at my feet. I want you obedient. I want you submissive."

Now she would be the good girl she was and let him off the hook. She would go and pack her bag, and he would take her someplace nice. His cock ached. His cock thought he was being an imbecile. He was going to sit up all night wishing he could have a beer when he could have lost himself in Beth.

She sank to the floor, the hardwoods creaking slightly as she fell to her knees. The yellow sundress belled around her as she allowed her hands to find her knees. She turned them over, palms up.

"Like this?"

Fuck yeah, like that. All thoughts besides the woman kneeling in front of him fled in an instant. His cock firmly took control, and the idiot who always wanted a beer in his hand went completely silent.

It was the Dom's time.

"Very nice, love." He let his hand find her hair. He pulled the pins that held the bun out, and her soft hair flowed out like a gorgeous sable cloud surrounding her face. "Better. You're not to wear your hair up when I'm around. It's beautiful, and I want to be able to touch it."

He shoved his hand in, fingers twisting lightly, and he raised her head to face him. "And, Beth, if you disobey again, the spanking won't be erotic. It will be a reminder to you to mind your Dom."

He didn't miss the way her eyes had gone soft, and her mouth couldn't seem to close. She was responding beautifully.

"Is this only for the night?" She asked the question with a slight frown. She seemed to be expecting an answer that wouldn't make her happy.

And he was going to have to give her one. He felt such a deep connection to the woman at his feet. He'd never quite wanted anyone the way he wanted her. But he had to be honest. "I don't know that I'm good for anyone in the long run, darlin'. And I don't intend to stay here. I'm working here for a year, and then I'm leaving. I'm going out west. I'm buying into a ranch, and that's where I'll live."

"That doesn't answer my question. Are you going to disappear in the morning? It doesn't change my answer. I still want this. But I would like to set my expectations."

He was going to have to teach her a thing or two. And that would take more than one night in the sack. "I'll be with you in the morning. And we'll talk. I think we could spend some time together, if you want to."

A Dom was worth more than just an orgasm. He could teach her how to stand up for herself. He could teach her to not need him.

He didn't like that thought, but it might be the best gift he could give her.

Trev sat back on the creaky sofa. He was going to spend the next year here in Deer Run. He'd have to work most of the time, but the thought of spending his off time with Beth teaching her about BDSM made his heart lighter.

He had a year until he got the money from his contract. He had a year to spend with her. "Come up here. Sit on my lap."

Now that the decision was made, he could take his time. His cock still throbbed in his jeans, but even that beast had quieted a bit. It would get its way. He would bury that cock deep inside her pussy and not leave for a really long time. He could be patient with her.

She took his outstretched hand and placed herself on his lap.

Trev looked at her. "Now, tell me how you like to be kissed."

Chapter Four

Bo drank down the beer and wished he was somewhere else.

Jimmy Nixon slapped another beer in front of him. "Damn, man, you're getting lucky tonight. Have you seen the way Clarissa is looking at you? I wish I was in your shoes."

He'd seen it. It was the way she looked at any man she hadn't gotten into the sack yet. There was nothing special about him to Clarissa except that apparently it was his turn. She'd gone through most of the men in the county who had a lick of money. She'd apparently discovered he had a trust fund he'd recently come into.

He hadn't bothered to explain to her that there was no way he was spending the eight hundred thousand his father had left him on anything except buying back into his own damn ranch. That codicil in Conner O'Malley's will had been the old man's last attempt to drive a wedge between his sons. Causing trouble between Bo and Aidan had been one of the old fucker's favorite pastimes. Giving Aidan the ranch but not the money to run it had been Conner's way of punishing Aidan for not sticking around. And giving him the money but not the land he loved had been his way of punishing Bo for not being Aidan.

Now he had access to the money, and he knew what he should do with it. So why was he hesitating?

"I think her tits are going to fall out of that shirt. Do you think those are real?" Jimmy asked.

He turned back to his friend. "No. She had them done last year. You didn't notice she went from next to nothing to Pamela Anderson?"

Clarissa's breasts were big and perfectly round, and he was kind of afraid they'd explode if he touched them too hard. They were like a water balloon someone had filled to the point of bursting. They weren't soft like…

What was wrong with him? Earlier in the day he'd been damned excited about getting in that girl's pants, and now he wasn't interested. Now he was sitting around moaning into his beer because he couldn't get the sight of Mouse's sad eyes when he'd dropped her off out of his mind. She'd seemed resigned and done with it all.

Was she done with him?

"I heard her talking to Melody in the hallway. They were going out to have a smoke. I think they're going to initiate you into their little club."

He fought to not roll his eyes. Melody and Clarissa thought they were wild because every now and then they shared a guy for the night. Bo didn't see the attraction. He only had one dick. What was the other girl supposed to do? Give him a foot massage?

In this particular case, his brother had the right idea. A woman could handle more than one guy. A woman had a whole lot of parts that required attention. She had breasts and a mouth and a soft pussy and a round ass she tried to hide under clothes that didn't fit. Fuck. He was thinking of Mouse again.

"I don't know. I might pawn her off on you tonight," he said, sliding the beer away. He'd only had the one, and now he didn't feel like getting even the slightest bit tipsy. He wanted to be able to drive. Maybe he should go talk to Mouse. He hated the way he'd left things with her. It made him nauseous. He'd acted like an ass around her all day.

Jimmy's mouth was turned down, and his brother, Brian, joined them. Brian looked like he was on his fifth whiskey. "What's wrong with you, man? You haven't been the same lately."

Maybe he wasn't the same because he was growing up and his

friends seemed to want to stay the same. They were still the same redneck idiots they'd all been in high school, except some of them had wives and kids. Jimmy had two kids by two different women, and here he was looking for baby mama number three when he didn't pay support to the ones he had because he couldn't keep a job.

This was why he spent a lot of nights at Mouse's place watching TV while she worked on other people's taxes or read a book. He told himself it was because his house was too quiet, but he enjoyed her company. She could talk about anything.

"I'm fine, man," Bo said. "I'm tired. It's been a long week."

It *had* been a long week. He'd had to completely reinstall a large portion of the east fence after straight-line winds tore it up. His shoulder had been aching for days. Mouse had fussed over him and made him put a heating pad on it.

Damn, his brother was right. He was such an asshole. He'd been using her for years. He'd gone to her for comfort and love and offered nothing real in return.

Brian snorted. He was older than Bo. He'd been in the same class with Trev.

Sitting next to Trev and having dinner had been a weird experience. Bo had always liked Shelley. The dark-haired woman had been popular, but in a sweet way, nothing like Clarissa's mean girl. She'd always been nice to Mouse. Bo had gotten to know her pretty well when George had gone into the hospital for his final days. Apparently Mouse had helped Shelley through her mother's final days, and Shelley had shown up to pay the favor back.

Sitting with Mouse and Shelley and Trev tonight at dinner had been a revelation. He hadn't been forced to laugh at dumb jokes or compare women's breast sizes. They had talked about politics and things happening in the world. Sure, he'd mostly listened, but he'd enjoyed that meal more than he liked to admit.

He'd missed Trev. *Asshole.*

"Bo's been spending too much time with that group out on his ranch, if you ask me. They think they're better than us because they came from the city." Brian had a real problem with anyone who hadn't been born in a town the size of a postage stamp.

"Aidan was born here," he argued, but there wasn't a lot of heat behind it. He was starting to get damn tired of this conversation.

"Yeah, well, he left as fast as he could." Brian tossed back his drink, swallowing the contents and slamming the glass on the bar when he was done. "And he's brought back those two. City snobs. Did you know that woman of his is trying to force the city to spend thousands of dollars so she can wash her hair in artesian water?"

Now Bo didn't try to stop his eye roll. *Idiots.* "Lexi is trying to get the city to upgrade the water filtration facilities that serve the school. And Lucas put up some of his own money for the project."

"Yeah, we don't want no money from gays."

This was the shit he put up with on a daily basis. "Well, you fight him then. I'm sure all three of your kids will be fine. They might be deformed, but at least they won't have taken homosexual money."

Why did he hang out with these guys? Habit. He'd been trying to fit in since the day he'd figured out it sucked to not fit in.

Brian scratched at his head. "Yeah. That's right. Hey, what do you mean by deformed?"

He was saved from having to explain that to a very drunk Brian by a well-manicured hand dipping into his shirt.

"Hey, what are you doing?" Clarissa practically purred in his ear.

Thinking about running as fast as he could. The whole thing with Clarissa had seemed like a fun idea, but she was kind of scaring him now. He looked down and saw her blood-red nails disappearing into his shirt.

"Yeah, Bo, how's it going?" Melody swept in beside him. She was a blonde, too, though hers seemed a bit more natural than Clarissa's. Melody's hand slid along his thigh.

He nearly jumped out of his seat. "It's going good, ladies. But I seem to be a little tired."

Clarissa cocked a hip, and that taloned hand of hers rode it. "What do you mean, you're tired? It's not even ten o'clock. We're supposed to head out to Angel's party."

Angel. He'd forgotten about that. Angel threw some wild parties that lasted for days. He had to work tomorrow. He'd promised his brother he would come in and meet the new foreman and pick up a feed order.

"You know I have to work in the morning. I think I'm going to call it a night."

Clarissa's mouth turned down into a pout that would do a two-year-old proud. "Tomorrow is Saturday."

"Yeah, the cows don't care. They don't stop eating because it's the weekend." Ranching was a twenty-four-seven job. And it was a great excuse to get out of something he never should have gotten into.

"He's gotta work hard because that brother of his is way too busy fucking his boyfriend to do real man's work." Brian belched.

Bo'd had just about enough of Brian. And he'd had enough of all of this. "Shut your fucking mouth. You don't know my brother. My brother damn near gave up his legs for this country. You will treat him with some respect."

Jimmy stood, his hands waving. "Hey, guys, there's no reason for this to get ugly. We're all joking around. That's all."

That was the excuse for everything. He'd said the same words a thousand times. *Don't fight. It's not worth fighting over. Laugh it off and let the good times roll.*

Maybe some things were worth fighting over.

"I think I'd like an apology." Bo stared at Brian.

Brian stood up. He towered over Bo. "Maybe you're gay, too. Everyone saw you sitting with Trev McNamara. Did big-city living give him a taste for boys?"

"Trev ain't doing Bo. Bo's not gay. And Trev's not either, though his taste in women sure has gone down." Clarissa's lips curved up like she had a secret she was dying to tell.

The music from the jukebox seemed to pulse through the bar. He could feel it in his boots. The place was too damn loud, and he didn't like the company. It was definitely time to leave. It was time to fucking change. He'd made too many decisions based on keeping his place in a group of people he didn't even like anymore.

"Now that we've got my sexual orientation out of the way, I think I'll head on home." He wouldn't. He was going to make a beeline for Mouse's place. Right after he stopped for some flowers.

Could he get flowers at this time of night? He wanted to apologize to her.

Damn, he wanted to treat her right. She was the only person in the world who ever stuck by him. It was past time to start treating her the way she should be treated.

"I don't know if I want this discussion to be over." Brian stood in his way. "I think it's about time the good citizens of Deer Run got together and forced your brother out. We don't need his kind around here."

He almost laughed. Aidan and the company he was invested in, Barnes-Fleetwood, had poured more money into Deer Run's coffers than the town had ever seen. There might be a large group of assholes who talked bad about his brother's way of life, but ninety-nine percent of them had profited from his business. If Brian wanted to show up at the O'Malley Ranch with torches and pitchforks, he would most likely do it alone.

And then Aidan would find a nice place to bury Brian.

"You do that, buddy." He wasn't getting into a brawl with some dickhead whose mind was way too small.

"You can't leave. I told everyone we're going to that party." Clarissa and Melody had formed a hair-sprayed phalanx in front of him.

He didn't want to fight with them, either. "I appreciate the offer, ladies, but I have to pass tonight."

"Hey, I was talking to you." Brian's meaty finger poked him in the back.

"Maybe you should sit down, Brian. I'll get you another drink." Jimmy tried getting in between them.

"Back off, asshole." The whole bar was starting to watch the scene playing out. He could hear the bartender on the phone, already calling the cops. Fights at The Rusty Spur were legendary.

"Are you planning on going to that pathetic whore?" Clarissa asked.

Bo turned to her, Brian utterly forgotten. He had a pretty good idea who she meant. Aidan could stick up for himself. Mouse couldn't. "What did you say?"

Melody seemed to be smarter than her friend. She took a quick step back. "Nothing. She didn't say nothing."

Clarissa didn't back down. "Yes, I did. I think you're planning on dumping me for that sad-sack little mouse who follows you around. Damn, I always thought she was a dried-up old prude, but she must be doing something right. Have you been fucking her all these years? She must have learned something from you since she's sleeping with Trev now."

Damn it. The story about the diner had gotten all over town, but it hadn't gone down the way Bo had hoped. "We had dinner with the man. Don't you go around trashing her reputation."

"I don't have to," Clarissa shot back. "She did that all on her own. Melody saw it, too. Old Mouse Hobbes left here with Trev McNamara wrapped around her. I guess he knows the real women of this town won't have anything to do with him."

Brian laughed behind him. "Bo couldn't even do Mouse Hobbes. Damn. Maybe I'll give that girl a whirl. I like my women with a little cushion, and after Trev's done with her, she should be experienced enough. Yeah, maybe I'll see what she's doing."

The whole world took on a strange red sheen, as though someone had put goggles with bloody lenses over his eyes. They were talking about Mouse. They were talking about his Mouse. The entire idea of that fuckhead Brian's hands on his sweet Mouse sent his fist rearing back.

Bo attacked the other man, fists flying.

In the background, he could already hear the sirens wailing.

* * * *

Mouse couldn't breathe. Sitting on Trev McNamara's lap was the most erotic thing that had ever happened to her. He wasn't pawing at her or making any aggressive moves. His hand was on her waist, and the other cupped her knee through the material of her skirt.

"Put your arms around my neck." He seemed calmer than before. His voice was a rich, dark blend of sensuality and command.

It was nothing like the times she'd been close to a man before. It hadn't happened often, and they had been boys, not men. She'd gotten into trouble the one time she'd gone to a party. Some drunk guy from two towns over had gotten her in a corner and put his hands all over her.

Bo had saved her.

But she wasn't going to think about Bo tonight. She let her hands find Trev's shoulders. Even through the cotton of his shirt, she could feel the supple muscles that covered his body. He seemed to be hard everywhere.

"Now, answer my question." The hand on her knee came up to brush across her bottom lip. "How do you like to be kissed?"

"Soft. And I don't like the tongue thing." That boy who had molested her had put his tongue all over her. She remembered it surging into her mouth. She couldn't stand it.

"Well, I'm going to have to fix that. Because I definitely want to put my tongue on you. But we can go slow." His words seemed to do exactly that. They seemed slow and languid, like he had all night and intended to use it.

It was utterly different from what she'd expected from him. He'd seemed so close to the edge. She thought he would throw her over the nearest surface and take her. A part of her wanted that. She would get it over with and know once and for all what it felt like.

Of course, she also hadn't expected him to tell her he wanted more than one night.

"Why don't you show me how you want to kiss?"

"I thought the Dom was supposed to do all the showing." She wasn't sure she could do this. It would be easier if he would take control. What kind of Dom was he?

The hand on her waist tightened. "The Dom is supposed to know what the sub needs. I know what you want. And I know that me turning you around and shoving my cock in isn't going to teach you anything. I will fuck you, darlin'. Don't doubt that, and when we get to it, I'll be in control. But we're going to start slow, and you're going to be ready to take me. Now, kiss me or lay over my lap for some discipline. I'm allowing you to control the kiss for now, but do not doubt that I'm still the Dom. Speaking of Doms, is all your knowledge from Lexi's books?"

"Yes. And some other books. We don't have a club here. I've

seen how Aidan and Lucas treat Lexi. It's different than what I would have thought." Lucas and Aidan worshipped Lexi.

"Yes, we get a bad rap. Now kiss me."

Mouse took a deep breath and moved in. She could do this. She wanted this. She pressed her lips against his. His lips were thick and perfectly made. Masculine but so sinfully beautiful they made her sigh. She'd watched his lips when they had sat together in the diner. Now she felt them under hers.

He didn't move. He simply let her explore. She was tentative at first, her lips dry and awkward. He didn't respond. Was she doing it wrong? She should stop. She didn't know what she was doing. She was being ridiculous.

She really was. He was a man. He was a man who had offered himself up to her, and she was thinking about quitting because she didn't get it right the first time?

Mouse shifted. She could feel his erection against her bottom. He was hard and ready, but he seemed to need something from her.

She ran her tongue across her lips and kissed him again. She kissed him the way she'd dreamed of kissing a man her whole life. She molded her lips to his and let go of her inhibitions. She might only get one shot at this, and she wasn't going to waste time worrying if she got it right. She wanted to feel. She kissed his mouth and the straight line of his jaw. She rubbed her cheek against his. His five-o'clock shadow nipped at her skin. She ran her nose along his neck, reveling in his scent. She kissed all along that rock-hard jawline until she found his lips again.

And suddenly she got the whole tongue thing. She wanted to taste him. She gently brought the tip of her tongue out to run along his plump bottom lip.

Trev groaned, and his hand wandered to her ass. "Straddle me."

She didn't want to stop kissing, but she did as he asked. She hooked a knee over him so she straddled him like she was riding a horse. A magnificent stallion. She gasped as his cock touched her pussy through the thin cotton of her underwear and the rough denim of his jeans.

He pressed up against her, bucking slightly. "Yeah, girl, you did that to me."

His hands were all over her backside. It felt so good. It wasn't like the other time. Trev wasn't groping, merely making her aware that he was here with her.

She kissed him again. From this position, she had full access. She planted her lips on his and kissed. He followed her lead, their lips playing softly against each other. But it wasn't enough.

"I want more." She forced herself to say the words. She was glad for how dark it was or he would have seen how much it made her blush.

"What do you want?"

She wanted him to not be so dense. He knew what she wanted. She could hear it in his voice, but he seemed determined to make her say it. "Open your mouth."

"I thought you didn't like that."

And he was going to make her admit she'd been wrong. "I want to try again."

"All right." His hands nudged her toward him.

This time, when she put her mouth on his, he opened for her. She took his face between her hands and let her tongue explore him. Trev's tongue glided along hers, all silky seduction. He let her lead, but there was no question in her mind that he was the man. His tongue felt strong against hers even as he let her lead the way.

She kissed him for the longest time, getting utterly lost in his taste, touch, and feel.

Her body felt like someone foreign had taken up in it. She felt sensual and confident. She could handle this man.

When she came up for air, she realized the game was about to change. His hand drifted across her back and wound into her hair. There was a little bite of pain that did strange things to her pussy.

"Are you feeling better now?"

She nodded. This was what he'd wanted. He'd wanted her in the moment with him, not a doll to play with. She was with him now. She was eager to find out what came next.

"Then show me your breasts."

And just like that, she was right back to shy. Her breasts weren't pretty. They already sagged. She had a couple of stretch marks, and she'd never even had a child. She was ten pounds overweight. It wouldn't go away no matter how much she rode that bike. She liked food too much. She needed to be on a diet.

Trev's hand smacked against her ass, forcing her attention back to him. "You look at me. I gave you an order. I want to see your breasts. Show me now or take ten."

He wasn't going to give her time to worry. She could show him her breasts, or he'd spank her and then she'd show him her breasts. Walking away wasn't an option. She brought her hand up and started to push the top of her dress down, catching the strap of her sturdy bra in her fingers. The zipper was in the back. When her shoulders were bare, she reached behind her.

"Let me." His hands found her zipper, and he lowered it slowly. The tips of his fingers traced her skin as he brought the zipper down to her waist. She shivered, but not from cold. Heat was lighting her up everywhere he touched. After he was done with the zipper, he laid his hands on her back and twisted the clasp of her bra with the ease of long practice. He'd obviously removed more than one woman's undergarments. He growled, the sexiest sound, as he peeled the bra toward him.

She fought the urge to cover herself. That was part of the old Mouse, the Mouse who'd never had a man take off her clothes in her living room. That Mouse didn't know what it felt like to have a man like Trev press his cock against her. That Mouse had never been soft and wet, her body melting along with her inhibitions.

This Mouse let her hands fall to her sides. Her breasts bounced out of their confinement. They were what they were, heavy, and the nipples seemed too big to her. They matched her wide hips and not-tiny waist.

Trev's chest rose on a harsh breath. His hands came out, and he went straight for her nipples.

"Pretty."

She held herself still, though her whole body felt like it was quivering inside. His fingertips found her nipples, and he brushed across them.

So why did it feel like he'd touched her pussy?

"And they appear to be sensitive, too," he commented. "Tell me something, love, has anyone ever touched these breasts? Ever played with them?"

"Tommy Smith grabbed one in seventh grade," she admitted.

He rolled her nipples in between his thumbs and forefingers. Again, a little bite of pain that lit up her flesh. She couldn't stop the moan that came out of her mouth or the way her back arched into him.

"Did this Tommy boy play with your nipples? Did he pinch them and roll them until they felt so tight they would burst? Did he clamp them with pretty jewels that kept the blood boiling?"

"No, he didn't have any jewels, though I was wearing a white shirt and he had jelly on his hands. It was lunchtime."

Trev sat back, his face utterly blank for a moment, and then it split into the widest grin. He threw back his head and laughed. The sound was masculine and joyous. Mouse thought she should be offended, but then realized he probably didn't laugh all that much.

His eyes were crinkled with delight when he looked back up at her, and she started to understand what real intimacy was. It wasn't merely having a man put his hands on her. It was laughing with him.

A picture of Bo slipped into her brain. She'd laughed with Bo a lot. But she'd never held him while she did it.

"Did they tease you all day, baby?"

Oh, the way he said "baby." They *had* teased her. At the time, it had been terrible, but now, in the quiet of her own house with his hands on her, she could laugh about it. A memory really was what she made of it. That was what her father had always told her. "I had a purple handprint on my left boob all day long. Well, someone was real nice to me and lent me his jacket."

"Was it Bo?" The quiet question suddenly seemed like a landmine.

"Yes." She and Bo hadn't become close until high school, but he'd always been nice to her. She wanted to be honest, but she didn't want Trev to think she was pining for Bo. Because she wasn't. Not anymore.

His face became serious again, but his hands found her breasts, stroking across her skin. "You know, some men can't see what's in front of them. He could come around."

"He won't. He's having too much fun."

"Is that what you're doing?"

She shook her head. "No. I want to find out who I am. I don't think I can until I figure out this sex stuff. Those books of Lexi's, they speak to me."

There. She'd said it. She hadn't said it to anyone, least of all Bo. She knew how he felt about it. Though he was a hypocrite since he had crazy ménage sex.

"They speak to you because you're submissive, love. You want to please the people around you, but you often don't know how to ask for what you want. There's a difference between enjoying a spanking and needing to have a Dominant partner in order to feel complete. You need a compatible partner." His hands found her nipples again. He twisted just a bit. "And if I'm right, we're very compatible. You like a bite of pain, don't you?"

He pinched down, the harsh flare sending shock waves to her pussy. Yes. She liked the bite.

"You don't have to say anything. God, I can smell it." He pulled her head forward, and now he took control. She felt the shift, the power moving between them. He brought her close and kissed her, his mouth dominating. His tongue thrust past her lips as his hand slipped down to her waist. He shoved her panties aside, and that clever hand slid across her pussy.

"Oh." Mouse squirmed at the touch.

He tugged on her hair. "No. You had your turn. Now it's mine. We do this my way for the rest of the night. I'm going to touch you. I'm going to find out all the ways to make you come. I'm going to sink my cock inside you, and you won't be a virgin anymore. Do you want that?"

She wanted it more than anything. "Yes."

"Then be still, or I'll tie you up. I'll do that eventually, but this first time, I would rather not." His hand slipped inside her pussy, taunting her. "You're wet, darlin'. You're hot and wet and ready for a cock. Let's make you even more ready."

She couldn't breathe when she felt a finger push inside her.

"Fuck, you're going to be tight. I'm going to be careful with you, Beth. It's been a long time since I did this."

"Took someone's virginity?"

He shook his head. "No, baby, had sex. I haven't had sex in two years. I've played around, masturbated until my eyes bulged, but I haven't done this in a long time. I need to make it good for you because I worry I won't last long."

"Why?" she asked. She needed to know.

He didn't pretend to misunderstand. "Because I didn't want anyone until I saw you."

Her heart clenched. She hadn't expected his sweetness.

"Come here. It's my turn now." He pulled her down and kissed her again.

His lips didn't stay for long. He kissed a path toward her breasts. She let her head fall back. She gave up trying to control anything. She wanted him.

He licked at her nipples. She had to steady herself, her hands clutching his shoulders. Her hips seemed to move of their own accord. His hand played around in her pussy, and something was happening down there.

She'd masturbated before. She'd even managed to bring herself to climax, but it was nothing like what was happening to her now. Trev's finger rode in and out of her pussy, curling up inside her as his thumb rubbed her clit in a rhythmic circle. When he pulled her nipple between his teeth, she felt the orgasm begin. It started low in her pelvis and bloomed like a flower opening its petals for the first time. She'd been able to give herself pleasure before, but this was different. This was a storm crashing over her. Mouse gave herself up. She rode that finger, trying to milk the feeling for all it was worth.

Trev released her breast, and she slumped forward into his arms. His hand came out of her pussy, and he wrapped his arms around her. She felt closer to him than she'd ever been to another person. She breathed in his scent, felt the heat of his skin. This was intimacy.

"Darlin'?" His voice sounded a little strangled.

"Yes?" She would say yes to everything he said from now on. And she would add that word that seemed to get his motor running. "Sir?"

He groaned. "Baby, we'll have time for protocol later. I'm

dying here."

Mouse sat straight up. She'd forgotten about him. How impolite. She'd had the best sexual experience of her life, and she'd forgotten about him. "Do you want me to lie down?"

She would let him do anything to her. It would hurt, but she would get through it.

He shook his head. "No, just get out of that dress and let me get a condom on."

He helped her up and then sat right back down on her couch. They weren't going to the bedroom? He reached a hand back and pulled the T-shirt he was wearing over his head. He fished out his wallet.

"I hope these things have a long expiration date." He tore open his pants, and his cock pulled free.

She stared. Wow. He was a work of art, and she couldn't even see his whole body. He was ripped everywhere. Sculpted shoulders molded into a chest she'd only seen the likes of on TV. His stomach was solid muscle and his…Oh, that part of him was gorgeous. Big and thick and long, his cock jutted out of his denims. She got a glance at round, heavy balls before his hand covered the stalk, stroking before he rolled the condom on.

She stood there, dress at her waist, and prayed she wasn't actually drooling.

"Beth, drop the dress." His voice had gone as hard as granite. "And get rid of those panties. You won't need them."

She shoved the dress off her hips, dragging the underwear with it. She didn't give herself time to think about the fact that she was naked in front of him. He seemed barely leashed. His face was dark and dangerous, but she didn't even think about calling this off. Her body was still humming from the orgasm he'd given her. She wanted more from him. She wanted him deep inside.

"Come on." He patted his lap. His breath seemed to saw in and out of his body. "Ride me. I'm worried I could be too rough. I only want you to take what feels right."

She bit into her bottom lip. Once again, he was offering himself up. So many men would have shoved her over and taken her, but he seemed intent on giving more and more. She scrambled to get back in his lap. He caught her before she tumbled into him.

"Slow, girl. We're going to go slow." His lips brushed hers as he settled her legs around his hips.

She felt the tip of that gorgeous monster at her pussy. She whimpered as he pressed up.

"That's pretty." His hands were on her hips, steadying her, but his eyes were looking down. "Lean back, darlin'."

She obeyed, leaning back slightly, and realized what he wanted. He wanted to watch. He wanted to see his cock disappearing into her pussy.

"Slowly."

She pushed down, inch by agonizingly sensual inch. He was big, but he'd prepared her. The slick moisture from her orgasm coated her pussy, facilitating the penetration. He filled her, stretching her pussy. The tight walls felt like they would break, but she wasn't ready to stop. It wasn't comfortable, but she wanted it.

He was perfectly still, allowing her to move. She found a rhythm. A little bit down, a little bit up. Each time she took him further and further inside. His hands moved from her hips, tracing a path to the cheeks of her ass.

"Damn, you feel good. So fucking good." Trev's head rested against the couch. He looked like a decadent dream.

Finally, after what seemed like forever, her hips met his, and she'd taken him all the way. She felt his hands tighten on her. One left her ass and began to tease her clit. It came to life again.

"Fuck me, darlin'. I need it bad." He looked up into her eyes, those dark-blue orbs of his slightly desperate.

She'd done this to him. Mouse Hobbes had reduced a man to begging, and she wasn't about to force him to wait. Her pussy protested the use, but her clitoris was more than ready to go. She rose up and let gravity pull her back down. Trev's hand pressed on her clit, and she fucked him up and down again, catching the rhythm.

She went off, her head falling back.

He took over, his body coming up. His hands found her hips again, and he shoved his cock up. She felt deliciously impaled as he pulled and pushed her onto his hard cock over and over.

He cursed and stiffened, holding her down, forcing her to take every inch as he came.

He fell back against the couch. His arms pulled her close, cradling her to his chest. She could feel the harsh rise and fall as he dragged oxygen in. The thunderous beat of his heart filled her ears. His hands moved across her back, soothing. His cock was still tucked inside her body, joining them together.

Mouse felt more peaceful than she'd ever felt in her life.

There was a slight creak and then a mighty groan.

Trev shouted as he started to roll, taking her with him as the ceiling opened up and rained down on them.

Chapter Five

Trev covered Beth as he rolled. He twisted his body, taking her with him in an attempt to avoid being impaled by a hundred long-dead antlers as they crashed toward the floor.

He put a hand on her head, covering her so he took the brunt of their fall. They hit the hardwood floor with an audible crash.

The floor shook as the hideous chandelier crashed into the sofa right where their bodies had been. Had Trev not moved, and quickly, he could plainly see that Beth would have been killed, her lovely, giving body impaled by the horns. His heart raced, and it had nothing to do with arousal this time.

"What happened?" She lay still beneath him, her hushed words a testament to her anxiety.

"The chandelier fell. It seems to have taken a good portion of the ceiling with it."

"I'm going to have to fix that." She clutched his shoulders.

He was weighing her down, his big body covering her smaller one. Talk about getting caught with his pants down. His cock was pressed against her pussy, and the damn thing didn't seem to understand that they had almost been killed. It was already getting hard again because Beth was right here. So much for not being aroused.

"How old did you say this house was?" Trev asked, wondering what else was going to go wrong.

"Really old. And I didn't exactly have an inspection done." Her face had contorted sweetly, as though she knew she was in trouble. "It was an impulse."

He rolled off of her. "You bought a whole house on an impulse?"

"I've always loved this house."

"Even though it was supposed to be haunted?" He'd had the holy crap scared out of him by Maudine Bellows as a kid. She was one mean old lady.

"I'm going to check to see if anything else is going to come down on our heads." He couldn't help but kiss her before he pushed off her body and got to his feet.

Damn, he hadn't even gotten his pants off. He pulled the condom off and managed to find a box of tissues. He rolled it up and tucked himself back in. He caught sight of Beth scrambling for her clothes.

"Don't." He'd wanted her first time to be on her terms, and with all the sweetness she deserved. He'd managed to keep it fairly vanilla. She'd enjoyed the experience and hadn't been too uncomfortable. Now it was time to start putting this relationship on the proper footing. He knew what he needed out of a relationship, and it wasn't vanilla.

Relationship. Eight hours in this town and he was in a relationship. He wasn't sure if that was a good thing or a bad thing, but it was the truth. Taking Beth Hobbes's virginity meant something to him. It meant that for the time being, he was responsible for her.

"You don't need clothes when we're alone."

"What?" She clutched the yellow sundress as she gingerly stepped around the damage.

He reached out and pulled it away, fisting the material in his hand. "I said you don't need clothes."

Her mouth came open as she shot him an incredulous stare. "Trev, we nearly died. I don't think we should be talking about my state of undress."

Because she didn't understand. "Begin as you mean to go. We need to start getting the rules in place. You and me alone equals you naked. Now, where's your bedroom? I want you to go and wait for me in bed. I'm going to check this out and make sure we don't need to call anyone tonight."

Her head shook slightly. "I don't think there's anyone to call. There's no emergency chandelier repair in Deer Run."

He gave her his best "badass Dom" stare. He'd perfected it over the last two years, and he'd been told it was sure to send every sub in a two-mile radius scrambling to do his bidding.

She took a step back. "Fine. But no one will come out at this time of night. And I don't think it's a good idea to call someone anyway. They might get the wrong idea about what's been going on out here."

"What's the wrong idea, darlin'? That we managed to shake the house so hard with our fucking we brought the roof down?" He actually kind of liked the idea. If it hadn't almost killed them both.

"Yes. That would be the idea I am trying to avoid. And then there's the problem that apparently I'm no longer allowed to wear clothes."

"Which won't be a problem because you'll be waiting for me in your bedroom."

"They'll still know you're here."

He felt his face flush. He hated that. She wanted to hide him? He couldn't blame her. Maybe he'd jumped the gun thinking they had something going. But he had to point out a few facts to her. "Honey, everyone knows you left The Rusty Spur with me. I suppose we can come up with something, but every person in this town is going to think you're seeing me."

Her face softened. She stepped close. "I didn't mean that. I don't care if they all know. I just didn't want someone walking in when it's still, you know, it's so obvious that we…"

He grinned and brushed his lips across hers. The room was a mess. Clothes had been tossed aside. It still smelled like sweet sex. "We'll wait until we've cleaned up to call. Now go on to the bedroom. I'll take care of this."

He could see how she fought not to cover herself. Her hands

moved restlessly at her sides, but she managed to hold her ground. "It seems funny that I'm naked and you have your jeans on."

He was starting a relationship with a woman who didn't understand D/s at all. She was submissive as hell, but she didn't understand what was required. He was going to have to have a talk with Lexi about those books. They apparently needed way more instructive information in them. "Me Dom. You sub. Sub's about to get spanked if she doesn't obey her Dom."

"Fine." She turned on her perfectly formed heels and strode toward the stairs. He got his first good look at her ass. Heart-shaped and perky, that rear end was the finest thing he'd ever seen. His cock twitched again. He loved the curve of her shoulders and the graceful hourglass of her figure. He was utterly obsessed with the sweet length of her spine and the dimples right above her cheeks. Her skin was perfect and creamy.

He wouldn't be happy until he'd fucked her ass. No way. He wanted all of her.

For the first time in a long time, he was looking forward to the near future.

He looked at the ruined sofa behind him. The hideous light fixture had actually punctured the sofa and embedded several horns into the old velvet. He couldn't fool himself. It had been a close call. He pulled the heavy chandelier out of the sofa and moved it the side, careful of the electrical wires and the crushed glass.

Twenty minutes later, he was pretty sure this house should be condemned. The doors creaked and shuddered when he opened them. The floor under his feet wasn't perfectly solid in places, and he was pretty sure there was a raccoon in residence. Now the second floor would be dangerous to walk on after the chandelier incident.

And he wasn't going to be able to get Beth out of here. She'd lit up when she talked about turning this old place into a show home. She'd sunk every dime she had into this project.

He was going to have to learn about home repair because he foresaw a bunch of it in his future.

One year. He had one year with her. He knew he wasn't good for anyone long-term, but maybe he could help Beth over the year he had. He didn't even try to tell himself that it wouldn't last a year.

The trouble would be walking away from her when he left for Colorado.

She'd felt so good, and it hadn't just been her silky-smooth body. It had been all about her trust and the sweet way she'd submitted. He'd gone easy on her because she was a virgin, but starting tomorrow, she would become his submissive.

His.

Years of training and he'd never taken a submissive. He shouldn't take one now, but he couldn't deny her. He'd had a primal feeling in his gut the minute he'd seen her. He should have walked away, but he'd never been great with the whole self-denial thing.

And now he had to deal with Bo O'Malley. Despite the fact that his former friend wasn't Beth's boyfriend, he was still a part of her life. And he had a feeling Bo wasn't going to like the fact that she was with him now.

He heard a phone ringing. He picked up Beth's dress, and two cells dropped free. His and hers. Hers was an old phone. It was cracked and looked like it probably didn't work half the time. She needed a new one. That would be the first order of business once he had his paycheck in hand.

He thought about the ten million coming to him in less than a year. It staggered him that once he could have bought Beth an amazing house many times over. Now every dime he had coming had to be spent on securing a future that didn't include football.

He needed a drink, but then he always needed a drink.

Trev looked down at the phone. He didn't recognize the number. It wasn't assigned in her phone, so he let it ring. He ignored the messages on his own phone. There would be time enough to deal with all of that tomorrow.

Tonight he wanted to sleep with Beth and forget everything.

He walked up the stairs and was pleased to find she had obeyed him at least once tonight. She was naked and waiting in bed.

Trev slid under the covers and had his mouth on hers before she could speak.

* * * *

Bo didn't like jail. It smelled bad, and the sheriff hadn't bothered to separate out the prisoners. He was in the cell with the same asshole he'd fought with. Luckily, Brian had passed out long ago, but Bo didn't really want to be around when he woke up.

"Hey, O'Malley, you ready for your phone call?" Sheriff Lou Mark yawned a little as though all the trouble had interrupted his very important nap.

Lou had been the sheriff for as long as Bo could remember. He was edging toward retirement. He filled out his uniform almost to the point of bursting and had been known to play checkers with his prisoners.

"Hell, yeah. I'm ready to get out of here." Bo shifted off the bench that served as Brian's cot and followed the sheriff out the door.

Only Bo and Brian had been brought in. Everyone else had either managed to flee or been deemed not dangerous enough to waste space on.

He picked up the phone to dial his brother's number. Aidan would give him a stern lecture, but he would be here as fast as his truck would carry him. Lucas would be right behind Aidan, making sure he found every loophole the sheriff had undoubtedly left open. And Lexi would come, if only to add much needed sarcasm.

His family. He could count on them, but Aidan's wasn't the number he dialed. His fingers seemed to be more in line with his heart than his head. The only person he wanted to see was Mouse. He wanted to see her sweet face and have her hold her arms out to him. Mouse wouldn't yell at him. Mouse would fuss over him, and he needed that.

And, by god, he was going to fuss over her, too. He was done fooling himself. He wanted Mouse, and his friends could go to hell.

The phone began to ring, and his heart sped up at the thought of being able to talk to her about this. He was going to tell her as soon as she walked in the doors to pick him up. The county lockup wasn't the most romantic place to declare his intentions, but he'd made her wait long enough.

He'd sat in that cramped, stinky cell where he was sure some serial killer had recently died and realized that he was being an idiot and had been his whole life. He let other people influence his decisions, and they were people he didn't even like. He'd looked down at Brian, who seemed to have some serious problems with sleep apnea, and realized he'd denied his feelings for Mouse so someone like Brian would accept him. He'd spent so much time trying to fit in that he had forgotten to figure out who the hell he was. He'd only been able to be himself with Mouse.

The phone switched to voice mail. He pulled the receiver back and stared at it like it was a foreign object. Mouse always answered her phone.

How mad was she?

"Hey, Mouse." He'd leave her a message. He deserved her anger. He'd been an asshole, but she would listen to the message. "It's me. I'm in trouble, girl. I'm in jail, and I need for you to come down here and pick me up. I know you don't like to drive, but I'm begging you, baby. Please come get me. I want to talk to you. I have a lot to say. And I went to jail, not Clarissa's. Jail. No sex in jail. At least I hope not. Don't leave me too long. I'll be waiting."

He hung the phone up.

The sheriff shook his head. "You're in jail and you call Mouse Hobbes to come get you? That girl doesn't even like to drive. And her car is a menace."

His jaw firmed. "A man calls the person closest to him in a time like this."

"A smart man calls his brother's boyfriend, who happens to be a lawyer."

"Lucas isn't Aidan's boyfriend. He's his partner."

Sheriff Lou groaned a bit. "I got no idea what to call the man. I only know I'm glad you're a dumb bunny. That Lucas Cameron is smart and mean from what I've heard. The last thing I need is a false arrest lawsuit. Not that Aidan is any nicer. I ought to let them have at that drunk in there. If I didn't have twenty witnesses willing to testify that you damn near decapitated the man with a pool cue, I'd let you go. I heard all the things the idiot said about your brother."

He turned to the sheriff. Lou Mark didn't live in Deer Run, but he'd presided over the whole county for most of Bo's life. "Most men would be on Brian's side."

97

The sheriff's eyes rolled. "You need to get out more, Bo. The world isn't as all-fired small-minded as Deer Run. And it's changing. You'll still find assholes like Brian, but there are plenty of folks who live and let live. Life is way too short to spend your time hating. Besides, I've got a sister who lives in Seattle, and she's a lesbian. She also makes the best chili I've ever had. I think the two are connected somehow."

Bo wasn't sure a person's sexual preferences had much to do with the ability to properly make chili, but he was intrigued by the sheriff's relaxed take on the subject. "Not many people around here agree with you."

"It's more than you think. The problem is that one or two strong voices shout out the softer ones. I admire the hell out of your brother. He served this country with honor, and no one has a right to tell him how to live his life. Too many people in this town live in fear that they'll get looked down on. That ain't no way to live."

The sheriff opened the door again. Brian snored loudly and turned over on the cot, showing off the fact that he didn't mind a little plumber's crack. Bo tried to shrink back.

The sheriff laughed. "Go on, now. I'm not cleaning out the other cell to spare your tender sensibilities."

"I don't mind if it's dirty." Dirty sounded better than staring at Brian's asscrack all night.

"Nope. In you go. Maybe this way you'll stay out of that bar. Jail is supposed to be a deterrent, son. But you can sit out here with me for a while." The sheriff's eyes lit up a little bit. "Mouse won't be here for a while, anyway. It'll take her an hour or two to find enough mice to power that car of hers. We could play some checkers. Hey, do you want some coffee cake?"

Anything was better than being stuck in there with Brian. "Sure."

The sheriff smiled. "Good. You get the checkers set out of my desk. I'll go heat up that coffee cake." He turned to the kitchenette door. Then he turned back. "Hey, don't you escape or nothing."

Bo gave him a proper salute. "Wouldn't think of it."

The sheriff nodded and disappeared. Bo found the checkers game and set it up. He pulled up the deputy's chair. He shouldn't have to wait too long. Mouse would be here, and they would talk. He would drive that cheap little car of hers back to her place, and they would figure out their future.

He was going to kiss Mouse, and not on her cheek. He was going to take her in his arms and lay her down. He was going to get inside her and finally make her his.

He was going to marry Mouse.

He felt a smile split his face. Something settled deep inside of him. He was going to be a husband and someday a father. The idea of Mouse with a baby in her arms warmed him. He would be a good father. He wouldn't let his son feel alone and adrift. His son would always know that he was there for him. He would never beat the shit out of his son and force him to seek shelter.

That night he'd gone to Austin to find Trev flashed across his brain. He'd been hurting. Aidan would have killed their dad had Bo gone to him. He'd gone to Trev because they'd had a real connection.

Trev had told him to go away because he didn't want to interrupt his party.

Mouse had gotten on a bus and come to him. She'd cleaned him up and held him. She'd given him a place to stay until his bruises healed and covered for him at school. Bo had made sure he was never alone with his father when he was drinking again. When the bottle had come out, he'd hightailed it straight to Mouse's place.

No, he wouldn't be anything like his father.

Mouse had always been his home. He could see that now. He was done denying it. He loved her. He was ready to start his future.

If she would only get here.

When the sheriff came back, Bo ate his coffee cake and waited for his girl.

Chapter Six

Trev came awake slowly for once. Usually his morning began with the rude awakening of an alarm clock going off full blast. His life at The Club had been carefully regimented, beginning with a workout session every morning at 5:30 a.m. Leo would be at his door before dawn, dressed in sweats and sneakers. Trev had gotten used to getting up early.

Early-morning light filtered through the filmy curtains that covered the windowpanes. It was a soft, white-and-yellow light that made everything seem gauzy and slightly unreal. He glanced at the clock on the bedside table. It was ancient, but it seemed to be working. 7:30. He let his eyes drift closed again. There was no hurry to get up this morning.

He turned and smiled as he felt soft, warm flesh against his body. Beth shifted in her sleep, the sweetest whimper coming out of her mouth as she curled into his body. Her head found his chest, her hair tickling his skin.

Beth.

Damn, he was in deep. He'd planned on introducing her to some bondage once he'd gotten into bed with her, but as soon as he'd kissed those sweet lips, he hadn't found the discipline to do anything but fuck her again. After he'd rung a couple of orgasms out of her, he'd come for what felt like forever. He should have fallen straight to sleep, but he'd found himself sitting up and talking to her.

He sighed and brushed her hair back from her face, feeling a sweet sense of peace. He hadn't felt this calm and happy in a long while.

He wasn't due out on the O'Malley Ranch for a couple of hours. There was plenty of time. He could drowse for a while and then get up, and he and Beth could make breakfast and talk some more.

Damn, he liked her. She was smart as a whip and had a sweetly sarcastic sense of humor that wasn't obvious on the surface. He was going to enjoy the next year.

He settled back down when he heard the door downstairs squeak. His eyes flew open. He was going to fix that door first thing. He gently eased away, reluctant to let her go, but god only knew what critters would wander into the house and set up a nest if he didn't go and secure the door.

Stretching, he looked back at his sleeping lover. She was turned on her side, her hands close to her face. The sun kissed her porcelain skin. How had she stayed a virgin for so long? She was tempting as hell lying there with those soft breasts and round hips. She was perfectly fuckable and so giving that she would be a perfect sub to the right Dom.

Was he the right Dom?

Deep inside he'd wondered if he would ever take a permanent submissive. He certainly hadn't expected one so soon. With his track record, he wasn't sure he should. What if he dove back down into that hole he'd spent years in? How would he take care of her? He wouldn't. He'd never been a violent drunk, but he'd been horribly neglectful. He couldn't think of a worse thing for a Dom to be.

He wouldn't go there. He wouldn't give in. Not today. Tomorrow would come, and he would have to make the decision all over again, but he was going to be okay today.

He stopped, an unwelcome sound reaching his ears.

Voices. He heard soft voices talking deep in the recesses of the house. They were muffled, but there was no mistaking it. This wasn't the raccoon or the wind. Every nerve went on full alert. Who the hell was in Beth's house? Whoever it was, they were about to find out that Beth Hobbes had a keeper who didn't appreciate early-morning visitors.

Unless they'd brought coffee. Damn, but he could use a cup of coffee.

He slipped on his jeans, careful not to wake his sleeping beauty. Who the hell thought to call her Mouse? Her beauty was quiet, but there was nothing mouselike about her.

The floor creaked under his feet, groaning as though it truly resented having to bear the weight of someone walking on it. This house was going to fall in on itself.

"I'm sure because I can read my bloody phone, Leo," a disgruntled voice said. That voice had a heavy Irish accent and a deep tone of irritation.

Liam O'Donnell. The man worked for McKay-Taggart, the security firm Julian used for everything from bodyguard services to investigations to figuring out where the addict ran off to.

"And might I add," the Irishman continued, "you have the same damn app on your phone. There was zero need to drag me to the back end of nowhere. And what time is it? Never mind. I can answer that meself. It's time for me to sleep."

"All that app tells us is where his phone is," Leo replied. "He could have ditched it. You're here in case we need to track him down. I was told you're good at that. So far, all you're good at is complaining endlessly."

"Thank you," Liam replied without a hint of irony. "No one ever takes my complaining seriously. It's an art form."

"Well, that's his truck out there in the drive. I wonder how he ended up here." Shelley's voice floated up to the second floor.

He sighed. He should have expected she would freak out. He'd forgotten to call her after he'd stomped out of the house in a fit of anger. Had she and Bryce been looking for him all night? That should have put his brother-in-law in a great mood.

"You said this was a woman's house? I can come up with a scenario on how he ended up here," O'Donnell replied. "Should I start banging on doors?"

Trev took the rickety steps two at a time because the last thing he needed was O'Donnell to start trying to find him. "I'm here."

His mentor stood in the living room looking down at the ruined chandelier. He looked slightly out of place in the old house. He was dressed in perfectly pressed slacks and a dress shirt. Which was odd, because Leo was fairly casual. He tended to prefer T-shirts and jeans when he wasn't in his leathers. Leo had apparently spruced himself up for the occasion. Leo Meyer was thirty-three, and despite the fact that he was an inch or two shorter than Trev's six foot five, there was no way to miss the commanding nature of the man. Leo had been his keeper those first few months. The fact that he was here now made Trev nervous.

The fact that he'd brought an employee of Julian's favorite security company with him made him way past nervous. Had they brought O'Donnell along to drag him back to Dallas? Well, they should have sent both Tags because he wasn't going anywhere.

"Hey, what's wrong?" He strode into the living room, ready to deal with the problem before Beth knew anyone was here.

Leo's eyes narrowed. "Well, you disappeared on your first night alone. Your sister was very concerned. She called me at midnight last night. I drove down to help her look for you."

There it was, that voice Leo used to let him know he'd fucked up royally and had better get straight. It was the same voice the Master Dom used on subs, and a part of Trev actually wanted to snarl a bit at his mentor. He would never let another man use that tone on him, but Leo had earned a lot of patience from him.

"And then he called and forced me from my beautiful lover's bed to come and help find you," O'Donnell complained.

Leo rolled his eyes. "What was her name?"

A smirk lit O'Donnell's face. "Sandy. Candy. Mandy."

"Which one?" Leo asked.

"All three." The Irishman winked Shelley's way. "That's why I'm in such a bad mood, darlin'. Got nothing to do with you. I'm leaving for England and a big job soon and Leo here won't let me say good-bye to me loves."

He was certain there hadn't been a lot of love in the Irishman's heart, but he was probably good with the lust. He turned to Shelley, genuinely remorseful. She'd gone to bed by the time he'd taken off, but it was obvious that her asshole husband had told her, and probably put the worst possible spin on it.

"Shell, I'm sorry. I didn't mean to worry you."

There were circles under his sister's eyes that told him she hadn't slept all night. "Bryce told me you left."

Bryce had basically ordered him to get out. After Shelley had gone to bed, Bryce had been right there in his face, telling him how he was going to ruin his sister's life and reputation. Bryce had gone over everything Trev had done wrong. In the end, he'd walked out rather than put his fist through Bryce's face.

"I thought it was best. I shouldn't have come down early. I should have waited until the foreman's house was ready for me." Only then he wouldn't have met Beth. If he hadn't come down a day early, he doubted he would have left the ranch for several weeks. At first, living on the ranch seemed perfect. It was almost like a halfway house. There would be eyes on him all the time. He wouldn't have a chance to fuck up. But now he wouldn't have a chance to see Beth. He didn't like that thought. "It's best if I stay away from your husband, sis. He doesn't like me, and I don't want to come between the two of you."

He didn't have to come between Shelley and Bryce. Leo was doing a damn fine job of that himself. There was no way to miss the heat between his sister and Leo.

Shelley's face fell. Tears clouded her eyes. "Bryce said something nasty to you. I knew it. He drove you to drink. The son of a bitch."

Leo's arm went around her shoulder. He pulled her close. Shelley leaned into him like it was utterly natural to find comfort in the Dom's arms. "He'll come back with me. We can start over if we have to. It's a setback. It happens all the time. This is nothing for you to worry about, sweetheart. I'll take care of it."

He glanced the Irishman's way as if to tell him to get ready in case Trev bolted. Unfortunately, O'Donnell had found a comfy chair and his eyes were already closed.

Trev sighed. They'd made a big drama out of a little thing. Well, sleeping with Beth had actually been a big thing, but it had nothing to do with his sobriety.

"I didn't drink."

Leo looked up over Shelley's head. "Really? You found yourself in a highly stressful situation and you didn't drink? Then where exactly did you spend the night?"

He wanted to tell his mentor to go fuck himself. He was an adult. He didn't need to account for his damn whereabouts. Except that he'd earned this treatment. And he knew that Leo wouldn't accept anything less than honesty.

"I started out at The Rusty Spur."

Shelley's hands tightened around Leo. The Dom soothed a palm down her back. It took everything he had not to roll his eyes and tell them to get a room. He had to admit, they made an attractive couple. Leo whispered something in her ear that had Shelley nodding and standing up straighter.

"It's all right, Trevor. We can get you back in rehab," she said as O'Donnell started to snore.

He longed for a day when rehab wasn't mentioned at least twice. "I didn't go into the bar. I sat out in the parking lot and thought about it, but I didn't go in, and I didn't drink anything stronger than a French roast. Now, if you two are done with the much-appreciated intervention, why don't you take Sleepy over there and go. I need to see if Beth has any coffee. Though I doubt the electricity in the kitchen works."

Shelley's head came off Leo's massive chest. "You didn't drink?"

"Nope." They might not believe him. "I was perfectly sober. Do you need me to pee in a jar?"

"Well, what did you do all night?" She huffed out the question as though flummoxed by the problem at hand.

He smiled, remembering exactly how he'd spent the night. Beth had been a luscious distraction. "Beth."

Shelley's mouth dropped open. "You slept with Mouse?"

He growled his sister's way. She threw up her hands as though conceding the point.

"Who is Beth?" Leo asked. "And why is there a deer herd on the floor?"

His mouth tugged up in the one-sided smile he always used

105

when particularly proud of himself. He'd used that smile when he'd won the championship and when he'd signed his pro contract. He used the smile now because this achievement was just as significant in Trev's new world. "She's my submissive."

Shelley gasped. "Did you pull Mouse into that kinky sex stuff?"

"It's more than sex, love. Now hush. He's safe and fine." Leo dropped his arms and strode forward. He stopped in front of Trev. "You took a sub? Formally?"

He could feel himself flush. To the outside world, what had happened the night before was nothing more than a common hookup. Inside the world that he'd grown to love, it meant something serious. He'd taken a sub. He hadn't begun her training, but he'd made his declaration. He'd taken her virginity. He wasn't going to pretend it hadn't happened. "There's not a lot of formality here in Deer Run, but I claimed her. She understands what it means. Sort of."

He'd claimed her in the sweetest way possible. He'd been her first man. He'd been the first man to be smart enough to see past that wall she built to protect herself. He'd been the first to see how sensual and hot she was. He was utterly amazed that he was the first to understand how beautiful Bethany Hobbes could be.

"What does 'sort of' mean?" Leo asked suspiciously.

"Did you tie her up? Do I need to let her out?" Shelley asked.

Leo stared back at her. Shelley rolled her eyes. God, she would be the brattiest sub if she ever walked into a club. "No one asked your opinion, love."

"I wasn't offering an opinion, Leo. I was concerned with Mou...Beth's circulation. Trev sucked at Boy Scouts. I was always better with knots."

Leo looked horrified. "You will never be allowed around a rope. And your brother has gotten better at Shibari. I've made sure of it. And yes, Shibari is kinky sex stuff." Leo turned back to Trev. "Sort of?"

He wasn't going to get rid of them until Leo was satisfied. "She only knows about it from books."

Leo groaned. "Not Lexi's books. Where the Dom always surrenders in the end? I've begged Aidan to spank her ass until she writes one of us who isn't a pussy."

"I like Lexi's books," Shelley admitted.

"They are not a true representation of D/s," Leo argued.

"They're a representation of love," his sister shot back.

"I suppose so." Leo stared at Shelley for a moment before turning back to Trev. Leo's face split into a smile. He held his hand out. "I am so glad to hear that you've taken a submissive. How did you hide this? No one knew you were seeing anyone."

He swallowed before he answered. "Um, I didn't meet her at The Club."

"He met her yesterday." Shelley still sounded slightly outraged. "And she's the most innocent woman I've ever met."

Leo's brows climbed up his forehead. "Really? That explains a lot."

Trev fumbled for words. "I've met her before. But she was a kid back then. We went to the same high school. We didn't run with the same crowd."

"Mou...Beth doesn't have a crowd. She has Bo," Shelley explained.

Not any more she didn't. He wouldn't tell her she couldn't see Bo anymore. He wouldn't come between Beth and her friend. Not exactly. He did intend to keep her so busy that she wouldn't have time for anyone except him.

"Bo? As in O'Malley?" Leo put a hand to his forehead as though trying to ward off one of the killer migraines he got from time to time. "Fuck. Please tell me you didn't screw Aidan's brother's girlfriend."

Shelley waved him off. "Mouse...Beth, god that's hard, isn't Bo's girlfriend. She's his friend and it's perfectly platonic. Don't get me wrong, she's one of the nicest people around, but she's very naïve when it comes to men."

Leo calmed a bit. "And she doesn't belong to Bo? Because the last thing you need is to give Aidan a reason to fire you. He's looking for one already."

That was news to him. He hadn't started the job yet. How had he already fucked up? "Why? I know what I'm doing. I thought he wanted me."

Leo's jaw tightened the way it did when he delivered bad news. "Aidan wasn't exactly thrilled when Julian asked him to take you on. He thinks you're dicey, and he knows you're only going to be here for a year. He would rather find a permanent foreman. He's doing this as a favor to Julian."

Trev felt his stomach turn. That was all he needed. Now he had to deal with the guilt and shame of being a fucking charity case. "Tell him it's fine. I'll go back to The Club. I can spend my last year of probation there. As long as Julian will give me a place to stay, I'll work for free. When I get my contract money, I'll buy my spread and no one will have to worry about me."

He still had a shred of pride. At least he was trying to have it.

"You can't leave. You just got here." Shelley's dark eyes practically pleaded with him.

And then there was Beth. He didn't want to leave. He'd spent one night with her, and the thought of not seeing her again had him in knots. He'd promised her he wasn't going anywhere.

"Slow down. I know this situation isn't perfect, but you can make it work. You didn't want to be stuck in The Club. That's why you decided on this path. You knew it wasn't going to be easy," Leo said.

He also hadn't known it was going to be so damn hard. A single vision of Beth's face as she'd rolled into his arms, her skin flushed from orgasm, her mouth smiling and eyes wide with wonder, flashed across his brain. "I'll stay. I'll keep my head down and get my work done. And I'll tell Aidan that he can keep searching for a permanent foreman. If he finds one, I'll work as a hand."

He couldn't leave her. Not after taking her virginity. He'd failed too many people over the years. He took his promises seriously. If he had to swallow some pride, it would be worth it to know he'd done right by Beth.

Leo sighed. "Well, we can work it out with Aidan. I didn't call him, by the way. I hoped to find you in the proverbial ditch somewhere."

Trev laughed. "Yeah, that would have been better than having to haul my ass out of a bar or jail."

"No, it wouldn't." Shelley looked from Trev to Leo, a frown on her face.

"Trev? Are you down there? I took your rules seriously."

He turned at the sound of Beth's soft voice. She reached the top of the staircase. She had taken him seriously. She wasn't wearing a stitch of clothes. Her gorgeous, curvy body was on full display. The only thing she was lacking was a collar. He would have to fix that.

"Well, hello." Leo's eyes warmed as he took in Beth.

Shelley slapped at Leo's arm, earning her a stare from the Dom.

"Hello, me darlin'." O'Donnell's eyes were open wide now as though he had a deeply ingrained instinct that told him when someone was naked and woke him up for the show. "See, that was worth making the trip for."

"Oh, my god!" Beth screeched the words, and her hands flew over her breasts and down to her pussy as though she couldn't decide which to protect. She stumbled as she tried to fly back up the stairs. Her nicely shaped backside came into view.

He needed some toys to go along with the collar. A whole training set of anal plugs would be required because he was definitely going to get his cock up that perfect ass.

"Trev?" she called out from what Trev assumed was her bedroom.

"Yes, darlin'?" He couldn't keep the amusement out of his voice.

"Did they see anything?"

He had to put a hand over his mouth to stop the laugh. "Nothing that wasn't lovely."

"It was a wonderful way to begin the day, Beth. It's very nice to meet you," Leo called out.

"Oh, my god!" The door slammed.

"Don't worry about it. She says that a lot." In the day they'd been together, she'd called out the deity's name several times.

Plaster drifted down from the ceiling, and the door slammed open again. Leo barely touched the railing to the stairs, and it came off in his hand.

Leo looked down. "Uh, this place is a bit of a fixer-upper, huh?"

Yeah, Trev had that in common with this old house. And he might have found the woman who could renovate him.

* * * *

Mouse slammed the door, her heart racing. She grabbed the sheet off the bed and wrapped it around her naked body. Trev had guests, and they had been treated to a vision of her *au naturel*. It was mortifying. What had she been thinking?

She hadn't been thinking. She'd woken up, and Trev hadn't been in bed with her. She'd decided to go looking for him. She hadn't even stopped to grab her robe. She'd simply obeyed him. He wanted her naked, and Mouse had waltzed through the house in the altogether.

Maybe she was the mess everyone said she was.

There was a light knock on the door before it opened, and Trev walked in. He carried her dress from the previous night and two cell phones with him. He was wearing a pair of jeans and nothing else. The jeans rode low on his hips, showing off the notches on his abs. He was a Greek god. What the hell was he doing here with her?

"Has anyone ever told you how pretty you are when you blush?" He asked the question with the sweetest smile on his face. He placed the dress and the phones on the bed.

"Who were those men?"

Trev crossed the room in two long strides. "That was Leo Meyer. He's sort of my mentor. The other guy is named Liam O'Donnell. He's an investigator of sorts, though I think in this case Leo brought him along to be muscle. Drop the sheet."

She pulled it closer. "I am not going to drop the sheet. I might never be naked again. I might shower with my clothes on from now on."

His eyes narrowed, and a low growl came out of his mouth. "We're alone."

"No, we're not. There are people in my house."

"They're downstairs. We're alone, and I want to see you."

That tone of voice really did something for her. How did the man manage to get her so hot with just a sentence? "Why are those men here?"

Trev stood in front of her. He didn't move a muscle, but she could feel his displeasure. He seemed to come to a decision. "Leo's here because my sister called him. O'Donnell's here because Leo uses his company for security purposes. Shelley was afraid I had fallen off the wagon. Leo came to help her look for me. O'Donnell came to drag my ass back to Dallas in case I needed rehab. You'll have to forgive them. Leo has spent the last two years making damn sure I didn't slip up, so he was worried about me."

Her heart softened a bit. "That's real nice of him. I still wish they hadn't seen my bottom."

"Oh, they saw more than that, but don't worry. Leo's used to being around pretty, naked little subs. He usually knows when to keep his hands off. Usually. And O'Donnell is apparently leaving the country, so we don't have to worry about him hanging around."

She was pretty sure Leo Meyer wasn't off somewhere thinking about how to get his hands on her. "Well, in the future, I would appreciate it if you would let me know when we have guests." She winced. She was assuming a lot. "I mean, I, when I have guests."

"You had it right the first time, darlin'. Now drop the sheet or we'll spend the morning on discipline."

He seemed to be big on discipline. And on having her naked. She dropped the sheet and was rewarded by the heat that crept into Trev's eyes. Those gorgeous orbs locked on her breasts.

"See, that's better." He leaned in and kissed her, pulling her body up against his, plastering her breasts to his chest. "Good morning, Beth."

Her heart thumped in her chest. It felt right to be close to him. This was how she'd always imagined it would be with Bo. A sliver of guilt knifed through her, but she cast it aside. Bo hadn't wanted her. Trev did, and she was crazy about him. In the course of a single night, he'd saved her twice, taken her virginity with kindness and patience, and sat up holding her and listening to her. Bo was good at listening to her, but she craved the intimacy Trev offered. It had been amazing to press their bodies together and rest her head on his chest. She'd never felt as close to a person before as she felt to Trev, as though the mere act of making love had bonded her to him.

And that was the way it was supposed to be. She sighed and wrapped her arms around him, no longer concerned with her state of undress. "Good morning, Sir."

He groaned. "Damn, I like that."

He did. She could feel the press of his cock against her belly. Trev was utterly turned on by the whole submission thing, and that was fine with her. She'd read about the lifestyle in Lexi's books and watched how it worked with Lexi's husbands/Masters, and it seemed like a nice way to live. She'd been responsible for herself and her parents for so long that giving up some responsibility seemed like a good thing.

Trev's hand gently tugged on her hair, a silent request for her to bring her head up. She was already catching on to his habits.

"Yes?" she asked.

"What are your plans? I have to go out to Aidan O'Malley's. I'll probably be tied up for most of the day, but I want to see you tonight."

Oh, she wanted to see him, too. There was a part of her that didn't believe he'd meant what he'd said the night before. She halfway expected him to be gone this morning. "I want that, too. And I have to go out to the ranch. This morning I'm working on some stuff for Lexi, but this afternoon I have to go into town to the bank. I'm getting a home improvement loan."

He frowned. "Are you sure about that? It might be better to hire out a bulldozer."

She wasn't going to let his attitude get her down. Nor would she allow it to change her mind. She simply sighed and cuddled again. "Nope. I'm making this house beautiful again."

His hand curved around her head, stroking her hair. "Explain it to me. I don't understand. This place is falling down around you."

No one understood, but Trev was the first one to ask her why. "You see a house that's falling down, but that's not what I see. Did you know this house was built in 1892?"

"I can believe it. And it hasn't been updated since then."

She laughed but continued on with her story. "It was built by a man named Milo Bellows. He brought his family from New York, and he was one of the first people to move into Deer Run. He ran a general store. He built this place with his own two hands. I can see him. I can see that man laboring over this house, praying to get it just right because this house was his wife's dream. He built it from the ground up, and his children grew up here. I can see them playing in the yard and running through the halls. How many people have walked through this place? How many sat on the porch and watched the sunset? How many sat in that big old dining room on Sunday enjoying supper after church? Those people mattered. They were loved, and they had lives, and this house saw it all. It shouldn't be torn down because it isn't perfect anymore. It's got a history, and if I make it beautiful again, then a whole other family can live their lives here and it will go on. The beautiful things in life should go on even when they have flaws."

He pulled her head up so their eyes met again. This time there was a grave look in his. He stared at her for a moment. "I'll help you, then. You tell me what you need."

A rush of pleasure crashed over her. "Are you serious?"

"Yes. But I have a few rules."

He always had rules. He seemed to need them. That didn't mean she had to follow them, but she would listen politely. "Yes?"

"Don't do anything dangerous. This house really is falling apart. I don't want you on the roof. I don't want you lifting anything too heavy. And don't go into the downstairs office."

"Why?"

He grimaced. "I'm pretty sure the damn thing could be made into a wildlife preserve. We need to call animal control before you clean out that room. There was a reason you got it so cheap."

His rules seemed perfectly reasonable to her. She'd been afraid he was going to throw down a dictate that required her to be naked while painting and refinishing. "All right."

He kissed her again. "Can you make some coffee while I'm in the shower? I couldn't find any downstairs."

"Oh, that's because I don't have any."

He groaned. "Baby, coffee is all I have left. We have to get you a coffeemaker."

"I'll pick one up when I go into town." She would have to remember to put the basket on her bike. It looked like she was going to the store. She glanced down and saw the phone. "Oh, you had a call last night. I forgot."

113

He grimaced. "Was it from a man named Marty?"

She nodded. "Yes. I would tell you what he said, but it was mostly a bunch of letters."

"Yeah, Marty's big on acronyms. Don't worry about it. He's not important. I won't be seeing him. And you got a call, too. It came in after you went to bed. Your phone didn't recognize the number, so I didn't mention it. It was after midnight. Probably a wrong number. I'll go heat up the shower. You do have hot water?"

"I hope so." She wasn't exactly sure.

Trev growled again as he headed into the bathroom. He seemed to believe it was a perfectly acceptable form of communication. She heard the water creak to life and picked up her cell. She didn't recognize the number, either, but there was a voice mail message. She sat on the bed, surprisingly comfortable with being naked, and listened.

Bo. His voice came over the line. There was no way to mistake the anxiety in his tone.

"Hey, Mouse. It's me. I'm in trouble, girl. I'm in jail, and I need for you to come down here and pick me up. I know you don't like to drive, but I'm begging you, baby. Please come get me. I want to talk to you. I have a lot to say. And I went to jail, not Clarissa's. Jail. No sex in jail. At least I hope not. Don't leave me too long. I'll be waiting."

Bo was in jail. He was in *jail*. And he'd been there all night. She quickly dialed the sheriff's department. A feminine voice answered.

"County Sheriff's Department. If this is an emergency, please call 9-1-1 because I don't deal well with stress. And if you're calling about a ticket, there's nothing I can do. Take it up with the judge. I don't get paid enough to listen to you complain."

As receptionists went, Wanda wasn't known for her friendly demeanor on the phone with strangers, but she'd been with the county forever.

"Wanda, it's me, Mouse Hobbes."

There was a surprised gasp, and then Wanda's voice went down a notch or two. "Good for you, Mouse. That boy needed a night in jail, if you know what I mean. It'll teach him not to go to bars. We can hold his ass for another twenty-four hours or so if you'd like."

"No, no. I don't want him to sit in jail. I didn't know he was there."

A sigh came over the line. "Hon, just admit it. There's no shame in a little revenge. That boy has had you panting all over him for years. I would have left his ass in jail, too."

"No, it's not about that. I have a boyfriend." That wasn't exactly the term Trev would want, but she wasn't about to call him her Master to one of the biggest gossips in town.

There was a long pause. "Holy hell, Mouse. Clarissa's been spreading the rumor that you done gone and took up with Trev McNamara. Tell me it isn't true. Hon, that man is bad news. I mean, he's gorgeous, but he's bad news. And from what I've heard, he's not really into foreplay."

"That's blatantly untrue. He's very much into foreplay." She couldn't let that rumor go.

"Really? He's gorgeous and into foreplay? That never happens."

"Well, it's true with Trev. Now, tell me how much it's going to cost me to get Bo out of jail." She didn't have time to gossip about her suddenly interesting personal life. She heard Trev shout. Apparently, she also didn't have a whole bunch of hot water. She mentally added a water heater to her ever-growing list of things she needed to shell out money for. She needed that loan.

"No charge, hon. Bo's a dumbass, not a criminal. The sheriff told me to let him go as soon as you showed up. Having to sleep close to Brian Nixon's drunk ass was apparently punishment enough. Just come pick him up."

"I'll be there soon." She flipped the phone closed.

Bo had called for her, and she'd been too busy with Trev to answer the phone.

She hurried to get dressed. Trev might not like how his morning was starting, but she was going to ask for a favor.

"Goddamn, that's cold." Trev's shout resounded through the room.

Yeah, she was going to have to fix that.

Chapter Seven

Bo hadn't slept a wink. His every muscle felt abused from sitting on the floor of the jail cell with cold metal pressed to his back. His skull felt like it was going to cave in. But that was nothing compared to the nausea in his gut.

Mouse hadn't come.

He'd played checkers for hours, letting the sheriff win game after game. All the while, he'd been sure that any minute Mouse would burst in the doors, all soft, feminine worry, and she would fuss over him. At four a.m., the sheriff had given up. He'd made Bo get back into the cell, and then he'd put his hat over his head and napped until his deputy had gotten in a few hours later.

Len Miller wasn't as tolerant as the sheriff. He was an asshole who needed to make up for his teeny-tiny dick with a badge and a bad attitude.

And Deputy Len was friends with that dickwad Brian, who seemed to be waking up. Bo watched him with narrowed eyes. His big body shifted on the cot, and he burped a couple of times before sitting up.

"What the fuck?" Brian wiped his eyes with the back of his hand. He immediately turned and vomited.

Bo's stomach churned. How long before they would let him call his brother? How long before Aidan figured out something was wrong? Bo was pretty damn sure everyone in town knew he was wasting away in jail, but Aidan rarely went to town, and he didn't talk to a lot of people about anything except business. Lexi had her head in her laptop most of the time. Lucas would be getting in from Dallas this morning. Maybe, if Lucas had to stop for gas, someone would mention it to him.

Otherwise, he was pretty sure he was stuck here until the sheriff got back. There was no way Deputy Len was going to let him go. He was enjoying the fact that Bo was in jail.

"You're the reason I'm here, ain't you?" Brian looked like his beauty rest hadn't put him in a better mood.

"I ain't. You're the reason we're here because you're an asshole." Brian had about seventy pounds on him, but he was through backing down. "And if you ever mention her name again, I'll kill you."

There was a chuckle from the deputy's desk. "Now that sounded like a threat, O'Malley."

"It wasn't. It was a promise." Mouse might not have shown up, but maybe he deserved that after the way he'd treated her yesterday. He would eventually get out of jail, and he'd show up on her doorstep—if it would hold his weight. He would show up, and he would get on his goddamn knees if he had to.

He loved her. It was right there in the center of his body, an odd sensation that warmed him. Even though he was sitting in jail, he was okay because he was finally going to make things right with Mouse.

"I don't think I like the way you're talking to me. You know, you used to be a good guy until you started hanging with the fags." Brian's fists curled in his hands.

And he was going to stop listening to that shit, too. He heard it all the time, and he took it. He was sick of taking it. His blood was starting to boil. He'd put up with it for far too long. "You know, I read somewhere that most prejudice comes from ignorance. That must be true because you're the most ignorant person I know. Now stop talking about my family, and we can avoid another fight where I set you on your ass."

"You didn't set me on my ass, you motherfucker." Brian managed to get to his feet.

Bo struggled to his. He could hear Wanda in the background. She was on the phone giving better play-by-play than an ESPN color announcer.

"They're going to fight right there in that jail cell, Patty. Bo called Brian a dummy. I know he is, but he doesn't like to be told that." Wanda kept it up.

Bo looked out at the deputy. Brian might have weight on him, but he was also hungover. Bo was tired, but his adrenaline was starting to flow. He clenched his fists. "Are you going to stop this?"

Deputy Len stood up. He walked around to the bars, nightstick in hand. There was a malicious smile on his weaselly face. He walked around to the front of the cage to where Brian held on. He shoved the nightstick through the bars, and for one moment, Bo was terrified the deputy was going to start in on Brian with the weapon.

Nope. It was worse. Bo shrank back, and Len handed Brian the weapon.

"Oops, I must have lost my hold," Len said with a sigh. "I hate it when prisoners get the upper hand, don't you, O'Malley?"

Brian clutched the evil-looking stick in his hand. Len leaned against the cell bars and yawned as though all of this was simply boring to him.

Wanda stood up at her desk. "What are you doing, Leonard?"

The deputy shrugged. "Well, I was trying to stop the prisoners from fighting. I dropped my nightstick. I guess I'll have to go get the Taser."

He had no doubt who the deputy would use that Taser on. This was going to get really ugly.

Brian wasted no time. He charged across the small cell, nightstick raised. Bo barely managed to avoid the swing of Brian's meaty arm. He ducked and rolled to the other side of the cell as the sound of wood striking metal clanged through the building.

God, that would have been his head. He looked for anything to defend himself with. There was nothing in the cell but a toilet and the cot, both bolted down.

He was fucked.

"Don't you dare touch him!" Mouse roared into the room. She practically threw herself against the bars, her arms coming through them as though she could catch the bigger man and keep him away from Bo.

"Mouse, you get back." Bo wasn't about to let that asshole get his hands on her.

"Lookee here, O'Malley. You got a mouse coming to your rescue." Len hadn't moved from his position. "Ain't that lucky for you?"

"Do something," she demanded, looking at the deputy. "He's going to kill Bo."

Len sighed. "I'll go get the Taser. It might take me a minute or two to find it."

"I suggest you find it sooner, Deputy. You now have witnesses to your improper use of police force. I assure you, if Mr. O'Malley comes out of this experience with a single scratch on him, you will be looking at a police brutality charge."

Bo looked out, and Leo Meyer stood beside the deputy's desk. He stared at Len, and suddenly the bastard looked like he gave a damn.

Shelley Hughes came running into the room. "What's going on? Why the hell does Brian Nixon have a weapon in a jail cell? Give me that."

What the hell was going on?

Bo pushed that bastard Brian out of the way. He was way too close to Mouse. "Don't you touch her."

Leo stepped forward before Shelley could get her hands on Brian. The big former Navy SEAL hooked an arm around each woman's waist and started to pull them away from the cell. Bo was about to express his gratitude when Mouse dug in. She tightened her hands around the bars.

"Let go, Beth." Leo's voice was calm, but there was a dark command behind it.

"Mouse, you let go!" Bo shouted his command. And then he ducked again because Brian didn't care that there were witnesses.

"Stop it!" Mouse yelled.

Leo used that muscle of his, and Mouse didn't stand a chance.

119

Bo thanked whoever had taught Leo Meyer to work out. At least Mouse wasn't in the line of fire anymore.

Brian lifted the nightstick, and Bo didn't have a damn place left to go. He looked out at Mouse. Tears were streaking down her face. She struggled against Leo's hold. Bo wasn't sure what had brought Aidan's friend to the sheriff's department, but he was damn happy the man was here. At least Mouse would be safe.

Bo closed his eyes and waited for his skull to crack.

There was a pop and then the sound of sizzling and a loud groan. Bo opened his eyes as Brian Nixon fell forward. There was a Taser probe in his back. His enormous body shook with the force of the electric current flowing through him.

A man he'd never met before stood outside the cage, yawning as he held the Taser in his hand. "Good thing me girls last night are into electric play or I wouldn't have had this beauty on me. I usually just shoot fuckers."

The man had a lyrical Irish accent.

Mouse had calmed, but Leo still had an arm wrapped around both women.

The deputy was back, his unused Taser in hand. "Who the hell are you?"

"Liam O'Donnell, and before you try to arrest me, you should know my boss is an asshole and he'll come after you if you toss me in that cell. I'm hopping a plane to England in two days and he doesn't like delays." The Irish guy tugged until the probe came out and Brian groaned.

"You let him out right now, Len Miller," Mouse demanded. "I'm going to hire a lawyer. I'm going to sue this whole county, starting with you."

"Yeah, that's right. He's some kind of Irish guy and he has his own Taser, which is a good thing because Len was not coming back in time, if you know what I mean. Now old Mouse is threatening to sue Len. And there's a really attractive man here who won't let go of Mouse and Shelley Hughes. Yes, I think so. It would serve Bryce right." Wanda kept talking.

"We don't need your commentary," Leo said to Wanda. He let both women go as Len opened the cell door.

Wanda looked up at him, utterly unintimidated. "You might not, but Patty sure does. Yes, hon, he's very bossy. I think so. Just like Aidan. Uh-huh."

Bo ignored her. He stepped over Brian's still-twitching body and muscled past the deputy.

"I don't care who your boss is," Len said to the guy named Liam. "You can't come into my station house and pull a weapon like that."

"He's working for Julian Lodge," Leo said.

Len stopped. "Huh. Now the way I see it, I'm probably lucky you were here."

"I'll have to tell Big Tag he's not the most intimidating person I know," Liam was saying as he yawned again.

Bo ignored them all, pulling Mouse into his arms. He'd never seen a more welcome sight than that pretty face looking up at him. Pretty? Hell, she was beautiful. How had he not seen it before? She wasn't flashy like Clarissa, but she had the loveliest eyes, and her hair was soft. She usually wore it up, but now it tumbled all around her shoulders and down her back. He let his hands sink into the silky stuff as he pulled her close.

"I'm sorry. I didn't get the message until this morning," she whispered.

"It doesn't matter." He squeezed her, enjoying the way her breasts felt against his chest. She was so damn sweet. His dick was getting hard. The adrenaline of the fight was still riding him. He wanted to kiss her right here and now.

She'd come. She hadn't been pissed off. He believed her. She simply hadn't gotten the message. And it looked like he wouldn't even have to ride on her handlebars to get back home. The thought made him smile.

"I'm glad you're here." He pulled back so he could look at her. Her eyes were still a little red, but there was a tremulous smile on her face. "I have some things I need to tell you. Can we go somewhere and talk?"

He'd thought about this all night. He had a speech prepared, and at the end, he was going down on one knee and asking her to marry him. There was no need to wait. He'd known deep down she was the one for him for ten years, since that night when she'd taken him in without a single question. She'd been his haven ever since. He'd been stubborn and stupid and focused on the wrong things. He knew he should wait and buy her a proper ring before he asked, but now that the moment was here, he was impatient to get on with the rest of his life.

"You ready to go?" a deep voice asked from the front of the room.

Bo knew that voice. He turned and saw Trev McNamara standing there, a ferocious scowl on his face. What the fuck was he doing here? Bo checked his temper. He didn't need to start another fight. There was a perfectly reasonable explanation for Trev being here. There had to be.

Mouse tried to take a step back. She was so shy. Bo wasn't going to let her be so shy anymore. He pulled her close again. It was time to start staking his claim.

"Did you try to ride that bicycle of yours all the way out here? Did Trev pick you up?" He looked over at Trev, not giving Mouse a chance to respond. "Thanks for picking up my girl. I'm going to force her to get more comfortable driving."

"I picked her up last night." Trev's eyes were on the place where Bo's hands held Mouse.

"Trev was nice enough to give me a ride to come and get you out of jail. Leo and Shelley came along, and Mr. O'Donnell didn't have a place to go. I think he drove down with Leo. Shelley was worried about you," Mouse explained.

Bo noticed she wasn't clutching him the way she had in the past. When he'd hugged her before, she'd practically inhaled him. She'd been starved for affection. Now he was going to drown her in it.

"Well, I'm fine. No need to worry now. What do you mean last night?"

She pulled away. There was no way to mistake the fact that she wanted to stand on her own. Bo felt the loss of her warmth as she stepped away from him.

"Wanda, do you need anything else? Can we take him home?" Mouse asked.

Wanda pulled the phone away from her ear. "Are you sure you don't want to hash this out here, hon? Bo seems to be in a fighting mood."

"No one's going to fight," Mouse promised.

Wanda sighed. "Well, then I guess you're free to leave."

"Now, Wanda, I am the deputy here." Len tried to reassert himself even as he checked Brian Nixon's pulse.

Wanda wasn't having it. "And I know your momma. How is she going to feel when I tell her you keep a bottle of whiskey in your desk? And I bet she doesn't know about your card game every Wednesday night when you're supposed to be at men's bible study."

Len proved he caved easily when given the slightest chance. "You're free to go."

Bo got a nasty feeling in his gut. Trev didn't look like a man who was doing a woman a simple favor. He was staring at Mouse like he was going to pounce any second. Trev looked predatory and possessive. What had he meant when he'd said he'd picked her up last night?

"I'm going to take Shelley home. She's been up all night, and I suspect her husband will wonder where she's been. I'll drop her off and meet you out at Aidan's." Leo put a hand on Shelley's back. She had flushed at the mention of her husband.

Bo doubted Bryce Hughes would even notice his wife was gone. He'd fucked almost every single woman in the county. The man seemed to prefer the trailer-trash girls of the world, and they loved him back. He'd noticed that Bryce always had people coming in and out of that real estate office of his, and at all hours of the night. Bryce liked to work late, it seemed. He felt bad for Shelley. She was a nice lady.

Leo turned to Wanda, pulling a card from his pocket. "You would make an excellent Domme, ma'am. If you ever decide to investigate the lifestyle, give me a call. I can get you into training."

Wanda stared down at the card, phone still in her hand. "A Dom? I don't know what that is. Patty, do you know why some man with a ponytail would call me Dom?"

"Does Aidan's brother not know about Beth and the quarterback?" O'Donnell asked.

Leo pointed toward the door. "We'll wait outside. Come on O'Donnell."

Leo, Liam, and Shelley walked out toward the parking lot, but Bo stared as Mouse walked straight up to fucking Trevor McNamara and put her arms around his waist. She leaned in to Trev's body like she belonged plastered against him. Trev sure as hell wasn't pushing her away.

"What's going on here, Mouse?" He suddenly had a terrible feeling that he knew.

Mouse gave him a shy smile. "Trev picked me up last night. I guess you could say we've decided to start dating. I hope you're happy for me. You've told me for years that I needed to find a keeper."

That was a joke. He'd said it a hundred times because trouble always seemed to find Mouse. He'd told her to find a boyfriend, too. He'd said it because he'd known damn sure she wouldn't find one. Certainly not an ex-football star with addiction problems.

"Yeah, I hope you're happy for us, Bo." The way Trev's hands curled possessively around Mouse's shoulders set his teeth on edge. That bastard thought he could swoop in and steal his girl, did he? "I want to get along with Beth's friends. I hope we can do that for her sake."

"Yes, Patty, Trev is being very polite. But I think Bo figured out what we've known all along." Wanda didn't bother to keep her voice down.

Bo flushed. He scrubbed a hand through his hair. He'd just gotten over what people would say about him marrying Mouse. Now he realized that losing Mouse was going to be even more humiliating.

"Are you ready to go? Do we need to take you to your truck?" Mouse asked. Her hand went to Trev's chest.

His truck was still out at The Rusty Spur. He hoped. Unless someone had towed it. Hell, the way the last twenty-four hours had gone, his truck might have been blown up by aliens or some shit. It would be fitting. "No. I want to go home."

The Rusty Spur was on the other side of the county. There was no way he was going to ride with them for twenty damn minutes watching Trev hang all over his Mouse.

Fuck. She wasn't his anymore. How had things gone so fucking wrong in the course of a single evening? How was he going to win her back before she slept with that asshole? Trev wouldn't wait long. Trev was used to all kinds of freaky shit, and probably a whole lot of it. He hadn't been picky. The asshole could easily give Mouse any number of diseases. No, there was no way he was going to let that happen.

The good news was Mouse liked to take things slow. She was the kind of girl who slowly pulled off a bandage, hoping and praying that it wouldn't hurt too much. She took six months to buy a refrigerator, looking at hundreds and researching to get the best price. He had a little time, surely.

He would still talk to her. Ten years couldn't be erased because one ex-football player gave her a ride home and then offered to drive her out here. He would wait until they were out at the ranch, and he would talk to her away from the glaring eyes of Trev. It could still work out.

She didn't realize that Bo wanted her. That was the trouble. Once she realized he was finally ready, she would leave all this talk of dating Trev McNamara behind.

"Let's get the hell out of here," Bo said, eager to leave the sheriff's office far behind him. He turned back to Wanda. "You'll be hearing from my lawyer."

She smiled brightly. "Lucas? I hope so. That man is delicious. You tell him to bring the paperwork himself. Yes, Patty. I know he likes boys, too. It's a little naughty. Have you seen him without his shirt on?"

There was no intimidating Wanda. Bo gave up and followed Mouse.

He hated the way her hand slipped down into Trev's, like it belonged there. Trev's fingers curled around hers, linking them together. Trev pushed out of the double doors and into the heat. Leo and Shelley were still standing outside. Leo's head shook as he looked at Trev's vehicle. Trev's old pickup was sitting in the parking lot, and it looked like someone was making his opinion known.

"Trev," Shelley started, her face sympathetic.

Trev stared at his truck for a moment as though the sight didn't quite register.

"What the hell? How did that happen? We were only in there for a couple of minutes. No more than ten." Trev dropped Mouse's hand as he walked around the truck. There, in big, black, spray-painted letters, was a message for Trevor McNamara, former hero of Deer Run.

Go Away

The Irish guy was taking pictures of the damage and telling Leo this better not take long.

There were squiggles and dots all over the truck, but the message was what Bo found important. Someone didn't want Trev in town. Someone was willing to trash his car in the sheriff's department parking lot, where anyone could walk out and see him.

Bo pretty much knew exactly how that person must feel. He wanted Trev out of his fucking town, too.

* * * *

Trev sat down in the cool sanctuary of Aidan O'Malley's office and waited. He could hear Aidan talking to his brother. Bo's voice was low, but he got the gist of the conversation. Bo was unhappy that Aidan was bringing Trev in as the foreman.

One more person who didn't want him around.

Something ugly was gnawing at his stomach. All he could think about was beer. He only needed one. That other part of him was whining. *Just one beer and I'll shut up. Don't you want me to shut up for a while?*

"I thought you might like some coffee." Beth stood in the doorway, a mug in her hand. She had on a well-worn pair of jeans and a button-down shirt that looked to be a size too big. It hung off her, but he knew the curves that were there.

Just like that, the voice fled. There wasn't a place for that whiny idiot when Beth was standing there looking like sunshine. And he

126

did need the caffeine.

"Thank you, darlin'." He held out his hand, and she crossed the room. Her eagerness was like a balm on his wounded ego.

"It's the good stuff," a sassy voice claimed. Lexi O'Malley stood in the doorway, a smile on her face. Lexi was a lovely woman with a sharp mind and, oftentimes, an even sharper tongue. "Lucas bought one of those single-cup makers. It's like heaven in a mug."

Trev took a whiff. It smelled dark and rich.

"It always tastes like motor oil to me. I prefer tea." Beth looked down at the mug as though trying to understand.

"It's all right, darlin'. You stick to your tea." He took a long drink. It was rich and bitter, and entirely wonderful. He had to be addicted to something, and all he had left was coffee.

"Mouse doesn't understand the call of caffeine, I'm afraid," Lexi explained.

"Her name is Beth." Despite his affection for Lexi, no one was going to call Beth by that name around him again.

Lexi stopped, and her eyes went back and forth between Trev and Beth, assessing and judging the situation. "You and Beth?"

She hadn't asked Beth. The question had been directed at him, and he couldn't misread the momma bear protectiveness behind it. "Me and Beth. And yes, I know what I'm doing."

She stared for a minute more. "Do you know what you're doing, Beth?"

Beth shook her head. "Not really, but I know I like doing it." Her face flushed as though she'd figured out what she'd said could be taken in a risqué fashion. "That wasn't what I meant."

"Yes, it was." Lexi's face broke into a huge grin. "Well, I have to say I'm happy for both of you. I've been trying to convince Aidan to bring Beth with us to The Club for the last year since she's…well…you know."

He nodded. Beth was a natural submissive. He hadn't met many. Even the subs in The Club tended to be more of the "submit in the bedroom"–style subs. "I know."

"I don't know. I have no idea what you're talking about." Beth's big eyes looked between them as though trying to decide what was going on.

There was a loud shout from the next room, and Lexi winced.

A tall man with raven-black hair strode into the room, his eyes laser focused on Lexi. He walked in and immediately crowded the small woman. His arms went around her, and Trev could hear his sigh as they connected.

"Hi, baby."

"Hi, Lucas." Lexi kissed him, her mouth finding his. Her arms wound around him.

Lucas O'Malley had, at one time, been known as Lucas Cameron. He was the scion of a political family, but he'd left them long before to live with his two loves, Lexi and Aidan.

Lucas nodded his way. "Hello, Trev. Beth."

He liked Lucas O'Malley. "Hello, Lucas. How's it going?"

He reached for Beth's hand, the impulse so overwhelming, he gave in.

Lucas didn't fail to note the exchange. "Well, that didn't take long."

Lexi smiled up at him. "You know I always said Trev had the Dom thing down. It's like a moth to a flame. Speaking of moths to flames, Leo's in town. Shelley Hughes called him last night when she couldn't find Trev and worried that he had found a bottle again. He's the reason we have Big Tag's crazy Irishman asleep on our couch. Leo brought him in to track down Trev. I think now we know what he found instead of a bottle."

Lucas smiled. "Seriously, dude, eight hours in this town and you find the sub."

Beth's eyes lit up. "Oh, now I get it. I'm the sub. I can handle that. I don't know why everyone is praising Trev, though. Maybe I'm the one who found him."

Lexi nodded. "Don't listen to the men, Mou…Beth. They need to have their egos stroked. It's why they became Doms."

There was another loud crash from the adjoining room.

Lexi winced again. "Except for that one. Aidan became a Dom because he likes the violence."

That earned her a playful swat from Lucas. "Don't you start that, brat. You know he's struggling with this."

Aidan opened the door to the office. His face was grim, but he smiled as he caught Lucas. "You're back early."

Lucas put a hand on his Dom's waist. Aidan was the Dom, Lucas the switch, and Lexi the sweetly bratty sub. "I finished up as fast as I could. I wanted to come home."

Aidan leaned forward and pressed his lips to Lucas's. "I'm glad, O'Malley. Now take our wife out of here or she'll run this damn interview."

Lucas winked at his partner and took Lexi's hand. He led her out of the room.

Trev looked up at Beth. "Go on, darlin'. I have to talk to Aidan."

Beth smiled down at him and followed Lucas and Lexi.

Just like that, the light left the room for him. He was back to darkness as Aidan frowned at him.

"You playing around with Mouse?"

"Her name is Bethany. Don't call her Mouse. She isn't some animal." Trev tried to keep his anger tamped down.

Aidan walked around the desk and slumped down into his chair. "Thank god someone finally calls her by her name. You serious about her? She's a damn fine woman."

That was the question. He could be perfectly serious. He just didn't know for how long. One day at a time didn't leave much promise for the long-term. What could he offer her if he couldn't promise much past tomorrow? "I care about her."

"So does my brother."

Bo cared. He'd seen it in Bo's eyes. Bo simply wasn't man enough to follow up on the emotion. "She's been alone for years. Don't make this sound like I walked in and stole her. You know what she is. Bo isn't a Dom. It would be a disaster if he got together with her. She would be his doormat. She would be miserable."

"I don't know if I would say she'd be a doormat, but I do get your point. My brother isn't a Dom."

"Not even close."

Aidan seemed to consider the problem. "But I don't know that I trust you, either."

He hated this. He hated being at someone else's whim. He'd spent so long being the freaking center of the universe that it rankled to have sunk so low. His hands curled around the arms of the chair he sat in. The need that was always there in the back of his head had taken up residence in his gut. It took everything he had not to get up and walk out.

"I can only try my damnedest to change your mind. Leo told me Julian called in a favor to get me hired on here. If you'll let me work as a hand, you can continue your search for a foreman. All I'm asking for is a year's worth of honest work."

Aidan's brow rose. He leaned forward. "I thought one of the things you required was a safe place to stay. The way Julian explained it, you need a babysitter."

Trev huffed. Julian had made it sound bad. "I think I have a place to stay. It's run-down, but I can handle it. I don't want Beth staying there alone."

"Out at the old Bellows place?"

He nodded.

"That place should be condemned."

Not if he had anything to say about it. Beth loved it. "It will be fine once she fixes it up. Look, I get you don't want me here. All you have to do is tell me no, and I'll go. I won't cause trouble between you and Julian. We can tell him I changed my mind."

"And then what happens to Beth?"

That was the million-dollar question. "I'll take care of her."

He wasn't sure how, but he would do it.

Aidan leaned forward, his eyes never leaving Trev's face. "My brother is under the impression that you're nothing more than a bump in the road for Beth. He's sure she'll come around to his way of thinking if I tell you to leave."

"Like I said, do what you need to do. I'll take care of Beth. She gave herself to me. I can't ignore that gift. I won't walk away because Bo O'Malley has decided to finally step up to the plate after ten years. He didn't want her until I set eyes on her."

Aidan sat in quiet judgment, the silence of the room oppressive. It gave Trev too much time to think.

He'd lied to himself. He'd been ready to break the night before. He'd put the coffee mug down. He'd made his decision. He'd shut the door to the truck, and he'd started the long walk inside. It was like he'd been pulled along by some invisible rope. He'd stopped fighting it. There had been a certain peace to laying down and accepting the inevitable.

And then he'd seen Beth and known he couldn't afford to give in.

She claimed he'd saved her. It was utterly the other way around.

"Will you submit to weekly drug tests?"

Aidan's words sent him into another spiral. And what fucking choice did he have? He had a year until he got his money and he could work his own spread. Maybe then he could afford to buy back some small shred of dignity. "Sure. I'll pee in a cup."

He was certain his whole face was on fire, but he kept his words measured and even. He drank his coffee. He thought about Beth as Aidan started going over all the rules.

He wished he was still in bed with her. Everything had been all right this morning. The world had been soft and warm. It had been a place where he hadn't ruined everything. It had been a place where he'd never chosen a drink or a line of cocaine over his family—one where he'd made his parents proud, where he'd shown up at his momma's deathbed and helped his sister get through it. When he'd held Beth, that real world—the one where he'd screwed everything up—had fallen away, and he was someone else. He'd been Beth's loving Master. He'd been someone she could count on. He'd been good for something.

"Did you get all that?" Aidan stared at him.

Yeah. The rules. He knew them by heart. Julian had drilled the rules into him every day of the last two years. They all came down to one edict—don't fuck up. "Yes. I know what to do."

"I think we can try putting you in charge for a while." Aidan sat back, his voice softening a bit. "You know how to work a ranch, right? You haven't forgotten?"

It wasn't the kind of thing he could forget. It had been his whole childhood. If he'd followed down his father's path, he might never have gotten into trouble. He would have been there when his mother had gotten sick. He would have made sure Shelley stayed the hell away from Bryce Hughes. He would have lived a quiet life.

Vanilla. Yes, it would have been vanilla. He would never have been trained to see the inherent beauty and value in someone like Bethany Hobbes. He would have ignored her like the rest of the town.

"I recently worked for your partner, Jack Barnes. I think he'll vouch for my skill."

Aidan snorted. "Partner? Don't let Jack hear that. Let me tell you something, I might be a Dom, but my father-in-law scares the crap out of me. Julian softened up after marriage. Marriage and a family simply refined Jack Barnes's talents for revenge. And he likes the hell out of you."

At least someone did. Which begged the question. "But you don't."

Aidan's mouth twisted slightly. "Jack doesn't have our history with you. Or rather, your history with my brother. I don't know what happened between the two of you. Bo is tight-lipped about a lot of things. I know you were a real good friend to him after I left for college. Our father was a bastard. You know that, right?"

Trev nodded. Conner O'Malley had been a mean drunk, and he'd liked setting his kids at each other's throats to see who would win. "Bo mentioned it."

"You were there for him all during your senior year. Why did you have to dump him?"

That was the pot calling the kettle black. "I went to college. The same one you went to."

The slight stain on Aidan's cheeks told him that Aidan wasn't unaware of his own guilt. "Yeah, maybe that's why I have trouble with you. You remind me of all the things I did wrong with Bo. How close were you? I remember him talking incessantly about you every time I managed to come home, and then one day, he stopped. He wouldn't even say your name. He said Mouse was the only true friend he had."

"Beth."

"His words, not mine."

Trev had to shake his head. "I don't know. I know that sounds horrible, but I don't know what happened. I got involved in the football season, and I ignored him. He called, and when I was at home and sober, which wasn't that often, I would talk to him. I liked

Bo. I never had a little brother. By my sophomore year, I was sober during the season, but the minute I wasn't playing, I was drunk or high all the time. I didn't talk to him much after that. I opted into the draft after my junior year. It was the last great season I had. It was the last season I stayed sober. The rest is history. I signed one huge deal and threw it all away."

Aidan sighed. "I'm worried about Bo. I don't know what losing Beth is going to do to him. He might not admit it, but she's been his anchor for years now. He's really upset that you're dating her. I think he's going to be even more upset when he discovers you've begun a D/s relationship with her. I would assume you've done that. Or, are you aiming for vanilla?"

Aidan said the word "vanilla" with a hint of disdain. Trev could reassure him on that point. "We haven't formalized anything, and she's going to require training, but she's amenable to the lifestyle, thanks to your wife's books."

Aidan's face suddenly turned youthful as he grinned. "Leo hates them. He thinks they make us all look like wimps. I like them. I like that all of Lexi's stories have happy endings." His face turned a little sad. "I know Bo made his own bed with that girl."

"It wouldn't have worked." He knew it deep down, but it didn't stop the guilt that formed a knot in his stomach. "Bo isn't a Dom. If I had to guess, I would say he's actually more submissive than anything else. He needs a strong woman in his life. He needs someone who will make decisions and allow him to be who he is."

Aidan's eyes became hooded. "A woman, or a man."

He felt his brows rise in pure surprise. "You think he's bisexual? I never got that off him. I always felt like he was looking for a big brother or a father figure, not a lover."

"I didn't say he was like me," Aidan corrected. "I said that he could use a Dom. You know it doesn't have to involve sex. I believe Bo really does care for Beth, and Beth cares for Bo. You wouldn't be the first Dom to find himself in a ménage because his sub needs it."

The words hit him like a lightning rod. Share Beth? Why the hell would he do that? Bo didn't want him here. He sure as fuck wouldn't want to share a woman with him. And he wasn't staying.

He wasn't good for anyone.

"Just think about it," Aidan said.

Trev didn't want to think about it. He was already wondering if he wasn't going to get Beth in trouble. Bo would be more trouble than he could handle. And it brought up a couple of questions. "You don't even like me. Why the hell would you want me in a ménage with your brother?"

"It's not that I don't like you." Aidan ran a hand through his hair. "I don't know you. I'm bringing you into my home, and that makes me nervous. But Julian assures me you're a good Dom. I would do almost anything to help my brother. I hurt him in the past. I didn't mean to, but I was one more male authority figure who walked away and left him alone. He needs more than I can give him. I believe he would be happiest in a ménage with a strong Dom and a female sub. Don't worry about it, Trev. He won't listen to me. He's determined to have a white-picket-fence lifestyle. I think he's still rebelling. Or he doesn't want to go through what I've gone through. It's hard to live the way we do, especially in a small town." He slapped at the desk and got up. He held out a hand, and Trev took it. "Just do your job. We'll get on fine."

He pushed himself up out of the chair, his heart still pounding. He couldn't share Beth. He just couldn't. He fucking needed her. He needed her right now.

"Thanks. I'll take a couple of minutes and then go out and meet the men. Can you give me half an hour?" He didn't want the fucking job. He wanted to walk away, but he couldn't. The need to get drunk off his ass kept rising with every damn word Aidan said.

"Sure. Take all the time you need. Will you think about what I said? Will you consider giving Bo a chance?" Aidan stared at him, his face a mask of blatant desire.

"I'll consider it. But Bo hates me. I don't know why, but I have to take that into consideration. He won't go down easy." Trev didn't want him to go down at all. He wanted to be left alone with Beth.

Was he the best man for her? With all the baggage he carried?

Fuck. His cock didn't care. He wasn't sure who would win that battle.

Aidan nodded. "A chance is all I can ask."

Trev walked out of the office door and closed it.

Beth stood outside, her eyes grave. He took a step toward her. He knew he shouldn't touch her feeling the way he did. Something ugly was inside him, but he couldn't help himself. He needed her. He needed her right fucking now.

"Where's the bathroom?" he heard himself say.

Beth took his hand and led him down the hall.

Chapter Eight

Trev closed the door behind them, locking it with a decisive click. The bathroom was small, but it would do.

He should walk away. He should get the hell out of Deer Run and find the first AA meeting he could, but he knew that sitting and talking to twenty sad-sack people like himself wouldn't give him half of what he needed. It wouldn't burn away the pain and humiliation of the day the way dominating Beth could.

Fuck, he was already addicted to her.

"I want to see you. Take your clothes off." He knew he didn't sound gentle or kind. He sounded cold. Beth stared at him for a moment, but then seemed to come to some decision of her own. Her hands went to the buttons of her blouse. The minute her creamy skin began to appear, the violence and rage inside him dialed down a notch.

He could handle this. He could manage to get through the afternoon without taking a drink. But he had to have her.

He leaned back against the door and finally let himself breathe. The interview with Aidan had his gut in knots, but watching Beth undress at his command settled something deep inside him.

She turned big, brown eyes up his way as she dropped her shirt and pulled at the latch of her bra. She struggled but got it undone.

Her breasts bounced free. His cock hardened in his jeans. Despite the fact that he'd had her twice the night before, he was hungry for her.

"Are you sore?" If she was, he wouldn't fuck her. He would find another way to slake his hunger.

Her lips curled up the slightest bit. "Just a little. I'm fine."

He didn't touch her, yet her nipples tightened. Those nipples were so lovely to his eyes—brown and pink and large. She probably thought they were too big, but all he could think about was getting them in his mouth.

"Tell me you want this." He needed to hear the words. "This won't be vanilla, darlin'. I have something inside me. I can dominate you, or I can go and find that bottle that always seems to call to me."

Her eyes softened. She really did need a keeper. When he told her something that would send most women running for cover, she looked at him with her big doe eyes and brought her hand up to cup his face.

"Trev, I want this. I want you. I don't care what happened before. I want the man you are now."

He wasn't sure the man he was now deserved her. "Bo wants you."

He was pretty sure that had come out with all the jealousy of a five-year-old fighting over his favorite toy.

She shook her head. "No. Not that way. If he does, it's only because someone else looked at me. Bo can be like a dog with two bones. If you left, we would go right back to where we were before. I would be his friend."

But she wanted more. She loved Bo. He could see that plainly on her face. She didn't love Trev yet, but he could take her, brand her. He had a shot that Bo didn't have. If he wanted Beth, he could make her his. He could bind her sweet heart by taking her body and introducing her to his lifestyle.

Aidan's words played through his brain. *Bo needs you, too.* He wasn't going there. He didn't have to share. He didn't. He wouldn't. He was going to keep her. Bo could find what he needed on his own.

"The pants, too. I want to see every inch of you." He wanted to do more than see her. He already wanted to throw her down on her hands and knees and force his cock inside. But that would only soothe his aching cock. He needed more. He forced himself to be still.

Her hands went to the button on the top of her jeans. She trembled a little as she pushed the jeans off her hips, dragging the cotton panties she wore with them. She toed off her shoes and stood before him completely naked.

Her face was tight with anxiety. He didn't want that.

"Are you scared?"

She shook her head. "Not in the way you think. I'm scared you're going to wake up and realize you don't want me. I'm scared you're going to figure out that I'm not pretty like the other girls you've been with. I'm kind of fat."

He wasn't about to put up with that. Her training began now. "Lean over the tub and place your hands flat on the marble. You are not allowed to make a sound. Later you can cry all you like, but we're not alone in this house. I'm going to spank you. You get ten every time you call yourself fat or make a disparaging statement about yourself. I won't put up with it."

Her mouth dropped open. "You're going to spank me?"

"I am. Now do as I said, or I'll up it to twenty. Right now, I'm using my hand. If you try my patience, we can move up to a paddle. I assure you Aidan has a few paddles around here. Maybe even a whip."

Her eyes filled with tears. "But I didn't know I wasn't supposed to do that."

"You didn't know you shouldn't think poorly of yourself? You didn't realize I won't let anyone talk bad about you?"

She stood a little taller, her shoulders setting back. She turned and grabbed the side of the big marble tub. She leaned over, and her round ass was in the air.

"Very good, love. That's what I want. You'll take your discipline quietly. Can you do that?"

"I can try." She sounded breathless, as though on the edge of trepidation and desire. It was right where he wanted her.

He opened the first drawer he found and praised Aidan O'Malley's obvious belief in remaining stocked on the important items in life. Lube and condoms. He pulled both out with no guilt whatsoever. He set them on the sink and regarded her lovely ass. He'd spanked subs before. He'd been spanked himself. He knew how to do it, but this seemed more serious than those playful times. This was *his* submissive.

He put a hand on her waist. She shivered and then tensed. "Relax. This will be over in a moment, and we can move on to the nice part. Although I truly believe you'll enjoy this, too."

He brought his hand down on her right cheek, a short, sharp slap. She gasped, and her head dropped forward. He smacked her again, loving the feeling of her skin against his hand. She heated up, her skin pinkening beautifully as he continued. He didn't count out loud, but in his head he marked each slap in his memory. The first time he'd disciplined a sub who mattered was a momentous occasion. The fact that she'd never been spanked before made it all the sweeter. He was her first.

He could be her only.

He put the thought aside as he slapped her cheek one last time.

Beth was panting. Her skin was flushed. He ran a hand along her ass, hoping he'd been right about her. He sighed as he felt it. Her pussy was soft and moist. He could take her right then, and she would be ready for him. She was submissive in every way. He could teach her to stand up for herself, to value herself, but damn, he wouldn't change this about her.

"Do you know how good you smell, Beth? I can smell how hot this pussy is. This pussy is dying for some cock, isn't it? You answer me properly. No lying."

"Yes, Sir. I seem to be very aroused. I'm rather surprised. I didn't think a spanking would do that to me."

"Didn't you? Are you going to tell me that you've been reading Lexi's books and it never occurred to you that you might like a big bad Dom to take control?"

Even the words seemed to be arousing her. He let his hand trace the petals of her pussy. They were plump and moist. Every word out of his mouth seemed to bring a fresh pulse of cream from deep inside her body.

"Yes, Sir. I did think about it."

"Did those books make you hot?"

"Yes, Sir."

"I'm glad, Beth. I really am." He would have to remember to thank Lexi later. For now, he was dying. He let his hand slide back. He had some prep work to do. "Do you know about anal sex, darlin'? Does Lexi cover that in her books?"

She tensed. "Yes."

"And you're afraid." It was all over her. He pressed his hand back against her pussy, finding her clit and giving it a little pull. She relaxed again. He would have to go slow.

"I'm a little nervous," she admitted. "I think it might hurt."

"I promise, you'll take the pain because it's going to bring you so much pleasure. Trust me. All you have to do is tell me to stop if it gets to be too much. I want you to give it a chance, but I don't want you to simply endure it. I'm going to use my finger today. Just one. Can you trust me?"

"Yes, Trev." He could hear the smile in her words.

This was what he needed. He needed to be reminded that he could still do something right. He could take care of her. He could be worthy of her trust. He parted her cheeks and dribbled the lube. Like the rest of Beth, her asshole was a lovely thing. Pink and puckered, he couldn't let himself think about how tightly it would grip his dick or he would come in his jeans. He lubed his finger up and placed it right against her.

"Don't tense on me," he warned. "Relax. It won't be so bad."

It would be amazing, but only after careful preparation. He gently pressed forward. The muscles of her asshole fought to keep him out. He wouldn't allow that. He pushed in, gaining ground. He pulled back and rimmed her gently.

Slowly and with great patience, he worked his finger in. Her asshole clenched around his finger, the muscle so tight he felt it in his cock. God, he couldn't wait to fuck her there.

And he couldn't wait to fuck her period. His cock throbbed. He needed her.

"Stay where you are. Don't move."

He quickly washed his hands and shoved his jeans off his hips. His cock bobbed out and then pointed toward her. His cock was a compass pointing straight at her pussy. He stroked his cock before rolling the condom on.

"I'm going to go and buy you a plug. I want to get this asshole ready for its Master. It's mine, Beth. Your ass is mine the same way this pretty pussy is mine. It all belongs to me. Say it."

"I belong to you." She said it with a shaky voice, but there was determination behind it. She paused, and then she sounded stronger. "Do you belong to me?"

Fuck, yeah. She was learning. "Yes, darlin'. That's what it means. I belong to you."

He lined his dick up and pressed home. She felt perfect. So tight and hot and welcoming. Her ass wiggled as she adjusted to his girth. She tilted her hips up, and he slipped in deeper. He pulled at her hips, shoving himself deep inside.

Beth moaned, the sound calling to him. He fucked her with purpose, every thrust bringing them closer together. He thrust in and out, enjoying the way she gradually moved from utter submission to jolting back against him. She wanted it. She was willing to fight for her pleasure. He loved the trust she put in him, but now there was a part of him that wanted her to be fierce. This was what he'd missed in other subs. Other subs had either been brats looking to top from the bottom or soft, sweet things who would wait for their pleasure. Beth was a mix of both. She was smart, and with the right man, she could do great things. Beth slammed her hips back toward him, and he nearly lost it.

He groaned and pushed his hand around her waist to her clit. The little nubbin was swollen and hot. He rubbed a quick circle and pressed in. He was rewarded by the clenching of her pussy around his cock, and she went off.

He let go. He felt his spine light up as the semen in his balls bubbled up and shot off. He pushed his cock in as far as he could go, binding them together.

He dragged oxygen into his lungs. All the previous humiliation had burned off in the face of her submission.

"Thank you, darlin'. I needed that."

He could breathe again. He was filled with her. He didn't need anything else. For now.

He kissed the back of her neck and helped her stand up.

* * * *

Bo stared at the bathroom door. He'd watched them disappear behind it a while back, but the shock was finally setting in.

There was no reason for Mouse to have walked into that bathroom with Trev McNamara besides the obvious one.

He was too late.

He stood there in the house he'd grown up in and wondered when it would feel comfortable again. How long would it take before he could walk down this hallway and not see Mouse wearing a smile he'd never seen before, shutting the door behind her— shutting him out.

The door opened, and Bo shrank back so they wouldn't see him. When he'd first realized what was going on, he'd thought about breaking down the door and beating the shit out of Trev. The rage had been right there in his gut, winding its way through his body and into his fists.

And then it hit him.

This was his fault.

Mouse walked out first, her eyes going to either side of the hallway as though she didn't want to get caught, but he didn't know why. Her skin glowed. Her eyes sparkled. Her mouth was swollen, and her hair mussed in an oh-so-sexy way. She was fucking beautiful. She was transformed, and not by him. Mouse was a different woman, well loved and happy.

Trev walked out behind her. He obviously didn't give a shit if anyone saw them walking out. He had a lazily satiated look on his face. He reached out and caught Mouse's hand, dragging her back to him. His hand cupped her face, and a soft look came over the former quarterback. Instead of closing his mouth over hers, Trev did something that made his heart ache. He leaned over and touched his nose to Mouse's in a sweet, affectionate gesture.

"Thank you, darlin'." Trev's voice was low and quiet and so

serious, Bo felt guilty, like he was seeing something too private and intimate.

She sighed and wrapped her arms around him. "I'm glad I could help, Sir."

Trev kissed her forehead. "Can you get into town okay? I can take you if you need me to."

She shook her head. "No. Lexi is going into town. She has some shopping to do. She'll take me to the bank and bring me back. Then I'll have my loan, and I can start my renovations."

Trev groaned. "Be sure to buy me a home repair book. I'm afraid I'm better with cars than I am plumbing. And electrical. And woodworking."

She slapped lightly at his chest. "It's not that bad. Well, it is, but it's going to be fun."

They moved apart, but Trev's eyes followed her. "And buy a coffeemaker, woman."

"I will," Mouse promised as she walked toward the kitchen. Bo had to move fast to avoid her. She walked by, her hips swaying in a sexy cadence.

This wasn't Trev McNamara fucking the first woman to come along. The man had feelings for Mouse, and they weren't shallow. And Mouse had never looked at him the way she looked at Trev.

Maybe because you never kissed her. You never dragged her in a bathroom because you couldn't wait one more minute to have her. You never told her how much you want her.

There was a rustling behind him, and he turned, startled. Aidan stood there, his face grim.

"I'm happy you managed to not attempt to kill my new foreman."

Bo closed his eyes. He'd tried to talk his brother out of hiring Trev. He'd used the incredibly intelligent argument that he didn't like Trev therefore Aidan shouldn't hire him. He hadn't been willing to admit why he didn't want Trev around. But then that was the trouble, wasn't it? He hadn't been willing to admit how he felt about Mouse, and now he'd lost her.

"I'm not going to hit Trev. It's your ranch. You gotta do what you think is right." All the fight had left him the minute he realized

Trev wasn't using Mouse and Mouse wasn't going to leave Trev because one dumbass man had finally come to his senses. It was like everything in life. Mouse would move on, and Bo would be alone. He would smile and party and be everyone's "friend," and no one would know him, not really. Everyone he ever opened up to had left and moved on.

At some point in time, he had to stop blaming the people who left and start blaming himself. Maybe his father had been right. He wasn't good enough.

"I don't like the look in your eyes. And you know this ranch is your home." Aidan crossed his arms over his chest.

His brother could talk all he liked, but Aidan owned the ranch. There was a reason Aidan hadn't turned over the foreman's job to him. He was good with cattle, but he was never going to be the boss. The rest of his life played out in his brain. He would stay here in the little house he lived in and grow old, all the while spending his nights with a bunch of people he didn't love. He would watch as Lexi and Lucas and his brother raised their odd family. They might cause the town to talk, but at least they had each other. Bo might be accepted by the citizens of Deer Run, but he wouldn't have a woman smile at him like Lexi did at his brother and Lucas, like Mouse had smiled at Trev. It was his fate.

He shrugged and tried to give his brother a careless grin. "Whatever, man. It doesn't matter."

"Are you just going to lay down?"

He hated that tone in his brother's voice. "I don't know what you're talking about. I'm going to get back to work. I have to pick up a feed order."

"Stop." Aidan strode to him and put a hand on his shoulder. "Talk to me about this. Don't put on a brave face. Talk to me. I'm your brother."

Yeah, Aidan was his brother. Aidan was his perfectly happy, heroic brother. Aidan had honorably served his country and fought back from a bullet to his spine. He'd taught himself to walk again. He'd told society to go to hell and found his happiness. Bo didn't want to explain to his perfect brother how thoroughly he'd fucked up. But he knew he wasn't getting out of this house without a fight unless he gave Aidan something. "There's nothing to talk about. Mouse found a boyfriend. I might not like him, but she seems happy enough."

Aidan stared at him. "Bo, you love that girl."

"Like a sister."

"Lying isn't going to help. You love her, and you're going to lose her if you don't take action."

"There's nothing to do, Aidan. She made her choice."

"She didn't know she had a choice to make," Aidan insisted. "But that's beside the point. You know I've never thought you would be good for that girl."

Yeah, Aidan had always insisted Mouse needed someone else. "Well, then you got what you wanted, didn't you? I would think you would be thrilled."

Aidan's fists clenched at his sides. "Damn it, you never understood me. I've always thought Beth needed a strong hand."

He was so sick of this shit. "A fucking Dom. You thought she needed a Dom."

"Yes, and I think I'm right. I think you've seen the way she looks today. She's a whole different person. Trev gave that to her. What if he could give that to you, too?"

It took all he had not to punch a wall. "Goddamn it, Aidan. I'm not gay."

Aidan sighed. "You don't have to fuck him. You just have to listen to him. You have to let him make you stronger by being able to rely on him."

"Trev McNamara is the last person I would rely on." Not after the way Trev had let him down. He had to hope that Trev had learned his lesson and he wouldn't let down Mouse.

"I don't know about that. I was upset that Julian strong-armed me into hiring him, but he's been through a lot. He seems to be solid now."

"Once a fucking addict," Bo heard himself say.

Aidan nodded. "Yes, he'll always be an addict, but at least he knows what his problem is. He knows what he can and can't do. Can you say the same?"

Bo didn't answer. He didn't need to. He slammed out of the

house in time to catch Mouse walking back in.

Her face lit up as she saw him. "Bo. Thank god. Lexi isn't feeling well. Any chance I could get a ride into town?"

Tell your fucking boyfriend to take you. It was right there on the tip of his tongue. He could tell her to go to hell and be done with her.

And never see her again? He wasn't willing to do that. He might never be willing to break with her.

"Sure."

He walked her to his truck, his heart in his throat. She might not be his, but he would always take her where she needed to go.

Chapter Nine

Mouse felt sick as she walked out of the bank lobby into the brilliant light of day. After the chilly office, the heat hit her like the blast of a furnace, but it didn't really sink in. All she could hear was the loan officer telling her she'd been turned down for her loan. The loan she'd been told last week would be a sure thing. She'd talked to the bank and gotten preapproved. Now she'd been turned down, and all they would tell her was that she lacked enough collateral.

She owned her property outright. The house itself might not be worth much in its current condition, but the land was worth far more than the amount she requested.

The stony-faced loan officer, who Mouse knew a couple of days before had approved a loan for Janie Harte who got out of prison last month and didn't even own her TV, hadn't been willing to listen to any arguments.

Tears blurred her eyes. How was she going to fix up the house? She'd counted on that loan. She'd never been so much as late paying a bill, but they'd turned down her loan?

She clutched the paperwork in her hand. She'd brought it all in, everything they had requested, and they hadn't even bothered to look at it.

She sniffled and looked down the street toward the feed store.

Bo was still there. His truck was in the parking lot. She needed to get it together before he came down to pick her up. She shoved the paperwork in her bag and started walking down the street toward Patty's. She would get a Coke and try to figure out what to do next. She could try another bank. It would take longer than she'd hoped, but she could do it. She didn't have much of a credit history. She'd never used credit cards, but she had land, and that meant something. She worked as an accountant for many of the businesses in town and had a part-time job as Lexi's assistant.

She thought about the list now sitting in her purse. She'd planned on ordering all her materials as soon as she had the loan in hand. She'd spent days picking out the right fixtures and lights and paint. She could see it in her head, but it would have to wait.

"Good afternoon, Mouse." Bryce Hughes stepped out of his SUV. It was parked in front of Patty's.

Of all the people she didn't want to see, Bryce was number one. He looked too perfect in his suit and tie. He didn't look like a man who got turned down for loans.

Mouse nodded and walked on by only to walk straight into another body. Mouse gasped as she came up against a man roughly her own height. He was slight, dressed in an impeccable suit, and his eyes were covered in oversized aviators. He carried a briefcase.

"God, what is the problem with you small-town types? Fuck. That was my foot, you know." The man had a harsh Jersey accent.

Mouse took a step back. Bryce was right behind her. He chuckled a bit as he helped Mouse steady herself. The man continued to curse, and she suddenly recognized his voice.

"You're that man from last night. You're Marty." This was the man Trev was trying to avoid. "You called on Trev's phone."

Bryce straightened up. "Marty Klein? The agent?"

Marty visibly puffed up. "It's good to know this isn't the absolute ass end of civilization. I thought I was never going to find my way around. Why Trev had to come to this god-awful part of the world, I have no idea."

"It's his home," Mouse pointed out. So far she wasn't at all impressed with Marty Klein, but it was apparent that Bryce was.

"He knows that, Mouse. This man has negotiated some of the

148

most lucrative deals in modern sports. Trev was his client. I assure you he knows Trev McNamara's history. And his family. I'm Trev's brother-in-law." Bryce put out his hand. The two men shook.

Mouse wondered if Bryce had lost his mind. Everyone knew Bryce Hughes had been cursing his brother-in-law's name since the day Trev had been fired from the San Antonio Bandits. Mouse didn't follow football, but she remembered that day. The whole town had been quiet, like a tragedy had happened. Bryce had been one of the men leading the talk about what a loser his brother-in-law turned out to be.

"Uh, yeah, Trev has a sister. I remember that. Sharon, yes. Lovely girl." Marty touched his ear. He had a Bluetooth in his right ear that acted as a receiver for his cell phone. "Go for Marty. Yes. Absolutely. I'm in Texas right now. Sure as fuck, I'm going to get this deal done. You tell them he won't come back for less than twenty million a season, and we're going to do a media blitz. *People*, *Sports Illustrated*, the whole shebang. Cokehead quarterback makes a comeback. Yeah. We'll be out there ASAP."

She stared. Trev hadn't mentioned Marty was trying to recruit him back into the pros, but she was pretty sure that was a tremendously awful idea. "He's got a job. Trev is working out at the O'Malley Ranch."

Marty rolled his eyes. "Who the hell is she and why is she talking? It doesn't matter. Where's our boy? Did he tell you about the sweet deal I have cooking in LA?"

Bryce looked suitably impressed. "No, he didn't mention that. They want to bring him in?"

"Didn't you hear? Their QB tore his ACL and he's on IR for the rest of the season."

She wished the man would use words rather than letters. "Trev doesn't want to see you."

Bryce stepped in, smoothly pushing Mouse back. "Don't worry about her. She's nobody. I'm family. My office is right over here. I can set up a meeting with Trev."

"Excellent." Marty began to walk off with Bryce. "You seem like a man who knows what he's doing. Maybe you can help me out. Tell me something. Is there anyone in this town who can hook me up?"

Bryce looked back, his eyes narrowing. He said something to Marty, but he whispered it. She watched them walk away and hoped that Bryce wasn't going to try to find some woman dumb enough to sleep with that nasty man. She was going to have to tell Trev to avoid Bryce for a while.

"Hey, you weren't in the bank. I popped in, but they said you were already gone. I thought stuff like that took a long time." Bo walked up, his boots resounding against the pavement. His dark-blond hair was curling over his shirt collar. He was so beautiful, but in a different way than Trev. His hand came out to touch her shoulder. "What's wrong?"

And he'd always been able to read her when he bothered to try. "I didn't get the loan."

She tensed a bit. Bo hadn't wanted her to buy the house in the first place. He would probably tell her it was for the best and now she could sell the land to a developer and move someplace safer and way more boring.

"Oh, baby, I'm sorry." Bo pulled her against his chest right there in the middle of Main Street. He wrapped his arms around her. "I know what that meant to you."

She froze for a moment. He usually kept his affectionate nature private. It was sweet to be held by him, something she'd dreamed of a thousand times. He still smelled like the soap from the shower he'd insisted on taking before they left for town. His well-worn cotton shirt was soft against her cheek, but his chest was all muscle. After a moment, she let herself sink into him. The tears were back. She couldn't hold them off when he was giving her a place to cry.

"I don't know what to do. They said I don't qualify. I have to have that money. I can't fix up the house without it."

His hand found her hair. "It's going to be okay. We'll find another bank. Hell, Aidan knows lots of people with money. You'll see. It's going to be okay. Now, come on, dry those tears and let's go get some pie. I was talking to Jerry at the feed store, and he said Patty had pecan today."

She loved pecan pie.

Relief washed over her as Bo began to lead her toward the

diner. She'd been terrified that Bo would be angry that she was seeing Trev. She'd played it off as nothing, but she'd been scared he would turn away.

Instead, he opened the door for her and started to ask her about her plans. He seemed interested for the first time. Bo ordered for them both and then gave her his full attention. He was quieter than she'd ever seen him before. Well, except for that night when she'd had to find her way to Austin to get him. He'd been quieter then. He hadn't talked for days. She didn't like to think about that night.

"Hey," Bo said, leaning over and putting a hand over hers. "It's going to be okay, you know. We'll find a way to get your house fixed up. Tell me something, is that boyfriend of yours going to be worth anything beyond hauling you into bathrooms in the middle of the day? Does he know anything about home repair?"

She flushed, but Bo had said the words with no accusation in his tone, just a sad smile on his face. She shook her head. "He told me to buy a book."

Bo sighed. "We're in trouble. Well, show me your plans. Let's see how screwed we are."

He gave her that smile that lit up her world and reminded her of all the reasons she'd fallen in love with him in the first place. He was a sunny presence. He always made her laugh, and deep down, he understood her.

Trev was her lover, but she would miss Bo. She would miss him so much.

She showed him her list, and by the time they were done, she felt better.

She would find a way. She would fix her house, and she would keep Trev and Bo in her life. She needed them.

* * * *

An hour later, Mouse had a small coffeemaker, some filters, and a pound of French roast in hand as she got out of Bo's truck and began to walk into her house. Despite the earlier problems, she was feeling unaccountably cheerful, and she knew why. Bo. She loved to be with him. She loved the way he teased her and got her to smile even when she was sad.

"Thanks," she said as he hopped out of the truck.

"You're welcome. You know I'll always help you out. No matter what happens with the guy you're dating."

She hadn't known it. Somewhere deep inside she thought he would go away someday. And why? He'd never gone away before. He hadn't exactly been with her, but he'd never let her down when she called. "Did you really get out of bed with Darla Jackson on prom night to come pick me up when my bike was stolen?"

She'd never asked. She'd heard the rumors, but she'd always thought they were made-up stories. No way did a guy give up sleeping with the head cheerleader to pick up a friend and then proceed to spend the rest of the night on her couch watching sitcoms and eating popcorn.

"She was mighty pissed with me. I don't think she spoke to me the rest of the school year, and she left for Dallas after that." His unspoken words were that many of their classmates had left. So many friends had gone and found lives elsewhere.

"Why would you do that?"

He swallowed once, and she thought he might not answer her. "I realized I didn't want to be with her. I wanted to be with you."

Tears popped up. These tears were frustrated. "I don't understand you." She took a long breath. It didn't matter. That was long past. "You're crazy, Bo."

He stepped close to her. Very close. She could feel the heat of his body. "I am crazy, Mouse. I have been for a really long time. But what if I wasn't crazy anymore? What if I came to my senses?"

The world felt like it slowed down as Bo's hand cupped her cheek. He smiled down at her.

"I've never told you how beautiful you are. That was definitely crazy." He smoothed back her hair.

"Bo." She wasn't sure what was happening. Her breath hitched.

"You're gorgeous, Mouse. And I love your hair down. You should always wear it down." He leaned over and pressed his lips to hers.

Warm. Soft and yet strong. Bo's kiss immediately lit up her every nerve. He'd pecked her on the cheek before, but this was utterly different. Those light busses had been a mere affectionate shift of lips against skin, but this was something more. This was purposeful. His lips brushed hers once and then again, her mouth opening under his. His tongue pushed into her mouth, a luscious treat. He pulled her against his body.

She'd dreamed of being close to Bo since she was a child. At eight years old, he'd punched Scotty Kirk for shoving her on the playground. Sometimes she could still feel the warmth of his hand in hers as he helped her off the ground and walked with her to the nurse's office. He'd sat with her as the nurse had bandaged her skinned knees, but all she'd been able to think about was how nice it felt when he'd held her hand.

Bo kissed her, his hands sinking into her hair. She felt her hips press against his, the strong line of his erection rubbing against her belly. She was getting soft and warm. Her breasts were heavy, the nipples peaked. She breathed him in. She'd always loved the way Bo smelled.

He'd been her first crush. Her first lust. Her first love. God, he'd been her first friend.

But not her first lover. Trev. How could she do this to Trev?

She pushed at his chest. "Stop."

His hands tightened. "I don't want to stop. We just got started. Baby, we waited so long. I want to make love to you. I want to do it now."

But *they* hadn't waited. He had. "No. I can't."

Bitterness welled up. He'd kept her at arm's length, taking what she gave him emotionally but not giving her what she needed physically. Trev had shown her what she needed.

She loved Bo, but she was starting to love herself a little, too.

"Mouse?" He looked at her, those blue eyes round and so much younger than his years. His face had fallen as though he couldn't quite believe what she'd said. His boots stirred up dust as he took a step toward her.

Never once had she refused him anything he'd wanted from her physically, but she couldn't hurt Trev.

"I have a boyfriend now, Bo." The words sounded stupid coming out of her mouth. Boyfriend? She hadn't actually been on a date with Trev. She'd slept with him.

"How can you choose him over me?" There was no anger in the question. He sighed with a sort of sad acceptance, like he'd always known it would happen.

It wasn't fair. "I didn't choose him over you. You never chose me at all. You never wanted me until he did."

"I love you."

"I love you, too." She did. She loved him with everything she had. "But you can't love me that way. If you did, you wouldn't have spent all of your nights with other women."

His fists clenched. "I didn't sleep with Clarissa."

She stepped away. "This isn't about Clarissa. It's about all the other nights."

"Damn it, I love you. I'm stupid. I'm just stupid. Can you forgive me?"

She felt her heel hit the front of the step. She didn't want to be here having this conversation with him. She didn't want to let him go. She needed him. Her whole system rebelled at the thought of letting him go. Trev wouldn't be around forever. He would leave, and she would be alone. Tears blurred her eyes. Why was he doing this now?

"There's nothing to forgive." Maybe she should take what he had to offer. She could walk into his arms and let Trev go instead. Bo would stay. He wouldn't leave Deer Run. He didn't have an expiration date, but he was only doing this because he knew she was with Trev. What would happen when Trev was gone? "Bo, you don't really want me. Not that way."

He reached out and grabbed her hips, pulling them together, slamming his cock against her. "Don't you tell me what I want. Don't tell me this isn't real."

But it wasn't. It couldn't be. He'd denied her for so long she couldn't trust it. And Trev needed her. Bo had never really needed her. She'd been a burden to him for so long. There had only been the one night he'd reached out and opened himself to her. That night when his father had crushed his world. Maybe Clarissa was right. Maybe she had held him back.

"I love you, Bo, but I can't be with you like this. I started something with Trev."

"He won't stay." He whispered the words against her forehead. "He won't stay with you."

"I have to see where it goes." Not only for her sake, but for Trev's. "No one goes into a relationship knowing how it will end. It requires a little faith."

"He isn't worth any faith, Mouse. He isn't. He's fucked up so many times. How many chances can one man get?"

"As many as it takes."

"Please, don't do this to us."

She pulled away. "I can't. I can't. I understand if you won't be my friend any more. You be polite when you see me."

How was this happening? Her heart ached. She'd lived twenty-five years without a soul who truly wanted her, and now she had to choose? It was brutally unfair.

"Polite?"

She nodded. "You owe me that. I came to get you that night. I protected you. I kept your secret, so I'm calling it in. You don't get to treat me the way the others do. You can ignore me, but don't you talk bad about me, Bo O'Malley."

She wouldn't be able to stand it. She couldn't live in this town knowing Bo was laughing with the rest of them.

"Mouse, I would never talk bad about you. I told you I love you. Fuck, Mouse, you're my best friend."

He could sound like a little boy at times. Maybe he still was deep inside. Maybe that was why he'd never been able to choose her. He was a boy unwilling to give up all the toys of the world for just one. Until he realized he'd lost it. Yes, when Trev left, he'd grow bored with her. His attention would wander, and she'd truly be alone.

"You remember that. And you be polite." She turned and hurried up the steps. She threw open the door. It was unlocked. Again.

She took a quick step back as she looked inside. It was also occupied. And not by the raccoon Trev had found. A man stood in the middle of her living room. He wore a dirty T-shirt and a shocked expression on his face. And he had a gun in his hand.

Chapter Ten

Bo felt like the world had opened up and threatened to swallow him whole. How could she think he would laugh at her? How could she even think that he would become like everyone else?

Walk away. That was the only thing to do. He should have known that there was no way she would stay. Trev McNamara moving back into town just as Bo got his shit together was proof positive that he wasn't supposed to be with anyone at all. People left.

People leave you because you aren't worth anything. You're the reason Aidan left home. You're poison, boy.

His father's voice resounded through his head. It was always there somewhere deep inside him. It whispered to him that he wasn't good enough. It was screaming now.

He'd lost Mouse. And he couldn't blame anyone but himself.

He turned to go, but instinct made him look back at the house one last time. Maybe there was something he could do for her. Not because it would get her back, but because he did owe her. He owed her for all those years when he kept her at arm's length even as she opened her soul to him.

The door banged open, and he heard something horrible.

There was no way to mistake the sound.

Gunshot.

He took those rickety steps two at time. He hit that crappy door at a full run, throwing his body into the house. He had to sidestep the now ruined box of the coffeemaker Mouse had bought. He kicked it to the side.

"Mouse!" He screamed her name, his heart pounding in his chest. Terror absolutely threatened to overwhelm him as he looked at the skinny man in the center of the room with the revolver pointed at the stairs.

He could smell the acrid scent of discharge and hear the scrambled hurry as Mouse tried running up the stairs. He got a flash of a slender man in a T-shirt, jeans, and a baseball cap as he raised the gun again toward the fleeing woman. The asshole wouldn't miss this time. Bo could see it. In that one point two seconds he had to make his decision, he could see that the bullet would tear through his Mouse and she would fall, and he realized that it didn't matter if she slept every night for the rest of her life in Trev McNamara's arms. He loved her. She was half of his heart, and she could stop him from acting on it—but not from saving her.

He did the only thing he could. He rushed at the asshole with the gun before he could fire again.

There was a shout and a terrible stinging sensation in his right bicep, but Bo remembered everything he knew about taking down a man.

Play it smart, Bo. Rush from your legs up. Send the power from the bottoms of your feet through your shoulder. Take him out at the waist. Breathe and hit him hard.

He hunched down and planted his shoulder squarely in the other man's abdomen. There was a whooshing sound as the man hit the floor, the air obviously leaving his body. He got to his feet, springing up and kicking the gun out of the asshole's hand.

"Mouse, call the sheriff." Bo stared down at the man. Damn, he was really more of a boy. Austin? Allen? He recognized the young man on the floor. He was from another town, but he often came into Deer Run with his mom and sister. Fuck. That kid couldn't be more than sixteen.

"You're bleeding. Oh, my god, you got hit, Bo." Mouse tore

down the stairs. Her eyes were wide with horror as she pushed up the sleeve of his shirt.

He was bleeding, but it wasn't serious. He could see that it wasn't anything beyond a scratch. He kept a boot on his assailant's chest. "I'm fine, honey. Go on and call Lou. Tell him he has a guest coming in." Bo felt his eyes narrow. "I hope you like checkers."

He heard Mouse on her cell phone and finally was able to breathe again. She was fine. The danger had passed. And now he could see that shooting wasn't the only thing the jerk had done. It looked like he was into graffiti, too.

Get Out

It was spray-painted on the wall of the parlor in a horrible lime green. It was the same color the hardware store had on sale the week before. He was a cheapskate criminal to boot.

"Are you the idiot who spray-painted Trev McNamara's truck at the sheriff's office this morning?" Bo asked.

What did this kid, who hadn't even been big enough to enjoy football when Trev was a high school god, have against the man? And this kid wasn't even from Deer Run.

"I ain't talking." The words came out in a hateful sputter. The kid tried to move, but he had fifty pounds on him. And now that he looked at the young man on the floor, he could see how fragile he was. The kid had moved past lanky and into gaunt. Bo searched his memory. Austin. His name was Austin, and he lived in a trailer park with his mom. He was bussed in to the county high school. He'd always been a little on the small side. He wasn't an athlete, but now the kid looked downright sick. There were scabs on his face.

"What did Trev ever do to you?" Bo asked, his voice softer now. He wasn't about to let the asshole up, but he wanted to understand what had brought this kid so low.

"Trev? Who is that? Are you talking about the druggie quarterback? What does he have to do with anything?"

"If you're not here to piss off Trev, then why the hell are you here?" A cold feeling started in Bo's gut.

The boy shook his head. His skin was a pasty white, like it

hadn't seen the sun in a very long time. "It's a job, asshole. I was supposed to spray-paint the truck and then break in here and fuck some stuff up. It's a job. Nothing more."

"Who hired you?"

The boy's skin flushed, and his eyes widened. "No one. No one at all. I was only looking for drugs."

"That's not what you said a minute ago."

But his head was shaking now. "I lied. I didn't mean it. I was making shit up. I was looking for drugs. I heard the lady who lives here has a lot of drugs."

Mouse? He could barely talk Mouse into taking ibuprofen when she had a headache. She'd read something about potential liver damage. No one in the whole state of Texas would mistake Mouse for a drug user. "Bullshit. You're scared. Who are you scared of?"

"I ain't talking. Not to you. Not to the cops."

Whoever had hired the little fucker had him scared shitless. He wasn't going to move. Bo had to hope Lou could muster up the energy to look somewhat threatening, but he doubted the sheriff would be able to get the kid to talk.

"Bo?" Mouse's voice pulled him out of his thoughts.

He turned his head, never letting up on the pressure keeping the criminal on the floor. Mouse's face was stark white, and it took everything he had not to pull her into his arms and promise her everything would be all right.

He couldn't do that. She wasn't his, not in that way. But at least he could say the words. "It's going to be okay. Why don't you call Trev?"

Bo could hear the sirens in the distance. Mouse ran to the door to let the police in, though he could have told her the door was kind of hanging on by a single nail at this point. No need for formalities now.

He hated it, but when the chips had been down, it hadn't been his father's voice that helped him. Never. But it hadn't been Aidan's, either. In that moment when he needed guidance, it had been Trevor McNamara's patient voice that had come to him. Trev had spent hours teaching him the game when no one else had thought he could learn it. Trev had been the reason he'd made the

159

varsity team his junior year. He'd never quite understood why Trev had been kind to him, but it had stuck with him, even after all this time. Even under all the bitterness, there was still some warmth for the man.

"I ain't talking." The kid was crying now.

Nope. He wouldn't talk. But that didn't mean he wouldn't figure out what the hell was going on. After all, when he'd left the big house earlier, there had been a real live investigator snoring on the couch. Perhaps it was time to put the Irishman to work.

* * * *

"Seriously?" Trev stared at the door. It wasn't where he'd left it. When he'd left this morning, it had been where doors customarily rested, in the doorframe. Now, long after the sun had gone down, the door was sitting on its side on the porch.

Beth smiled at him, a hammer in her hands. She'd changed into a pair of overalls with a collared shirt underneath. She'd slung a tool belt around her waist. It was pink and slightly prissy looking. It didn't quell his desire for her. It merely made him want to shove his tool where it would do the most good. "There was an incident a couple of hours ago. I took care of it, but the door suffered. I've already reset the mountings. Now I need a little muscle to get the sucker in place, and it'll be good as new."

He seriously doubted that, but he picked up the heavy door anyway. His back protested, but he managed to hold out until Beth was satisfied. She turned her wrench and hammered something into place. When she pronounced it finished, he let go and hauled her close. Her time controlling things was done for the day.

"Hello." He smiled down at her. There was a little sweat on her brow, but she still smelled sweet, like hard work couldn't possibly mar her femininity. So fucking soft.

Those pillowy lips raised in a smile. "Hi."

He loved how breathless she was when she talked to him. He wasn't about to let her know that he felt the same damn way. He was the Dom. He was supposed to stay in control.

Damn, it had been a long day. O'Malley had put him straight to work. He'd thanked Leo as he left because if Leo hadn't insisted on vigorous workouts during his rehab, Trev doubted he would have survived the day. As it was, all he wanted to do was cuddle up with Beth and make love to her over and over again. Well, and get fed. He would really like some food. But mostly the lovemaking stuff.

He closed the door. He was damn happy to see that she'd attached a proper deadbolt. He found it strangely sexy that his lady knew how to install a deadbolt.

"I like the lock, darlin'." He twisted the handle, satisfied it worked smoothly.

"I'm good with a drill. My dad taught me."

He pulled her close. "I can show you how good I am with a drill."

She laughed, her amusement sparking something light in him. The day might have been difficult, but it seemed to melt away now that he was here with her. "I think I know how good you are."

She had a sweetly sexy smile on her face, and his ego about doubled because he knew he'd put it there. He kissed her, surprised at how comfortable this whole "coming home" thing was. Even in this rickety old place. He looked around. Beth seemed to have had a busy afternoon.

"Painting?" Trev asked, looking at the back wall of the parlor. The parlor walls had been painted an odd orange color. Now there was a large swath of white. It looked white. She had the lights off, so he couldn't discern the exact shade.

She shrugged. "I wanted to try a couple of looks. I'm eager to get started."

"How did things go at the bank?"

"It was all right. There was some trouble with the door when I got back home, but Bo handled it. Oh, and I bought that coffeemaker you wanted, but I had an accident with it. It kind of went in a million pieces. I promise I'll get another one tomorrow."

"Bo?" He couldn't help the growl. He'd talked to some of the hands. They all liked Bo, but they were universal in their praise of how many women he could get into bed with. He'd done almost every girl in the county according to the hands. All of them except Beth Hobbes.

"He's my friend."

There was something about the way she said it, a tightness to her eyes that told Trev she wasn't telling him everything. A bit of his calm slipped away. He thought about pursuing it and decided against it. What if she told him she loved Bo? What the hell would he do then?

"I need to get cleaned up. I thought we could pick up some dinner in town and come back here. Is that okay?" Beth lifted herself up on her toes and brushed her lips against his. She immediately went back down, a look of horror on her face. "Was I supposed to do that? I've read some books where the Dom doesn't want the sub to touch him without permission."

He wrapped his arms around her. "Touch me all you like, darlin'. We're not performing a scene or training. We're just Trev and Beth right now."

Her arms tightened around him. "Good. I didn't think I would like that part."

He wasn't the type of Dom who required a total power exchange. He'd seen it, and it worked for some, but he'd never be twenty-four-seven. In the end, he wanted to be taken care of too much, and not because he'd ordered the sub to do it. Beth's arms around him felt like caring, not the rote, practiced touch of long-held formality.

He kissed her long and slow as his mind drifted over the way he wanted this relationship to go. Submission in the bedroom. Long evenings of her naked at his feet. But part of the point to his dominance was to teach her how to stand up for herself. To give her a feeling of self-worth that seemed to be lacking, though she had no reason for it. She was lovely and worthy, and he needed to show her all of those things. Some submissives needed the complete exchange, to lose themselves in another's dominance, but for Beth, it was different. A Dom could free her.

His hands moved lower, his groin becoming distinctly engaged in this "hello" kiss.

And then his stomach growled.

Beth pulled back, a laugh bursting from her lips. "I won't be more than ten minutes."

He watched as her backside swayed in her overalls as she scampered up the stairs. His dick and his stomach warred, and he promised both they would get what they needed. He would have her undress in the truck on the way back from picking up the food. She would take it all off and sit on his vinyl bench seat while he told her everything he had planned for her tonight. Her pussy would be wet by the time they got home. She would leave a spot on his seat, and he would fucking let it sit there. His whole cab would smell like her. He could surround himself with her.

He started to go up the stairs. His cock had definitely taken over. His stomach protested, but weakly, as though it knew it had a crappy argument. He was on the second step when he heard her phone ring. He thought about letting it go, but damn it, he knew who it was. He knew deep down.

He crossed the space between the stairs and the front hall table in three long strides and looked down at the number. Sure enough. Bo O'Malley.

Aidan's words haunted him as well as his own damn fool memory. They had been friends. More than that. They'd been close. Bo had been the kid brother he'd never had. Bo had looked up to him for something more than his ability to toss a football and get laid. He wasn't sure what had made him befriend the younger man other than the fact that he looked lost among the larger players. He could remember hearing his teammates laugh about the fact that Aidan O'Malley must have gotten all the muscle and intellect in that family. He'd known that the kid had heard it all. He'd watched as Bo had sunken into himself.

Fuck. Aidan was right. Goddamn it. He wanted to kick something. He didn't need this. He wasn't responsible enough to take care of his own damn self. He didn't have to do it. He didn't.

Almost as if his fucking hand had a mind of its own, he picked up her cell and flipped it open. He was going to tell Bo off. He was going to tell the little shit to find his own woman. He needed a Domme, not a Dom, and sure as hell not him. He didn't need that shit.

"Mouse, it's me. Don't talk. I got some stuff to say and I need to say it." Bo slurred his words, and Trev could hear the sounds of thumping country western music in the background.

He sighed. "Bo, it isn't…"

"Hush, now, girl. I told you. I need to say this. I love you, Mouse. I always loved you, ever since we were kids, but it turns out I'm not very good at it. Hell, I ain't been good at much of anything. I know that. But what you said today was wrong, Mouse. How can you think for one second that I would treat you like that? It doesn't matter that you picked Trev. It doesn't matter."

Trev knew he should hang up. "Bo, this isn't Beth."

Bo went on as though he hadn't heard a thing. "I would never treat you like the rest of the people in this town do. And I won't be polite. I love you. There's not a damn thing polite about it. When I see you on the street, I'm going to smile, and I'm going to talk to you because that will be the best part of my whole day. I'll ask about you, and I'll even ask how that fucker Trev is doing. Sorry. I'm a little drunk, baby. I know we can't be friends the way we were. I know that. Hell, I even get why you picked him. He's already taken care of you in ways I never have. That's what I feel the worst about. I should have been strong enough. I should have told the world to fuck itself and been with you. I don't know why I'm like that. I'm broken inside, I guess. But if you ever need anything, Mouse, you call me. I'll be there. I won't fail you again. I won't. God, I want to fade away, but I won't do it because someday you might need me, and I'm going to be there. And if that fucker breaks your heart, then I'll kill him. I know he's bigger than me, but I don't intend to play fair. I'll follow his ass, and I'll get him when he's unaware. I swear it. I love you. I'm sorry. I won't call again, but I needed you to know that."

The phone clicked dead, and Trev cursed. His stomach and his cock were going to have to wait because his conscience had taken the forefront. He couldn't leave the bastard out there. Anything could happen to him. Bo was drunk and hurting. It was a toxic cocktail. He would know all about those. He wrote a quick note to Beth and ran back to his truck. He sighed as he put it in reverse. He wouldn't have his sweet sub naked on the bench seat. He would have drunk Bo in his cab. It likely wouldn't smell like Beth's arousal. It would smell like puke. Yep.

Shitty damn night.

And he had the additional problem of a promise he was about to break. He drove toward Aidan's ranch as he dialed a familiar number. Leo picked up, and Trev prayed he hadn't hightailed it back to Dallas. If he had, then Trev was going to have to ask Aidan to come with him, and that might be disturbing. He was going to top the hell out of Aidan's brother, and despite the fact that Aidan had asked him to do it, it might be difficult to watch.

"What's up, Trev?" Leo's voice came on the line. Trev could hear Lexi laughing in the background.

Trev laid it out for him. There wasn't a lot of time for explanations. "I'm going to a bar. I need you to come with me."

"Uh, no. Not just no, but hell no. What happened?"

"Bo happened. I have to go and drag his ass out of a honky-tonk."

"No, you don't," Leo said, his voice stern. "I'll let Aidan know. We'll handle it. You don't need to walk into a bar at this stage."

Trev rolled his eyes. What did Leo think would happen? He wasn't going to turn into an alcohol-crazed maniac at the sight of a beer. He really wasn't. Something deep and calm settled in Trev. He wasn't even going to be tempted. He had a job to do, and it was far more important than that whiny asshole who lived in his soul and wanted to drink himself into oblivion. This wasn't only for Bo. This was for Beth. Beth needed Bo, too.

Hell, this was for himself.

"I'll be fine, but I would prefer to have you with me. I promised I wouldn't do this, but I have to break that vow."

Leo was insistent. "No, you fucking don't. Aidan can do it."

"He's my sub, Leo." There. He'd said it. He'd said it out loud.

There was a long pause. "Are fucking kidding me? Two days in this godforsaken town and you take two subs. Tell me something. Does Bo know he's taken a Dom?"

"Not yet, but trust me, he'll understand after tonight." Trev pulled up into the driveway. "Are you coming or not?"

"Li, get off the damn couch. I need you to come with me," he heard Leo say.

Trev watched the door. It flew open, and Leo was in the cab of

165

the truck in a heartbeat, pulling the Irishman along. Trev didn't bother to wait. He took off toward The Rusty Spur. The faster he got there, the less time Bo had to fuck up and get himself in serious trouble.

"I thought I was investigating the graffiti now," Li complained as he sat back in the cab. "How did I end up back in this damn truck."

"We're going to a bar," Trev said flatly.

"Oh, that's a different story. Let's go, mate." Liam seemed far more eager to come along now.

He would likely be disappointed when he realized they weren't there to drink. Leo had brought him along to ensure that everyone came out of the bar. He would argue that he wasn't going to be tempted, but it was easier to simply go along with it.

"This is a mistake," Leo said. "I'm fine with you taking Beth as a sub. Beth isn't going to be any trouble at all from what I understand. Bo is going to be a train wreck."

Liam had been looking at his phone. His head came up now. "Wait, I thought the kid was straight."

He tightened his hold on the wheel. "I'm not planning on having sex with him. I'm planning on topping him."

"What's the point in topping someone if you don't fuck 'em?" Li asked with a frown.

"Go back to sexting that waitress you met." Leo turned to Trev. "Bo doesn't even like the lifestyle."

Trev had thought about this all day. "Because he doesn't want to recognize it in himself. I'm going to give him a choice. He can get with the program, or he can lose what he loves. He needs this. He knows it deep down, but once he figures out Beth needs it, I think he'll come around."

Leo stopped for a moment. "That could work. You know Aidan has been worried about his brother for a long time. He says their father was always really hard on Bo. Aidan was kind of like you."

Trev snorted. "What? Addicted and irresponsible?"

"Smart. Great at school. Popular and athletic."

Yeah, but Trev had thrown all of those things away. "Bo was good at football. He was an excellent linebacker."

"After you took him under your wing and forced the rest of the team to accept him. I talked to Aidan about it. I can fill in the blanks. Am I wrong?"

"No." He'd pretty much done exactly that.

Leo was quiet for a moment. "Do you ever wonder why you did that?"

He knew where Leo was going. "Because deep down I was a Dom, and I recognized what he needed."

"Yep. Are you sure you can handle this? You haven't been outside The Club in years. This could end up being very stressful and chaotic."

"Then I'll make it unchaotic. Isn't that what I'm supposed to do? Impose order?" If he couldn't manage it, then he'd turn in his leathers, but he had no intention of fucking this up. "I can handle it."

"He can handle it. Stop being such an old lady, Leo," Liam said. "How far is it to this bar and do they have waitresses?"

Leo slapped a hand on his thigh, ignoring Liam altogether. "The fact that you called me makes me think you *can* handle this. All right, then let's take that boy down. After what happened today, I'm surprised you're not still spanking your sub. I expected that girl's butt to be red for days."

The gravel crunched under his tires, and the truck rolled toward the honky-tonk. It was utterly dark this far from town. "What are you talking about? Why would I spank her? All she did today was fix the front door and start painting a wall."

Liam chuckled. "I'm glad he's not the one paying me bills. I take it the girl thought you wouldn't find out. Bo must have not told her he hired me. I was planning on talking to you tomorrow about who might want you out of town."

This was about what happened to his truck? "Pretty much everyone. The list is long. You don't need to look into it. And why the hell would Bo hire you?"

He half expected Bo would hire someone to murder him, not try to find out who painted graffiti on his truck.

Leo whistled. "Wow. That girl is in real trouble. Do you have your kit? I have rope in my Jeep if you need it. You might need a spreader. I'm sure Aidan will let you use his barn. It's fully equipped for a torture scene. What are her hard limits? You might want to push those."

"What the fuck are you talking about?"

"I think you should ask that pretty sub of yours," Liam said with a shrug. "I make it a point to stay out of lovers' quarrels."

"I asked you, Leo." He could see the lights up ahead.

"I ran into Shelley at dinner earlier," Leo said.

"I bet you did," the Irishman said with a chuckle.

His sister was walking a thin line. If someone like Liam noticed, everyone would soon. "She's married. I wish she wasn't, but she is. Cheating would kill her."

Leo's mouth tightened. "I'm not sleeping with your sister. I won't lie. We have an odd connection, but she made her choice when she married that man. I'm friends with your sister. Nothing more. She needs a friend since her husband is such a fucking douchebag."

"Holy shit, you asked her to leave him." How much had been going on? Leo was a happy, affable guy on the outside, but Trev knew he kept a lot hidden.

"I haven't touched her if that's what you're worried about. I haven't kissed her or laid a damn hand on her, and I won't. But I'm worried about Bryce. I'm worried he could be violent. He fits a certain profile. I believe he's been emotionally abusive toward your sister, and that can certainly turn physical. The truth of the matter is I would like to do an investigation into his background. Starting with his financials. I've got O'Donnell looking into it."

"This town is full of secrets," Liam agreed. "If only it had a bloody Hooters."

Crap. Once again he'd been so involved in his own shit that he'd missed his sister's problems. "I'll take care of it. She's my sister."

He didn't have the money to hire someone like O'Donnell, but he would find it. Somehow. If Bryce was shady, he would figure it out.

Leo's eyes narrowed. Sometimes it was easy to forget that Leo had been a SEAL and not the team's medic. He'd been deadly, and though it didn't show up often, that warrior was on his face now.

"I'll take care of it." He shook his head as though to clear the violence of his thoughts. "She would be horrified if you started looking into her marriage. She wants to protect you. Trust me on this. Let me take care of your sister. I'll let you know if McKay-Taggart finds anything."

Li shoved his phone in his pocket. "Oh, I'll find something. I met the fucker today. He's got that look about him."

Trev wasn't sure having a "look" meant Bryce was anything but a douchebag.

"Besides, you have enough on your hands with that sub of yours," Li continued. "After all, Beth was shot at this afternoon. Don't you go thinking I'm moving down here. I'll have to send someone else in because no one is taking my London assignment."

Trev nearly turned the truck into a ditch. "What?"

Leo handled it all with a calm sigh. "Some kid named Austin Hall was in Beth's house when she and Bo came home. The sheriff thinks he was looking for drugs. At least that's what the kid says. He took a couple of shots at Beth, but Bo took him down. The sheriff says the kid's in pretty bad shape, though not from Bo."

"The kid's into meth," Li explained. "I tried to talk to him, but he was pretty high at the time. I don't know. The sheriff ain't the brightest bulb in the box. He thinks it's about drugs, but it's got me nose itching, if you know what I mean."

He did not, but that didn't matter now. Trev forced himself to go very calm. His first instinct was to turn the truck around, find Beth, use the rope in his kit, and prove to her all the reasons she shouldn't lie to her Dom. "All she told me was that there had been some trouble with the door, but she'd handled it."

"Bo had a scrape, but that was the extent of the physical damage," Leo offered.

"She didn't even call me."

"She was probably afraid to," Leo said. "I don't mean she was afraid of you. I mean she was afraid of being troublesome. She's submissive, but she doesn't understand the lifestyle yet. She doesn't want to be a burden."

Neon reds and blues lit up the night as he pulled into the parking lot. God, he'd loved this place once. He'd been allowed in

169

despite the fact that he'd been underage. He'd been the quarterback who led the team to a state championship both his junior and senior years. He'd been a damn hero, therefore everyone looked the other way when he had a beer or two or ten. It had all started here.

Crap, he wanted to be back in The Club. Things had been easier there. He'd known there was no way he'd be allowed to step out of line. He could spend his evenings working with subs who never lied or tried to cover anything up. There wasn't anything *to* cover up. Besides the occasional scene, he had no real ties to any of those subs.

That had been fantasy. This was real life. In real life, he could fuck up all he wanted and people would help him along. In real life, in real relationships, he had to deal with the fact that he was going to get angry and irritated even with the best-behaved sub. Because she wasn't merely a sub. She was a woman, and women were irritating and aggravating and the only thing that made life really worthwhile. Fuck, he was in love with her.

He was going to spank her ass red.

He shoved the truck in park and got out. Now that he knew how serious it had gotten, he agreed with Bo's plan. "Liam, I need you to find out everything you can on the kid who shot at her. If he was the same person who spray-painted my truck, I want to know."

"I'm already on it." Li looked up at the sign. "Now this is more like it. Why didn't you take me here in the first place? I think better with a beer in me hand."

Li strode in.

Trev hung back, Leo standing beside him.

"So we go in, kidnap Bo, and get out." There wasn't a hint of worry in Leo's voice. It was as though he wholly approved of the plan. "You know, I always did think Julian put far too much faith in contracts. A good kidnapping followed by some time on the rack. That's what some subs need. A claiming. Everyone loves a good claiming. Lexi's right about that. Now the whole 'Dom submits to the sub to prove his love' stuff is complete crap, but she's right about the claiming part."

Trev stopped and faced his mentor. He was a pain in the ass sometimes. "I'm not claiming Bo."

"Really?"

"Not in that way. I'm not taking him home and fucking him. It's not going to be that way."

Leo shook his head. "That's what you all say. Then the butt sex starts."

Trev turned. Leo was utterly obnoxious at times. This was one of those times. "I'm planning on talking to him."

Leo slapped him on the shoulder as he fell in step with him. "That's your first mistake. I don't think talking to Bo is going to help. If you want your very own crazy three-way, you're going to have to make it happen."

"One of these days, Leo, you're going to end up in a crazy-ass threesome, and I'm going to laugh. I'm going to sit back and laugh."

Leo shook his head. "Not going to happen. A. I'm not even close to bisexual. B. Not interested in sharing."

"I've met your brother. You have the same taste in women." Wolf Meyer would probably have been all over Shelley, too. The Meyer brothers were incredibly different, but the same in some ways.

They reached the front steps. Trev got a little sick to his stomach. It had been years since he'd been inside a bar, and now he was going into the belly of the beast for a man who might hate his guts.

"I'll kill myself before I share a woman with my brother. Wolf is intolerable. He's my brother and I love him, but I want to kill him half the time. He has no organizational skills. He throws his clothes everywhere. He's a slob, and he still eats like a five-year-old. I can't live with Wolf much less share a woman with him." Leo was looking at him with an outraged expression. It was actually slightly prissy.

All of his fear fled. He'd managed to make big, tough Leo Meyer look like a prissy schoolmarm. He could handle this.

Trev strode through the doors of The Rusty Spur certain everything was going to be fine.

Chapter Eleven

Nothing was ever going to be fine again.

Bo scrubbed a hand through his hair as the bartender set another whiskey in front of him. Someone sat down next to him and ordered a beer, but Bo didn't turn the man's way. He stared at the glass in front of him. He wasn't so far gone yet that he couldn't think, couldn't see Mouse's pretty face turned up to his telling him they couldn't be together. He wasn't sure anything would obliterate that sight.

He pushed the drink away. He was drunk enough. It was probably time to figure out how he was getting home.

"Hey, Bo." Clarissa slid on the barstool next to him. Her blonde hair was tucked under a fashionably crushed, pink cowboy hat. Her breasts were practically hanging out of her tank top. "Sorry about last night. That Brian can get mean when he's drunk."

"He wasn't the only one." He hadn't forgotten what she'd said about Mouse. Did she honestly think she could call his best friend a pathetic whore and he'd still sleep with her? Probably. That was his reputation. He'd take anything they dished out and laugh it off.

He was the pathetic one.

Her hand slid across his. "Don't hold that against me. Every woman you've ever dated hates that girl. I don't intend to be another of your girlfriends who takes a backseat any time Mouse Hobbes scrapes her knee. You can't blame us for disliking her. I was mad that you were dumping me for the night. I had big plans. I still do. I get it now. You didn't want Melody. You only wanted me."

He nearly came off his barstool as her other hand found his thigh. He knew one thing for sure. He couldn't have Mouse, but he loved her, and he wasn't about to start up with another woman. Now that he knew he really loved her, he couldn't accept what Clarissa was offering. "I don't think so."

Her cold, brown eyes rolled. She leaned forward, and her hand tightened on his thigh, dangerously close to his cock. Her voice was low as she leaned in. "Come on, Bo. Don't be an idiot. No man turns me down. I'm not about to be made a laughingstock in this town. I won't let anyone say Mouse Hobbes took a man I wanted. Now you're going to get up off this barstool, and we're going to get out of here. Or I'll tell everyone here you're just as queer as your brother."

He froze. He didn't have Mouse anymore. Did any of it matter? And he was starting to hate these people he'd thought of as his friends. But did he really want this fight? Would it do anyone a lick of good? He felt slightly frozen.

"Or you can take your hand off him before I'm forced to do something I don't want to do." A low, menacing voice cut through the thudding music.

Bo swiveled the seat around and saw Trev McNamara and Leo Meyer staring down at Clarissa. He was damn happy they weren't staring at him. Both men looked ready to commit murder or something worse. Clarissa turned on her stool, her hand coming off his leg. She looked Trev up and down, her lips curling up. She didn't seem to pick up on what Bo was seeing. He was pretty sure they weren't sizing her up for a fun night.

"Damn, Trev, you look fine. It didn't take you long to find your way back here. But then everyone knows Trev McNamara likes a good time." She actually smiled and leaned forward, letting her hand trail down his chest.

"You get your hands off me right now." There was no way to mistake the coldness in his tone.

She turned toward Leo.

Leo shook his head, dismissing her. "I'm not interested, either. Go find easier prey. And think twice before spreading rumors about Bo. I can make your life hell, and quite frankly, I would probably enjoy doing it. I get bored."

Yep, Leo was one scary dude, and Clarissa seemed to finally get the point. She stood up, and a look of fury crossed her face. She opened her mouth.

"I wouldn't if I were you." Trev's face was a stony mask. Maybe Trev was a little scary, too.

Clarissa turned on her perfect boot heels and strode away.

"Now you've done it." He turned back to his whiskey. It looked like he was going to need it after all. He reached for it, but Trev's hand whisked it away. He shoved it down the bar where Leo handed it back to the bartender.

"I think you can consider Mr. O'Malley's tab closed until further notice," Leo informed the bartender.

"Hey, I was drinking that," he protested.

"Not anymore you aren't." Trev sat down on the stool next to him. His face had softened.

"You don't have any right to tell a man what he can and can't do." What the hell was Trev doing here?

"I'm exactly the person to listen to about this. That whiskey isn't going to fix your problem. Let's get out of here. We can talk about Beth."

Fuck. Trev had obviously heard his message to Mouse. "I'm not going to talk about this with you. I'm not going to try to kiss her again if that's what you're worried about. She picked you. You win. I lose. Now leave me be."

"What if neither one of us had to lose?"

Bo stopped. What was Trev saying? Fuck. He knew exactly what Trev was saying. It wasn't anything he hadn't thought of himself in the hours since he'd realized Mouse wasn't going to leave Trev for him. How could he not think about it? He had living, laughing, loving proof paraded in front of him every day that a relationship like that could work.

"I don't like men." That was why it couldn't work. He wasn't bisexual. No matter what his father said. He didn't begrudge his brother and Lucas. Hell, Bo loved Lucas like a brother himself. Lucas was part of his family, but he didn't view other men as sexual objects.

Trev sighed. "I don't have sex with men, either. I know it seems like I've done just about everything decadent the universe has to offer, but I haven't done another dude. I don't have a problem with it. I'm simply not intrigued. Rest assured, I'm not after your dick."

Bo finally looked at Trev. "Fine. I don't like you."

Trev seemed nonplussed about that fact. "We got along once. We could get along again. For Beth's sake."

Crap. His cock twitched at the thought. Hadn't he had enough to drink that his cock should be asleep now? He had a sudden vision of Mouse, her gorgeous pale form surrounded by their tanned skin. She would be so fucking small in between them. They could turn her from one to the other, kissing her at will. She would be a pretty doll between them. They could lavish her with pleasure in a way one man alone couldn't.

"I don't think Mouse would go for that." No way was this going to happen. And even if she did want it, would he be able to do it? After what Trev had done? What had Trev truly done? He'd closed a door in Bo's face. And Bo had walked away. That was what he always did. He always walked away. And he never really tried. He expected that it would all go bad. He expected that if he fought, he would lose.

Wasn't that what he'd done with Mouse?

His head was swimming with alcohol and possibilities.

"You are going to call her Beth. I won't allow you to call her by that nickname anymore," Trev said, his tone stern. "Her name is Beth. That's one of the rules."

Rules? There were rules now? "I think I'll call her whatever I like."

He tensed as a big hand went around his neck, and he was hauled off of his barstool.

Trev looked down at him, his eyes narrow and his face as hard as a rock. "You will show her some goddamn respect. Whether you end up accepting my proposal or not, if I ever hear you call her by that demeaning name again, I will beat the fuck out of you. You can't take care of her while you're putting her down. And you sure as fuck can't take care of her until you start taking care of yourself."

Bo put a hand on the barstool, trying to regain his balance. The whole world felt like it had tilted, and he wasn't sure where he was going to land. "What is that supposed to mean?"

"What were you about to do with Clarissa? Tell me what your solution to that problem was." Trev said the words like he already knew the answer. *Bastard.*

There was nothing that said he had to be honest. "I was about to tell her to go fuck herself."

The man who had been sitting beside him chuckled. "No, he wasn't. He's lying. I watched the whole bloody thing."

O'Donnell was here? Wasn't he supposed to be out there investigating that Austin kid? "Hey, I thought you were working for me."

O'Donnell hefted his beer. "I'm off the clock, mate. And I'm excellent at reading people. You were going to leave with her to keep the peace, and you would have ended up sleeping with her for the same bloody reason."

"I was not going to sleep with her." He damn straight knew that. "I wasn't going to touch her."

"You weren't going to stand up for yourself, either," Trev said, letting him go.

Bo took a quick step back. He rubbed the nape of his neck. "I wasn't going to sleep with her."

Leo crossed his arms over his chest. "I doubt that. I believe you would go into the situation thinking that. But would you honestly be able to make the decisive effort it would require to put her off? She's an aggressive woman. Would you be able to tell her effectively that you didn't want to sleep with her? Or would you fall into the situation because it's easier to do what she wants than it is to piss her off?"

"I wouldn't have slept with her." He said it with a stubborn bent to his words, but he could see some truth to what they'd said. He didn't like to admit it, but a whole hell of a lot of his life had been about keeping the peace and fitting in.

It had cost him Mouse. *Beth.* Her name was Beth.

What would have happened if Beth had made the first move? Would he have gone along with it? Would they be together now? Would he be happy?

Trev's hand came down on his shoulder, though this time there was an air of almost fraternal affection in the gesture. "It's all right. It's like anything else. Standing up for yourself is something that has to be taught in some people. I can help you."

He'd heard that before. "Yeah, I'm not buying the shit you're shoveling. I bought it once. Not again. I might not be the strongest man around, but I'm sure not a fool."

Trev's face fell. "Can we talk about this? I don't remember what I did to you. I was a different person. I'd like to talk this out for Beth's sake. Can't you see she's going to be miserable without you?"

"Fine, then you can leave, and I'll take care of her." Even as he said the words, he realized how selfish they were. Mouse…Beth deserved better. And how would he take care of her? According to his brother, Beth needed more than he could give her. Beth needed a Dom. He wasn't an idiot. He knew about the books she read. She was interested in the lifestyle. How could he say he loved her when he wasn't even willing to explore something she needed?

Trev took a step back. "I'm not going anywhere, and you know it. And I don't have to be here. I have the girl. I don't have to share her. She's mine now, and she'll stay that way. But I lo—care about her. It's my job in this relationship to make sure she has what she needs. I think she needs you."

Leo had taken on a distinctly professorial tone. He was more relaxed and infinitely more grating on Bo's nerves. "Bo, Trev is trying to be giving. Maybe we should take this someplace quieter and have a session. I think there are a lot of emotions here that need to be talked about."

"Are we in couples counseling?" The idea horrified Bo.

O'Donnell spit out a mouthful of beer, he was laughing so hard.

Trev threw Leo a look. "Can you stop?"

Leo shrugged. "You're the one who wanted to talk to him. I told you it was a mistake, but if you insist on talking, we should do it in a professional setting. I can probably make do with Aidan's office.

177

Oh, we could even have a talking stick. You're not allowed to speak unless you're holding the stick. It forces you to really listen to the other person. Although easily distractible people play with the stick."

"Don't make me go with him." He did not want to end up in some weird therapy. Trev suddenly seemed like the safer bet.

And there it was. Trev was right. He would have gone with Clarissa. He would have allowed himself to fall into a situation that was bad for him. Hadn't he been doing that all his damn life?

"Don't listen to Leo." Trev shook his head. "He's being obnoxious so you'll turn to me. He's a manipulative son of a bitch."

"The bastard has a PhD in manipulation," O'Donnell said with a nod.

"That's fair," Leo allowed. "But I believe I just proved my point. Bo, Trev is offering you something most people in your position never get. Do you love Beth?"

He nodded, unable to say the words.

"I know you don't want to hear this, but she needs more than you can give her right now," Trev said, his voice gentler than before.

"Because she's submissive." He hadn't wanted to acknowledge it because he couldn't be her Dom. He knew it. He also knew how Lexi and Lucas had blossomed under his brother's care. He'd seen the way Mouse…fuck…Beth had clung to Trev after a single night with him. "I don't understand it."

"Are you willing to try?" Trev asked.

If it meant not losing half his heart? "Yes."

Trev smiled. "Then we'll get through this. But we should have that talk first. I don't understand what I did to you."

"Are you really off the drugs?" He had to know. If Trev had fought his way back, maybe he deserved to be heard. He wasn't sure if he could trust the man, but he'd said he was leaving in a year. He'd told Beth he was leaving, and he wouldn't be taking her along. What if Trev could bring them together, help him be what she needed? He didn't have to love the man. Hell, he didn't even have to like him. He only had to listen.

Trev scrubbed a hand across his face, a weary look in his eyes. "I've been sober for two years. This is the first time I've walked into a bar since the day I stopped drinking. Contrary to what the shrink over there believes, I don't even want a drink right this second. I honestly want to get out of here. The smell is bugging me."

Bo stood for a moment, really looking at the man. Was he lying? Why the hell would he lie? What did Trev gain from any of this? If he was telling the truth, then what did Bo lose by at least talking to the man? He stood to gain everything he wanted. "All right. Let's get out of here. I probably shouldn't drive."

"Well, look at who's here. See, Marty, I told you where we would find your boy." Bryce Hughes stood in the doorway with a smallish man in a suit.

Trev's face had gone a stark white.

Leo got up off his barstool and stood beside Trev. "Bryce, I don't think Trev wanted to speak with Mr. Klein."

Li stayed on his barstool, but his gaze had narrowed and he no longer looked casual.

"Don't be ridiculous," the man in the suit said, his voice nasally and quick. "Trev likes to play hardball. Always has. He likes to string 'em along. Exactly like I taught you, brother. I was pissed that we missed the meeting today, but the fuckers are now offering us even more money. Idiots. We're going to come out of this with a huge payday."

"No." Trev seemed to have a hard time getting the word out of his mouth.

O'Donnell slid off the barstool.

Marty rolled his eyes. "Don't be a moron. We can't hold out for more. Twenty million for this year. If you take them to the playoffs, you get a million-dollar bonus. And their current QB is thirty-two, practically ancient for a football player. We can squeeze a five-year contract out of them. Now, take a little pick-me-up, and let's go catch a flight out of this hellhole."

"I'm not going anywhere." Trev stood his ground.

Bryce frowned. "You damn sure better. Do you have any idea what your mother's medical bills cost?"

Trev's jaw tightened. "I know."

Bryce pointed an accusatory finger Trev's way. "Your sister is still paying them."

Trev took a step back as though shocked at the news. "I thought you paid those off."

Bryce snorted. "No way in hell. Why do you think your sister works two jobs? She wasn't my mother. I told Shelley to let it go to default. It wasn't like your mother left a whole lot to inherit anyway."

"Think about it, Trev," Marty said, sounding like the devil on Trev's shoulder. "You could pay off your mom's bills with one check. Your sister wouldn't have to work two jobs anymore."

Bryce smirked. "She's at the second job right now. She's tending bar at a strip club up the road."

"Bastard," O'Donnell cursed under his breath.

"What?" Leo's question rang through the bar. "You let your wife work in a strip club?"

There was only one strip club anywhere close to Deer Run, and Bo didn't like the idea of Shelley Hughes working there. It looked like Trev liked it even less. He'd paled visibly.

Marty kept up his pitch. "Let's get out of here, my man. We can be in LA in a couple of hours, and all your problems will be solved tomorrow."

Leo started to get into Bryce's face. Trev put a hand out, stopping him.

"Don't make this worse on Shell. Please," Trev said.

"Trev, if you go back into that life, you will slide back into all of your problems." Leo's fists were clenched.

Trev's face had taken on a blankness that Bo recognized. He'd seen it on his own face many times. It was the mask he wore when he knew he had to do something he didn't want to do.

"I'll be fine."

"Damn right you will," Bryce said. "Maybe you can wash some of the tarnish off your name and start giving back to this family."

"How do you want me to play this, Leo?" O'Donnell seemed to understand the whole confrontation was ripe with potential violence.

Leo merely frowned at Bryce.

Marty slapped Trev on the back. "Don't worry about a thing. Bryce here set me up. We'll get out to LA, and I'll make damn sure you feel good, if you know what I mean."

He wasn't sure what the man in the suit meant, but he had a feeling that going to LA would be bad for Trev.

Although it might be good for Bo. "You planning on taking Beth with you?"

A hollow look came into Trev's eyes. He looked like a man who had just realized his life was over. "No. I won't take her with me."

He wouldn't take her with him because he knew what would happen. Bo could see that plainly. He could also see how much it was going to cost Trev McNamara to get his sister out of trouble. And it was obvious that the man had changed. Bo couldn't fool himself. Trev hadn't done anything since he'd come into town except stop Bo from hurting Beth and try to get honest work. And he'd offered to share a woman he clearly cared for because she needed it.

And Bo needed it.

If Trev left, he might never figure out what Beth needed.

"This is a huge mistake, Trev." Leo's jaw had formed a hard line.

It was. And the shrink was going to stand around talking the problem to death. Frustration bubbled up in Bo. Wasn't this just the way everything went? It was sure as fuck the way his life always seemed to go. The moment he thought he was making progress, some asshole stepped in and screwed it up. He was goddamn sick of it. He was sick of the Brians of the world tossing their prejudice around. He was sick of the Clarissas, who thought they could have any damn thing they wanted. He was sick of the slick-suited guys who thought they owned everything. He was sick of himself for never fighting.

Leo could try to talk the problem to death, but Bo was done talking.

He pulled back his fist and plowed right into that asshole in the suit. He went straight for the fucker's face. Bo heard a satisfying crunch and a howl of pain. Yeah, that felt good.

"Bravo, boyo," O'Donnell said with a wink.

"Bo!" Trev barked out his name.

Bo looked at Trev, who glowered disapprovingly, but Leo was

smiling.

The man he'd hit was still howling. Bryce was growling into a cell phone, probably calling the cops. Damn. He was going to jail again, but this time it was going to be worth it.

Like always at The Rusty Spur, the minute the first fist flew, the bar exploded. It was as though violence was simmering right there at the surface, waiting for any excuse to let loose. Almost immediately, Bo felt someone tug on his shirt and a fist smash into his face.

"Hey, asshole, what did you do to Clarissa?" One of Clarissa's old boyfriends shoved another fist into Bo's face.

"Fuck off!" Trev threw himself into the fight. The man might have sworn off liquor, but it seemed he hadn't sworn off fighting. Trev pummeled the guy, tossing him aside when he was done.

Bo lashed out at the next man Clarissa had sent. He could see her standing outside the fray, a humorless smile on her face. Arms and legs tangled in a violent display as the world became a mad mix of fierce joy and righteous pain. He welcomed both.

He punched out at anything that came too close. The music suddenly seemed louder. The lights brighter. Everything seemed to come to life as he realized he wasn't alone in the fight. Trev was behind him, their backs almost touching.

"We're going to have a talk about your lamentable lack of control, Bo." Trev plowed his fist into Brian Nixon's gut.

"Yeah, well, we're going to have to talk about your bossiness, McNamara." But he could feel the grin on his face.

"Fuck!" Bryce Hughes screamed as he started to run, pushing against anyone in his way. "I will sue you, asshole."

His nose looked broken. Bo couldn't miss the satisfied smile on Leo's face.

The doors to the bar flew open, and the sheriff and both of his deputies charged in.

Bo was still smiling as they put him in the back of the squad car. Trev was shoved in after him. This time he wasn't alone.

Chapter Twelve

Mouse paced. She walked through her house which now had a sturdy door and locks on every entryway. She'd made sure all the windows were solid. She'd even checked the attic to make sure there was no way someone could get in through there. She'd done everything she could with the tools she had, and still Trev hadn't found his way home.

A note. She'd gotten a note saying something had come up, and he'd be back later. That was it. And he wasn't answering his phone. It kept going to voice mail. What had happened?

A million scenarios played through her brain—none of them good. She'd tried his sister, but her phone had gone straight to voice mail, too.

She sat down on her rickety stairs, phone in hand. Why had he left? She'd worked so hard in the short time she'd had to obliterate that nasty message the young man who'd attacked her had left. She'd put two coats of primer and three coats of paint on the wall, and for the life of her she could no longer see the words. Trev wouldn't have been able to see them. She'd been worried he would leave to protect her, but she didn't want to be protected. Not like that. Had he seen it somehow or found out about what had happened and that was why he'd left?

Or he might have changed his mind and this was his way of telling her.

The phone in her hand buzzed. She flipped it open as quick as she could. "Trev?"

"No, hon, it's Wanda."

Wanda? Why was Wanda calling? There was only one reason Wanda called, and that was to spread gossip about the people who got hauled into the sheriff's department. Mouse's heart fell. "What did he do?"

"Which one, hon?"

She sat up straighter. "Trev, of course."

"Well, I had to ask because both Trev and Bo got their butts hauled in along with that pretty Irish fella, who had way more weapons on him than is right, and the attractive man who thinks I would make a good Dom DeLuise. That's not flattering, mister. I don't care what you say." Wanda sounded like she was talking to someone else. "Seriously, Mouse, you have to get your men under control. Lou is in a crappy mood now because he had to hose down the second cell. No one uses that second cell, and now it's full of puke. When you think about it, this is your fault. If they think I'm cleaning up after a bunch of drunk-ass twenty-year-olds, those boys are wrong. I have shit on both those deputies, and I won't hesitate to use it. I got my nails done this afternoon. Do you know how much Sue charges these days? Well, let me tell you, I'm not wasting these nails on cleaning."

She heard Wanda take a breath. It was the only chance she was going to get. "Wanda, what did Trev and Bo do?"

"Oh, they did what all those boys do. They got in a fight. Why boys need to beat on each other I have no idea."

Mouse got to her feet and started looking for her keys. *Damn it.* She was going to have to drive. She hated driving, but apparently Trev had gone looking for Bo and they had fought. Fought. Oh, that was absolutely the last thing she wanted. "Is Bo still alive?"

There was a laugh, and Wanda was talking to someone else. "She wants to know if you're still alive, Bo."

"Hell, Mouse, I'm not exactly fragile. Beth, I mean, Beth. Damn it, that hurt, Trev." Bo sounded far away, but she got the idea.

"Wanda, you have to separate them." She found the keys to the ancient car her father had left her.

"Oh, Trev wouldn't let Bo go into the other cell. He did this whole thing where his eyes got cold and suddenly all the men in the room do what he tells them to do. I don't get that. I would have done what I wanted, but that look does seem to get to the men. So he and Bo and the other two are in one cell, and everyone else is in that second cell, and let me tell you, that man from New York City is getting on my nerves. We should be able to send him to a bigger lockup for that accent alone. How am I supposed to follow that? He talks so fast."

But Mouse was out the door. Like it or not, she was driving, and she had to hope that her car was going to get with the game plan.

* * * *

Trev felt cold deep in his gut. He'd taken care of everything he'd needed to, and now he could let the guilt wash over him. He sat down on the hard bench and looked over into the second cell where Marty held a compress over his nose. He sat sullenly among the other men the sheriff had managed to catch.

"You're an asshole, Trev. And your choice in friends has gone way downhill." Marty spat out the words.

Trev merely leaned back against the bars. His last set of friends had been a bunch of druggies and dealers and Marty himself. He kind of thought Bo was a step up. And Leo. *Crap.* He'd gotten his mentor tossed in the can. He looked over where Leo stood in the corner talking quietly to Jimmy Nixon. He hoped Leo wasn't having to listen to crap about how city folk always came into town and ruined everything. He'd gotten enough of that from the deputy.

Liam had promptly found the second bench and taken a nap. It appeared the man could sleep anywhere. He was mumbling in his sleep. Something about hot pants.

And now Beth had been called to come get them all. His heart ached. He was going to have to tell her he was leaving.

"Fine. I'm an asshole. When does our plane leave?" Trev had to do it. He needed the money now. He had to get his sister out of debt.

185

She couldn't go on working in a strip club.

And where had his brother-in-law gone? Why wasn't he attending this party? Trev had seen Bryce with Deputy Len and assumed they would all end up in the same cell together. Why had Bryce been allowed to walk away?

"You can't go." Bo turned to him. "You can't leave Deer Run now."

Bo was a mystery. Trev didn't understand him. Bo hadn't even spoken up when the deputy had tried to separate him. He'd seen the way Bo's whole body had stiffened at the thought of getting thrown in jail with Brian Nixon, the same man who had tried to separate his head from his body this morning, but he'd taken it with almost willful acceptance. Now Bo wanted to protest?

"I would think you would be happy about it." Mere hours before there had been nothing Bo wanted more than to see his ass leaving town.

There was a long pause. The hum of conversation around them seemed to relax Bo, as though he didn't want anyone to hear what the two of them were saying. "Tell me why you wouldn't let me in that night."

He searched his memory. "What night are you talking about?"

Bo's eyes became hooded. "You don't even remember."

He sighed. His whole body felt like it was weighed down. If he could sink into the floor, he would. The desire for a drink was raging now. *Just get through the next five minutes, Trev.* He could handle it. He had to. Sure he could. He hadn't been able to handle fame and all the crap that went with it in San Antonio. How the fuck was he going to do it in LA? He would take some of that money he would get for signing and hire two guys whose only job was to make sure his ass didn't stray. If he did, they would beat the shit out of him. The minute he sniffed a beer or started to walk into a party, they would beat the impulse out of him. Yeah, that might work. He was sure O'Donnell's boss knew some guys.

"My dad tried to kill me that night."

Bo's words shocked Trev out of his misery. He turned to Bo. "What are you talking about?"

Bo shook his head. "I shouldn't have said that. I don't want to

186

talk about it. Look, that's all over. The thing is I came to your apartment in Austin that night and you told me to go away. You said something about me not being dressed for the party."

"I had a lot of parties. It could have been any of them." There was a sick feeling in the pit of his stomach. This event was obviously important to Bo, and he couldn't even recall it.

"You really don't remember."

He shook his head. Shame threatened to choke him. "I wish you would talk about it."

Bo shook his head. "We can let it go. It changes things now that I know you don't even remember. Maybe you really were a different person."

"That addict is still inside me." He was screaming right now.

"Well, don't let him out again." Bo's demeanor changed. He sighed and settled back as though trying to get comfortable. "So, how does this thing work? You know, the whole 'sharing Beth' thing. I mean, if she says yes, of course."

"Well, I wasn't going to ask her exactly. I was going to strip her down and see how she felt when she had two mouths on her girl parts. That's when the yes, yes, yeses start." Except they wouldn't now. He would be in LA, and he didn't dare take Beth with him. He wanted to. He wanted to order her to pack up and come with him. She would be the reason he stayed sober. She was his responsibility, the person who kept him grounded, the person he couldn't let down.

But he would.

Bo chuckled. "Damn, that actually sounds hot. Are we going to tie her up? Maybe we should make a game plan. We have some time. She'll either have to find a ride or worse, she'll drive. We could be here for hours."

Trev ran a frustrated hand through his hair. "We're not going to tie her up. I have to leave."

"No, you don't."

"Did you hear a word Bryce said? My sister is working at a strip club because she can't pay the hospital bills. I can't let her down. I don't have a fucking dime until next year. I can't leave her there."

Bo shrugged it off. "I have eight hundred thousand dollars in the bank. You can pay me back later. Now, do I get to order her

187

around, too? I don't know how good I'm going to be at that."

Trev stared at him for a moment. He'd said it so casually. "You would do that? You hate me."

Bo leaned his head against the bars, his eyes closing as he spoke. "I don't hate you. I don't know how much I can trust you, yet. This doesn't make us friends, but I like your sister well enough. And that money doesn't mean a damn thing here. What the hell am I going to spend it on? I came into that money last year, and I haven't spent a dime of it. I thought about asking to buy into the ranch, but Aidan's got his own family now. He's going to want to leave that ranch to his kids. I wouldn't be any good at my own ranch. I can work a herd, but the business part makes me nervous. So, I've got a whole bunch of money and not a damn thing to do with it. Beth cares about you. It would break her heart if you walked out now. I'm not doing this for you. I'm doing it for her." He opened his eyes and turned to Trev. "The question is, are you man enough to accept it?"

It rankled. It was charity, and he knew it. What would his sister want? It was a question Leo forced him to ask whenever he thought about something like this. When making a decision that truly affected another person, he had to take her feelings into account. It sucked. Shelley would want him to follow the path he'd planned. That was the whole damn reason she'd never mentioned it. His sister loved him. Making a unilateral decision that could cost him his sobriety wouldn't help her in the end. He was the only family she had left. Bo was offering him a chance to fix the situation without causing another problem.

Sometimes being a man meant swallowing his damn pride.

"If I'm getting involved in this, I have to know I mean something." Bo turned away as though he didn't want to look at him anymore. "I can't be a third body. I know the way this goes. You're going to be the big guy, the one with all the authority, and I'm mostly okay with that. But I can't just be a dick to be used in bed and ignored out of it. If that's all you want—a third to please Beth—then you should count me out."

Bo wanted to matter. He got that. "Thank you. I'll take it. I'll find out from the hospital how much the bill is. And I'll pay you back. With interest."

Bo turned to him.

"Fine, without interest."

"I'm not a fucking bank."

"Understood." He didn't have to go. He felt a smile sneak across his face. How was it that he'd reached his lowest point and finally found the people who mattered? His sister. Leo. Beth and Bo. Years and years he'd been a football god, and it was only when he had not a dime to his name that he found real friends. "Thank you, Bo."

A sunny smile lit Bo's face. "No problem."

Marty stood at the bars. "Hey, McNamara and I have an early-morning flight to LA. When are we getting out of this piss pot? I swear to god, I'm going to sue the fuck out of this town."

"You can try. We ain't got any money, so good luck, mister." Wanda went back to admiring her nails.

"And Trev's not going anywhere," Bo announced. "He has a job. He's a cowboy."

Marty's eyes went wide. "Have you been talking to Dallas? Behind my back?"

He laughed. It was genuinely freeing. "No, Marty. I'm not that kind of cowboy. I'm the 'spend all day on horseback, get knee-deep in cow shit, and get paid next to nothing' kind of cowboy."

And it was the best job in the world. He'd loved football, but he'd loved the game more than anything else. The rest of it—the business part—had nearly killed him. He just wanted to play. He hadn't picked up a football in two years, but he suddenly wanted to. He wanted to get the ranch hands together on a Sunday and play a game of touch. He never felt freer than when he was looking for a target to throw to.

If he'd been a different man, his talent and his personality would have meshed. He wasn't that man. He couldn't handle it. Life was a choice. He chose to live and not burn out. Some people might never understand, but he'd chosen to live the day he'd walked away from the game.

"I'm not going anywhere, Marty. Go find someone else to exploit. And don't call me. I'll never step onto the field again. Not a professional field. Now, leave me be. Bo and I have a game to plan."

It would involve rope and a paddle because he intended to let Beth know what she was in for the next time she hid something from him.

Leo smiled over at him before patting Jimmy on the shoulder and passing him a business card. "Call me tomorrow. We'll set up a session. It's going to be all right."

Trev raised a brow. Leo shook his head. "Patient confidentiality. But god, I could build a whole practice off this town." He stared down where O'Donnell was snoring in between talking about boots not being right. He shook his head. "And this one must actually work for therapy. Brilliant investigator but totally fucked up." He turned to Bo. "Are you going to be able to handle this? Beth lied to her Dom. This is going to be an ugly scene."

Bo's eyes found his. "Lied?"

"By omission," he clarified. She hadn't mentioned the fact that she'd been shot at. It was a hell of an omission.

"Fuck, I told her you would find out. I told her to call you. Hell, I hired an investigator. I don't know how she thought she could hide it." Bo talked fast.

"You aren't in trouble, Bo. Though now that we have a deal, I expect that you would call me in if something like that happens again. So, she fixed the door and painted over the bullet holes?"

Bo groaned. "Nope. She painted over the words on the wall. 'Get out.'"

He closed his eyes. Those words had been meant for him. A huge part of him wanted to slink away. It would be better for everyone if he left. Beth and Bo were going to be tainted by his presence. He opened his eyes to find Leo and Bo both looking at him expectantly.

If he left, this town would eat up Bo and Beth again. *Fuck it.* He was better for them. The town could go to hell. Bo and Beth had made their choices. The town could hate him all they liked, but Beth was his. Fuck. Bo was his. Not in any sexual way, but Bo had recently become his responsibility in a way that meant something to Trev.

Trev raised his voice to make sure Wanda heard him. As long as Wanda heard, everyone in town would know what he'd said. "I will beat the living shit out of the next person who tries something like this. I'm not going anywhere, and this town better get used to it. I'm here for a year, and then we'll see what happens, but I'm not going to let some asshole make me run out on my friends."

Leo stood, a brilliant smile on his face. "The man learns. I am the greatest therapist in the world." He pointed to the five men in the opposite cell. "Group rate, gentlemen. Give me a call. I can fix you. Well, maybe not you. You offend me. But the rest of you are more than welcome."

"Did you hear that, Patty? Yeah, I think the ponytailed man is some sort of cult leader. Right here in Deer Run. Yep." Wanda was back on the phone.

"I can handle whatever this town tries to throw at me," Bo said, sitting back. "This is what she wants, right?"

Trev turned to him. "I have a question for you. Were you with her when she walked into that house? Or did she call out for you to help her?"

Bo's face tightened. "I only knew she was in trouble because I heard the gun go off."

"Is that the way she should have reacted? Or should she have called out for you?" He asked the question because Bo needed to understand his place. "I don't care what had gone on with the two of you. She should have called for you. If she belongs to us, then she has to learn to take care of herself, and that damn straight includes asking for help when some asshole is shooting at her."

A hard look came into Bo's eyes. "I can handle it."

Trev was suddenly pretty sure he could. And that meant he'd gained a partner.

The door to the sheriff's office opened, and Beth ran in. She was dressed in jeans and a bulky shirt Trev intended to burn. Her wardrobe was getting an update. He stood, Bo beside him as though they had practiced the move.

"I'm here to pick up Trev and Bo." She was breathless as she spoke to Wanda. She finally turned, and a little stubbornness firmed her chin. "I hear the two of you have been fighting. You should both know that I won't put up with it."

Trev narrowed his eyes. The only thing that kept him off her

191

were the bars between them. "You won't put up with it?"

She swallowed but seemed to find her courage. "No. I will not. You two should make up."

Bo chuckled beside him. "Oh, I think Trev and I are fine now. You could say we talked it out."

She stared for a moment. "Well, I'm glad." She turned back toward Wanda. "Can I take them home now? I mean, I'm going to take them to their homes, of course."

Wanda's eyes widened. "Of course."

Trev wasn't going to let her get away with that. "Are you really in?"

Bo nodded.

Then it was time to stake a claim. "You can take us back to your place, Beth. There's no reason to hide. I slept there last night. I'll sleep there tonight. So will Bo."

"What?" It came out of Beth's mouth with a little squeak. "Bo?"

"That's right, Beth. I ain't calling you Mouse anymore. Trev won't allow it. And I am definitely spending the night," Bo insisted.

Wanda continued her play-by-play. "That's right, Patty. Both of them. Just like Aidan and Lucas."

"No!" Trev and Bo both managed to shout it at the same time.

And then Bo laughed. He laughed long and hard, shaking his head.

The sheriff sighed as he opened the cell door. He looked back at Beth. "Can you take the long-haired fellow with you? He's made two of the men in the next cell cry like babies. If you leave him here, they'll all be throwing fits."

"They aren't throwing fits. They're having breakthroughs," Leo assured the sheriff as he walked out.

"I'm going to actualize my own perfect being," Jimmy Nixon proclaimed through his tears.

Leo gave him a thumbs-up.

Trev walked out after him. He walked straight to Beth and pulled the ponytail out of her hair. "I told you to wear your hair down."

He would have quietly reminded her another several times to

get her into the habit of obeying him when it came to her hair, but she'd pushed him. She didn't get a reminder.

"It looks beautiful down. You need to leave it that way." Bo stood close to her but not touching.

"It feels so soft. Try it." He was going to have to ease Bo into this.

After a moment of hesitation, Bo let his hand drift up and stroke her hair. There was something sweetly innocent about the way Bo's fingers drifted into Beth's hair. His eyes took in the soft brown stuff. Beth's hair was threaded with sable and wisps of dark blonde. Bo touched her, petting her hair as if it satisfied something inside him. And then he did something Trev hadn't expected. His hands wound through that silky hair and tightened.

"You didn't call out today." Bo's voice was harder than he could remember. "When you were in trouble, you didn't let me know."

He could see the way her breath hitched the minute Bo's voice had deepened. If her pussy hadn't gone soft and wet when Bo had clenched his hand in her hair, he would give up his throwing arm.

"You were mad at me," Beth reminded Bo, her voice soft.

Bo forced her head up. Maybe Trev wouldn't have to ease him in. He seemed more comfortable with it now. "I would never be mad enough at you that I would let some fucker shoot you. Don't you forget that. Now, give me the keys because I'm not sitting in that Pinto for the hour it would take you to drive us home."

He plucked the keys from her hands and strode out without a backward glance.

Beth stared at him, her mouth half-opened. It was good that she was aware of Bo, but Trev wanted her aware of him, too. "And we're going to have a talk tomorrow about lying to me. I should explain that omitting pertinent facts is the same as lying. You better pick a safe word, darlin', because tomorrow, you're going to need it."

"Not tonight?"

He forced himself not to smile. She sounded disappointed. "Tonight is for something different, but you better enjoy it. I'm not going easy on you tomorrow. And you can tell Patty that, Wanda.

Beth Hobbes's butt is going to be red tomorrow because she defied her Dom."

Wanda shook her head. "What is you people's obsession with that man?"

Leo laughed. "You three go on ahead. I'll call Lucas. He and Aidan can take me and Li back to the scene of the crime. We'll get your trucks back to Beth's place for you. I was out the minute someone mentioned a Pinto. Seriously, they explode. And I prefer to travel in a vehicle that doesn't require me to fold my body in two."

"You're getting a new car," Trev said as he took her hand and walked out into the night.

Chapter Thirteen

Bo put the car in park and prayed his dick still worked. The freaking tin can Mouse drove had him bent in half. Beth. Fuck, that was hard. He was hard. Damn it, he was so hard.

Was he really about to do this? Was he going to fuck Beth while Trev watched? Or would he be the one watching? Could he watch her writhe under Trev?

Beth took Trev's hand as he helped her out of the car. Trev had forced her to go over every instant of her afternoon, from getting turned down at the bank, to cleaning up after the man who had shot at her. He'd been ruthless in his questioning. He'd forced her to tell him everything, right down to how it had made her feel.

Scared. Bo could have told him that. He'd been pretty fucking scared when he'd realized someone with a gun was trying to kill her.

"Beth." Trev's voice was as dark as the night. "Do you understand why I'm angry? This relationship won't work if you don't even trust me enough to tell me when someone's tried to hurt you. I want you to think about this. I require trust from you. I'm willing to give it, too. And now you have to think about whether you can handle the both of us."

Bo stilled. He hadn't even thought about the fact that she might say no. Shouldn't this whole Dom thing preclude her from saying no? Shouldn't Trev simply tell her what he wanted, and she would do it? Even as he thought it, he knew this was one of those things his brother had tried to talk to him about. D/s wasn't some crime perpetrated against the weaker player. It was a power exchange. In an exchange, something had to be given. First and foremost— permission. Beth had to say yes.

He couldn't stand the thought of being left out. It had been surprisingly easy to make the decision to share her. The minute Trev had made the offer, his cock had jumped up, started singing, and bounced around with joy.

The truth was he actually thought it might be for the best. He already felt different. He felt stronger. He might wilt if she said no.

"I can handle it." Beth smiled at Trev and put a hand out to Bo. "I want this. I want it so much."

"Remember that tomorrow, darlin'." Trev pulled her close. Bo envied the easy way he dominated her. "Tonight is going to be easy. You've had a hard day. You'll take a simple spanking, and you'll serve your Masters, but tomorrow is going to be rough."

Masters?

"Bo tops me, too? I don't know about that." Beth looked at him, her lips frowning. "I can still remember a time when he cried because he broke his crayons."

Trev looked over at him, too, though there was challenge in his eyes. Bo felt his pulse hitch. He could choose. He could top Beth, or he could be another sub. Trev would always be the alpha, but it was up to Bo where his place would be. His choice and his responsibility. If he chose to be a sub, Trev would take care of him. At least, that was the way it was supposed to work. If he chose to top Beth, he would have to not only take care of her, but change the way he viewed himself.

He reached out and gripped the back of her neck, loving the silky-smooth feel of her skin and the way her lips softened. "I'm not a kid anymore." Hell, he wasn't even the same man he'd been a couple of days ago. Realizing he loved Beth and losing her, seeing her almost die, discovering that Trev might be different than he'd thought—it all combined to form a changed version of himself. And he liked the man he was becoming. "And I will top you. Don't you think I can't do it."

"Are you going to kiss me?" Beth asked.

Fuck, yeah, he was going to kiss her. He tightened his fingers in her hair, but he asked Trev first. It seemed right. Trev was sharing her. "Can I kiss her?"

Trev chuckled. "You don't have to ask. We're not doing a scene tonight. This is how this works. I'm in charge during discipline and scenes. I expect both of you to come to me with your problems, not because I don't think you can't handle them, but because we're in a relationship. I'll talk to the two of you about all the things going on in my life. Trust me, you'll hear more than you want about how I need a fucking drink. We're in this together. But she's yours, too, Bo. Kiss her."

Bo looked down at her, tears suddenly threatening. For years and years she'd been the center of his world, and just like the fucking sun in the sky, he'd taken her for granted because she was always there.

"I love you, Beth." The words didn't come from his mouth. They were pushed out of his heart.

Her hands came up, cupping his cheeks. "I love you, too."

She always had. All of his life, he'd looked for the one person who could anchor him. She'd been that anchor, not holding him down like a lodestone, but keeping him grounded in love and affection when the rest of the world seemed dark. She'd been his everything, even when he'd ignored her. She'd been the quiet presence he could count on. He owed her everything.

"This is it. You understand? This isn't sex. This is the rest of my life. I won't ever leave you. I won't ever touch another woman." Nothing felt as freeing as making that pledge. He was twenty-five, and now he had his purpose in life, to make sure she was safe and happy.

Tears had formed in her eyes. "Do you mean that? Because I don't think I could stand it if you changed your mind."

He was going to have to show her. "Never."

He lowered his head to hers, and his mouth brushed the softest lips he'd ever kissed. She sighed into his mouth, and he couldn't mistake that single sound for anything but submission. His whole

197

body tightened. His hands found that silky hair again as his tongue touched her lips, licking and seeking entry. Her mouth flowered open under his, and he truly tasted her sweetness for the first time. Their tongues played, hers shyly at first, and then with a soft, insistent demand. He pulled her close, feeling her breasts against his chest, her hips seeking his. His cock practically thumped against his zipper, begging to be let out. He wanted to shove her to the ground and get his cock inside. He needed to know she was his.

And he needed to make it good for her.

"Come on, you two." Trev's voice sounded slightly strangled. "We should move this inside. We can't be sure when the next idiot is going to paint something we own in an attempt to run me out of town."

"That was why I didn't tell you." Beth's arms wound around Bo's waist. "I thought you would walk away. I'm sorry."

"Trev assures me he isn't going anywhere for a while," Bo replied, trying to gauge Trev's reaction.

Trev's hand came out and smoothed back Beth's hair. "You accepted me as your Dom. That means you accept all the shit storm that comes with it. Do you want me to leave? Because this could be bad for you. The people in this town will give you both hell for being involved with me."

Bo seemed to be forever in this position. But now he had a ready answer. "They can go fuck themselves."

Beth smiled. The expression held a confident grace he'd never seen on her face before. "What Bo said."

"Then come in the house." Trev turned on his heels and started for the door.

Bo looked down at his best friend. "Are you sure about this? You seem to care about him. If you want, I can walk away, and I promise we'll still be friends." He couldn't stand the thought, but he was beginning to understand this stuff. She should have all the options laid out. She should know what she was getting into and that the men she was getting involved with wanted her to be happy.

"I do care about him. I think I'm falling in love. I know I've never met anyone like him, but I love you, too. And he's not staying here forever. He's moving west in a year. He told me. He could teach us a lot. I want to explore this thing."

He heard the urgency in her voice. "You want to try this out? You want me to spank you? You want me to tie you up?"

He wasn't so sure about it. His cock was sure. His cock was ready for anything that got it closer to her pussy, but Bo wasn't sure. He'd known real violence. Could he really give her what she seemed to need?

"I want to try."

He laced his fingers through hers. Trev was waiting at the door. "Then we'll try."

He was done being selfish. His selfishness had kept them apart for years. She'd given so much to him. How could he refuse her?

Trev's eyes nearly bore a hole through them as they walked up. He seemed different than before, stronger, more in control. He seemed to be bigger, taller, as though he took on extra height the minute he decided to become the Dom.

"The rules haven't changed, Beth. Don't think because Bo is with us that it changes anything. You know what to do when this door closes, and you know what position I want you in. I require obedience tonight. You'll have pleasure, but I'll have submission."

Position? She was going to get into a position?

She nodded, her face tranquil as she passed him. She didn't seem even close to nervous. A calm had settled over her that he didn't feel yet. Trev stopped him, putting a hand on his chest and allowing the door to close.

"Give her a minute. We should talk."

God, the man was going to talk him to death. Plain old vanilla sex had way less talking. "I thought we already did that."

"I'm going to be rough with her. I need you to watch her. You'll see what she wants."

Rough? He wasn't sure he liked the sound of that. "You haven't known her very long. How can you be sure what she wants?"

"Years of training. I know you think this is all bullshit, but I've spent years watching submissives. Watch her. See what she needs. Sex isn't some bodily exchange. It's a dance, and she needs you to lead."

Fuck. He was a terrible dancer. He had two left feet.

Trev laughed as though he could read his mind. "You'll be fine. Give her what she needs, take care of her, and then it will be your turn."

"Why the fuck are you doing this? Don't give me that crap about this is what Mou...Beth needs." It was too perfect. He couldn't trust it.

Trev suddenly stared at something in the distance. "She does need you. And maybe I need you, too. I'm always so close to the edge. It's always right there. I've fucked up so many times in so many ways, and I can't even give a good excuse for it. All of my life I was the golden boy."

And all of Bo's, he'd been the damn whipping boy. He opened his mouth to explain that his position had been worse, but Trev kept talking.

"I was the one everyone looked up to. I was the one who would win the game. I was the one who scored near perfect on my SATs. I was the one who got all the girls. And all I wanted was a damn beer because it was too much pressure. I couldn't handle it. What other people saw as this charmed life, I knew it was one long fall waiting to happen. Don't get me wrong, I loved the game. But I hated the other parts. I hated the pressure. I hated the fact that I couldn't trust a single person around me because they all had an angle. You didn't have an angle."

"Sure I did. I wanted to learn from you. Hell, in some ways I wanted you to protect me." It was sad, but it was the truth. Maybe Trev hadn't had it so perfect.

"And apparently I didn't do a good job of it." Trev sighed, some of his confidence gone.

And he finally understood Trev McNamara. Trev McNamara felt too much. He wasn't a man who could accept the gifts he'd been given with a laid-back air. It was too much for him. He didn't feel he'd earned it no matter how much time he'd spent in training. He'd been surrounded by people who didn't truly love him, who'd used him, and he'd felt it too much. He'd deadened those emotions with alcohol and drugs.

A deep calm settled in Bo's chest. He'd had the opposite problem. He'd never been wanted by his father. His mother had died long before she could have branded him with love and affection. His brother had cared, but he had his own life. Bo had deadened the pain by withdrawing, even from himself, by floating through life, trying to get along, never fighting.

Beth had done the same. She'd allowed things to happen to her rather than stand up for herself because she'd never been taught how. Her parents had been quiet academics in a town where no one valued them.

Aidan was right. He needed Trev, but by god, he'd figured out that Trev needed him, too.

"I won't let you fuck up. I know I'm smaller than you, but I swear I can be meaner. I see you come close to a beer, I'll find a way to kick your ass. And I'll be here to take care of Beth. You don't have to worry about that."

The Dom was back. "See that you do. Keep your mind open tonight."

Trev was doing that whole "intimidating" thing Aidan did whenever he was about to go to the barn. Bo knew what went on in the barn, and it wasn't anything having to do with the ranch. The barn was his brother's personal dungeon. Trev was prepping for some play, but Bo hadn't missed the way his eyes had softened at the promise of an ass kicking.

Trev opened the door, and Bo walked through feeling infinitely better. He supposed when his brother had talked about the lifestyle, he'd always thought he'd get ground beneath "the Dom's" boot. He wasn't a Dom. But he wasn't exactly a sub, either. Not once had he thought that he could bring something to the relationship. Trev might be the only Dom in the world who needed what Bo could give him.

Then he wasn't thinking about anything but the woman on the floor in front of him. He'd thought he was hard before, but the sight of Beth naked and waiting had his balls drawing up.

Beth sat in the middle of the hallway completely naked. Her spine was straight, but her head bowed submissively down. Her hair was a soft halo around her head, falling to her shoulders and brushing her breasts. *Fuck.* He was looking at Beth's breasts. Free from confinement, they were more beautiful than he'd imagined.

Round and soft, with pretty pink nipples that begged to be pulled between his lips and suckled. She'd hidden that gorgeous body underneath shapeless dresses and bulky blouses. Now he could see how her small waist curved into feminine hips.

"Very nice, love." Trev put a hand on her head. "Spread your legs a little. I see you did as I asked."

"Yes, Sir. I shaved."

Trev tipped her head up. "You're beautiful, Beth. Your pussy looks lovely."

She smiled and her eyes came back to Bo. "He said I looked like Sasquatch."

Trev coughed. "I didn't put it like that."

She shrugged. "It's okay. I didn't have any reason to groom down there before. I like how it feels."

Trev's eyes narrowed. "Did you touch yourself?"

"I'm not sure how else I was supposed to shave," she replied.

Trev's hand bit into her hair. "You know that's not what I'm asking."

"He wants to know if you masturbated." Bo was well aware that his voice had taken on a dark quality. He was primed to fuck, but Trev was going to make him wait. Well, maybe he could play this game, too. "He wants to know if you touched your pussy, if you played with your clit. Did you touch it, Beth? Did you circle it with a finger and then shove that same finger deep inside your pussy? Did you get creamy and wet? Did you fuck that finger until you came?"

Beth's eyes were as wide as saucers as she looked up to him. "No, I just shaved. But that sounds real nice, Bo."

"It does, doesn't it?" Trev had a steady smile on his face. "Tell me something, Bo. Have you ever seen a pussy as pretty as this one? Spread those knees and show him."

After only a moment's hesitation, her knees widened, and he had to catch his breath. Her pussy was a work of art. It was plump and yet delicate. Her skin was a glorious pale ivory, but he could see the pink from her pouty folds. She was already turned on. She was already aroused, and no one had touched her. Trev was right. She needed this.

And he needed her.

"Wider." The word sounded foreign coming out of his mouth. He didn't recognize the deep tone. "I want to see more."

"Obey the man," Trev commanded. "He tops you. I suspect he could be convinced to spank you, as well."

She would want him to. Aidan teased Lexi about it all the time. Every time he mentioned spanking her, Lexi's face would flush. Beth's fair skin flushed now, and he was pretty sure it wasn't with embarrassment.

"Show me, or I'll give you five," Bo demanded.

Trev chuckled. "A whole five? We need to talk about proper punishment, partner." His expression changed, and his voice took on a deep, slightly sinister tone. "That will be twenty for you, Beth. That makes forty because you already have twenty coming from lying to me earlier today. And at least an hour without an orgasm."

Beth's knees spread wide really fast.

Her clitoris was a jewel at the top of her pussy, poking out of its little hood. It was pearly and pink at the same time, shining in the low light from the moisture that already coated it. She looked primitive and tempting sitting there, presenting her pussy to him. He stood over her, looking down at the gift being offered to him. He felt bigger than he had before, oddly stronger. Trev had asked him a question.

"No, I've never seen a prettier pussy. I've never seen a more beautiful woman. I think this one might need two men to take care of her."

Trev got to his knees behind her, his palms finding her torso and skimming up until each hand held a breast. Her whimper went straight to Bo's cock. She shivered as Trev flicked her nipples with his thumbs.

"I can tell you this pussy is tight. So fucking tight, and her breasts are very sensitive. You liked me sucking on your nipples, didn't you?" Trev asked.

Her eyes closed as Trev rolled her nipples. "Yes."

Bo watched as the fingers playing with her tightened, and Beth let out a hiss. She seemed to understand what that punishment meant.

"Yes, Sir," she corrected.

Trev continued playing with her breasts, but his eyes came up to meet Bo's. "She calls me Sir when we're playing. Would you like her to call you Sir?"

He shook his head. "No. I want her to call me Bo. I want to hear my name when I'm fucking her."

Trev nodded shortly, and then his mouth was close to Beth's ear. "Say his name, darlin'. He wants to hear it."

Her mouth curved, her pink tongue coming out to wet her lips. "Bo."

She'd said his name a thousand times, but never with the breathy anticipation she used now. She'd transformed from the quiet little mouse he knew to something different. She was submitting, but she seemed to find strength in it.

"Let's get the hard part over with," Trev announced. "On your feet. Go and grip the back of that monstrosity of a couch and present that ass to your Masters. It's a count of forty, and then tomorrow we'll discuss this situation further. You aren't allowed to hide things from us. Not ever."

She pouted up at him. "I didn't want Bo to get hurt."

Trev hugged her, his arms going around her torso. "I understand that, darlin'. I really do. But I can't allow it. Bo, what would be worse? Being injured or knowing she was being hurt and you couldn't do anything?"

No question. "I couldn't live with myself if she'd died in this house and I was driving away. My life would have been over."

"I feel the same way," Trev added. "I appreciate that you don't want us hurt, but you can't take away our right to protect you. Protecting you, making sure you have what you need, knowing that I'm important to you—these are the things a Dom gets from the relationship."

"You seemed to get a little more than that last night," she said, biting that hot bottom lip.

Trev's hand smacked her ass, but there was a smile on his face. "I'll get that, too. You could turn into such a brat. I'm going to enjoy watching you grow. Now, do as I told you. I want to get to the part of the evening where I fuck you."

Beth held out her hand toward him. Bo moved close and helped her up. He took the opportunity to pull her close. He wished he'd been smart enough to chuck his clothes, but he could still feel the way her nipples poked at his chest.

"You want to get spanked?" He needed to hear her say it. He wasn't sure exactly what was going to happen, but he was nervous about it.

"Yes. I know it's weird, but I think I'll like it," she admitted.

"No more waiting. Do as I told you." Trev's impatience was etched on his face.

Trev strode across the room and picked up a leather bag. He unzipped it as Beth let go of Bo and walked to the living area of the house. It was dominated by an antique-looking sofa. It was the type of sofa that went in old-fashioned parlors, when the lady of the house would serve tea or something. Maudine Bellows would probably roll in her grave if she knew her perfectly kept parlor was being used as a place to spank her home's new owner. He was pretty sure Maudine had never grasped the wooden back of the sofa and arched her back, presenting her ass high in the air the way Beth was. Of course, Maudine Bellows had probably never once had the look of anxious anticipation that lit up Beth's face.

He let his fingers find the buttons of his shirt. He wasn't going to make the same mistake twice. He wanted to feel that soft skin against his. He chucked off his shirt, tossing it to the floor. He noticed Trev had removed his as well, though he had folded it. Bo picked his up and followed Trev's example, folding it neatly and making a pile of his clothes. Trev worked methodically, as though he had all night and he would take every second of it. Bo was impatient, the need to fuck riding him hard.

"She's sweating. Trust me, the anticipation of what we're going to do to her is going to make it even better." Trev was down to nothing but his jeans, and even those were unbuttoned. He reached into the leather bag and pulled out a small piece of pink plastic that had been rolled in a towel. "Hold it by the base. I bought it earlier today. I was late getting home because I had to drive two towns over to find a toy store. It's been sterilized. I don't want to have to stop to do it again."

"Sterilized?" Bo held the stiff plastic by the base.

Trev grinned. "Oh, yeah. Trust me, she'll be grateful I'm a deep believer in sterilization when I shove that up her ass. We have to make sure every toy is fully cleaned. Thank god. I thought I forgot the lube. That would have been embarrassing."

Bo felt his face nearly go up in flames. Forgetting the lube was embarrassing, but shoving a piece of plastic up his girlfriend's ass was perfectly normal?

"It's the only way to prepare her. How did you think this was going to work? Did you think we would take turns? We will tonight, but eventually we'll take her together. That's what a ménage is, Bo. Are you sure about this? If you like, we can simply date her separately. I don't like that option, but having let her know she could have us both puts me in a corner."

He'd known this would happen. He'd known what Aidan and Lucas did to Lexi. It wasn't that he was against it. But it certainly wasn't something he'd ever thought he would do. "No. I want to do this."

"Excellent. Then let's get her punishment out of the way." Trev strode forward after handing him the tube of lube.

Yep, he'd fallen down a rabbit hole. When he'd woken up this morning, the last thing he'd thought he would be doing by midnight was holding a butt plug and a tube of lube, getting ready to watch his best friend get her ass spanked by a former professional quarterback. Of course, he'd woken up in jail with his face way too close to Brian Nixon's butt crack. This was a definite upturn in his day.

Trev stood over Beth, his big body making hers seem small and delicate. There was no way to mistake the erection the man was sporting. It matched his own.

Trev's hands ran down her spine toward her ass. He cupped the globes and leaned over to kiss that place where her back flowed and curved into the cheeks of her ass. "Your safe word is 'bunny.' If you say the word 'bunny,' I'll stop everything I'm doing and we'll talk. We're going to take this slow. We're going to find where your boundaries are. And then I'm going to push them. You can make as much noise as you like tonight, darlin'. There will be times when I demand silence, but not tonight. We're pushing Bo's boundaries tonight, too. It's a count of forty, and then I'm going to work a plug into your ass."

He could see the way it made her shiver. He looked down at the plug. It was dainty and pink. It was smaller than his cock. He would bet it was smaller than Trev's, too. "Is this a starter plug? Because otherwise, I don't see what good it's going to do. It's tiny."

"It looks pretty big to me," she said, her eyes wide. "If it's so tiny, maybe you should try it."

"Oh, you should spank her for that." He wasn't about to take a pink plug up his ass. He had standards. "That was rude."

Trev sighed. "You're going to be like two kids, aren't you? And for your information, Bo, that *is* a starter plug. We'll work that pretty asshole open until she can handle a cock. And if she struggles, there's always ginger root. I'll find a nice big piece of ginger, and I'll carve it into the shape of a cock. I'll work it into your ass, and every time you clench, the oil will burn. I promise, after an hour of figging, you'll learn not to fight your Master when it comes to anal sex."

"Who the hell figured that out? Who sits around and thinks, hey, maybe I should shove some ginger root up my ass so it won't clench anymore?" He couldn't help but laugh. "Sorry. I know this is supposed to be all serious and stuff."

Trev grinned at him while he ran his hands along Beth's body. "It's not that serious, buddy. It's sex, and it's supposed to be fun. And Leo teaches a class. I've never seen anyone who could whittle a more perfect penis than that man. But I assure you, our Beth won't be laughing. That fucking ginger root burns."

"You?" He couldn't imagine Trev doing that.

"Hell, yeah. I'm not going to do anything to her I haven't tried myself. I might laugh about this, but I take it seriously. Now, I'm going to spank her ass, and then I'm going to teach you how to plug this pretty asshole." Trev's hand arced and the sound cracked through the room.

Beth gasped. Her perfectly porcelain skin went pink. "Oh, my god."

"That's not a count." Trev held back as though waiting for

something.

"One." She seemed to struggle to get that word out. Her head fell forward with the second slap of Trev's hand. "Two."

Trev seemed merciless. He spanked her over and over, waiting when she didn't give the count. Beth's body practically vibrated with each slap of his hand. He spanked her ass, moving each time so both globes got attention, both became hot pink. Bo couldn't look away from the sight. He'd thought it would turn him off, but it had his cock twitching. What would she look like tied to one of those big *X*s as Trev used a whip on her?

Over and over, Trev slapped her ass, the only sounds in the room the heavy cadence of flesh hitting flesh and her moans.

"Thirty-eight." Her voice had softened. She seemed less tense than she had been at the beginning. Her body moved with each strike, but her muscles seemed more languid now, as though she'd accepted the pain. "Thirty-nine."

Trev's face was as hard as rock. One more smack and he was done, but Trev stood there looking down at his handiwork.

"Forty." Beth's voice came out in a heartfelt sigh.

"How do you feel, darlin'?" Trev's voice was low, and he sounded as out of breath as if he'd been the one taking the spanking.

"I'm good." She sounded like she'd finished a race.

And he felt like an idiot. He was just the guy holding the plug. Trev and Beth had shared something. Bo hadn't been a part of it.

"Come here." Trev gestured him over.

He took his place beside Trev. Beth's backside had an almost red sheen to it. It looked rough and painful. It was strangely beautiful.

Trev put a hand on the small of her back, offering her to Bo. "Test her. I can see you're fighting this. You think she shouldn't want this, but I assure you, she does. Run a finger through her pussy and tell me she didn't want that."

He hated the fact that he couldn't simply accept it. Watching Beth get her ass spanked had gotten him hotter than he could have imagined, but too many years of trying to fit in had him fighting his own impulses. His impulse had been to jump in. And he'd kept silent. Why did he always do that?

He took the out Trev had offered him. He held the plug in one hand and with the other tested the folds of her pussy.

He nearly groaned when his fingers slid easily through her juices. Beth was soaking wet, her pussy pulsing against his fingers. He had no doubt that if he touched her clit, she would howl as she came. Her hips moved as though trying to take his fingers deeper.

Trev smacked her ass again. "No moving. If you steal an orgasm, we'll start your real punishment tonight. Do you understand?"

Beth stopped immediately. "Yes, Sir. It feels so good."

Fuck, yeah, it felt good. She clenched around his fingers. She would be so tight around his dick. He gently stretched her, scissoring his fingers deep inside. There was no question about it. Beth had loved that spanking. It had her ready to go. He didn't need to do anything else. He could force her to her knees. He could mount her and ride.

But there were things he had to do first.

"Show me how to work this thing." Bo held up the plug. If he was in, he was going all the way.

Chapter Fourteen

Mouse breathed a sigh of relief as Bo moved his hands away from her pussy. It was hard not to move back and try to take his fingers deeper. She'd been close, but she didn't want to disappoint Trev, and she definitely didn't want to start whatever punishment Trev had in mind for her tonight. Tonight was about finally being with Bo. She didn't want anything to screw that up.

Not even Bo himself.

She'd been nervous leaving the two of them alone as she'd undressed, but she knew nothing she could say would make Bo comfortable about the D/s stuff. He had to see it.

From the tent in his jeans, it looked like he was well on the way to accepting what she wanted.

Her legs ached, but she didn't move. It felt too fresh, too fragile, for her to do anything but pray this continued. As Trev and Bo talked, she tried to remain quiet, hoping they would form a bond. This wouldn't work if it was only about her. Trev and Bo needed to care about each other, too. It would be the only way to keep Trev.

Contrary to everything she'd said, she had zero intention of allowing Trev to waltz off at the end of this year. Something had changed inside of her, and it had everything to do with Trev McNamara. She'd loved Bo all of her life, but it had been a long, slow slide with Bo. With Trev, there was a fire inside. She wanted both, and she intended to make it happen. A year was a long time. Anything could happen.

"I never thought about anal sex," Bo said, his voice tentative.

She wanted to snort. Bo hadn't thought about anal sex? She was pretty sure Bo had done everything with everyone.

"So you're a newbie?" Trev's hands still smoothed over her. He hadn't stopped touching her once since he'd begun his "punishment." He kept her sensitized, on the edge.

"I guess I don't see the allure. But I'll give it a try," Bo allowed.

She felt Trev's chuckle all along her skin. "You don't see the allure? I can explain it to you. Part her cheeks. We need to make sure we get the lube all over her. Truly good anal sex should be easy. Easy in, easy out. Of course, it doesn't feel that way on your dick."

She groaned as she felt hands parting the cheeks of her ass. She bit into her bottom lip. She was a girl who'd never had sex until yesterday, and now the two most important men in her world were staring at her asshole.

She nearly jumped when she felt a touch.

"Don't you move, Beth. This is our time. Your time will come. For now, we want to play with your ass, and you're going to let us." Trev's dark voice sent a thrill through her.

Every time he used that deep, pitch-black voice on her, she wanted to tremble, and not from fear. There was something about his voice when it got smooth and hard all at the same time that sent her into a froth. Her whole body ached, and not in a bad way.

"It feels different than a pussy." Trev spoke as a single finger started to rim her. Dark sensations flooded her brain as she felt that digit circle her. It pressed slightly in. She was almost certain it was Trev. He'd played with her ass earlier. He'd seemed determined to take her there. "The heat is different. It's tighter. And you have to fight your way in. It grips your dick the whole time you're fucking it. In and out. It doesn't matter. This pretty asshole will hold you like a fist. You'll feel it on every inch of your cock."

Now there was another sensation. Something wet hit her, causing her to clench.

It earned her a smack. The hard pain of Trev's hand against her ass quickly morphed into warm pleasure.

"I might have to find that ginger root, darlin'. You will not keep me out of this ass. This ass is mine. It belongs to me. I'm going to fuck it because it belongs to me." Trev pressed his finger in.

She gripped the back of the settee, hoping she didn't damage it by digging her nails in. It was such a wicked sensation. It was pain and pleasure in a single package. That finger was ruthless, tunneling in and stretching her.

Trev continued his exploration. "If you aren't interested, I understand. You can take her pussy. I don't mind fucking this ass. It's a pretty ass. It will be my pleasure to take it over and over again."

"Fuck, no. I want to try it now. I never thought of it that way." Bo sounded outraged at the thought of only having access to her pussy. She bit back a laugh.

Suddenly the fingers retreated. "Then put that plug against her ass and work it in. Do it slowly. Just a little bit at a time until she accepts it. I'm going to clean up because our sweet sub is going to take care of me before you monopolize her time. I assume you want to fuck her."

"Hell, yeah. I might not ever stop."

"That's why I think I should take what I can," Trev said before she heard him walk away.

Something harder than a finger pressed against her.

"Don't tense, Mou...Beth. Don't tense up." Bo held the plug against her ass, but she could hear a strain in his voice.

"That's hard when someone's pressing plastic in your bottom."

"Don't make me laugh, Beth." The plug pushed in a bit and pulled out, gaining ground with each stroke. He fucked her with the plug. "Baby, I'm so happy to be here with you. I love you, Beth."

Her heart swelled. "I love you, too."

She'd said it to him before, but it was different now. It was real. This wasn't about friendship. It was about forever.

The plug slid home, and she sighed. Tension prickled along her spine. She was so damn...aware. Aware of her body—every inch, every nerve, seemed alive. Aware of her heart. She was so full of hope.

"Isn't that pretty?" Trev's voice returned. "I love the way that looks. Beth, love, remember what I said about clenching?"

"Yes, I'm not supposed to do it." She would have to keep Trev away from the herb section of the grocery store. He seemed to be far too creative.

"In this particular case, I would clench if I were you."

She gasped as he tugged her up and found that she did need to clench to keep the plug from sliding out. He leaned down and hooked an arm under her legs, hauling her against his chest. She looked up into his face. Trev McNamara was one of the most beautiful men she'd ever seen. He still belonged on the cover of a magazine. His pitch-black hair fell over his brow. Stark blue eyes looked back at her. He looked like a fallen angel.

Bo looked like he was still hanging on to heaven. Dark-blond hair and a perfect face stared down at her. He wasn't as tall as Trev, but his shoulders were broader.

"I think we should take this upstairs," Trev said. "She's made the bedroom somewhat comfortable."

That was damning her with faint praise if she'd ever heard it. "You should have seen it before I got hold of it. Let me tell you, Maudine didn't believe in comfort."

Trev started toward the stairs. She had to wrap her arms around his neck. She felt so small in his arms. She'd never felt as delicate and feminine as she did when Trev carried her around. She also had to work to keep the plug in her bottom.

"Don't lose that plug." Trev's slight grin told her that he knew she was struggling. Then his mouth flattened. "Bo worked hard to plug that pretty asshole."

He took the steps quickly, Bo following behind. "It wasn't hard. I could totally do it again."

"Not the point." Trev swept her into the bedroom. "Tell me something, love, have you ever had a man in your mouth?"

She shook her head. "No, Sir."

He placed her on the bed, the soft cotton of the comforter a pleasant coolness on her backside. "I'm honored to be your first, darlin'. Bo, help her to her hands and knees. She's going to suck me off, and then she's all yours. Feel free to play with her all you like. As long as she takes care of me, you can do whatever you want."

A long, slow smile slid across Bo's face. "There is something I've wanted to do for a while."

She had to take a deep breath. Bo's hand came out, and he helped move her into position. It wasn't easy. The plug didn't really want to stay in her backside. Bo's hand slid between her cheeks, pressing on the plug, making her nerves jump with the deep-seated sensation. She got to her hands and knees. Trev stood at the foot of the bed, his hands at the fly of his jeans. Slowly, he eased the zipper down and pushed the jeans off his hips along with the boxers he wore. His cock bobbed out, the thick, heavy organ already rock hard and slightly wet at the tip, as though the play they had performed had affected him as much as it had her. Trev's big hand stroked his cock from base to bulb, forcing a little bit of semen to squeeze from the tip. His cock was gorgeous. She wouldn't have imagined how beautiful a dick could be, but she adored Trev's. It was plum colored, and she could see the vein that ran across the stalk throbbing. His balls were tight and round, so heavy they swung with his every stroke.

"This shouldn't take long, girl. I swear, I've had sex every way, in every damn position, but one look from those big eyes of yours and I feel like I'm fifteen and trying this out for the first time." His free hand came out to pet her hair. "You make me crazy, Beth. You have no idea how much my life changed when you walked into Patty's."

Bo chuckled behind her, his hands sliding along her legs. He'd gotten out of his clothes, too. "I knew we should have tried the Burger Barn that day, but no, Beth had to have Patty's pie."

Trev's smile lit up her whole world. He didn't smile often, but when he did, it shone from more than his face. He looked younger, less burdened, when he smiled like that. "You should be thankful. I suspect if she hadn't needed a slice of Patty's pie, you wouldn't be about to taste her."

"High five to that, my brother," Bo said.

She gasped as he slid between her legs, and she felt the first long lick of his tongue.

"Oh, my god!" Her womb clenched. Everything that was feminine inside her seemed to light up at the slow caress of his velvety tongue.

"Fuck, you're sweet. I always knew you would taste so sweet." Bo's words reverberated against her pussy. She heard him groan before he pulled one side of her labia into his mouth and gave it a suckle.

Her arms shook. Bo was eating her pussy. That was what they called it. She'd imagined it would be horribly embarrassing, that she wouldn't be able to enjoy it because she would be worried about how she tasted, if she was smothering him.

That wasn't the way it was at all. She couldn't think of anything past how soft and warm that tongue felt on her pussy. And the sounds Bo was making didn't make her think she tasted bad. He was sucking at her flesh like it was the sweetest peach he'd ever tried, and he didn't want to miss a drop of her juice.

Trev brought her attention back to him. "It's my time, darlin'. If I don't get in your mouth soon, I'm afraid I might come all over my own stomach. We'll go easy this time. Tomorrow, not so much. Tomorrow, I'm going to tie you up, and you'll suck both of your Masters."

She felt Bo's soft shout of approval against her flesh as Trev pressed his cockhead to her lips.

"Open up for me. Take me in."

She opened her lips, Trev's cock slipping behind her teeth. He was big. Even the head of his monster cock stretched her jaw open. She let her tongue come out to taste him for the first time. Her senses were surrounded with his touch and taste and smell. He'd obviously had a shower out at the ranch. He smelled clean and masculine, all soap and musky man. His arousal pulsed on her tongue. It was salty and warm. She lapped at the slit on the head of his dick, begging for more of his taste.

"God, Bo, she's a fucking natural. Her mouth is incredibly hot. It's so fucking small." Trev's voice sounded strangled. His cock fucked into her mouth in short strokes. He held her head with one hand, his cock with the other. She'd only taken a quarter of him, and she was already struggling. But he tasted so good, she wouldn't even think about stopping.

Bo's tongue fucked her pussy, spearing her, making her gasp around Trev's cock.

"Oh, she liked that, man. Do it again." It seemed Trev could feel her pleasure.

A long stroke of Bo's tongue had her writhing. She fought the instinct to sit on Bo's face and force him to make her come. It wouldn't take much. She was close. Her whole pussy pulsed with the need to come, but she had to take care of Trev. Bo's tongue fucked her in long, languorous strokes, each one punctuated with a little teasing lick to her clitoris. It was enough to make her howl, but not send her over the edge. It was maddening. She tried to focus on the cock in her mouth.

"Baby, I'm close. Suck me hard." Trev's hand tightened in her hair, and he pulled her head forward, forcing her to take more of his hot length.

She groaned around the cock in her mouth. Trev's dick took up all the space. She tried to relax. She wanted more of him. She wanted to take all of him in and swallow as he hit the back of her throat, but he was too big, and she was far too inexperienced. She would have to practice. She would have to suck him over and over until she got it right. Mouse was a perfectionist, and she wanted to be the best oral sex Trev McNamara had ever had.

She gave up trying to get her tongue around him and sucked. She felt her cheeks hollow out as she suckled the dick in her mouth.

"Oh, god, girl, you're killing me. Relax. Let me fuck your mouth." Both of Trev's hands tangled in her hair. He held her hard and fucked deeply into her mouth. Bo never let up on the slow slide of his tongue. Between the hard, relentless cock in her mouth and the languid tongue in her pussy, she was pretty sure she was going to die if something didn't let up soon. All the while, Bo played with the plug in her ass, the jangled sensation reminding her that they claimed every inch of her body.

Then Trev groaned, the sound coming from deep in his chest, and warmth covered her tongue. His cock jerked, giving up in long jets of fluid. She swallowed down Trev's essence. Again, it was so different than she'd imagined, so much more intimate and

216

wonderful. She had a part of Trev inside her. She had a piece of him filling her. She wasn't afraid of his punishment tomorrow. She was looking forward to tasting Bo, to learning the difference between them.

Trev's thrusts slowed, and he popped out of her mouth. She kept sucking as he softened, not wanting to give up her treat. She licked him one last time before letting him go.

"That was amazing, darlin'. I couldn't have asked for more." Trev's breath sawed in and out of his chest. There was a fine sheen of sweat covering that gorgeously cut torso, each rippling muscle a testament to his athletic grace. "Bo, she's yours. Take her. Fuck her."

She was on her back in a heartbeat. Bo flipped her over and covered her body with his big one.

"You taste like honey, baby. You taste better than anything I've ever known." His blond hair was cut close to his head, giving him a stark look without his ever-present Stetson. He looked different than her happy-go-lucky friend. He pushed her legs apart with his own, making a place for himself. His cock pressed against her pussy, sliding in her juices. She could still see her arousal on his lips and chin. He didn't bother to clean up.

Sex was sweaty and dirty and so, so good.

"Bo, don't you slip inside her without a rubber." Trev stood at the foot of the bed, watching. He tossed Bo a foil packet.

She couldn't miss the fact that Trev's cock, flaccid and docile mere moments before, was already straining again. It rose from his perfectly trimmed nest of pubic hair, pointing toward her as though she were a magnet.

Bo cursed over her. He sat back on his heels and took the proffered condom. He ripped through the package while she finally took in his cock. God, he was practically Trev's twin. Trev might be a bit longer, but Bo's cock was so thick. She doubted she would be able to close her hand around it. Bo fisted his cock before slipping the condom over it and settling himself back between her legs.

He leaned over and covered her, their bodies touching. Chest to chest. Legs tangling. Feet mingling. His cock twitched against her pussy, moistening itself. He brushed his nipples to hers.

217

And then he leaned down and kissed her nose.

"I love you. You've been half my soul for so long I didn't even recognize it until you were gone. Forgive me." His words were a benediction across her skin, making her whole body sing with the recognition of her soul's mate. One of them anyway. Somehow, she'd gotten two. Somehow, she'd been blessed enough to have found two men to complete her.

"You're forgiven. I love you, too, Bo. Forgive me for hiding from it. You should know I won't let you take it back. You're mine now. I won't let you go. I'll fight for you. And you should tell Clarissa that I don't share my man. Either of them."

"I made a monster." Trev laughed over them, his cock in hand. "You should watch it, Bo."

But Bo was still serious. "Not another woman, Beth. I swear it."

Bo leaned over and kissed her long and hard. She could taste herself on his tongue and lips. His tongue tangled around hers as he thrust his cock up and inside her. He groaned into her mouth, but held himself still, allowing her to adjust to his girth.

She felt deliciously pinned by him. His weight held her down, pressing her into the bed.

"Fuck, I can feel the plug. She's so fucking tight." Bo came up for air and looked to Trev, as though trying to bring him into the experience.

"Imagine how it's going to feel when that's me in her ass." Trev's voice was pure seduction. "We'll fill her up. She's going to be packed with cock. We'll have to be damn careful because no matter what your sexual orientation, the feel of another cock sliding against yours is intensely stimulating. We'll make her scream before we fill her up."

"Damn, Trev, are you trying to make me go off?" He looked down at her. He flexed inside her, his face contorting with pleasure. "You feel so good, baby. Is this all right?"

No. It wasn't all right. He was moving far too slowly. It was pure torture. "More. I need more."

She pressed her hips up, and he slid in another inch or so. His pelvis ground down against her clit, sending shock waves through her nerves. "Please, Bo."

218

Bo eased himself up onto his hands. He thrust forward. "God, just a little more, Beth. Take me all the way to my balls."

Trev knelt down, his face close to hers. "Relax, you can take him." Trev kissed her earlobe. "You were made for your men."

She wrapped her legs around Bo's waist, hooking her ankles together, watching his face as he slid deeper into her body. He stretched her. He pushed inside like he was trying to fuse them together. She felt so close to him.

"You two look beautiful together." Trev's voice whispered in her ear.

Bo found a steady rhythm, his pelvis grinding down on hers. His cock slid in and out. She fought to keep him in. Every long, hard drag of his dick brought her closer to that glorious edge, and then she fell over it. The orgasm covered her body in pleasure. She barely recognized the cries that filled the room as her own.

Bo stiffened above her. His mouth opened, and he called her name while he came, not the one she'd been branded with as a child, but the name her parents had given her, the name she seemed to be reclaiming. He pumped into her over and over again, pleasure evident on his face and in his voice. He finally slumped down, his head nestling in her breasts.

"I love you, Beth."

And Beth Hobbes knew in that moment that she wouldn't think of herself as Mouse again. No little mouse ever claimed such men. No mouse could handle them. No mouse could keep them. But Bethany Hobbes would.

"I love you, too. I love you both." She put a hand out toward Trev. She knew it was a risk to tell Trev, but she was done being scared. She wouldn't hide her love. It filled her with confidence and warmth. Her love for these two men was proving transformative. If he didn't want it, then that was on Trev. She wouldn't take back a second of the time she'd spent with him.

Trev took her hand and put it to his heart. She could feel it beat under her fingers. "Thank you. I'll try to be worthy of it. You can't know what it means."

He didn't say it back, but her big bad Dom had some hang-ups of his own. Trev had been hurt, too. She could understand his reluctance to throw himself in. She wouldn't let it hold her back.

"Then make love to me."

"Are you sure? I don't want you sore." But she could see the longing on his face. His body was stiff with arousal. He didn't want to walk away.

Bo looked up, his forehead wrinkled in dismay. He nuzzled her breast with great affection. "Does that mean I have to move?"

He said it with a pout, but he rolled off her. He got to his knees and hauled her up.

"What are you doing?" She'd expected Trev to roll on top of her.

"I'm sharing." Bo pulled her back in his arms, his chest to her back. "I'm sharing with my friend."

Trev had another condom in his hand. His eyes seemed to water for a moment before he shook it off. He ran his hand through her pussy. "Look at that. It's all pouty and red."

Bo's hands found her breasts. He played with her nipples. "I think we should keep it that way. I think one of us should be on top of her all the time."

Trev moved to cover her. The sweat from his body mixed with Beth's and Bo's. She loved the fact that she was covered in them both. His cock found her pussy, and he pushed in. "Always. This sweet pussy needs a cock inside it all the time."

Beth wasn't sure about always, but it felt good now. Trev stretched her all over again. She was sore, but it seemed like just another sensation to be had. Trev pressed in relentlessly until she could feel his balls hit her ass. She was so aware of the plug filling her.

She leaned back as Trev started to thrust. Bo's arms were around her, his voice whispering to her. She was sexy. She was a goddess. He was never going to let her go.

Beth gave up and let her men take her over completely.

Chapter Fifteen

Trev came awake to the sound of a large truck rumbling into the driveway. He stiffened at the sound. It was Sunday. Who came out on a Sunday morning at what appeared to be the butt crack of dawn?

Beth turned in her sleep. Her hips were barely covered by the sheet. She looked gorgeous in repose, her mouth open slightly, hair caressing her cheek.

And Bo was nowhere to be found. Trev eased out of bed and looked out the window, careful not to let in too much light.

He and Bo had been rough on her the night before, taking her twice each. She'd fallen into an exhausted sleep hours before. She would need her rest for what he had planned later in the day. There was still punishment to be meted out. It was even more important now that Bo was involved. Though he'd shared equally with Bo the night before, he wanted the younger man to understand that he wouldn't allow either of them to be in danger.

He peeked out the window, praying the town of Deer Run hadn't decided to come at him as one big mob. He had a sudden image of the townsfolk with torches and pitchforks. He knew there were men out there who would move on rather than bring two people into their exile, but from what he could tell, this damn town hadn't given Beth or Bo anything good.

He was better for them. It was enough for him. He'd learned long ago that what other people thought didn't matter. Love mattered.

He'd thought the word again. Fuck, he was in so deep. He was pulling Beth and Bo around him like a security blanket, trying to cobble together a family. He couldn't stay here. He'd promised to buy into the Glen Ranch in Colorado. He couldn't go back on that. He didn't even want to. His life couldn't be here. He needed to do something with the money he had coming to him. He had to build a future with it, and he couldn't do that here.

But did he want a future that didn't include Beth? Did he want to cut Bo loose again?

The truck pulled to a stop in the circular drive. Trev could see Leo had been as good as his word. Both his and Bo's trucks were parked beside that ball of terror Beth drove. That car had to go. His knees ached at the thought of being inside it again.

Carlson Home Everything Store was emblazoned on the side of the truck. Bo bounced off the porch. There was a light happiness in his step that had been missing before. He couldn't hear what Bo was saying, but he was speaking to the driver animatedly.

Another vehicle pulled up. This was one Trev didn't want to see. He quickly donned his jeans and threw a T-shirt over his head.

He made it to the front porch in time to watch his brother-in-law pull up in the Escalade that looked ridiculously out of place in a small town. Bryce opened the door and slid out. His face was puffy, his nose taped from the fight of the previous night.

"You son of a bitch. You caused this. This is all your fault. If you think for a second I'm going to sit back and take this, you're wrong, Trev." Bryce stalked toward him.

Bo hopped down from the back of the truck where he'd been helping the driver unload what looked like building materials. There were long boxes of flooring, cans of paint, and a multitude of tools in the back of the truck.

"What's going on?" Bo asked, looking between the two men.

"I'm not sure. Bryce, I didn't lay a hand on you." Trev had been damn careful to not touch his sister's husband. The last thing she needed was for Bryce to get angry.

"No, you didn't. Your fucking friend did, though. You know, that asshole who keeps sniffing around my wife? He says he slipped. Well, my lawyers are about to slip and sue the fuck out of him." Bryce touched his nose as if to make sure it was still there. "I'm not talking about the fight. I'm talking about you turning down Marty. You can't turn him down. You need to get the fuck out of this town. You're ruining your sister's life."

His stomach did a turn. He'd wrecked Shelley's life before. She'd married this asshole because he hadn't been around to stop it. If he'd been half the big brother she deserved, he would have been there to meet Bryce at the door and scared his ass off. He would have run a background check and known the man down to his last parking ticket.

Actually, that still wasn't a bad idea. Liam was still in town the last he'd heard. What could it hurt to have him run a check? As far as he knew no one had checked Bryce's background.

"He's not going to LA." Bo's chest had puffed out as if he were ready for his third throwdown in as many days. Trev was going to have to work on Bo's lamentable habit of beating the shit out of people.

"No, I'm not," Trev assured him, putting a hand on his shoulder.

Bryce's mouth dropped open. "Tell me you're not fucking him, too. Mouse Hobbes is bad enough. You can't have gone queer on me, too. You shouldn't be around that little shit anyway. Do you know what his brother's into?"

Trev's fist tightened. He could practically feel Bo's face go up in flames.

"His brother is one of the reasons this county still has a population attached to it. If the O'Malley Ranch picked up its business and left town, you wouldn't have a damn person to sell a house to. And if you call Beth by that name again, I won't hold back. I love my sister, but Beth belongs to me. I won't allow anyone to insult her. And I'm the only one who gets to call Bo a little shit."

Bo actually laughed. "Nah, Aidan does it all the time. Hey, do you think that Marty guy is going to sue me? Everybody else is getting sued. It's only fair."

Yep, Bo was going to keep him on his toes. "Let's hope not, buddy. Why don't you finish up with whatever you were doing? Is this Beth's order? I thought she lost the loan."

Bo's face lit up. "I stole her notepad. She had all the things she was going to order on it. I figured I could loan her the money."

Yes, he could see Bo doing that. He needed a keeper. "Do you have any left? After what you're loaning me and Beth?"

"A couple hundred thousand."

He said it like it didn't matter. How had Trev managed to find the only two people in the world who didn't give a shit about money or fame? Luck. Cosmic good luck. "She's going to appreciate this."

Bo's hand went to his back. "And I ordered a California king-size bed this morning. I wound up on the floor. I think that bed up there is at least fifty years old."

And he bet it had seen more action in a twenty-four-hour period than all the days before it combined. "Yeah, I'll be grateful for that."

Bo disappeared into the truck again.

"You're going to ruin all of their lives, you know. People are already talking." Bryce, bitterness etched on his features, watched Bo and the driver haul out a huge box.

"Let 'em talk." They'd talked before Trev came back to town. They would talk after. He wasn't going to let gossip ruin his happiness.

"And everyone knows about what happened yesterday. You pissed off a bunch of people in this town. You're the most hated man in the county. Do you think that kid will be the last one to come after you? How many people do you have to hurt before you realize you aren't wanted here?"

He felt his face fall. Would someone really come after Beth again? It seemed incomprehensible that someone wanted to hurt him physically over a couple of articles. He'd gotten the cold shoulder from people, but no one had tried violence. He could handle his car getting trashed. He had insurance, and people would stop when they realized he wasn't going anywhere.

Why would someone break in? It didn't make a lick of sense now that he thought about it.

Bryce kept talking. "And you should take those two with you.

Yeah. That would be for the best. Why can't you go back to Dallas and take your playmates along for the ride? Your new girlfriend isn't going to keep her clients for long once they find out she's sleeping with two men. No one is going to want a pervert accountant."

He shrugged. From what he could tell, Beth didn't really like her job. She preferred to work for Lexi, though that wasn't full time yet. In the meantime, he had the feeling moneybags wouldn't mind taking care of her. Once Trev came into his cash, he would work to take care of them all.

Was he really thinking that far ahead? He had to stop that. He didn't know what was going to happen past tomorrow, much less a year from now. He had to keep his head in the now or he could drown. And the now unfortunately involved his brother-in-law.

"You don't care at all, do you?" Bryce's forehead was ruffled in consternation.

And Bryce cared too much. "I'm not going anywhere. And if my sister wanted me gone, she would have been here herself. So that begs the question, why the hell do you want me out of town so badly?"

"I told you." Bryce backed up toward the door of his SUV. "You're bad for business. I don't want to be painted with the same brush as you. You have this town in an uproar."

Did he? It hadn't seemed so bad. He hadn't been terribly surprised by his welcome, but Bryce was moving into hyperbole. "It's going to settle down. Something else will come up, and the town will move on to the next scandal."

"I can see you don't care. You don't care about anything, obviously." Bryce opened the door to the SUV. "Whatever happens, know it's all your fault."

He felt his eyes narrow. That sounded like a threat.

Bryce drove away, his tires squealing when they hit the pavement.

"Your brother-in-law is an asshole. You know he cheats like crazy, right? He's got women going in and out of that office of his at all hours of the night." Bo walked up carrying a box.

He'd heard the rumor. Why was his sister putting up with this?

And why was Bryce so blatant? "How do you know about the women?"

Bo shrugged. "Everyone knows. I even heard Clarissa and her gang go to see him every now and then. I don't know why. It's not like he's attractive or anything. I asked her about it once, but she told me to mind my own business."

Oh, but this was his business. "I think it's about time we checked on my dear brother-in-law. I've only met him a couple of times, you know. I wasn't even at Shelley's wedding. After I got fired, Bryce treated me like a leper."

"Don't listen to him. He's not worth your time. Now, where do you want this? I know Beth doesn't have one, and it seems to be your vice now."

Thoughts of his brother-in-law fled in place of a deep and abiding affection for the man in front of him. "You got me a coffeemaker. Wait. You had to have ordered that yesterday. Didn't you hate me yesterday?"

"Sure, but I loved Beth. I figured I could at least try to make friends with you. I didn't want to lose her. Even if she couldn't love me back. It was important to stay in her life, you know. So I thought I would give this as a sort of peace offering. Now I'm glad I did it because you seem cranky without caffeine."

Bo bounced past him. Trev turned and saw Beth walk out. She'd put on PJ pants and a big T-shirt. Her eyes were wide as she looked around her. He couldn't hear what they said, but Beth launched herself into Bo's arms.

Trev glanced down the road where Bryce's SUV had left dust in its wake.

What the hell was that man hiding? Trev intended to find out.

* * * *

Beth looked at the boxes strewn across the living room, a sense of excitement building. It was all here. All her fixtures, the flooring she'd picked out, the paint she'd selected, the new lights. Everything. She glanced up at Bo, who was fiddling with the new coffeemaker.

"Are you sure?"

He turned slightly. He looked scrumptious in nothing but low-slung jeans and his boots. "I'm sure. I wasn't doing anything with the money. Besides, I'm just paying you back. Remember how you used to loan me lunch money?"

"Bo, that was like two dollars and twenty-five cents. This is fifty thousand dollars' worth of supplies."

He shrugged as he pushed the button that started the coffeemaker. "I never paid you back. Consider it interest."

"Bo," she started. The last thing she wanted was for him to think he had to buy his way into a relationship with her. "I love you. You don't have to do this."

He turned. "Are we in this together or not? I want to be a partner. I get that this body is enough to make any woman salivate, but I'm more than a hunk of a gorgeous man."

She couldn't help her smile. He always made her laugh. And now she didn't have to stop herself from doing what she'd always wanted to do when she was with him. She walked straight into his arms. "We're in this together. And I'll take the interest. You'll see. This house is going to be beautiful when I'm done."

"At least you got rid of that chandelier thing. It gave me the creeps. And can we get rid of the room with all the heads?"

The office was a monstrous altar to the Bellows family's love of hunting small woodland creatures and stuffing them. "Yes, that's going to go. I'm knocking down one of the walls to make a breakfast nook. It's going to be light and airy."

She was so excited she could hardly stand to wait. The first thing she intended to do was to move that antler chandelier to the curb. She went up on her toes and kissed his mouth before walking over to where Trev had stashed the fixture. She shook her head. It had probably been too heavy for the ceiling. She would more than likely need the boys to carry it out. She reached out and tested it. It was remarkably light.

She lifted it. It was heavy, but not as heavy as she'd expected. She managed to heft it up. What had caused that chandelier to fall if not sheer gravity?

"What's going on? You shouldn't be lifting that." Bo walked

227

into the dining room, putting down the mug of coffee he was carrying.

"It's not bad." She set it down and looked for the fixture that had held it to the ceiling. It was still attached to the base. She'd thought it would be old and ragged, but the fixture was shiny and well kept. The screws were in near-perfect condition.

Why had it fallen?

She walked into the living room and stared up at the hole in the ceiling. She couldn't see through to the second floor, and there was surprisingly little damage to the ceiling around it. She would have expected more raggedness to the spot, but it was almost as though the thing had simply fallen on its own.

Or had it had help?

She needed to get a closer look. She needed to get up there and feel the wood under her hand.

"Is everything okay?" Bo asked.

She gave him a sunny smile before crossing to the kitchen again. "Absolutely. Though I'm going to need to find a ladder."

She opened the junk drawer and found the key to the garage. She was pretty sure she would find what she needed there.

She walked back into the living room and noticed Trev coming in from the porch. The front door opened. Beth felt a deep sense of satisfaction that it made no sound. She'd done a very good job with that door. Trev strode in. His hair was still mussed from the night before. There was a pained expression on his face.

"He needs coffee," Bo said, putting the mug in her hand and giving her backside a little pat. "You should go and feed the beast. I think that should be your job."

She grinned up at Bo, the mug warm in her hand. "Will do."

She walked to Trev, whose whole face changed as he caught the scent of the coffee.

"Thank god." He sniffed it before downing a long swallow. "Good morning."

She kissed him, brushing her lips against his. "Good morning to you, too. Enjoy your coffee. I'll be right back."

She slipped past him and out of the front door. The morning was beautiful, dewy and warm. She didn't bother with shoes, letting her feet sink into the thick grass. She turned and looked back at the house. A deep sense of satisfaction settled in her chest.

"Well, don't you look like the cat who swallowed the canary."

Beth closed her eyes before turning to face Clarissa. It was Grand Central Station at the Bellows place today. No. It was the Hobbes place. It was hers. And she was done allowing women like Clarissa to intimidate her.

Clarissa was dressed in shorts and a tank top. It was obvious she'd been jogging. Clarissa's place was roughly a mile down the road. She probably jogged this way every day. Beth decided to go with friendly first.

"Good morning, neighbor."

Clarissa's eyes narrowed. "I thought you were going to sell this place."

"Who told you that?" She hadn't mentioned anything about this place to anyone outside of Trev and Bo and the gang out at O'Malley Ranch. Beth seriously doubted that Lexi had been gossiping with Clarissa.

Clarissa simply smiled. "Everyone knows you got turned down for that loan."

"Really? Everyone?" Since when did her banking practices become everyone's business? "There are other ways to get money. I took a loan from a friend."

Clarissa's eyes narrowed. "I bet I know how you got it. So Trev has some cash hidden away?"

"No. Bo loaned me the money."

Red flushed along Clarissa's skin. If she'd thought for one moment that Clarissa had real feelings for Bo, she would have kept her mouth closed, but Bo didn't mean anything to Clarissa but another man in her back pocket.

"Bo and I are together now, and not just as friends. He's my boyfriend. I would thank you for respecting that," she said.

She heard footsteps on the porch and turned to see both of her men step out. Trev leaned against the front post while Bo simply stared at Clarissa.

Beth fought not to blush. "And Trev's mine, too. You should stay away from him as well."

229

Clarissa's fists clenched. "I'm going to talk to every single client you have. No one is going to want you doing their taxes anymore. You can't expect that you'll have a job once everyone knows what a whore you've become. How are you going to pay Bo back then? Oh, I guess he's getting what he wants out of you. It's going to take a lot of blow jobs to get rid of that debt."

Trev straightened up. Bo opened his mouth, but Trev put a hand out. She got the message. They were behind her, but this was her fight. And she had a decision to make. She could play it safe and hide, or she could embrace the woman she was becoming.

"Somehow I think Bo will be kind when it comes to paying him back. And I have it on the highest authority that my blow jobs are worth a lot of money." She managed to get through it without laughing, but it was right there. There was a strange joy in telling off this woman who had dealt out such misery. "I think I can safely quit doing people's taxes and helping with their accounting and concentrate on fixing my house."

"Don't forget the blow jobs," Bo called out.

"And blow jobs. I need time to give a whole lot of blow jobs."

Trev shook his head but was silent as he took another long swallow of coffee.

Clarissa leaned in, her voice tight with anger. "After I get through with you, your name won't be worth a thing in this town, Mouse."

"My name has never been worth anything. And it's not Mouse. My name is Beth, so when you start telling everyone what a slut I am when I've had two men in my whole life, you get it right. You tell everyone that Beth Hobbes is a whore and proud of it. You're the pathetic one, Clarissa. You're the one who tosses away men like they were used napkins. I love them. I won't give them up. You can't scare me away. You can't shame me into it. Consider me an immovable object and get on with your own life. I don't care what anyone thinks. That's what you never understood about me. I never cared. I never tried to fit in. I was patient and waited until the right men came along. Now go back to your workout. You're going to need it."

Beth turned before Clarissa could say a single nasty word. She nodded at her men. "I'm going out to the garage to look for a ladder. I'll be right back."

She walked away, her heart pounding. She was really going to do it. There was no way to keep her clients. Some of them might not care, but she doubted the pastor of the Baptist church would allow her to do their monthly bookkeeping after he heard about her crazy threesome. And the principal of the school wouldn't want it known that his accountant paid back loans with blow jobs. She felt her face flush. She'd actually said that.

It didn't matter. Bo would take care of her. She approached the garage. She should shy away from the idea of being supported financially, but what was the use in being a couple—or a threesome—if they didn't depend on each other? She was confident that she could bring this house back to life. She could make it beautiful again, and it would pay out. She would be able to pay Bo back and have some money left over for her next project.

And the citizens of Deer Run could go hang if they didn't like it.

She stopped and stared at the door to the garage. It was a detached garage. She'd only been in it once before. It had been stuffed to the point that she'd known she couldn't get a car in there. All three of their cars were parked in the circular drive. At the time, she'd simply relocked the garage and promised to put cleaning it out on her never-ending list of things to do.

But it looked like someone had decided to move that project up a bit.

The lock that had been on the door lay on the ground next to the garage. Someone had cut it and tossed it aside. She reached down and grasped the handle, afraid of what she would see. The door squealed in protest as she opened it.

The garage was in shambles. The neat piles of boxes and magazines and old newspapers had been overturned and stomped on. It was utter chaos, as though the people who had trashed the place hadn't been sure of what they were doing so they had touched every single item in the place.

What the hell was going on?

"Wow, Maudine was kind of a slob." Bo stood behind her.

But she hadn't been. Maudine's house might have been stuffed to the gills, but there had been a pattern to it. Everything had been neatly stacked.

Trev stood beside him, coffee mug in hand. "Someone's looking for something, and they don't care how they find it. I think we were wrong that first night, darlin'. I think someone was in this house."

Goose bumps raced along her arm. "What on earth would I have that someone would want?"

"Maybe it's not about what you have," Bo said. "Maybe it's about Maudine."

"Maudine was a shut-in. She rarely went out, and when she did, she was nasty to everyone. She didn't have a single friend."

"She had a relative," Bo supplied. "Barry Bellows was her nephew, but I don't think they were terribly close."

"But Barry was close to Bryce. Barry was Bryce's partner. Fuck. Who was your loan officer?" Trev reached out and grabbed her hand, squeezing it reassuringly.

"Kevin Jones."

Bo frowned. "I saw Kevin having dinner with Bryce not two days ago. Bryce sends all his clients to Kevin for loans."

"I'm seeing a pattern here," Trev said. "But I don't know what to make of it. Does Bryce have any connection to that kid who took a shot at Beth?"

Beth shook her head. "That kid's name is Austin Hall. I talked to the sheriff about him when they brought him in. He's been in and out of trouble, mostly drugs. I heard someone say that his father deals meth and possibly some other stuff. The sheriff thinks Austin is afraid of his father."

"Everyone knows where to go for drugs in this town. Nelson Hall cooks meth, but he changes the place so often the cops out here gave up on finding him. But none of that explains why he would send his son in here to shoot at Beth." Bo reached down and picked up a box. It looked like it held old towels. Maudine hadn't been big on throwing anything out. "And what was he looking for?"

"And what's his connection to my brother-in-law?" Trev's face had taken on a stony look.

"Bryce wanted this place. It was only luck that the shelter put it up for auction while he was out of town." She'd always known she'd lucked out. Bryce would have outbid her in a heartbeat.

"I think it's time I had a talk with my sister. And put a couple of feelers out on my brother-in-law." Trev shook his head as he looked at the mess. "I think we can kill a couple of birds with one stone."

"Which birds are you planning on killing?" Bo asked, setting the box down. "Because it's Sunday, and the Cowboys are playing. Beth's TV here is crap. I thought we could go out to the ranch. Lexi makes Sunday dinner. It's the only time she cooks. I would hate to miss it."

A sadistic grin lit Trev's face. "I think the ranch suits my purposes. I believe we owe our sub some punishment. Oh, and look, someone was nice enough to leave us some rope."

Trev pulled a carefully wound length of rope from his back pocket. The rope was fairly thin, and there looked to be a lot of it.

"No one left that." She was starting to wonder how uncomfortable this punishment would be.

Trev grinned, but it was a predatory thing. "No. I brought that myself. This rope is special. It's made from jute. Have you ever heard the term *'hishi karada?'*"

Just the way he said the word made her breathless. Bo moved out of the garage and closed it. The mystery would wait for a while.

"No. What does it mean?" Beth asked.

"It means I get to dress you today, darlin'."

Chapter Sixteen

"You look really pretty, Beth." Bo couldn't help but look into the backseat of his cab as they turned down the road that led to the ranch.

Beth frowned at him, her eyes narrowing. "I look naked."

"Yeah, that's what I meant."

Trev snorted as he drove. Though it was Bo's car, Trev had insisted on driving. *Control freak.* He was getting used to it. And it meant he could look at Beth, who lay across the back bench.

"You don't like the dress I made for you?" Trev asked.

The dress Trev had "made" for Beth consisted of nothing beyond the jute rope he'd pulled from his kit. Trev had ordered Beth back inside the house where she'd taken off her clothes and submitted to him. He'd watched as Trev wound the rope around her body. Beth's hands were tied in front of her body, the rope twisting in a pattern that formed an odd dress. He'd gotten hard as a rock watching the rope wind around her breasts, forcing them to thrust out. The rope wound all the way down her body, holding her legs together. And the rope descended into the valley of her sex, splitting her pussy and the cheeks of her ass.

Beth hadn't been able to walk by the time Trev was done. She'd been thoroughly trussed up like a pretty sex toy waiting for her

Masters' use. She'd knelt on the ground, obviously waiting for the sex to begin, but Trev was way kinkier than that. The minute he was done with his elaborate ties, he'd announced it was time to head out to the ranch. And he'd picked Beth up and loaded her in the truck, naked breasts and all.

"What if we get pulled over?" Beth asked.

"You're in a seat belt, darlin'." Trev seemed to be in a much happier mood now that he'd had some caffeine and gotten his morning bondage session in.

Bo felt good, too. "Two in fact."

"And whoever pulls us over isn't going to care that I'm naked?"

He had an answer for that, too. "If we get pulled over, I'll throw this blanket over you. It's okay. I use it on horses."

"Nice, Bo," Beth replied, sarcasm dripping.

Trev chuckled. "Maybe we should try pony play. I think she would look good with a tail."

"I know what that is, Trevor McNamara. I am not letting you shove a horsetail in my backside. Consider that a hard limit."

Bo couldn't help but laugh. She sounded so prim and proper for a woman wearing a rope dress. The whole time Trev had been tying her up, he'd explained Shibari to Bo. It was Japanese rope bondage. Naturally, Leo taught a class.

Trev slapped lightly at the steering wheel. "I blame Lexi for that. Imagine. I find that most elusive of prey, the natural submissive. I manage to take her down, to make her mine, and Lexi writes a book that explains all the ways for a sub to manipulate her Dom."

"A contract isn't manipulation," Beth retorted. "And shouldn't we talk about this? Shouldn't we talk about whether or not I want my vajayjay on display?"

Trev turned to him. "Bo, there's a ball gag in my bag."

"I'll be quiet," Beth said quickly.

"I think I have something I could gag her with," Bo offered. His dick had been hard as a rock ever since she'd taken her clothes off.

"We'll get to that." Trev turned up the long driveway.

The house came into view. Bo stared at it. Sometimes he hated that house. There was a reason he'd moved into one of the smaller houses on the ranch the minute he'd been able to. That house held a lot of bad memories.

"We're going to talk about it, you know." Trev was looking at him, his face set in a serious expression.

Bo didn't say a word, merely watched as his brother stepped out on the porch, Lucas at his side. Trev had to park behind a Volvo. Ike, Aidan's big mutt, was trotting across the yard. "Hey, isn't that your sister's car?"

Trev nodded. "Yes, I want to talk to her. I thought it best we did it away from her husband."

Aidan waved as he stepped down from the porch. Bo took a minute. His brother loved him. He knew that, but he'd never shared what had happened that night with anyone but Beth. Was he ready to open up to Trev? Hell, was he ready to trust Trev? He was happy with where they were, just starting to wrap his mind around it, but to tell him what had happened was to show Trev a piece of his soul he wasn't sure he wanted to share.

Lucas looked into the back of the truck. "Ah, it's going to be one of those days. I look forward to them."

"Oh, my god. I'll take the blanket now. I don't care if it smells like a horse." Beth's whole body had turned a bright shade of pink the minute she'd realized Aidan and Lucas could see her.

Trev got out and quickly moved to open the back door. "No, you won't. And think carefully before you use your safe word. This is the lifestyle, darlin'. You're not going to shock anyone here. What do Doms do with their pretty subs in Lexi's books?"

Bo was going to have to read Lexi's books. Apparently they were a how-to manual of some kind. *BDSM for Dummies.* He hopped out of the cab and went to stand by Trev.

"They show them off," Beth replied.

Trev turned his eyes to Bo. "Is this not the prettiest sub you've ever seen?"

Bo watched Beth relax a little. She was getting turned on, and more than that, she was gaining confidence. She never would have handled Clarissa the way she had this morning without Trev. Bo had wanted to save her, but Trev had explained that part of her training was to learn to stick up for herself. She wasn't a fragile flower. She was an amazing woman, and hell, yeah, he wanted to show her off.

He smiled down at her. "You're gorgeous, baby. And I really do want to watch that football game. Seriously, if you had wanted to stay home, you would have fixed the satellite dish first, but no, you had to make the bedroom all pretty."

Trev hauled her out of the cab like a piece of luggage. "Come on, sweet thing. Aidan and Lucas aren't going to blush."

"No, I'm already thinking about how to get Lexi to turn her bratty mouth on me so I can truss her up, too." If Aidan was shocked by the fact that Bo had come over for Sunday dinner with a woman dressed only in some rope, he didn't show it.

"She's being punished for far more than a bratty mouth." Trev had her over his shoulder, her gorgeous ass in the air. The rope split her cheeks like a thong.

"She lied and didn't let us protect her," Bo explained. Just thinking about it made him angry all over again.

"I tried to explain that." Beth wiggled on Trev's shoulder.

Without really thinking about it, Bo reached out and smacked her ass. "There's no explanation for letting some asshole shoot at you and not even calling out my name."

Aidan's eyes got wide. He turned to Trev. "I thought you were going to take him as a sub."

Trev shook his head. "He's not really a sub. He's Bo. He's different. And I'll train him the way I think he needs to be trained. I do not expect, nor welcome, your interference. This is between me and Bo."

Aidan took a step back. "He's my brother."

"And he's my partner. I don't give you advice on how to deal with Lucas."

"I'm fine, Aidan." The last thing he wanted was for Trev and Aidan to throw down. He could smell dinner, and the game was about to start. And he really wanted to get to the part of Beth's punishment where he got to shove his cock into her mouth. "I'm happy. Stay out of it."

Lucas put a hand on Aidan's shoulder. "Careful what you wish for. Your brother already seems different. Now, let's head inside. Trev, your sister is waiting on you. She and Leo have been sniping at each other since she walked in the door. It's funny."

"Can I get into the barn?" Trev asked. "She's got at least four hours of this."

"Four hours?" Beth practically shouted.

Trev smacked her ass now. "I can make it more. It's only fair. You shaved a good year off Bo's life."

"Yep." He could still remember the terror he'd felt. It had only been matched by that night his father had asked him to come into his office. Bo shoved the memory aside. "I think four hours is fair."

"Traitor." Beth's face was deliciously red, and her lips pouted.

Bo gave her a wink that had her huffing as Trev walked her toward the barn.

Leo stepped out of the house, his face red and his fists clenched. He looked like a man ready to hit something, but his expression eased quickly into the placid look he normally wore. "That is an excellent tortoiseshell design. You've been practicing. Ah, and you're obviously an indulgent Master. You've tied that perfectly. She's going to enjoy that."

"I'm not enjoying it now," Beth complained.

Bo smacked her ass again. It was actually kind of fun.

Leo reached out and patted Bo's back. "Ah, Bo, exploring your inner Master. Very nice. You wanted to talk to me, Trev? You need to talk fast because I'm heading back to Dallas as soon as I can. It's been pointed out to me that I'm only causing trouble here."

Bo watched Trev's face tighten. He shifted Beth off his shoulder and passed her to Bo. She was a sweet handful, and her breasts poked out of their bindings like flowers waiting to be plucked.

Trev passed him a small bag. Bo was pretty sure he knew what was in it. "You'll know what to do with that. Settle her down in the barn. I believe Aidan has a place for her to rest while she thinks about what to do the next time someone shoots at her."

Bo knew his way to the barn.

"Are you sure he's treating you right?" Aidan asked, walking behind him.

"It's fine. What, did you talk to him or something?" Bo didn't like that thought.

"I asked him to consider taking you as his sub."

Bo felt his eyes roll. "Thank god he didn't listen. I'm not a sub. I'm really not. Trev offered to share Beth with me, not spank my ass when I'm bad. Though I suspect he would kick it. And he might kick yours if you keep putting your nose in our business. Seriously. I will help him."

Aidan stopped and allowed Bo to walk into the barn on his own.

Bo placed her gently on the long cot Aidan affectionately referred to as the rack. He rolled her to her side. A deep sense of love rushed across him. He was getting used to the crazy lifestyle Beth wanted. "You comfortable?"

Her lips curled up. "As comfortable as I can be while tied up fifteen different ways. Kiss me and I'll feel better."

He could do that. He leaned over and kissed her, brushing his lips against hers, reveling in her softness. He let his hands find her breasts. "I think you're beautiful like this. I'm beginning to understand why this lifestyle is so tempting. It's the only time I get to be in charge of anything."

He pulled the bag up and opened it, letting her see the anal plug and lube Trev had sent.

Beth groaned. "Seriously?"

"Maybe next time, you'll mention someone's trying to kill you." He rolled her over and pushed her knees up. Trev knew what he was doing. She was perfectly placed for what he needed to do. He lubed up the plug and pushed the rope over so he could get to her asshole. "Damn, that is pretty."

"I thought you didn't like anal sex."

Bo placed the plug's tip to her asshole. "I changed my mind. I want to fuck you every way I can. I want to try everything. I think I was hesitant before because I didn't love those other women. I want it all now. I want it because I can trust you. You won't hold anything against me."

"Never, Bo." She groaned as he started to fuck her with the plug. "Oh, god. Oh. Oh. Oh."

And Bo finally got what Leo had meant when he'd praised Trev for being a kind Master. The rope dress he'd made hit Beth's clitoris any time he touched her backside. Plugging Beth was going to prove to be a pleasurable punishment. Maybe Trev hadn't meant for that to happen, but he doubted it. Trev wasn't some sadist who only got pleasure from another's pain. Trev was a Dom because he needed it. Because he was out of control without it.

Maybe Bo needed it, too. Aidan was wrong. He didn't want to be someone's sub. He didn't want to be taken care of. But he did want this.

He pressed the plug in as Beth cried out. Her legs twitched, but there was nowhere for her to go. She was caught.

He let the rope slide back into place. "Can you do that on your own?"

She wiggled, and the glaze that came across her eyes told Bo yes. "Do you think Trev knows?"

"I think he knows. Now behave. I'll see if I can't get Trev to relax your punishment a little." He'd like to have her on his lap while he watched the game. He and Trev could pass her back and forth.

The door to the barn came open, and Lexi O'Malley entered, her hands full of her laptop and a glass with a straw. Beth gasped.

"Aidan told me what was happening. Oh, he tied that well. Aidan's not so good with rope. I bet that knot feels really good."

Beth's whole skin flushed.

"Do you want a blanket?" Trev hadn't given him specific instructions.

Lexi looked between Bo and Beth. "Oh, she's worried about being naked? Seriously? I could get naked, too. And I bet she got plugged. Yeah, I'm not going to join in on that one. I get that enough on my own, but I thought, while you're all tied up and stuff, we could work. I need to brainstorm the end game of this book. I've been talking to Serena about it and she pointed out a few problems. Hang on. I'll get her on the line."

Serena Brooks was an author friend of Lexi's. They'd bonded over having the same agent and the fact that they were both living the ménage lifestyles they wrote about. Serena had recently become Serena Dean-Miles when she'd married two of McKay-Taggart's employees.

"Hey, Serena," Lexi said into her phone. "I know you're

240

packing for London, but I've got Beth here. You know, Mouse. Well, she's Beth now."

"Thank god someone stopped calling her that silly nickname," a feminine voice said over the line.

"Yeah, she's found a superhot ex-football player Dom and my brother-in-law is topping her now, too," Lexi explained. "They've got her tied up and plugged right in the middle of my barn. I thought it would give us some time to go over that last scene you critiqued for me."

"She's tied up in a barn," Serena mused. "Beth, can you describe that to me. I'd like to take notes."

Beth's eyes swung up at Bo.

"Your punishment is complete, baby." Bo couldn't help but smile as he stepped away.

Lexi was already talking about external plots and wrapping up something with secondary characters as Bo stepped outside. He could still hear Lexi talking.

It wasn't the same place. It wasn't the home where his father had pulled a gun on him and let fate make the decision whether he lived or died. Everything had changed. His father was dead. Time had moved on. He'd survived, and his father hadn't managed to force him and his brother to hate each other.

He was alive, and he was in love.

Bo stepped toward the house. For the first time in years, there was nothing in his heart but hope.

* * * *

"So you started asking around about Bryce?" Trev asked Liam O'Donnell the question, hating the look in Leo's eyes as he watched. Despite the fact that Leo's face was perfectly placid, there was no way to mistake the hollow look in Leo's eyes. What had his sister said to put that look on his mentor's face?

O'Donnell had joined them after Bo had taken Beth off to the barn. The Irishman had a beer in his hand and a packed duffel at his side. "I didn't ask around. Certainly not here. I'm a stranger. I could put on my Midwestern accent and it wouldn't make a difference.

They know I'm staying out at the O'Malley Ranch. They won't talk to me."

He was no help. "What exactly do you plan to do then?"

"I called a friend of mine last night after our unfortunate incarceration. Usually I would call Adam, but he leaves for London tomorrow. You've met Julian's in-house security, I assume?" Liam leaned against the front porch railing. He continued when Trev nodded. "Chase sent me a report this morning. I can give it to you. Bryce's financials are interesting in that they show a very middle-income man. Yet he paid cash for his Escalade. That car was eighty thousand dollars. Now, Shelley's financials are a bit different."

"You ran my sister's financials?" Trev hadn't expected that, and from the way Leo's jaw had tightened, he wasn't happy about it either.

Leo's eyes went cold. "Your sister has an account in the Caymans. Chase can't crack into it. Do you know what kind of security Chase can't crack?"

Liam grinned. "He's wanted by several foreign governments for hacking. The only reason the US hasn't arrested him is his work with the CIA. Big Tag likes the hell out of him but mostly that's because Chase is OCD and Big Tag is an asshole who likes to play pranks."

Chase Michaels, along with his twin brother Ben, was The Club's resident private investigator. The two Doms were known for being able to ferret out information that no one else could find. They'd been selected and trained by McKay-Taggart. "Why would my sister have a Cayman account?"

"Because she's laundering his money," Leo said under his breath.

"That's my assessment, too." Li took a long swig from his beer can.

What the hell was going on? Trev simply couldn't believe his sister would do anything illegal. "Bryce is a real estate agent. Why the hell does he have dirty money?"

Leo shrugged. "No idea. It could come from any number of things. He could be embezzling. He could be evading taxes. I don't know."

"Here's what I do know," Leo began. "Bryce has spent a lot of time traveling. I just asked Shelley about his travel habits. She claims to only know about some trips to Austin for conferences and training seminars. Either she doesn't know or she's not willing to tell me the truth."

Liam took over, speaking in more academic tones than Trev had heard him use. "According to his flight records, he's been to Washington D.C. and Mexico City. We can't track him once he hits Mexico City. He could have gotten anywhere from there. His passport doesn't show anything beyond Mexico, but he was gone for weeks at a time."

"How is Shelley involved?" What had his sister been through with this guy? And what was Bryce's angle?

The stony expression was back on Leo's face. "I don't know. She claims she doesn't know about any of it. I've been told in no uncertain terms to stay out of her business. I'm taking Li to Dallas to catch his flight. I'm not coming back. She doesn't want me here. If you need anything, call me. Ben and Chase are taking over the case while Li's in England."

Trev put a hand out. "Let me talk to her."

Leo shook his head. "No. She's made it plain that she's happy where she is. She doesn't want to be rescued. For all I know, she's perfectly happy with whatever her husband's doing. So I'm going to leave and stop fucking up her perfect life."

"Leo, I don't know what's happening with her, but that doesn't sound like my sister. If she's involved in something bad, she has a good reason for it. If she said something terrible to you, it's probably because she's trying to protect you."

The laugh that came out of Leo's mouth didn't hold an ounce of humor. "And that's even worse. Look, I haven't slept with your sister. I haven't touched her. She's married. I have a lamentable habit of falling for women who are, shall we say, unobtainable. I'm not in love with your sister. I'm interested in her because she's lovely, submissive, and attached to another male. I can at least be honest with myself about my own flaws. I need to spend some time figuring out what I want. I can't do that here."

Trev's heart ached for both of them. "I'll take care of her."

243

"According to her, she doesn't need any help," Leo replied bitterly. "At least she probably won't threaten her own brother with a restraining order. Bring Bo and Beth to The Club. I would love to see you. And call me. I expect to talk at least once a day for the first few weeks. Just because your sister hates me doesn't mean you're off the hook."

Leo turned and stalked off, his keys in hand.

Liam shook his head and hefted his duffel. "He's totally in love with your sister. I've got to text that whole conversation to Big Tag. I get bonuses when I bring him good drama." He sobered a bit. "But seriously, she's in trouble, mate. I don't believe for a second she's capable of hurting a fly, and that means her husband is the one making her do it. Leo can't see around his butt. That's how hurt the fucker is. Talk to her. See what you can find out and call Ben if you need some backup. I don't know how long the English operation will last, but I'll keep tabs on what's happening here."

He was looking at that beer in the Irishman's hand. "I appreciate it."

Liam finished the can. "And stop thinking about this shite. You don't need it. You have better things to do with your time. Me, I got nothing but this beer."

"It doesn't have to be that way." He could get Li to a meeting, but it wouldn't work if he didn't have something he wanted more.

A resigned look came over his face. "My story ain't ending the way yours will. I screwed my life up a long time ago and there ain't no going back."

"There's always a way."

He shook his head and crushed the can. "Not for me."

"Hey, promise me something." It was an impulse. "Keep your mind open while you're in England. Sometimes a change of scenery helps."

"Maybe," Li allowed.

"And if you get the chance to find some happiness, take it, Li. Take it with both hands and don't look back."

Li tossed the can in the trash and hopped off the porch, getting into Leo's Jeep. It wasn't more than a minute before the Jeep was flying down the road.

"Is he gone?" His sister's voice sounded small and fragile.

Trev turned, ready to give his sister a piece of his mind. All thoughts of yelling at her fled when he saw the way her mascara had run down her face. His sister was always perfect. Since the day she'd discovered makeup and boys, she'd presented a perfect façade. It was gone now, and he could see the girl she'd been. He cursed and pulled her into his arms, wrapping his sister in a bear hug. "What are you doing, Shell?"

Her head moved against his chest. "I don't know anymore."

He held her for a moment, allowing her to cry, trying to be the solid rock he should have been all these years. Shelley had been on her own for far too long, and that was his fault. "Why did you marry him?"

She pulled away, wiping her eyes with her hands. "I can't tell you that. But you have to know that you're not the only one who can screw up in a huge way. Um, I had to marry Bryce, or he would have sent me to jail. Don't ask me. I'm not going to bring anyone else into this. Bryce didn't have anything to do with what I did. He didn't force me to commit a crime. But he did use it to his advantage."

And Bryce would pay for that. Trev decided not to push his sister on her secret. He could figure it out. She could go on believing no one knew, but he would find out and protect her. "What's your husband into?"

Her fists clenched at her sides. "I don't know. I think it's something bad. He doesn't talk to me, you know. Look, at first, it wasn't so bad. Bryce can be charming, and there was this odd part of me that wanted to make it work."

Because Bryce had, in effect, "claimed" her. He could see how his sister had fallen for it. Leo was right. Deep down, Shelley was submissive. She was looking for a strong man to take care of her and empower her. Bryce was not that man. And the one man who might have been able to do that was flying down the road toward Dallas. "Why do you have an account in the Caymans?"

"I have no idea. I swear to you, I didn't know that account existed until the investigator showed me. It's apparently tied to my decorating business. I let him do my books. I'm not good with money. I just want to do what I do, you know? I thought about hiring Mouse...Beth to do the books, but Bryce threw a fit. He said he didn't want to lose the money, that he could handle it. Actually Barry was the one who handled it before he died. That was when everything seemed to change."

"Barry Bellows?"

Shelley nodded. "He was Bryce's business partner for six years. They started the real estate company. Barry had family here. He's the one who brought Bryce to Deer Run. They met in college. After Barry died, Bryce seemed to lose it. He's paranoid. I'm not allowed to answer the phone anymore. He goes on long trips. Sometimes strange people show up at the house at odd hours of the night."

"Like who?"

"Do you know a man named Nelson Hall? He owns a garage two towns over. I've seen him with Bryce several times. Bryce told me Nelson was going to do some upgrades on his Escalade. Really? At two in the morning?"

Trev closed his eyes. They had talked about the man earlier. He was the meth dealer. "Nelson Hall. Yes, I've heard the name. And he has a son named Austin."

He would have to send all of this to Ben and Chase in a report.

Shelley nodded. "Yeah. He's in trouble with the law a lot, from what I hear."

Trev could guess what kind of trouble that was. A nasty pattern was being laid out. He just couldn't figure out how his brother-in-law was involved. "Beth said Bryce tried to buy her place."

"I love that house. I actually talked to him about trying to buy it when Maudine was alive. There was talk that she would need the money for a nursing home, but Bryce said no. He didn't want to spend the money. Then he flew into a rage when he got back from Austin and found out the house had been auctioned off."

What had changed? He didn't bother to mention to his sister that her husband hadn't been in Austin. He'd flown to Mexico City.

Trev needed to talk to a few people, but he had a horrible suspicion. It still didn't explain why Bryce would suddenly want Beth's house, unless he needed the money he would get from flipping it. But any money he would have gotten from the house

246

would be months away. Bryce had talked about turning the whole place into a small shopping center. He would need to first buy the place and turn around and sell it, after getting through all the red tape of rezoning the property for business.

Shelley's voice trembled as she spoke. "He hates you, Trev. You need to stay away from him. I don't think he's stable anymore. It's why I had to send Leo away. I'm worried about both of you. Bryce was so angry when you came back into town. He thinks it makes him look bad. He's obsessed with his perfect image."

"Enough to kill someone over it?" If he discovered that Bryce was the one who sent Austin Hall into Beth's house, nothing would stop him from hurting his brother-in-law.

"I hope not, but then, I don't really know him at all. You know, I haven't even slept with him in over a year. I'm nothing more than a doll he takes out and shows off. I hate him."

He pulled his sister back into his arms. He hated Bryce, too. And he was going to figure this out. His sister was in danger. "You're not going back home."

"Have you listened to anything I've said?"

"Listened to and made a decision. You're divorcing that asshole. You can stay with me and Beth and Bo for a while. I have some questions to ask. If I don't like the answers, I'm sending you and Beth to The Club, and you'll stay there until I deal with Bryce. Is that understood?"

She shook her head. "I don't think that's a good idea."

"I know I haven't earned the right to protect you. I know I left you high and dry for the majority of our adult lives, and it's not fair that I'm coming in and dictating to you now. You did what you had to do to help our mother, but that's over now. The medical bills are paid off. I'm going to get you out of this situation with your husband. I'm back now, and I'm taking care of things."

Her face turned up to look at him. "The medical bills?"

"Bo's paying them off, and I'll pay him back in a year."

"Trev..."

He wasn't going to listen to arguments about this. "No. I won't accept anything less. If I have to tie you up and force you to Dallas, I will. If I tell Leo everything you told me, I assure you, he'll help

247

me. He'll have a bodyguard on you before you can take another breath."

"I don't think Leo Meyer will have anything to do with me again." There was a sad longing in Shelley's voice.

Trev wasn't sure if there was anything he could do on that front. In the two years he'd known Leo, he'd come to realize that the former Navy SEAL was an unbelievably tolerant man, but once he was done, he was through. He felt for his sister.

"I'm going to sit down and have supper, watch the game with Bo, and deal with Beth. After that, I'm going into town for a few hours. I have some questions to ask. I expect you to stay with Bo. I expect you to mind him."

She frowned. "I don't know that I like the sound of that."

"You're my sister, but I'll tie you up, too. Oh, I won't treat you like Beth. I'll leave your clothes on, but you won't find the experience pleasant."

"I don't know that I like the new you." But he caught a hint of a smile through her tears.

"Get used to it, sister." He looked at her, his sister. No one else in the world knew what it had been like to grow up in their house. No one else knew how it felt to be loved by their parents. Each family's existence was strangely individual, no matter how many events or emotions were universal. Only Shelley knew how their father had tickled them and called them "little bugs." Only Shelley knew how their mother's banana bread tasted on a cold morning. Only Shelley knew what it meant to mourn them. "I love you, sister. I failed our parents. I won't fail you."

The tears were back. "Oh, Trev, she knew. Mom knew you were in rehab. Let me tell you about the day I fell in love with Leo Meyer. It was a week after you accepted the deal. You were still in the hospital under observation. Leo explained how hard detox could be on a body. He came to see our mom in the hospital. He sat down beside her, and he promised her that you would be okay. He swore to her that you were ready to change. When our mother died, she was so proud of you."

He felt tears prick his eyes. "I had given her nothing to be proud of. I had fucked up every opportunity given to me."

"And yet you chose to fight. You chose to fight for your life and your sobriety. God, you make it sound like you've had it easy. I can't imagine the pressure you were under. Not many men would have the strength to walk away. You could have been one more cautionary tale, but you did it. You got through it. You get through it every day. She's proud of you. She's proud of how strong you've become. She's proud of how you take care of the people around you. She's proud of the man you've become."

"How can you say that?"

"Because I'm proud." She wrapped her arms around him, her love surrounding him.

Trev looked over her shoulder and saw Bo standing there. He'd heard everything. Trev felt himself flush with shame. Bo was one of the people he'd let down.

"I'm proud, too," Bo said, his voice choking for a moment. "And I can speak for Beth when I say we wouldn't be where we are without you. I need you to know that I forgive you."

His gut tightened. "Will you please tell me what happened?"

Bo's face turned down. "My dad got drunk one night in my junior year. Aidan had left town. Aidan was his golden boy, but he was angry that Aidan was pursuing music as a career. He didn't think that was a masculine profession, if you know what I mean. Well, Dad got snockered, and he beat the shit out of me. I thought he was going to kill me. He pulled out his old Colt and shoved a bullet in it. He put it to my head and pulled the trigger."

Trev's blood ran cold. How could someone do that to his own child? "Bo, I had no idea."

Bo simply shook his head. "I think Dad was shocked that he'd done it, too. He dropped the gun after it didn't go off that first time. I ran. I ran to Austin, but I realized that if told my brother, Aidan would have killed our father."

Trev sighed. He couldn't imagine it. He couldn't imagine how helpless Bo must have felt. "Why didn't you call the cops?"

Bo shrugged. "Because they would have put him in jail and then Aidan would have had to leave college to keep the ranch afloat. Because I didn't want to go into foster care."

"I turned you away, didn't I?" He wished he could remember

249

the night. Wished he had been a different person.

"You weren't mean about it. I'll give that to you. You were never a mean drunk. You told me to get cleaned up and find some black-and-white clothes so I could join the party. But you wouldn't let me in until I was dressed properly."

The annual Black and White Ball at his frat. Of course. He'd always been plastered for that. "I'm so sorry. I didn't know what I was doing. Well, I did. I knew what I risked every time I took a drink. Where did you go?"

Bo smiled. "Beth came and got me. I think that was the night that really solidified our relationship as friends. I started spending more and more time with her. I started to love her."

Shelley walked up and gave Bo a hug. "I'm sorry to hear that. How could you have ever come back here?"

Bo patted her back, accepting the affection. "The strange thing was after that night, my father actually calmed down. He never hit me again. We got along for a while. He was still a mean bastard, but he kept his distance. I stayed on because I didn't have anywhere else to go, and I moved into the guesthouse. It was better after that. I loved this ranch even when I hated my dad."

Guilt threatened to overwhelm Trev. "But I could have helped you."

Bo shook his head. "Everything happens for a reason. I believe that now. We're here today because we did stupid shit and got our asses kicked. We made mistakes and we learned from them. That's what brought us here. I wouldn't take a single one back. I wouldn't be anywhere but right here, right now." He cleared his throat as though banishing the deep emotion he felt. "Now, dinner's ready. You two need to come inside. Apparently, we're going to need our strength. Lexi already made a plate for Beth and headed out. She's got five different plotlines to read to her. I think I saw Beth crying a little."

Trev laughed, the feeling of shame leaving him in an instant. He felt lighter. "Well, I don't want to keep your stomach waiting."

Shelley stepped away from Bo. "I agree with Bo. I've made mistakes, too. Now's the time to start fixing them. I'm going to wash my face. I'm sure I look a mess. Does Bo have to follow me to the bathroom?"

He was fine with his sister's sarcasm as long as she didn't fight him on Bo's bodyguard duty. "I think Aidan's bathroom is safe enough."

Bo frowned, crossing his arms over his chest. "I don't know. I hear sometimes women get assaulted in there."

Trev snorted. "Damn, you heard about that, huh? Well, how about after the game, we go out and visit our sub? You know, we promised we would give her a little something."

"Eww!" Shelley put her hands over her ears. "Too much info, brother."

Bo and Trev were laughing as they entered the house together.

Chapter Seventeen

Beth looked up as Trev walked into the barn, Bo hard on his heels.

"So, what do you think? I mean, I had the beta hero save the day in my last book. I think it's time the heroine kicked some ass." Lexi had a corkboard with about a hundred notes plastered to it.

Beth was sure they were an incongruous sight. The serious writer, going over plot and storyline, with her personal assistant, who Lexi'd had to prop up with pillows so she could comfortably sit because said assistant was naked and bound in a whole lot of rope. They'd spent the first ten minutes of the session going over how it felt to be tied up. Serena Dean-Miles was serious about taking notes. Luckily, she was also serious about packing for her trip. Now they were plotting out what Lexi liked to call "end game." "And when was the last time you had the Dom save the day?"

Lexi bit into her lower lip. "I guess it's been a while."

She shook her head. Since Lexi had started writing, she'd become known for her kick-ass heroines and quirky small towns. "It's time. Throw Aidan a bone. Let the hero save the day."

Lexi shrugged. "Fine. I guess the alpha has to save the day every now and then. Hey, guys! How did the game go? I'm glad you're here. I was just telling Beth that I should get a masculine opinion."

Bo's eyes flared in panic. "Uh, I don't read much."

"The Dom should definitely save the day, Lexi. Now, your Master requests your presence." Trev's deep voice didn't leave a lot of room for disobedience.

But Lexi was a brat to the end. Beth admired that about her boss. "Fine, but I'm not doing the dishes."

She grinned at Beth as she gathered her things. "I'm so glad you're in the lifestyle now. We can have fun. I'll show you all the best ways to top from the bottom."

Trev growled Lexi's direction.

Lexi took a step back. "Fine. Maybe not." But the minute Trev's back was turned, she mouthed the words, "I totally will," and slipped out the door.

"I love my sister-in-law, but I don't think she's a good influence on Beth." Bo frowned at the door Lexi had closed.

Trev shook it off. "Lexi is a brat of the highest order. She'll be good for Beth. And besides, I don't think Beth is about to let us choose her friends."

"Not for a second." She was ready to obey Trev in the bedroom and in things that made sense, but she wouldn't mindlessly follow him.

"Mind me now," he said as if he could hear her thoughts. "Let Bo turn you over. I want to play."

She could see that he did. His cock strained against his jeans. There was a slightly desperate look to his eyes. "What happened?"

"Nothing to worry yourself about. I've had an emotional day. And I spent two hours watching Lucas and Aidan enjoy a six-pack of beer between the two of them. I don't begrudge them, but it has me on edge."

"Damn it. I didn't even think about it. I had one, too. Fuck, Trev, I'm sorry." Bo ran a hand through his hair.

Trev waved him off. "You aren't an alcoholic. I can't expect the world to stop because I can't handle a drink. But I need something else. The whole time I watched them, I told myself that if I got through it, I would earn a prize."

The dark look in his eyes told her exactly what prize he meant. Her breathing sped up. "I think you definitely deserve a treat, baby."

She was his treat. She was his addiction now. And she was so happy to be it. She was addicted to him and Bo. She was addicted to wanting them, to loving them.

"Bo, did our sub figure out how to use the ropes to her advantage?"

Bo grinned. "I might have helped her figure that out."

"How many times did you come, darlin'? How many times did you rub your clit against the rope?"

"Not too many. Twice. Once with Bo, and then Lexi took a break. I didn't mean to. I wiggled and it happened." It had felt so good, she hadn't exactly fought it. She'd been disappointed that Lexi got back so quickly.

Trev nodded. "Well, I think two still deserves a spanking. Bo, where does your brother keep the crop?"

"Uh, it's a ranch," Bo pointed out. "There are crops everywhere."

"All right, smart-ass. Do you want in on this or not? Get me a crop."

Bo saluted. "Yes, Sir."

Trev lifted her easily, turning her over. She loved how it felt to be picked up by Trev. She relaxed and allowed Trev to move her into the position he wanted her in, face down, cheek to the side, knees bent, ass in the air. The plug tried to escape, but the rope held it in.

Trev groaned his pleasure at the sight. "Bo did a damn fine job."

"I'm getting good at shoving stuff up her ass." Bo was back with a soft-tipped crop in his hand.

"I think she's ready." Trev's hands smoothed across the skin of her ass. Each pass of his hands moved the rope slightly, affecting her clit and anus.

"Ready? Shit, are you serious?" Bo's breath came out in a sigh. "Fuck, I want that."

Beth shivered at the thought. Both of them at once. She wanted that, too.

"But first, we owe her some discipline," Trev said.

Beth nearly howled as the crop came down on her ass. The pain was jarring, but even as she flinched from it, the rope rubbed her clit. It rubbed all along her pussy and the crease of her ass, pressing on the plug, making her backside light up with nerves that had never come to life before.

"I made this dress for your punishment and your pleasure, darlin'." Trev sounded more in control than he'd been before. "That's my fucking job in life, to see to both. To make sure you're safe and you have what you need, and that includes my crop against your skin."

She bit into her bottom lip to stop from calling out. He struck again, high on her ass. It changed the way the rope rubbed and pushed at the plug.

"I'm your Master, Bethany Hobbes. I'm the center of your world. You're damn straight the center of mine." He struck lower. Her clit threatened to go off again.

He'd been that from the moment he'd saved her at The Rusty Spur. And Bo had been the sun in her sky for longer than she could remember.

The crop hit her again, this time from another direction.

"Never again, Beth," Bo said. "You can't treat me with any less respect than Trev. I might not have trained the way he did. I might never be the Dom he is, but by god, I will be what you need."

Bo seemed to have found his own crop. They took turns whipping her ass. The pain would flare, and then the rope would do its work. She felt heated and desperate, caught between the pleasure and pain. Over and over, they struck, pausing between to stroke her, to tell her how well she was doing.

Tears caught in her eyes, a cry in her throat. She'd spent the day trussed up and trapped, and she'd never felt freer. She was becoming someone she liked, someone who fought back and believed that good things could happen. Love had come in the strangest form, changing her forever, and she wouldn't give this up for all the picket fences and good opinions in the world. All of her life, she'd sat back and waited. She'd waited for love, hoping it would come her way.

Love was worth fighting for. Love wasn't something that came quietly. It had roared in and changed her soul, and she wasn't about to let it go. If Trev McNamara left in a year, she would follow him.

She would take Bo's hand and follow him because this was her family, and she would never give them up.

"She's crying." Bo dropped the crop. He put a hand to her face, his voice tortured. "Trev, she's crying."

She found herself turned over and in Trev's arms, his face staring down at her. His hair was mussed, his eyes warm. "She's feeling."

She gave him a watery smile because he understood. "I love you."

His eyes closed briefly. "I don't know why, but I'll take it. I know I'll be bad for you somewhere down the line, but I need you. I fucking need you."

He took her mouth, dominating it. His tongue surged against hers in a fierce dance, and his arms tightened, caging her as neatly as his ropes. Beth gave as good as she got. She played with him, opening and submitting as fiercely as he dominated.

"Help me get her out of these ropes." Trev was breathless by the time he was done.

She felt Bo lifting her up so he could undo the ties at her wrists. Her hands came free. Trev caught them and brought them forward. His hands rubbed along her arms.

"Are your arms okay? Was the tension all right?" Trev's hands rubbed circles in her skin.

She pulled him close. "My arms are fine. But there are parts of me that need your attention, Sir."

He groaned. "You know that kills me, darlin'. Do you want both of us?"

"More than anything."

"Then get that ass in the air. Bo, we need condoms and lube."

Bo slammed both down on the rack. He'd taken off his clothes and stood in front of her, his gloriously cut body a work of art for her eyes. Every muscle seemed tense, and his cock jutted up, almost reaching his navel. Bo had gotten awfully comfortable being naked around Trev. "Ahead of you. Now I want equal time."

Bo's hand cupped her neck and pulled her to him. His mouth closed over hers, tongue seeking entry. His hands ran over her breasts. They were still sensitive from the bindings.

Bo's mouth traced a path from her lips to her neck and shoulder. He dropped kisses all along her skin. "I love your breasts. They're perfect."

His head lowered, and he sucked a nipple in his mouth.

"I love them, too." Trev groaned before taking the other between his teeth.

Beth let her head fall back as they feasted on her. Someone's hand gripped her ass while another dipped into her pussy.

"Fuck, she's so wet." Trev came off her breast and sucked his fingers into his mouth. Beth could see his tongue whirl around like he didn't want to miss a single drop. "I have to have more of that."

He shoved her knees apart and sank down. She watched as his dark head lowered between her legs.

Bo watched as well. "Oh, do you want Trev to eat your pussy, baby? I love eating your pussy. It's my favorite dessert. One of these days, we'll lay you out on the dining room table after dinner and have our sweet treat. That pussy of yours is better than any pie."

"Should I make her beg?" Trev asked, his eyes going to Bo's.

"Do you think she would?" Bo got behind her, propping her up. His hands cupped her breasts.

"I will." She wasn't ashamed of it either. It felt good.

"I want to hear her ask. Baby, you never cuss. Say it. Ask Trev in that oh-so-polite voice of yours to kindly eat your pussy. Ask him to thrust his tongue straight up your cunt. Ask him to not stop until your pussy juice is all he can taste." Bo's words heated her skin.

Trev's fingers slid along her pussy, parting her labia, making her want more. So much more. "I think I need to hear it, love. I need to hear you ask."

"Please, Sir. Please eat my pussy."

"Since you asked so nicely." Trev lowered his head, his eyes never leaving hers, and swiped at the lips of her sex.

She would have come off the bench if Bo hadn't been holding her up. Trev was utterly relentless. His tongue slid through her pussy, fucking into her cunt briefly before starting over again. He sucked the petals of her pussy into his mouth and groaned at her taste.

"Fucking sweet," Trev said before sliding a single finger deep

257

inside. "And this pearl is so pretty."

"Give it to her good. I need to fuck so bad. My dick is killing me." Bo's hands tightened around her breasts. She could feel his cock against her back, his hips thrusting a little. He tongued her earlobe. "God, I want to fuck you, Beth. I want to fuck your pussy while Trev takes your little asshole. I want to feel you between us."

He bit her earlobe gently, the small pain sending tingles all the way to her pussy. That finger of Trev's curved up and hit the perfect spot as he sucked her clit into his mouth.

She came, her body jerking as the orgasm invaded her veins. Bo covered his mouth with hers, drinking down her cries as she shuddered in his arms.

Trev gave her one last lick. "Bo, get her on top of you."

Bo rolled a condom on and reached for her.

Trev shucked his jeans, his normal grace fleeing. He struggled out of them as though he couldn't stand for them to spend another second on his body.

Beth lay back in Bo's arms, feeling utterly boneless. She was so suffused with pleasure, she couldn't move, preferring to allow Bo to place her whatever way he would. He got onto his back and pulled her until she was on top of him. She loved the way his skin felt against hers, warm and smooth and safe. He smelled good and clean, though the woodsy scent of his arousal was starting to take over. Bo felt like home.

"Ride me, baby." His cock thrust against her pussy, seeking access.

Beth roused herself. Her pussy had been satisfied, but she wanted more. She wanted to be caught between her men, surrounded by them.

"Are you ready?" Bo asked.

She reached down and guided his cock to her pussy. She pressed her hips down, impaling herself on his dick. "I'm more than ready."

* * * *

Trev watched Beth lower herself onto Bo's cock and realized that this was so much more than sex. He needed them. His cock throbbed painfully. He hoped he had the dexterity to get the fucking rubber on. He stroked himself, telling the beast to calm down.

Bo's eyes dilated with pleasure as Beth's hips rolled.

"Don't you come, Bo. You don't come until I get in that ass and then we go together." Trev barked the order, satisfied when Bo's eyes sharpened.

"You better hurry then because she feels so tight. God, I love fucking you, Beth." Bo's hands went to her hips.

Trev climbed on the rack. He didn't have a ton of time, and his dick didn't want to wait either. "Hold her cheeks open. Beth, lean forward. Touch your breasts to Bo's chest."

Her asshole came into view along with the pink plug Bo had worked into her anus to prepare her for this act. Trev felt his cock weep at the sight. She was pretty, so trusting, lying there allowing him to touch her, to fuck her. She was everything he could have hoped for. He reached out and touched the plug. The muscles of her ass squeezed it tight. There was a ginger root in that girl's future. He couldn't wait.

But now, all he could think about was how that asshole would squeeze him. He pulled the plug out, twisting a little as he did. It would be a tight fit, but he would manage.

He squirted lube on his thumb and pressed in, trying to coat her rectum in the slippery stuff. Beth groaned. Tight. She was going to be so fucking tight. He could feel Bo's cock in her pussy.

Trev caressed the globes of her ass. They were round and perfectly made. They were pink from his crop. The evidence of her submission made his balls draw up. Beth trusted him. Beth needed him.

He forced the rubber over his dick, promising himself they would all get checkups and Beth would get on birth control because he wanted to ride that ass bareback. He wanted to fuck her every morning and know that some piece of himself was inside her all day. He wanted to know that he and Bo filled her pussy and her ass.

He lined his cock up, emotion threatening to choke him. She'd given him so much. He'd been her first man. Trev had had a ton of sex, some of which he didn't even remember, but he'd never made love the way he did with Beth. He'd never shared the way he did with Bo. These two people, these loving beings who opened themselves to him—they were his first. He'd fucked too many women to count, but he'd never needed a single one the way he needed these two.

He loved them. Fuck, but he loved them.

He pressed his cockhead to her. She was so small compared to him. "Relax, Beth. Bo, kiss her. Distract her."

Bo eagerly took her head between his hands and devoured her mouth. Trev could see their tongues playing. Bo was more dominant than Trev had imagined. He'd taken to it quickly, not because it was his nature, but because it was what Beth needed. That was Bo's nature—to provide. He'd simply never been given the opportunity to learn how to do it.

While Bo kissed her, Trev pressed in. He pushed inside her in little strokes, gaining ground with each pass. With each foray, his dick threatened to explode. He pulled her hips forward. His cockhead slipped inside. Trev groaned. So good. He pressed forward. Beth's skin quivered under his hands. He heard her moan as he pressed in.

He pushed forward, forcing her to take his cock. Bo kissed her, their heads moving in time as Trev pressed in until his balls touched the cheeks of her ass. He held himself still, enjoying the heat of her ass, the tight clutch of her ass around his dick.

"I'm in." He barely managed the words. He was overwhelmed by the feel of being balls deep in Beth's ass, Bo's cock millimeters away, only a thin piece of skin separating them.

Bo's head fell back. "Thank god. She's killing me. Her pussy keeps clenching on my cock, and I thought I would die when you slid against me. I get it now. I totally get it. You okay, baby?"

Beth turned her head slightly. He could see the strain on her face. "I'm dying. Please fuck me. Please."

Trev couldn't wait any longer. He pulled out and tunneled back in. Her asshole clung, fighting to keep his dick and fighting just as hard to keep him out. This was what he loved. The constant friction on his cock. Every nerve in his body was aware of her. His every sense filled with her—her heat, her sweet scent, her softness engulfed him. He felt infused with her.

He fucked into her ass, his hands circling her waist. He felt Bo, their limbs mingled as they pleasured their shared lover. Beth was small between them, a beautiful, delicate angel who had brought them all together. She rode Bo, shoving her ass back to take Trev. She worked with them, fighting for her pleasure. She was so different from that first night when she'd shyly allowed him to take her. This Beth reached for her men. This Beth clutched them and made a place for herself.

God, he loved this Beth.

Over and over, he drove into her ass, her cheek hitting him as she pushed back against him. He was getting close. His balls were drawn, and his spine tingled. He wasn't going to last.

He reached around and felt his way down her torso to that place where her body met Bo's. He found her clit and pressed down as he pushed deep inside with his cock.

Bo bucked up as Beth's head fell back. She cried out as she came, her body quivering under his. He could feel Bo's cock twitching against his as he came.

Trev let go. He pushed in, fusing them together as he came in jets of semen. It flowed from his body in a great wave. He kept fucking until he couldn't anymore, his body falling forward. They were heaped together, the three of them, their limbs mingling. Beth turned toward Trev.

He let his head find Beth's breast. Peace washed over him. He didn't need anything but this strange family in that moment.

He swore he would protect them.

Chapter Eighteen

Beth looked up at Trev, painfully aware that they weren't alone in the house. Lucas, Lexi, and Aidan had politely left their living room to give them some privacy, but Shelley was still here.

"You mind Bo." Trev stood in front of her, clean and freshly dressed. Aidan had taken pity on the fact that she hadn't fixed the water heater yet and offered them a place to shower. Lexi had loaned her some jeans, a bra, and a shirt, but she'd laughed when asked about underwear. Apparently Lexi's men weren't great believers in it.

"Are you sure I can't go with you?" She hugged him. It came naturally now. She wasn't sure why Trev needed to leave without them.

"I have some questions I need to ask. It's not something I can do with you, darlin'. No one would talk to me if I had something as sweet and innocent as you by my side. They wouldn't buy the act."

She snorted. "Innocent?"

He shook his head, his face soft as he looked down at her. "I don't care what you do in the bedroom. You're innocent. How many men have you had?"

"Two and you know it."

"How many men have you loved?"

That got to the heart of the matter. "Two."

He touched her nose with his, an affectionate gesture. "Innocent."

She'd hoped she was at least a little dirty. "Why don't you take Bo with you?"

He brushed his thumb across her lower lip, staring as though trying to decide how much to tell her. "I don't want to involve him. He's innocent, too. He can drink beer and get into fights, but there's a piece of Bo that's as innocent as you. I have to go see some people I wouldn't want either of you to meet."

She didn't like the sound of that. "Tell me what you're doing."

His eyes hardened marginally.

"Please."

He groaned but pulled her close. "I'm going to ask a few questions about Bryce Hughes. I think he's into something bad and I can't wait for the investigators. I need to figure out how dangerous he is and if he has any connection to the odd things that have been happening around your place."

She frowned. "Like the chandelier falling?"

His eyes narrowed. "You know something you're not telling me?"

She hurried to get the words out before he reached for some more rope. "It's just a suspicion, but I think the chandelier had help. Why would someone want a light fixture to fall? They couldn't possibly have known we would be sitting there."

It didn't make any sense.

"No, they couldn't have known, but I also don't believe that kid was looking for drugs. I need to figure out who that kid was coming after. You should know that if I find out he was really coming after you, I'm going to have your ass in Dallas under lock and key, and I won't take no for an answer. I should know something in a couple of hours. I want you and Shelley to pack a few things and come back here to wait for me. We'll decide how to proceed after I know something, but I don't want you to spend another night in that house."

Her heart clenched. That house was special to her. "Trev, I can't leave. I need to get to work. At the very least I need to figure out how to protect the house. It's all I have. Every dime I have is sunk into that house."

And it hit her.

"That hole in my ceiling is going to cost me a pretty penny. Pennies I shouldn't have because I couldn't get a loan. What if someone's trying to force me to sell the place because it no longer is a doable project? If I couldn't get a loan, I would have to sell. I wouldn't be able to fix it up. Is there something I don't know about the property? Is some big development firm interested in it?"

Trev's mouth flattened. "I don't know. If there was, you would think they would make you an offer. No big firm is going to send someone in to loosen your chandelier. They might have the property condemned. I'll have Ben and Chase look into it. I need to figure this thing out, not only for you, darlin'. I need to know if my sister is married to someone dangerous."

"She'll be fine," Bo said, coming up from behind. He nuzzled the back of her neck. "I'll take care of our girl. We'll hit the house, grab some stuff, and lock up the best we can. We'll be right back here waiting for you."

"Beth, pick up some clothes for Shelley. I don't want her to walk into Bryce's house again."

"Trev!" Shelley came up from her place on the couch. "I can't simply leave."

"Yes, you can," he replied grimly. "Did you talk to Lucas like I asked?"

Shelley's big brown eyes turned down. "I did. He got a big smile on his face when I told him I wanted a divorce, and I swear his mouth suddenly had fangs. Do lawyers grow fangs when they sense a good case?"

Beth had heard Lucas say he loved taking douchebags like Bryce for everything they were worth. At least Shelley had a lawyer who would go to the mat for her.

"All the more reason for you to not walk back into that house." Trev had made his decision, and Beth didn't think he would be moved.

She walked up to Trev's sister, slipping her hand into Shelley's, squeezing reassuringly. "We can go shopping tomorrow. It'll be fun."

Shelley took a deep breath. "All right. I think I can handle a little shopping. Though maybe we could drive into Austin. The only place to buy clothes here is Gwen's Emporium, and she stands there and shakes her head when I try to buy a V-neck. She always asks if I really think my boobs are going to fit or if I want them to spill out all over the place. I won't even tell you what she says about low-rise jeans."

"Austin it is." She didn't want to admit that Gwen always told her she had such modest taste. She didn't want to be praised for her modesty anymore. It was time to give the girls some breathing room. "I think I might like some V-neck shirts, too. And really low-rise jeans."

"Now, we should talk about that," Trev said, his eyes narrowing.

"Says the man whose idea of fashion consists of thirty yards of rope. Let the woman be. I think Beth's ass is going to look gorgeous in some tight jeans," Bo said with a healthy leer.

Yes, dressing was going to be fun from now on. She finally understood why women spent hours shopping and picking out the right clothes to wear. She made a mental note to take the trunk of clothes she'd found in Maudine's bedroom with her. The fifties style seemed to suit her. She noticed Bo was holding something in his hand. She rolled her eyes. "You are not bringing Roxanne."

Bo pulled his Remington Model Seven rifle to his chest, clutching it the way he would a woman. "You don't listen to her," he said to Roxanne. "She doesn't understand. No, sweetheart, after everything we've been through together, I'm not dumping you for her. She doesn't even take short action magnum cartridges."

Beth cocked a hip. That rifle was not sleeping in her bed. "And Roxanne doesn't take double input. You think about that before you bring her to bed with you."

Trev doubled over. "You are both insane. Bo? Seriously? You named your rifle?"

"Well, tell me you didn't name your favorite football. Beth had like a thousand stuffed animals, and every single one of them had a name. And she slept with all of them. They're in a box waiting to be picked up and moved. And my rifle is way more useful than a faded pink hippo named Horace," Bo argued.

She opened her mouth to give Trev a piece of her mind, but Shelley was smiling.

"He called it Troy, after Troy Aikman," Shelley said with a laugh. "He slept with that football. He carried it around for years. And, at one point in time, he named his biceps. Smith and Wesson. Because they were his guns."

Trev flushed and shook his head. "Brat."

Shelley hugged her brother. "You bet. Now go and do what you need to do. I'll follow Bo and Roxanne's instructions."

"Finally a woman who respects you," Bo whispered to his gun, but he gave Beth a wink.

She couldn't help but kiss him. He was crazy, and he was going to make their lives so much fun. Her heart skipped a beat as she looked at Trev and Bo together. So different and yet they fit. She was suddenly looking forward to the rest of her life.

When Bo hustled her into the cab of the truck, she held Roxanne for him.

* * * *

Bo pulled up to the house, his mind on the events of the afternoon. He could still feel Beth plastered to his body. Despite the shower he'd taken, he swore he could still smell her arousal. It had been the hottest sexual experience of his life. And he was worried.

Trev hadn't said he would stay. He knew it wasn't fair, but he wanted commitment. A couple of days before, he'd wanted nothing more than to see Trev McNamara's back as he walked out of town. But now he couldn't imagine it. He couldn't imagine a life with Beth that didn't include the Dom. For the first time, he was excited. He had so much to learn from Trev, and not merely about how to bind Beth's breasts.

He looked through the front window as he parked Aidan's truck behind Beth's "car." He knew he should pull closer so Trev would have space when he came home, but he didn't want to run the risk of breathing on the Pinto and having it explode in a fiery mass. Yeah, she was getting a new car, and she was learning to drive it properly. He took Roxanne from Beth's hands and eased out of the cab. He opened the door for the women and looked around.

Everything was quiet. The late-afternoon air was cool and calm. Everything seemed to be the way they had left it. Trev had him paranoid.

"Come on. Let's get what we need and get back to Aidan's."

Beth frowned, looking at the house. "I don't want to leave it. Now I'm nervous that I'm going to spend the night at Aidan's and someone will have taken a wrecking ball to it when we come back. I wanted to get started so bad."

Shelley put an arm around Beth. "It's a beautiful place, and it's going to be standing when we come back. When Trev is satisfied that Bryce is nothing more than a douchebag, we'll return, and I'll help you. This is my specialty, you know. Before Bryce talked me into refurbing politician's offices, I used to flip houses. I love working with my hands. And I am handy with a jigsaw."

Beth smiled, her face lighting up. "Good, because I have about two thousand square feet of bamboo flooring to put in."

Bo groaned. He got the feeling there would be a whole lot of home improvement work in his future. "Let's get this done."

He took the porch steps two at a time and opened the front door, allowing Beth and Shelley to enter. The women walked into the front hall, chatting about stained concrete and how to best knock out the wall between the office and the kitchen.

"Stop." His heart raced as he heard the sound. It was quiet, but the floor above them creaked with an unmistakable pattern. Someone was walking on the second floor. And it wasn't Trev.

He put a finger to his mouth. Beth's eyes widened, and Shelley reached for her hand. "Stay here."

As quietly as he could, he walked up the stairs, sticking to the side where there was less chance of a creak alerting whoever was upstairs to his presence. He wasn't taking any chances this time. He held his rifle, his finger on the trigger. It was just like hunting, he told himself. Patience would win the day.

"Fuck." Bo heard the soft curse and the frustration behind it. Bryce Hughes was here. Trev had been right, but Bo would be the one to figure out the mystery. He intended to call in the police, but not until he had a few questions answered for himself.

"Come on, come on. Barry, you were such a fucker. Goddamn it. If I could kill you twice, I would."

Bryce sounded past desperate. The words came out of his mouth in a harsh whisper, as though the dead man could hear him speaking from beyond the grave. Bryce had killed his partner? Barry Bellows had died in a car accident, and no one in Deer Run had really looked much past that fact. Had Bryce set up that accident? What the hell was he looking for in Beth's bedroom? It sounded like he was tearing the place apart.

He eased up to the second-floor landing and onto the carpet runner. He could move more freely now. Bryce was making enough noise for both of them. The door to Beth's bedroom was open, and even from his vantage point, Bo could see that Bryce had been hard at work. Beth's pretty comforter was on the floor, feathers from the pillows littering the hallway. Bryce stood in the center of the room with a sledgehammer. He pulled it over his head, the wall that separated the bedroom from the bathroom his obvious target.

"Stop right there." He wasn't about to let this asshole start tearing out walls. That was Beth's job.

Bryce stopped, staring at the rifle aimed solidly at his chest. The sledgehammer fell to the floor with a crack. Bryce turned, his normally perfect hair disheveled. His lower lip was busted, blood oozing onto his chin. One eye was swollen. It looked like a purple egg had made a nest of his face. "I have to find it."

"What?"

"They're going to kill me if I don't find it. It has to be here. Why else would Barry have come here? He hated that old bitch. He fucking couldn't stand her. He hid it here, the bastard. I built this business. I was the one with the contacts. He had no right to hold out on me. He tried to fucking blackmail me. No one blackmails Bryce Hughes. I showed him. I showed him."

Bo took a deep breath. Bryce Hughes seemed to have found that "edge" everyone talked about, and he'd gone straight over in a happy swan dive. "I think we need to go downstairs and wait for the sheriff."

Bryce's head sagged. "No cops. Cops won't stop them. I have to find it. Fuck. I have to find it or we're all dead. You're an idiot. You should never have walked in here. You're supposed to be at Aidan's. Shelley said she was meeting you all out at Aidan's for the afternoon. Now we're all dead."

"Bo?" Beth's soft voice nearly made Bo's heart stop. He turned, ready to yell at her to get her ass out of here and take Shelley with her.

Beth and Shelley stood in the doorway, their faces sheet white.

"Beth?"

"You told me I had to tell you the next time someone tried to kill me." Her voice was strained, a tight whisper. "Well, someone's ready to kill me again."

"I told you he'd kill us all." Bryce shrank back.

Bo turned and saw an immaculately dressed man. He was roughly six foot three and wore an air of disdain, as though the world always disappointed him. He also carried a .45 in his gloved hand, pointed straight at the back of Beth's head. His other hand was on her arm, keeping her close to his body. Beth was his shield.

"I need more time. It's here," Bryce insisted.

The man with the gun shook his head. "You made a deal with my employer. You took my employer's cash in exchange for your products. You set yourself up as a distributor. No one forced you to do that, Mr. Hughes. But we do expect to get what we paid for. I want the drugs now. We've been more than patient. It's been months. You, put down the gun or I'll shoot both of the women. I assume at least one of them is yours."

Bo let the rifle drop. Roxanne wasn't going to help him out now. Terror threatened to claw at his insides. One slip of that man's finger and Beth's life would be over. His life would be over.

"Look, mister, I can see you have some business with Bryce here. I can't stand the man, myself. Why don't you let me take the women, and you can conclude this transaction in private?" He was pretty sure it wouldn't work, but he had to try.

"Call me Carlo. I think we're going to be friends, Mr. O'Malley. Yes, I know all the players in this sad little town. My employer pays me well to keep up with everything. Including his product. You see, Mr. Hughes here started out as a small-time meth dealer. I believe your employees work out of a trailer park in another town."

"Bryce, what is he talking about?" Shelley's hands shook.

Bryce's hands shook. "Shut up, Shelley. This isn't any of your business."

Carlo chuckled, though the sound was slightly sinister to Bo's ears. "It *is* your business, darling. He used your business to do an enormous amount of our work. He's laundered money through it. He's gotten us some incredibly interesting information with which to blackmail certain politicians. It isn't easy to get drugs over the border these days. It certainly helps to have a few, shall we say, influential people in our pockets. You weren't aware of the hidden cameras you placed in your clients' offices when you redecorated? I can see not. It was probably smart of you to keep your wife out of it, Hughes. Now, Mr. O'Malley, get to your knees, please, and allow Mrs. Hughes to use the zip ties I carry around for such an occasion. It's shocking how often I find the need to tie people up in my line of business."

Bo felt his whole body harden, every muscle screaming for him to not allow this to happen.

Carlo's eyes narrowed. "I wouldn't play the hero, Mr. O'Malley. You might be able to take me down, but not before I kill her. The instant I see you move, I will put a bullet through her brain. Is that an acceptable outcome? Do you not believe that I will kill someone? I think you need a demonstration of my willpower. Mr. Hughes, as you obviously can't even manage to properly search a home, I have no further use for you."

He watched in utter horror as the gun in Carlo's hand moved slightly and he fired, the discharge pounding through the small room with the force of a grenade. Beth screamed, trying to put her hands to her ears, but Carlo held fast. Shelley stood in shocked terror.

And Bryce Hughes stood in the middle of the room, perfectly still for a moment, as though frozen in time. Then blood bloomed from the neat hole in his forehead. He tottered, as though his body wasn't sure which way to fall. It seemed to take forever for him to find the floor. All the while, Bryce stared out, his eyes as blank as a doll's. He hit the floor, and time seemed to speed up again.

Shelley cried out. Carlo tightened his hold. Bo wanted to run, to tackle the fucker, but he couldn't risk it. Beth's left ear was bleeding. Her face was so pale. He couldn't stand the thought of her hitting the floor, her body still forever, her strong heart silenced.

Bo got to his knees, his hands behind his back. "Shelley, you've got to do as the man says."

"Excellent, Mr. O'Malley," Carlo said with an approving nod. "Mrs. Hughes, bind the young man's hands, and then this one here will bind yours. We're going to see how well Miss Hobbes knows this house. Bryce was convinced his partner hid a half a million dollars' worth of cocaine somewhere in this house. You can find it, or I'll start killing your friends."

"I can find it," Beth promised, her eyes finding his as Shelley slipped the zip tie on and tightened it. He could feel Shelley's hands shaking.

He had to pray Beth could do what she'd promised.

* * * *

Trev pulled into the rickety trailer park and sighed. The whole place had an air of neglect he recognized. This was one of those desperate places. Every city and suburb had them. Every small town, too. This was a place without hope and that few escaped from. It was definitely the place to get drugs.

It had been remarkably easy to get the information he wanted. Everyone was willing to buy that he wanted to score. Apparently Marty had come through, drinking and asking the same questions. He'd been looking for drugs for his client. No wonder no one believed him when he said he was straight. His former agent had blown his reputation before he'd even had a chance to settle in.

He'd hauled himself into The Rusty Spur and in fifteen minutes knew where to go for meth.

Nelson Hall. Bryce's good friend. Nelson Hall, who had sent his son to do his dirty work, who obviously let his son test the product.

He stopped the truck. There were three teens standing around

271

smoking.

"Hey, can you tell me where to find Nelson Hall?" Trev asked.

The only female of the group pointed down a thin, gravel road. "He's the last one on the road, but I don't think he's there. His son is."

Apparently, juvie wasn't what it used to be if Austin Hall was already out. He nodded and prepared himself. It was a stupid plan, and he couldn't help himself. He had to know. He started down the road.

Fuck, what was he doing? He was putting himself in harm's way. He was going on a drug buy. He wasn't supposed to be getting close to this life again, but he had to. He was supposed to be working O'Malley's herd, marking time until he came into his money and got the chance to work his own herd. He wasn't even going to stay in this town. He was leaving.

A vision of Beth between himself and Bo assaulted him, her body twisting as she tried to kiss them both, her heart big enough to handle her men.

He'd started the relationship because she'd seemed to need him, and he'd needed a distraction.

Some fucking distraction.

She'd wormed her way into his heart, and he wasn't sure if he could live without her. It was his lot in life to never be able to do anything halfway. The only time he didn't feel was when he was drunk. Love for Beth was rolling in his veins and with it the acknowledgement that he loved Bo, too. Bo was the brother he'd never had, the person who might have been able to save him if Trev had given him half a chance.

Could he make it work? Did he even have the right to try?

Trev stopped the truck in front of a ramshackle single-wide that had seen way better days. Austin Hall sat on the steps outside the trailer.

The kid looked far older than his sixteen years. His face was covered in sores, and when he smiled, Trev could see that his teeth were already showing the effects of meth.

Thank god he'd never gotten into meth.

"Should have known you would show up. When Dad heard you

got back into town, he said we should up production."

Trev barely managed to not clock the little shit. The need to kill the kid was right there. He'd taken a shot at Beth. But hurting some sixteen-year-old meth head who probably didn't have much of a chance of seeing his seventeenth birthday wouldn't fix things. He let his face go slack and tried to keep his hat slung low so no one noticed how clear his eyes were. "I need a fix, man. Bryce Hughes told me this was the place to come."

He flashed a wad of cash to let the kid know he was serious.

"Bryce would know." The kid was dressed in jeans and a hoodie, his sneakers worn. Earbuds dangled around his neck.

"Hey, shouldn't you be in jail or something? I heard you took a shot at someone." Trev held his breath. Either the kid would buy that Trev's brother-in-law would send him here, or he would walk away.

The kid shrugged. "That was a mistake. No one was supposed to be in that house. I wasn't trying to kill the bitch, and then her dumbass boyfriend caught me. Luckily, we got a judge or something on tape fucking a prostitute. So I'm out. No one can keep me in jail. Bryce slapped the fuck out of me, though. Your brother-in-law is an asshole. Did he find the shit?"

Austin hopped off the steps. He had a cigarette in his hand.

Trev tried to play it cool. So Bryce was looking for something, was he? And he was willing to involve a kid, to hurt a kid over it.

He would be willing to hurt Beth and Shelley, too.

"He's not my blood, man. I don't claim him. And no. He hasn't found a thing. He's panicked about it, too." He shoved his hands in his pockets and tried to look a little desperate.

The kid took a drag off his cigarette. "Dad told him he shouldn't have gotten involved with those mob guys. That's some bad shit, but you know Bryce. He talked about moving upmarket. I don't know why we had to start dealing coke. No one does coke out here. He's turned us all into some freaking middle men, you know. Like we're some kind of business with plans and shit. Dad's been cutting the pure stuff Bryce brings back from South America and selling it to gangs and the freaking mafia. Stupid asshole. Now they're going to come down on all our heads, and all because he pissed off his partner."

A wealth of things began to fall into place. Bryce was in deep, and he was going to drag everyone down with him. "He thinks Barry stashed something at the old Bellows place?"

Austin laughed. "Ain't that funny? Old Maudine Bellows died not even knowing she had a half a million dollars' worth of coke in her house. Barry hid it good, too. I couldn't find it. I don't know how you find fucking anything in that house. Talk about a hoarder. I could barely move when I searched the garage. Hey, is that why you're fucking that girl? Does Bryce have you looking for it, too? Dude, he promised me ten grand if I found it."

Nausea rolled. His brother-in-law was the money behind the county's drugs. And apparently he'd been blackmailing politicians. How far was he in? There was no question about it. Shelley and Beth would be in Dallas by nightfall under the protective glare of Julian Lodge. He would set Ben and Chase, the super twins, on this and protect his family.

His family.

Beth and Bo were his family. He couldn't pretend. He couldn't say he would take it one day at a time and let life sort itself out. They were his. They would be his tomorrow. They would be in his heart no matter what he did, and if he walked away, he would regret it for the rest of his life.

He knew enough. He needed to get them out of town. He had no deep desire to play the hero.

"So, how much do you want?"

Trev stared at the kid before realizing what he was asking. "Uh, I changed my mind. I'll just go get a beer."

Big mistake. The kid stared at him as though trying to decide something.

"She's your girlfriend, isn't she?"

Trev was silent, trying to decide if the kid would call Bryce.

Austin's face fell. "I didn't mean to hurt her. I didn't want to. I panicked. Mouse is a nice lady. She probably doesn't remember it, but when I was a kid, she helped me out. My bike got a flat, and she stopped and made sure it was working again. She's real nice. I wouldn't have hurt her."

There was a long moment of quiet before the kid spoke again. "The mob sent a guy to deal with Bryce. Someone from New York. I overheard Bryce and my dad talking. God, don't tell them I told you. They would fucking kill me. They were going back to that house they sent me to. The mob dude said he would kill Bryce if they didn't find the drugs. You need to tell her to stay away."

Sheer panic threatened to overwhelm Trev. He'd sent them home. "Call the cops."

Austin's eyes were old and tired. "Who do you think's been watching the place? One of the deputies has been on the payroll for years. Only the sheriff is clean, but he's retiring soon."

Trev pulled a card out his pocket along with all the cash he had. He jotted down Leo's cell on the card and handed Austin both. "That's three hundred dollars. It's yours if you'll call that number and tell the man who answers what's going on. Tell him Shelley's in trouble, and we need him. He'll know what to do. You don't have to say anything else to him. Austin, please. You don't have to live this life. Help us."

He was putting all his faith in a meth head, but he'd dumped his phone once he'd hit town and Marty wouldn't stop calling. He had to get to Beth.

"There's no way out." But Austin's fingers were already pulling the phone from his pocket.

"That's what I said six hundred and ninety-three days ago." It was how long he'd been sober. It was how long he'd had to give to the universe before he'd found his life, his Beth. "And the man who answers that phone is the reason I'm alive today. Thank you."

"Yeah, um, the football dude wanted me to call you. Someone named Shelley is in trouble."

Austin continued to talk as Trev raced to his truck and peeled down the road.

He prayed he would get there in time.

Chapter Nineteen

Beth's hands trembled as she stood in the hallway. She could still feel the cold press of metal against her head, though Carlo had moved on to standing behind Bo now.

"I don't know where to start." She felt powerless. It was a big house.

"You seem like an intelligent woman. Where would you hide half a million dollars' worth of cocaine?" Carlo's voice was oddly calm, as though he was merely asking an academic question.

"I wouldn't touch half a million dollars' worth of cocaine."

Carlo smiled, seemingly amused by her. "As I said, an intelligent woman. Now prove how smart you are or your boyfriend is going to join Mr. Hughes."

Bo sat still, his face betraying nothing, as though he didn't want to show her his fear. But she was afraid. She was so afraid for him.

"She doesn't know anything." Shelley wasn't being as stoic as Bo. She was pissed and didn't mind telling the dude with the gun. "It would be faster if you would let me help her search."

Carlo chuckled and put a hand on Shelley's hair. "Yes, I'm sure you would like that. Do you know what your husband offered me in exchange for not beating him to death? He offered me you. He said you were a hellion in bed. I like a touch of spice in my women.

Perhaps I'll take you with me when this is over. A woman as pretty as you is always a valuable commodity. Your skin is so fair."

"Don't you fucking touch her." Bo growled the words.

Carlo pointed the gun at him. Beth felt her heart stop. "I don't need you, Mr. O'Malley. I suspect the girl will try to save whoever she can."

"You do need him." Beth squared her shoulders. "I swear to god, if you kill him, I won't help you. I've been in love with that man since I was five years old. If you put a bullet in his brain, you'll have to kill me, too. How long do you have before someone shows up out here? How many people can you kill before someone notices? This is a small town. I doubt no one's noticed you. Did you take a room at the motel? Did you have dinner at Patty's? Trust me, someone noticed you, and everyone is talking about the smooth Yankee. And everyone will blame you if we end up dead."

"I could simply disappear," he offered.

"And your face will be everywhere," Beth argued. "This isn't the city. This is the middle of nowhere. A murder like this will be all over the news. How helpful will your employer find you then? Think about that before you kill the man I love."

Carlo's eyes became cold slits, his handsomeness almost reptilian in the moment. "I take your point, Miss Hobbes. Take mine. I don't have long. I need to find what I came for, or I have no use for any of you. My employer would rather keep this quiet. If I don't have to dispose of bodies beyond Mr. Hughes, I would welcome that. I would rather leave you tied up for the authorities to find. That would not make a huge news story. But I will kill you all if I don't get what I want."

Beth nodded. She took a long breath. She hated the fact that Bryce's body lay in front of the door to her bathroom, but Carlo wasn't moving it.

"Shelley, what do you remember about Barry?" Barry had been the one to hide the drugs.

"I remember he was an asshole." She sighed. "Honestly, now a lot of things make sense. I remember hearing him and Bryce..." She choked on the name, her eyes going to the body, but she took a breath and visibly calmed. "Barry and Bryce had a huge fight before

Barry died. Before Bryce killed him. None of it made sense at the time. Barry kept insisting that Bryce was cutting him out. He said he wouldn't be cut out. I guess he was talking about the drugs."

"And it would have been easier to hide them here than his own place. That would have been the first place Bryce would look," Bo reasoned.

"Maudine was sick the last few months of her life. It wouldn't have been hard to hide something from her. I didn't think she and Barry were that close," Beth explained.

"They weren't," Shelley said. "When he started to visit her a couple of times a week, everyone thought it was because he was getting in good before she died. He told Bryce as much. He told Bryce that all the old lady ever did was watch TV and write in that journal of hers. He said she probably wrote pages about him since she didn't have much else to write about."

"The journals. Of course." Beth started to cross the room, excitement lighting her step.

"Careful," Carlo warned.

She held her hands out. "I have to get a box out of the closet. The woman who owned this house kept meticulous journals all of her life. They're in the closet. Maybe she saw something. She would have written it down."

Carlo nodded slowly toward the closet door, the warning clear in his eyes.

She opened the door and pulled out the box. She took a moment, searching for anything she could use. The closet was full of housedresses and sensible shoes and blankets. Nothing that would help.

"Miss Hobbes."

Beth opened the box and pulled out the newest journal. "Found it. Give me a second."

She scanned the last several weeks of Maudine's life.

"*Barry visited again. Vulture. The vultures are circling as my life comes to an end. He can't fool me. I never even liked his father.* And then she talks about her cats. There's a lot about her cats in here. Apparently Mr. Sprinkles had bowel issues."

"Beth," Bo said, his mouth a firm, authoritative line.

She skipped the sections on cats. "Here we go. *Barry the vulture came again today. I don't know why he bothers. He's always on his phone. He never really listens. He offered to clean out the barn, though. Why, I have no idea. No one has used the barn in fifty years.*"

Beth looked up. "The barn. We should look there."

Carlo nodded. "We will look there. Mr. O'Malley, you will join us. I believe I will leave Mrs. Hughes. Her mouth has proven to be difficult to deal with. I can solve that problem for you, darling. I probably will. I'm intrigued. I believe you will make an excellent hostage. Otherwise, I might not make it out of this piss hole. Sleep well."

He brought the butt of the gun down on Shelley's head. She sank to the floor.

"Is she alive?" She wanted to go to Shelley. If Trev's sister was dead, she would be devastated.

"Her head is extremely hard. She'll be fine. On your feet, O'Malley." Carlo kept the gun on Bo as he struggled to his feet.

Bo's hair was in his face. He tossed it back. "It's going to be okay, Beth. It's all going to be okay. I'll be okay no matter what happens."

She knew what he was saying and dismissed it utterly. He was telling her to run if she had the chance. He was telling her that he'd rather die than watch something bad happen to her. But she could take whatever would happen if it meant they came out of this alive. She wasn't fragile. She wasn't timid anymore, either. She was his woman. She was Trev's woman. She was going to survive.

Carlo nudged him with the gun. Bo moved forward. He tripped and fell against her. They went tumbling to the floor.

"Baby, he's not going to let us live." Bo's plaintive words were whispered in her ear. "Run. Run and find Trev."

Carlo held the gun to the back of Bo's head. "I suggest you get up, O'Malley. I'm not fooling around."

"Sorry," Bo mumbled. "I tripped. I'm not used to walking around without the use of my hands."

Beth fumbled to get up. She stooped to help Bo.

"I love you, baby," he whispered. "You run. You leave me

behind and don't look back. You tell Trev to take care of you."

"Move away from him," Carlo ordered.

Beth stepped back. She looked at the man she'd loved since she was a child. He'd been a strange child, quiet and yet filled with pride and rage. Tender and yet quick to anger. He'd been her friend even when it hurt him. He'd been afraid to move beyond friendship, but even that slight fell away in the face of his love for her. They'd been each other's silent strength. It had taken Trev to get them to speak.

"I won't, you know." She didn't care that Carlo was listening. Bo needed to understand. She wouldn't run. She wouldn't leave him behind. She would stand beside him even if it meant she died.

"You're going to get in serious trouble, Bethany Hobbes."

"I already am."

She turned and started to walk down the hall. She heard Bo shuffling behind her.

"I warn you, I have a hand on him. If he 'trips' again, I will be forced to fire." Carlo's deep voice cut through the quiet of the house.

She took the stairs carefully. Bo was probably right. No matter what he'd said, Carlo would probably kill them. He wouldn't want to leave any witnesses. Carlo was lying. He might take Shelley with him, but Shelley wouldn't survive the experience. She would disappear somewhere south of the border and then she would wish she was dead.

She walked across the lawn like an automaton, focusing on her feet. One in front of the other. She crossed over the grass and the drive. The barn loomed in front of her. She hadn't been inside. It had seemed dark and foreboding. Most of the land had been sold to the O'Malleys and the livestock auctioned off long before that. Beth had planned on either tearing the barn down or turning it into a guesthouse.

She hadn't planned on it becoming her tomb.

"Open the door, dear," Carlo ordered. His politeness seemed a nasty, suspicious thing.

She would find the drugs. She would find them, but Carlo might not like the way she handed them over. She wouldn't allow Bo to die. And if she went down herself, she would go down fighting.

* * * *

Trev parked a half a mile away. He didn't dare get closer. He needed the element of surprise. If Leo did his job, it wouldn't be too long before the sheriff made his way here.

At least he hoped it would be the sheriff.

Fuck, he was on his own. Bo had taken a gun. Maybe Trev was panicking for no good reason. Maybe Bo had realized something was wrong and gotten Beth and Shelley away. Bo might have started talking to his brother and put off bringing Beth out to her place. They could be perfectly safe.

In the distance, he saw Aidan's truck. Bo had borrowed it because they'd all come in one truck, a happy family off for a Sunday afternoon.

They were here.

Trev moved off the road and into the woods that separated the Bellows home from the Gates house. Clarissa's house was a mile down the road, too far away to hope for help.

He ran through the woods, deeply grateful that he'd kept to a fitness regime that rivaled any pro athlete's. He didn't even break a sweat as he sprinted, his body moving with the grace of long training. He avoided the trees and stones, leapt over the small creek. He was barely breathing hard as the Bellows House came into sight from behind a swath of trees. He slowed, forcing himself to stop. He wanted to run into the house. He wanted to scream and fight, but panicking wouldn't help them.

The barn came into view. The big structure was solid but in deep need of paint and refurbishment. Odd. The doors were open. He was absolutely sure they had been closed when they had left earlier in the day.

He stared across the expanse. The barn was on the other side of the yard, in the back of the house.

And then he saw Bo. There was no mistaking the sandy-blond hair or the broad set of his shoulders. Bo's hands were caught behind his back. He was on his knees. A man loomed above him.

"You will bring it to me." The man's voice carried across the yard.

A gun. It glinted in the late-afternoon light. It was pressed to Bo's head.

Trev closed his eyes. He had no doubt who the man in the suit was talking to. Beth or Shelley. Hopefully both.

Beth walked out, a package in her hand. Wrapped in plastic, he knew exactly what it was. Cocaine. A lot of it. So much it would cost both she and Bo their lives if he didn't find a way out.

"You will put it in Mr. O'Malley's truck and get the rest for me. If you move in any way other than the one I've directed, I will kill him."

Play it safe. Play it safe, darlin'. How many trips would she have to make? How much time did he have?

A million scenarios ran through his brain. He could cause chaos by running at the man with the gun. It would give Beth a chance to flee. It more than likely signed both his and Bo's death warrants, but it gave Beth a shot.

She wouldn't take it. She would try to save them.

He could try to make his way around the house and sneak up on the other side. He could quietly make his way up behind the man and take him down. If he made even the slightest mistake, they were all dead.

Every way he went the odds were hell.

He was stuck watching without even a gun. He looked around. What was he going to do? Take the asshole down with a stick?

A large rock sat at his feet. It was jagged, with edges that could cut through skin.

He felt utterly impotent. A scream lodged in his throat as Beth walked back across the yard. Was he going to stand here and watch them die?

What the fuck was he going to do? Throw a rock at the asshole's car?

Trev stopped, so much of his life falling into place.

For years he'd cursed the talent that had led him to the football field. It had seemed a useless thing that had only led down a path to ruin. Now it might be the only thing that saved him.

Trev McNamara had been praised for having the strongest arm

in his class, the most accurate arm in a decade. He could throw a football through a ring at forty yards, never once touching the target. He'd been forced to hold back, or his receivers complained that he threw too hard.

His arm had caused him nothing but heartache.

And every second of that heartache had led him here, to this place where he had only one way to save his love, his friend, and his sister. Every moment of his life, each lesson he'd learned, had brought him here. In a single second, the ache he felt morphed into something different. Strength. He had survived. He had fought.

And he would win.

Trev McNamara picked up the rock. It filled his palm, the weight reassuring. It would do the job. Fifty yards. It was only fifty yards. He'd thrown for far longer than that and with far less on the line.

He took a deep breath, the air filling his lungs. He dropped back as though coming out of the pocket. It was a habit from years of playing. His vision focused, the world narrowing to a pinpoint—an inch of skin right in front of the man's ear. His target.

He brought his arm back and let the rock fly.

One last Hail Mary.

And Trev took off. If he failed, he would go down with them. His eye tracked the rock as it flew through the air, and his heart soared. He knew his aim was true. His throw had been quick, accurate, and deadly.

The man with the gun didn't stand a chance. There was a sickening thud that split the air, the sound of rock hitting soft, vulnerable flesh.

He saw the rock connect, nearly burying itself in the man's head before bouncing back and falling to the ground.

"Trev!" He heard Beth's scream as she dropped the package she carried. Her eyes were wide with horror.

The gun at Bo's head hit the ground a single second before his captor. The man in the suit fell to the grass, his body crumpling at an odd angle. Beth kicked the gun away. Her arms went around Bo, checking him for injuries. She kissed Bo and then got back up.

Beth ran for him and launched herself into his arms. He caught her, happy to hold her, to know that she was alive.

"Trev. I thought we were going to die. Oh, god, I thought I wouldn't see you again. And Bo. He was going to kill Bo. Shelley is okay. She's inside the house. He knocked her out. Oh, it was horrible." She sobbed against his chest.

He wrapped his arms around her. She'd been stoic before, but now her softness broke through. His brave Beth. How had anyone ever called her a mouse? It seemed to him that Beth had held it together in the face of terrible danger. She'd managed to stay calm and keep Bo and Shelley alive. He would never be able to pay her back for that. But he would try. Damn, but he would cherish her every day.

"I love you." He couldn't hold it back. The words flowed freely now. They were nothing but the truth. "I love you so much, Beth."

He was going to marry her. The present wasn't enough. He wanted a future with her and Bo.

"I love you, too."

Bo's voice broke through the emotion. "Uh, I would love everyone if one of you would mind getting me out of this zip tie and away from the dead dude. He's not breathing. You were like David and Goliath."

No. He hadn't needed a sling. Just fifteen years of training.

He helped his partner up. He stared at Bo. He needed to make a few things clear. "Don't get used to this place. I know it's your home, but I have to leave in a year's time. I'm buying into a cattle ranch. Our ranch. We're moving. You and me and Beth."

Bo's face flushed. He nodded, too choked up for words.

Beth wrapped an arm around them both, her soft body a conduit for them.

Trev completed the circle, wrapping his arms around them, hugging them tightly.

In the distance, he heard the sirens, but they no longer mattered. He was safe.

Chapter Twenty

One year later

"Well, you wanted it to be a family home again." Trev smiled down at Beth, who was looking up at her handiwork one last time.

The old Bellows place shone in the early-morning light. It was a jewel of a house. Every room had been lovingly refurbished into a place any family would be proud of.

But it wasn't his home.

Lexi O'Malley stepped out of the truck and reached behind the seat to lift her infant son from his car seat. She held the tiny boy in her arms, Lucas and Aidan at her side as they stared at the house they would raise their family in.

"Beth, it's so beautiful. I can't tell you how much I love it." Lexi cooed down at her boy. "This is your home, Jack. You're going to love it here. And your aunt and uncle will be here this weekend, though they're really more like cousins."

Bo stepped out of the house, the last box in his hand. "I thought we'd carry the coffeemaker with us. Those hotel room coffeemakers can't keep up with Mr. Caffeine."

Beth's arm snaked around his waist. "He loves his coffee."

Not as much as he loved her. And Bo. Damn, but he loved his

friend. Weeks and months of working beside him had solidified their partnership. He couldn't imagine his life without either of them now.

And they were following him to Colorado.

Aidan held out a hand as Lucas led Lexi up the steps. "Thank you. For everything."

Aidan's genuine admiration had done wonders for his ego. "Anytime, brother."

"I hear your sister is on her way to The Club."

Trev had to smile. His sister had spent the last year recovering from her injury, her marriage, from life itself. She'd closed up her business, shocked at how many clients her husband had managed to blackmail. She had an old ally looking into it for her. Liam O'Donnell was trying to untangle the web Bryce had woven so Shelley could feel safe again. The Irishman was a completely different human being after he'd come back from the English assignment. He hadn't come alone. He'd come with a wife and had promptly begun meddling. He'd help Shelley deal with FBI agents and DEA agents. After she'd dealt with the fallout of Bryce's death, she'd gone into her shell, but it seemed to Trev that she was starting to come out of it. After spending a weekend with Avery O'Donnell, she'd announced that she needed a fresh start, and she wanted to explore D/s. Trev had called Julian, and Julian had offered to take her in and find a Dom to train her.

But she hadn't gone to Sanctum. No, Shelley was going to The Club, and Leo Meyer was in for a surprise.

He had the O'Donnells to thank for that, too.

"She'll probably cause a ruckus." It was one of the things she was awfully good at. He was going to miss his sister, but he knew she would be in good hands.

Aidan grinned. "I might have to go and see that. Y'all call us from the road. Let us know you're okay. I need to get in there or Lexi will have moved all the furniture herself."

Beth stood by the truck, her hair shining in the light, a soft, confident smile on her face. And a ring on her finger. Two in fact. Bethany Hobbes was now Bethany McNamara-O'Malley.

"Are you ready?" Bo wrapped an arm around her waist and

kissed her. "I bet you'll have a whole new house to work on."

Her eyes gleamed at the thought. "I hope this James Glen doesn't mind a little home improvement. I'm looking forward to it. And seeing Colorado. It seems like a big adventure."

Suddenly every damn day seemed like an adventure. They got in the truck, and Trev turned the engine on. He pulled up the drive, the road ahead of him. His heart nearly skipped a beat. He'd never imagined that he would make this trip with people he loved.

"I don't know about that town," Bo said, bringing him back to reality. "Who names a town Bliss?"

"I think we'll fit in," he replied with confidence. And if they didn't, they would be okay. They were a world in and of themselves, an island of peace he'd found. He didn't need Bliss. He'd already found it.

He turned the truck west, toward Bliss and their future.

* * * *

Leo, Shelley, and a surprise visitor from Colorado will return in *Siren in Bloom*.

Author's Note

I'm often asked by generous readers how they can help get the word out about a book they enjoyed. There are so many ways to help an author you like. Leave a review. If your e-reader allows you to lend a book to a friend, please share it. Go to Goodreads and connect with others. Recommend the books you love because stories are meant to be shared. Thank you so much for reading this book and for supporting all the authors you love!

Sign up for Lexi Blake's newsletter
and be entered to win a $25 gift certificate
to the bookseller of your choice.

Join us for news, fun, and exclusive content
including free short stories.

There's a new contest every month!

Go to www.LexiBlake.net to subscribe.

Siren in Bloom

By Lexi Blake writing as Sophie Oak
Texas Sirens, Book 6
Coming November 6, 2018

For Leo Meyer, being the Dom in residence at The Club has been a perfect life. But when the only woman he ever loved walks back into his life, his world is turned upside down.

Wolf Meyer has been restless since an injury ended his career with the Navy SEALs. Hoping to reconnect with his brother, Wolf accepts a job with Julian Lodge. His first assignment is to train Shelley McNamara, a gorgeous sub with a troubled past.

Shelley came to The Club to heal her wounded heart. She never dreamed that exploring her dark fantasies with her new Master would leave her caught between two brothers.

Lost in Bliss

Nights in Bliss, Colorado Book 4
By Lexi Blake writing as Sophie Oak
Coming September 25, 2018

Laura Niles fled Washington, DC, with her career in ruins and her love life decimated. In her desperate flight, she found a home in Bliss, Colorado.

For years, Rafe Kincaid and Cameron Briggs have searched for the only woman they've ever loved. The FBI agents couldn't share her before and it tore them apart. Now they have tracked her down and they want answers.

When her former loves bring the full force of the FBI with them, Laura knows Bliss is in for a rough ride, because a killer has been watching and waiting for a second chance.

About Lexi Blake

Lexi Blake is the author of contemporary and urban fantasy romance. She started publishing in 2011 and has gone on to sell over two million copies of her books. Her books have appeared twenty-six times on the *USA Today*, *New York Times*, and *Wall Street Journal* bestseller lists. She lives in North Texas with her husband, kids, and two rescue dogs.

Connect with Lexi online:

Facebook: Lexi Blake
Twitter: authorlexiblake
Website: www.LexiBlake.net

Sign up for Lexi's free newsletter.

Made in the USA
San Bernardino, CA
04 September 2018